"Don't fi~~ght me~~. I need you.

"And you need me," Beau whispered, using the most persuasive tone he could muster. His fingers moved in tiny caresses on her, feeling her womanly warmth through the wool shawl and cotton dress. She had a delicacy of frame that pleased him. "Let's marry," he said, "and thus fool the fate that awaits us."

"If I do, what will you expect of me?" she asked, her voice trembling. "Will I take your name only?"

The question seemed an insult to his tender dreams of wedded bliss and clearly indicated her feelings toward him. "I confess, the thought of a child of my own intrigues me...."

Dear Reader,

Welcome to Harlequin Historicals, where we hope you'll find a lot to be thankful for this November.

Fans of Bronwyn Williams will be pleased to see that Dixie Browning and her sister, Mary Williams, have written another book in their popular Outer Banks Series. In *The Mariner's Bride,* young seaman Rogan Rawson marries a woman for the sole purpose of keeping an eye on his wayward stepmother, only to discover that nothing is ever that simple.

You will also find *Season of Storms,* from Kate Kingsley (our one hundredth book by the way). It's the tale of a wayward son of the Creole elite and an independent heiress. Readers of contemporary romance will recognize the name Laurie Paige. In the author's first Harlequin Historical, *Wedding Day Vows,* an Englishwoman trades her release from Newgate prison for her hand in marriage.

Last, but not least, I would like to mention Nina Beaumont. This first-time author lives in Austria, and her wealth of knowledge and experience lend a powerful flavor to *Sapphire Magic,* the story of a cynical Austrian count and the woman who melts his heart.

Please keep an eye out for *Historical Christmas Stories 1991.* The collection features Lynda Trent, Caryn Cameron and DeLoras Scott. You won't want to miss it!

Our best to you and yours during the upcoming holiday season.

Sincerely,

Tracy Farrell
Senior Editor

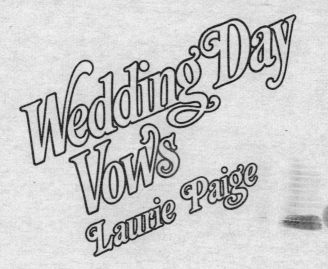

Wedding Day Vows

Laurie Paige

Harlequin Books

TORONTO • NEW YORK • LONDON
AMSTERDAM • PARIS • SYDNEY • HAMBURG
STOCKHOLM • ATHENS • TOKYO • MILAN

Harlequin Historicals first edition November 1991

ISBN 0-373-28702-X

WEDDING DAY VOWS

LAURIE PAIGE

loves delving into history via journals and diaries. One of her favorite periods is the American Revolution and the years following it. When she and her family are engaged in another favorite pastime—hiking the Sierras—she easily imagines they are pioneers exploring a new land. Ideas for books seem as endless as the sky over her head and the earth beneath her feet.

We are such stuff
As dreams are made on . . .

—William Shakespeare
The Tempest, IV, i, 158

Chapter One

Wednesday, May 15, 1790

Roselynne Moreley held her father's arm and guided him along the line as the prisoners hobbled forward at the guard's command. The leg iron was heavy around her ankle, the skin chafed from the tuggings of her fellow captives. She was tired to the point of exhaustion after a fortnight in the custody of the king's troops, but fatigue couldn't quell the jolt of fear she felt when she gazed upon Newgate prison. The moss-shrouded walls exuded a chill like that of the grave.

"Remember this place, Father?" she asked, holding her fright at abeyance. "'Tis Newgate. It was once the western wall of the city until the town outgrew its bounds."

Roselynne waited for several seconds, but no answer came from her father.

"It was called Westgate then, until Henry I rebuilt it and named it Newgate," she continued on a note of desperation. "The gatehouse has been used as a prison for centuries. Do you remember speaking of it when you were preparing your essay on prison reform?"

She searched his face for signs of understanding, for one spark of awareness concerning their circumstances and the uncertain fate that awaited them. There was none.

Fear raised its ugly head like a viper, its fangs bared to strike her vulnerable courage and destroy it. She closed her eyes briefly. *Don't be afraid,* she counseled her failing spirits. *All will be well.*

By now, Charles would have spoken to the duke, who should have returned from his Scotland trip a sennight ago. The duke, a rich, powerful man, would go straight to the authorities. Soon there would be an order for their release. She opened her eyes.

The damp stone confronted her, mocking her expectations and depressing her momentary hope of rescue. This was not a nightmare that would disappear with the dawn. The sun had risen hours ago, and the day was all too real.

Her bones ached from the long trip in the cart. The guards had rambled from one town to another, gathering the prisoners to bring to Newgate. She glanced about the yard in pity.

A dozen or more wretches were hooked together behind or before her father and herself. They waited in the courtyard while the gaoler decided where to put them. He had argued loudly over the matter with the captain of the guard when they had arrived an hour ago. Now the two had gone inside the massive doors and left the prisoners shackled, standing in the midmorning sun, with no water or food to give them strength and comfort.

Her gaze lighted on a window set high into a corner turret. She spied a man there, visible in the sunlight, his appearance made sinister by the bars that cast shadows across his features. A beard further darkened his grim visage.

Even from the distance she could see swelling and bruising around his eyes, and apprehension shivered through her. Prison guards were notoriously cruel.

She stared as if she were in a trance while fear renewed its hold upon her. Clutching her shawl with one hand and her father with the other, she fought for control of her emotions. Forcing her gaze past him to the soaring sky beyond the tiled roof, she watched a bird fly down and land at her feet.

Her father stared at the pigeon pecking at the dirt between the cobbles. His expression didn't change, but suddenly he took a step toward the plump bird.

The rattle of the chains alerted the half-dozing guard nearest them. The man sprang toward Mr. Moreley, the butt of his gun raised to deal the older man a stunning blow.

"No!" Roselynne cried, throwing herself in the way, her arms flung wide to either side as if she would defend her fa-

ther from a whole battalion of attacking warriors. The iron strap circling her ankle dug painfully into the skin. "He didn't do anything. He was just looking at the dove."

The soldier glared at her, then at her father. "Git back in line. Step back." When the old man failed to respond, he raised the gun again, his eyes flicking nervously over the prisoners.

"Don't you dare hit him!" Roselynne said in the most authoritative tones she could muster.

"He's nought but a half-wit," the soldier said. "He'd hardly notice a little tap."

"A blow from one like you was what damaged his mind and made him like this in the first place. You should be ashamed to even think of striking a defenseless old man who only wants to look at a harmless bird."

"Mayhap he can ketch it, dearie," a woman, coarse in manner and speech, called out behind them. "I've a notion I could eat the bloody thing, feathers'n'all. When do we get some breakfus' at this fine inn?" she demanded.

"Yeah," chorused the man shackled beside her.

"I wants me eggs and 'am, I do," another said with a gap-toothed grin. He spat into the dust.

The soldier swung his gaze from one to the other as the calls continued and grew louder. Roselynne saw him glance toward the gaol as if hoping for relief. His eyes shifted back to the row of ragged prisoners as their taunts grew louder. Another minute and he would have a riot on his hands.

"Silence," he bellowed.

That brought only a momentary lull, then the heckling began again, more ominous with each muttered demand for food and water.

"Water, me arse," the woman cackled. "Bring me a glass o' your best champagne, Charlie, an' be quick about it."

"Coo, Henny, you ain't never tasted champagne in your life."

"I 'ave, too. Onct a gent came to the inn where I've been wiping tables from dawn to dark, and he brought a bottle. I shared a bit o' it with 'im."

"Go on, 'e never gived it to ye."

"I didn't say 'e did. I took a little nip when 'e weren't looking. What 'e didn't know didn't hurt 'im none, now did it?"

A dirty, ragged lad of no more than ten years sang out, "Bleat, bleat, we're poor sheep, give us som'pin good to eat."

The prisoners leaped upon this bit of doggerel and sang it louder and louder. They stomped their feet and rattled their chains to keep time. Roselynne tugged at her father until he stepped back into the relative safety of the group and away from the arc of the musket should the soldier swing it at them.

"Hee, hee, hee," laughed the woman behind her.

The massive door of the prison was flung back on its hinges, and the gaoler burst out of it, a "cat" flying over his head as he cracked its nine barbs in a menacing display of authority. The singing stopped.

"There'll be none of that," he said. His eyes, sunk deep under bony sockets, seemed fired with embers straight from the hearths of hell. "Bring them water," he ordered a young private, who hastened to the well and a bucket hanging there. The gaoler swung to the other guard. "What happened here?"

The man shifted from one foot to the other. "The old man, 'e started it. Broke line, 'e did. I was just trying to git 'im back when *she* jumped in."

Roselynne, her fears dispelled by righteous anger, spoke to the gaoler. "My father was curious about a bird, that's all. He moved one step to look at it, and this . . . this *miscreant* accosted him for no reason."

"A miscreant, that's what 'e is," Henny agreed vigorously.

"Keep a civil tongue in your 'ead," the corporal ordered.

"Attention!" The captain of the guard emerged from the dim interior and stood beside the gaoler. "Finish up with that bucket," he ordered the private, then turned to the gaoler. "I have discharged my duty. The prisoners are in your hands now."

Motioning to his men, he mounted and rode off, the guards and the empty cart that had transported the human baggage following him along the road that led out of town.

Roselynne watched them leave, a wistful expression flicking through her eyes. She had wished to see the last of the cart when she was riding in it and her bones seemed ready to poke through her skin, but now she saw it as a last symbol of freedom. An awful loneliness rose to her throat, threatening to choke her.

"'Ere you go, duckie, some water."

"Thank you."

Roselynne took the bucket from the woman behind her. Henny, she'd been called by her friend. She looked to be in her forties. Her hair, which had once been red, was showing streaks of gray at the roots. She was buxom in an overblown way, like a lettuce past its prime, a bit wilted around the edges but not yet given to decay. Her smile was friendly, and her blue eyes shone merrily. Roselynne smiled back.

"Here, Father," she said, "drink this and you'll feel better." She talked to him as if he were recovering from an illness, although there were no signs that he comprehended anything that happened.

Holding the dipper to his lips, she let him drink until he turned his head and would take no more, then she helped herself and passed the bucket along when she finished.

Exhaustion returned after the excitement of the past few minutes, and with it, remorse for her wayward temper. That was part of what had gotten them into this troubled mire in the first place. Her accursed, unpredictable temper.

When the troops had come to arrest her father—for sedition, if one could credit such a ridiculous charge!—she had reacted impulsively and tried to stop them from chaining her gentle parent, a country vicar and a scholar, like a common thief. The soldier had struck her, and her father had tried to stop him. Another guard had battered the older man with the butt of his musket, thus causing the loss of his wits.

For the entire fortnight, the time it had taken to gather and transport them and the other prisoners to London, he had not spoken once. It distressed her greatly to see his brilliance so dulled and his manner so changed.

She looked with longing toward the west where the little caravan of troops was disappearing around the bend. Toward the northwest, in a land lovely beyond measure, was her home.

Would she ever again sleep in the snug bedroom under the eaves and dream of a handsome brigand carrying her off to some wild land the way heroes in novels did? Would she and

Charles ever again go rowing on the Lake of Ullswater while he cautiously explained his prospects to her?

Beau St. Clair grinned as the confrontation below settled down. His lower lip cracked and a drop of blood oozed to the surface at the movement. Grimacing at the slight pain, he went to the table, ran his finger over the grease congealed on the pewter plate and rubbed the lubricant over his lips.

Still sore from the beating he had taken at the hands of the turnkey and his minions, Beau stretched out on the bed and closed his eyes. Be nice to have an armful of lively woman to frolic with before a nap, he thought. Perhaps that would quiet the seething of his mind over his predicament and help him get a good sleep.

He thought of the woman in the courtyard. She was feisty enough to be entertaining. Her courage in defending the old man to whom she was shackled spoke well for her character. However, it wasn't her character that interested him at the moment.

His body surged with vigor below his belt for the first time since his arrest for murder four months ago. He was to be hanged June 3, nineteen days hence, a date approaching with terrifying speed and awesome slowness. For the first time, the realization that he might really die hit him.

He, Beauregard St. Clair, doomed in the prime of his life? he questioned his fate with a mocking defiance of the event. Struck down at the tender age of twenty-nine, to die in a foreign country with no one to mourn him, no wife and children to carry his name forward? It seemed an unfair legacy.

His body protested his demise with a heated reminder that he was yet a man, alive and functioning in all parts. If he could but have a few hours of bliss before he donned the hangman's noose. It was a thought to cheer a man's heart and restore his courage . . . at least for a time.

Restless, he rose and went to the window. The captives were seated on the filthy cobbles and had received their breakfast of hard bread and water.

The young woman—he had discerned her tender years during the time she had looked toward his window—was urging the old man to eat his ration. She had better see to her own meal as the rest of the wretches were doing, or it was liable to be snatched out of her lap and gobbled up by another.

Beau's attention wandered down the line and returned. She was now breaking off pieces of the bread with her fingers and eating it with a show of delicacy. She had probably worked in some great house and picked up the manners of her betters.

He wondered what she looked like beneath the dirty, unkempt clothing she wore. A shawl, too warm for the day, was tied around her shoulders, hiding what lay beneath her dress from his curious eyes. His imagination supplied what reality did not.

Ah, there might be bounty there to please a king. Her breasts would be warm and firm, the nipples rosy at the tips. He would kiss them, taste them, suck that tender treat until she went limp with passion. He looked again at her face, much drawn to the promise of a passionate interlude between them.

Her hair was bunched into a chignon at the nape of her neck. It was brown in color, a soft shade neither dark not light, but medium in tone with golden lights where the sun hit it. Her face was an oval, the type painters liked to use as models for saints.

A harsh chuckle escaped him. He certainly hoped she wasn't inclined in that direction. For a coin, the turnkey would bring her to him for the night, then he would ask her preference—him in his private cell or many in the common. He would also have to purchase a bath for her.

"Bowes," he yelled through the small window of his door. "Bowes, come here, you lazy rascal. I've an errand for you."

Roselynne felt her legs tremble as she stepped over the threshold. *Newgate.* The horror stories learned in helping her father with his research loomed greater and greater in her mind. The inside was worse than she could ever have envisioned.

The stench almost closed her throat, and she could hardly draw breath. The walls were blackened with soot and mildew. The stone floor was damp. In addition to rats and fleas, she imagined leeches and other silent, slimy things hidden in the dark, dirty corners. She drew closer to her father.

Whatever happened, she wouldn't let anyone further harm her quiet, scholarly parent. All her life, he had treated her with respect, his discipline firm as befitted a vicar, but fair as befitted a man of great moral conscience.

With the death of her mother five years ago, he had assumed that role, too, advising her on the relationship between men and women when he saw that she and Charles Osgood were growing fond of each other. Charles was secretary to the Duke of Wainsco, and had become a frequent visitor to their modest vicarage.

She closed her eyes and leaned against the cold, clammy wall when they were told to halt in a dim corridor. Perhaps even now, as they waited here in this hall, a release was on its way. By now, Charles would have spoken to the duke and arranged a pardon from the king or whatever had to be done to rectify this corruption of justice.

She looked at her father, standing quietly in his chains, his frailness accented by hollows beneath his cheekbones. John Jacob Moreley, a seditionist? The idea was too ridiculous to be contemplated. His modest essay had concerned the will of the people to be governed. She had read every word. 'Twas nothing in it advocating the overthrow of the king.

The entrance of the gaoler caused her to straighten her shoulders and stand upright. The shackles were at last being cast off. Her turn came. She lifted her skirt and held out her leg. When the iron was removed, she sighed in relief. Her right leg had ached for days from the unaccustomed weight.

"Here, Father, let them remove the king's bracelet. We are no longer his favorites, it would seem," she said with brave irony, tugging at his trousers to bring his leg forward. He moved as she ordered with no change in expression. Once, he would have chuckled in delight at her quip.

Roselynne blinked back the tears that stung her eyes. Now was definitely not the time for missish behavior. Beneath her skirt, she worked her ankle in a circle to restore its free use. Her right leg felt lighter than her left, a strange sensation.

"Listen, all," the gaoler ordered. "We'll have no fighting in the cells, else you'll feel the 'cat' laid to your scrawny backs. It leaves a pretty stitchery of scars. Show them, Mr. Bowes."

A huge man stepped forward and yanked up his shirt. Slowly, with a toothy grin, he turned so they could see his back. It was a mass of crisscrossed, welted scars, terrible to behold, worse to think how the flesh must have torn and bled.

"Mr. Bowes was once in the service of his majesty's navy. He is familiar with punishment and prefers to mete it out rather than receive it. Isn't that so, Mr. Bowes?"

"Aye, it is."

Bowes swiveled and stared down the line at his audience. His great head blended into his shoulders with hardly a curve to indicate the placement of his neck. He reminded Roselynne of a bear, his eyes cunning but without the intellect the animal probably had.

The gaoler finished his warning lecture and left the hall. Bowes grinned, licked his lips and looked the little troop over. Like a vulture picking the best morsel, she thought. To her horror, his eyes alighted on her . . . and lingered. He sauntered over, his enormous girth pitching from side to side.

"You, come with me," he ordered, pointing at her.

"No," she said.

His small eyes narrowed. "None o' your sauce, girl. You'll do as I say, or suffer the lash for't."

Roselynne stretched herself to her full five feet four inches. "I must stay with my father. He needs me." She clutched his arm with icy fingers.

"Coo, she speaks the truth, ducks," Henny spoke up. "The old man cain't wipe 'is nose without 'er to do it for 'im."

"Quiet, you old crow. If I want to hear you sing, I'll tell you the tune." His gaze threatened Henny.

"Thank you, Henny," Roselynne interceded before the brute lost his temper and hurt the woman. When his attention focused on her again, she motioned toward Mr. Moreley. "My father is . . . was . . . is," she said firmly, "a vicar in the Ullswater district. He suffered an injury to his head—"

"I ain't here to listen to no sad tales. You're to come along with me. A gentleman wants to see you."

Roselynne's heart rose to her throat. She had read that the guards sold female prisoners to others for the night.

She lifted her chin and said in the haughtiest tone she could muster. "My father's parishioner, the Duke of Wainsco, will hear of any harm done to either of us while here. Even now, he may be speaking with the king to correct this error of justice.''

Bowes stared at her, puzzlement on his broad face. "I'll talk to you later," he muttered. "All right, on your feet, you mangy curs, or it's the tickle of the lash you'll feel on your backsides. Up, now. Come along.''

He shoved them toward a door made of iron bars hinged to the stone. In a few minutes, all of them were locked into the cell.

Roselynne glanced around in despair. Two chamber pots were its only accoutrements of civilization.

"There ain't even a blanket or pile of straw to warm a man's bones," one of the men grumbled, eyeing the dank cell that was hardly big enough to accommodate them if they all tried to sleep at the same time.

The gap-toothed prisoner glanced at the three women. "Don't always need straw to warm a bed." He chuckled deep in his chest and made a lewd sign with his great slab of a hand.

Roselynne pushed her father into a far corner and took up a protective stance next to him. Henny edged her way over until she was beside them.

"Gonna be trouble," she muttered. "Are ye a virgin?''

Roselynne felt as if her skin were suddenly too tight for her flesh and bones. She was trapped in her female body, a thing she had never before felt. Evil invaded the cell. It seemed to draw around her, like the constriction of a python about its prey.

She spied the chamber pot near her feet. Perhaps it would do for her purposes. It was the only weapon at hand.

"I's cold," the smaller man whined.

"So get a coat," the other advised.

The men prisoners crept against the walls. The big, gap-toothed man and the small, whiny one stood like an island of menace in the center of the cell. The small man looked at the clothing the others wore. His eyes fell on Mr. Moreley's thick wool coat, somewhat dusty but in good repair.

"I'll take that one," he decided, pointing toward their corner.

"Indeed, you will not," Roselynne stated.

"Are ye telling me I cain't take that coat?"

"Yes." She faced the petty thief, outwardly calm, and prayed her inner anxiety didn't show.

The big man laughed as his companion shuffled indecisively. "Are ye goin' to let a skirt tell ye what ye can do, Neddie?" he demanded.

"You, Gramps, 'and over th' coat," Neddie said. Mr. Moreley didn't move. "Tell 'im to 'and it over," he said to Roselynne.

She shook her head. "He needs its warmth more than you."

"I wants it!"

"No."

Neddie glanced at his cohort, who gave him an encouraging grin, and entered the battle again. "Me friend, Mr. 'Inkle, here, don't take lightly to 'is friends being un'appy. Ain't that right, Mr. 'Inkle?"

Hinkle nodded, his glance running over Roselynne as if sizing her up for a meal. A tremor of fear edged through her body when Neddie took a step forward.

"If you bother us, I will see that you're punished," she said. She remembered Hinkle's name. He was a cutthroat who had led a small gang in terrorizing widows and defenseless people in a county south of her home.

"Are ye threatening me?" Neddie laughed at this.

"I'm giving you fair warning."

"Go on, get the coat," Hinkle advised, giving his friend a push toward the corner.

The prisoners, including the other woman, seemed to flow in the opposite direction, away from trouble, all except Henny. When Neddie advanced another step, Roselynne stooped and picked up the chamber pot.

"You shall be sorry if you come another step this way," she warned.

She held her ground, ready to fling the contents at him. While the thief didn't seem to be a man of great cleanliness, she hoped that even such as he would think twice before chancing the unsavory leavings of the pot.

"The old man prob'ly 'as fleas," he decided. Pulling his own ragged coat under his skinny flanks, he settled on the floor and leaned against the stone wall. He gave Roselynne a malevolent glare while his friend laughed at him.

She relaxed slightly when the large man also settled with his back to the wall. For the moment, peace reigned.

"A good show, duckie," Henny complimented her. "I couldn'a done better, meself." She motioned to the floor. "Sit 'ere, lassie, and tell me your name and 'ow ye came to be in 'ere."

Roselynne told her brief tale.

Henny asked about her mother and clucked in sympathy upon hearing of Mrs. Moreley's death. She gazed at the youngster across the cell. "They's many a h'orphan about nowadays, what with all the wars the king 'as got into. I lost me own man more'n ten year ago, it was, over in Ameriky."

"I'm sorry," Roselynne said. "It must have been a terrible sadness to you. My mother died of the influenza. I miss her still."

Henny dabbed at her eyes with a dirty rag she pulled from her sleeve. "Aye, and yer father 'as lost 'is wits, ye say?"

Roselynne sighed. "Yes. I am very worried about him. The soldiers wouldn't let the doctor in our village look at him."

"May'ap 'is mind will return," Henny consoled. "We'll stay together and 'elp one another, eh?"

"Yes," Roselynne agreed. "What unkind fate brought you to this cold place?"

"Well, uh, it were this way, you see. I sorta took a fee for dinner and a bottle when the gentlemum were sleepin' like."

"She doped 'im and robbed 'im," the other woman suddenly called out with a knowing grin on her face.

"That never was the truth o' it," Henny denied. "'E promised me the coin, then passed out afore givin' it t'me. I only took the one what was promised. 'E lied when 'e said I stole it all."

Roselynne smiled in understanding. "I'm sure, whatever the man said, you did only what necessity dictated."

"That's right," Henny declared with a glare at her friend.

"Well, things will improve tomorrow," Roselynne said, sure they would. Soon Charles would come with the pardon. Perhaps she could help Henny to win her freedom, too.

"If we live through the night," Henny said.

Roselynne followed her glance. Hinkle was staring at her with a malicious gleam in his eyes. Chill bumps raced along her spine. Before a new dawn broke, she might have wished she had gone to the gentleman the turnkey had mentioned. Her hand tightened on the handle of the chamber pot.

Chapter Two

"She refused to come, guvner." Bowes gave a shrug of his massive shoulders to indicate the vagaries of female minds.

"How did you put it to her? As a threat?" Beau asked. He speared an asparagus stalk and dipped the end in the cream sauce before biting the tip off.

"Told her it was a gentleman wanted to speak to her. She said she had to take care of the old man, her father, it was."

"Her father?" Beau was surprised.

"Aye. 'Pears she's a lady. Talks like one, hoity-toity. Claims to be on fair terms with some duke. Wainsco, I b'lieve she said. Don't know in what capacity." He grinned.

Beau cut a piece of succulent beef, roasted to a nicety by the French chef of the town house and delivered to him by a footman. He chewed slowly while he mulled over this last bit of information. Now that he recalled the incident, he realized she had spoken in cultured tones when she had defended the old man.

"Did you get her name?"

"Moreley. John Jacob Moreley and his daughter, Roselynne," the turnkey answered.

"Their crime?"

"The old man wrote a paper, something about trying to get the people to overthrow the king. I'm not sure about the girl. I guess she was in on it."

"They haven't been tried yet?"

"Nay."

"And they were tossed into a common cell with that sorry bunch of thieves and rascals?" At Bowes's affirmative nod, Beau frowned, wondering if she was an innocent. What an awakening she would receive at that mob's hands. He dug a coin out of his pocket. "See that she isn't harmed this night. And find out all you can about them and report back."

Bowes caught the flipped coin and tucked it out of sight. He nodded amicably and opened the door.

"Tell the crone to come up when she finishes her chores. I have several errands I want her to run before nightfall."

"Aye, guvner." Bowes locked the massive wooden door behind him and ambled down the corridor, his great hulk heaving from side to side like a galleon in full sail.

Roselynne drank the watery soup from the bowl and used the piece of bread to scoop up the few grains of barley that stuck to the bottom. She glanced at her father and saw he wasn't eating. Feeling guilty for gobbling her own gruel down instead of helping him eat his, she lifted his bowl to his lips.

"Drink this, Father. It will give you strength. Take it now. There, isn't that good? 'Tis plain but nourishing."

With patient urging, she got it and the bread down him. He had always had a fussy appetite. Her mother had taken pains to fix the freshest, most pleasing food for him. Roselynne wondered what he thought of the fare they received now.

"Not much longer, Father," she whispered. "I'm sure Charles is on his way with a letter from the duke. Perhaps Wainsco himself will speak to the king on our behalf. Don't fret on it."

She peered into his eyes and saw only vacancy. A rush of hopelessness caused her eyes to mist over. She blinked the tears away before they could gather and fall.

She buttoned his coat around his neck. As night drew nigh, the fetid air in the prison seemed to grow colder. Across the narrow cell, the two thieves watched her. The third woman leaned into the far corner, already asleep. Snores issued from the dark cavern of her mouth.

"She were always a bitch," Henny said matter-of-factly. "I never trusted 'er for a minute. I shouldn't wonder if'n she didn't take the extra coins and turn me in."

"What was she arrested for?"

"Debts."

"Oh." Debtors prison was a common fate of many. Once they might have been transported to the New World to work their indebtedness off, but that route was closed after the war.

"You, there," Bowes called through the bars. "I'd speak to you. Come here. The rest of you stand back."

Roselynne realized he meant her.

"Go on to the door," Henny advised. "'E cain't 'arm ye from there. I'll keep my eye on yer pa."

Roselynne rose stiffly and walked to the iron bars. Hinkle and Neddie moved to the opposite wall where room was rapidly made for them. She realized that, whatever might happen come dark, she could expect no help from the other men. They were too afraid of the robbers.

"What is it you want?" she asked.

Bowes leaned down to whisper close to her ear. "There's a nice gentleman who'll give you a place for the night. He's not so much to look at, but he's clean and a decent sort."

"What kind of place?"

He drew back to stare at her in the lamplight. "Are you gammoning me, girl? You know what I mean. He'll give you supper and a bath, too, if you should want one. Aye, and pay you well. You might can buy a private room for you and your old man."

Roselynne stared at the turnkey. "You mean, for a price, I can have a room to myself?" She should have remembered that. Bribery was the way of prison life, she'd read.

Bowes grinned slyly. "It might can be arranged."

"How?" she demanded.

"If you did me a favor, I might do one for you."

"Your favor being that I go to this *gentleman* and lie with him?" She spoke bluntly, wanting to be sure she understood. If anyone had told her a fortnight ago she would be standing in a cramped cell, bargaining her virtue for food and bed like a girl of the street, she would have had the person arrested for slander.

"Aye."

"No."

His eyes narrowed in warning. "You'll be doing yourself a favor, too. He's rich, and he'll treat you good, not like these scurvy bastards in here'll do."

Roselynne thrust her chin forward. The turnkey would say anything to win her to his purpose. He would probably receive another coin for delivering her to his patron. She must look gullible indeed if he thought she would leave what little safety she had in here for the unknown comfort he offered.

"I will not leave my father," she said firmly.

"Now listen, girlie—"

"And you cannot make me."

"I wouldn't be too certain of that," Bowes snarled. "Get back to your corner, then, and let me hear no pleas for help afore the morning comes."

"I will be all right."

Legs trembling, she returned to her place and sat down between her father and Henny. The older woman patted her arm. "There, ducks, ye're safe for now," she whispered.

Bowes shouted to the room at large. "I'll have no prowling and mewling around in the dark, laddies. Your backs will look like mine come the morning if I have to come in here to settle you down. You hear?" He looked them over malevolently, then left, taking the lamp with him.

Only a faint light entered from the high window as twilight deepened into dark. May 15, Roselynne thought. Caesar had been warned of the ides of March; she would be wise, she thought, to be as wary of the ides of May.

Beau had hardly finished his breakfast of eggs, fresh berries and cream, served with warm French croissants, before his attorney arrived. "You're zealous in your work," he said, noting the early hour.

"Your note said you had urgent business, so here I am," Bernard Clayburgh announced, taking a seat opposite Beau across the table. "Perhaps you would be kind enough to pour me a cup of tea?" His voice was pleasant, its tone deep and resonant.

"It's coffee."

"Yes, you Americans prefer the evil brew and have induced the unwise among us to indulge in the same." The attorney's smile was dry. "Well, give me a cup. I've not had breakfast."

Beau smiled. Under different circumstances, he would have enjoyed playing lord of the manor, but this morning's business was too serious. "Have a roll."

"I think I might." Clayburgh selected one and, taking Beau's knife, liberally spread it with butter and jelly.

"Tell me the law about a man taking on his wife's debts so that she may be released from prison upon his death," Beau requested when the other man finished and sipped the coffee.

Clayburgh was visibly surprised.

"An odd question, I know, but I have reasons," Beau said.

The attorney didn't speak right away, a characteristic of his that Beau found comforting. He liked a man who thought things through before replying. "What is it you would know?" Clayburgh asked. "You have the gist of it. That is the law."

"What if the woman didn't have debts, but was imprisoned on a minor charge?"

"What charge?"

"Attacking a soldier while trying to prevent the arrest of someone else."

"If you consider that a minor charge, what, pray tell, do you think of as a major one?"

Beau chuckled at the irony. "Sedition."

Clayburgh looked amused. "I'm afraid you've lost me in the maze of your thinking. Forgive my simple mind and speak plainly. She was arrested for sedition after attacking a guard?"

"Her father was."

Comprehension dawned on Clayburgh. "I'm beginning to see the light, as one might say, though your reasoning is still murky." He paused and steepled his fingers together. "Correct me if I'm wrong. There is a young lady whose crimes you wish to take to the scaffold with you so that she might be free. Her father was arrested for inciting others to overthrow the king and she . . . ?" His voice trailed off in question.

". . . Was arrested when she tried to prevent the soldiers from taking him."

"Hmm," the lawyer said and waited.

"They've not been tried and sentenced yet," Beau continued. His brow quirked humorously. "I think I need not tell you time is of the essence."

Again the dry smile flitted across Clayburgh's thin lips. "From your viewpoint, I'd say it is of *grave* consequence, if you'll forgive the pun. It is not meant cruelly."

"No offense taken." Beau waved the matter aside. "My question is, if she and I were to wed, could I take her fine or sentence for her? We'd have to petition the king for a pardon for her father, since his is the greater crime."

Clayburgh stared into his coffee as if reading some message in the vapors that rose from its surface. "You don't ask for much, do you?"

Beau grinned and shrugged.

"The king isn't feeling too sympathetic toward you Yanks at the moment. Neither is he apt to be indulgent of seditionists, having lost a major source of wealth in your colonies."

"I know 'twill be difficult, but not impossible for a smart man." Beau looked with meaning upon his attorney.

"Even flattery cannot change an impossible fate," Clayburgh warned softly. "Nevertheless, I appreciate your confidence in my small skills. All right, I will see what can be done."

Beau stood and shook Clayburgh's hand. "Use whatever funds you need. Find out all you can. By the way, do you know someone named Wainsco?"

"Of course. He's a rather powerful duke. Not an intimate of the king, but one whose word carries weight. Why?"

"He's known to the Moreleys. He may be able to help. Also, can you arrange a special license? I want to be ready to move on this if all works out."

"A man of action. I like that," Clayburgh murmured. "On a business level, I think we would have enjoyed a long term of mutual benefit. A pity you're about to hang."

"As my granny used to say, it isn't wise to count the chicks before they're out of the shell."

Clayburgh studied Beau for another moment. "You still wear the marks of your last attempt at escape. Do you plan another?"

Beau shook his head. "One never knows what the fates might have in store, though. Another opportunity with better odds may present itself."

And next time he was determined to succeed. During the last attempt—while being returned to gaol after his final appearance in court, where he had been sentenced to hang—he'd thought the gods must be with him. The guards had forgotten to put the leg shackles on him, nor had they tied the cords very tight around his wrists. He'd worked them off easily.

He'd made his break, but to no avail. Extra guards had been posted outside the Bailey, and he'd run right into their trap. Mr. Bowes had taken great pride in teaching him a lesson.

If he got another try at freedom, he would be very careful who knew of it. There was no need for anyone not directly involved to have the story.

"Nay, the chances are slim, perhaps none," he added as the attorney stood to leave. "I have another plan."

"Are you going to share it?"

"I thought you would have figured it out by now. The estate I inherited isn't entailed, thus I intend to marry and leave an heir with my name . . . and my wealth."

Roselynne woke from her dream and lay staring up at the ceiling. In the dream Bowes had taken her against her will to another cell, high in the turret of the building. He had opened a door and showed her inside. There, she faced the man she had seen in the window yesterday. Up close, his face was more than merely sinister. She saw he was a monster.

Horns protruded from his forehead in two curved spikes. His eyes were fiery red, and his gaze made her skin crawl as if with a thousand bugs. When he smiled, his long, deadly fangs were exposed to her horrified gaze.

She shuddered and tore herself loose from the nightmare. It was morning, and she was safe. The three of them—her father, herself and Henny—lay against each other like a stack of cordwood, chopped and ready for use.

Henny stirred and groaned. "Oh, me aching bones," she muttered, sitting up and rubbing her eyes.

Roselynne smiled at Henny. "The night is past," she said.

"Aye, but 'ow many do we 'ave to go?"

"Not many. Soon my father and I will be free, I'm sure. The Duke of Wainsco will get this straightened out. He is the employer of... a dear friend of mine."

"A sweet'eart, is 'e?"

Roselynne hesitated, then nodded. "When I'm free, I'll see what I can do about you. Would you take a job if I could find one for you?"

"Aye, I'm right good in the kitchen, I am, or waitin' table. I don't take to washing clothes, though."

"Then it's settled. You shall come home with father and me. I'd love to have you near. You're a good friend and true."

"'Ere now," Henny said with a sudden sheen in her eyes, "I ain't no better'n I ought to be, but I'll be your friend, never fear." She grinned at Roselynne.

Their friendship sealed, they talked of their future. By the time their bread came for breakfast, they had decided Henny would serve meals and clean for the Moreleys.

"And I must see about a barrister to aid the duke in our defense if we are to get out of here and execute this grand scheme of ours. I have a little money with me—"

"Shh," Henny said, glancing at the other occupants. "They's like to cut your throat for a penny, duckie."

Roselynne finished her crust and woke her father to partake of his. "I'm going to ask the turnkey to get us a lawyer, Father," she told him. "I fear we may need his services, no matter what Charles will be able to do for us."

She was increasingly worried at not hearing from Charles in all this time. The innkeeper at the village had assured her he would pass on the news of their predicament. The hostler was a man known to her all her life and she knew he would keep his word.

After Roselynne drank her ration of water, she stood and moved from leg to leg to exercise a bit. Bowes came to the door and peered in. He motioned to her to come close.

"So you made it through the night," he observed.

"As you can see, I am well."

"The guvner has sent his lawyer to talk with you. Will you go and listen?"

Roselynne was perplexed. "Who is this gentleman and what does he want from me?" she demanded.

"St. Clair be his name. The lawyer is Clayburgh, known throughout the city as a fair man," he added.

"You seem anxious that I speak with him. How much is he paying you to convince me?"

A faint red flushed Bowes's ears. "He said he'd give me a crown if I could get you to listen to him or the lawyer, either one."

"I have only to listen? 'Tis no trick to separate me from my father?"

"Nay. I think it would do you much good to listen. St. Clair's a generous man, he is."

"Show the lawyer to me. Bring him to the door."

Bowes looked as if he would like to say something harsh to her, but he finally nodded and left. In a minute, he returned with a gentleman dressed in an immaculate superfine morning coat of forest green, buff breeches and white waistcoat. A cravat of snowy linen was expertly tied around his neck, and he carried a silver-headed cane in his hand.

"Miss Moreley," he said with a slight bow. "I cannot blame you for your distrust, but my intentions are harmless. Will you hear me speak on my client's behalf?"

She nodded. "Henny, would you watch my father?"

"O' course, dearie. Never ye fret."

Bowes unlocked the door, and Roselynne followed him to another room, the lawyer behind her.

"Bernard Clayburgh, at your service," the lawyer said as soon as they were alone. "Would you take a cup of tea?"

"Yes," she said, her mouth watering at the aroma of cinnamon toast coming from a platter. Orange slices were artfully arranged on another dish, reminding her of rays of sunshine.

"Help yourself. I've eaten."

She shook her head. She would not be bribed with a piece of toast, no matter that it smelled like ambrosia from heaven.

"I represent Beauregard St. Clair. He wishes to speak to you and explain his case himself. His . . . proposition may surprise you, but I assure you, he is in dead earnest." He paused and smiled slightly at some jest she didn't understand.

"Cannot you tell me?"

"He asked to present his case in person. At his request, I have looked into your circumstances. I would advise you to cooperate with him."

Her eyes flashed with anger. "Who gives this Mr. St. Clair leave to delve into my affairs?"

"He took it upon himself—"

"Then perhaps he found I do not need his scheme nor your advice. We shall soon be free—"

"And if you're not?" he interrupted smoothly. "What do you think will happen to you ere too long in that crowded cell?"

"I will ask to be moved today."

"So, you will not listen at all?" Clayburgh gave a dry laugh. "St. Clair will be disappointed. He thought you looked a most sensible young lady."

"How could he think that? We have not met."

"He apparently saw you arrive yesterday."

Roselynne thought over the day. She had met no one other than the gaoler and his minions such as Mr. Bowes. A fragment of memory passed through her mind, that of a face watching from a high window. She shook off the nightmare.

"You could at least listen and make your judgment after you have the facts before you. Isn't that the way to make a wise decision?" he asked.

She smiled slightly. "I can see you have your true calling. You are most persuasive. All right, I will see this client of yours and hear him out."

"I will call him at once." Clayburgh went toward the door.

"Wait! What is he in prison for?"

"I will let him tell you." He left the room.

Roselynne stared at the tray while she waited. The aroma teased her nostrils cruelly, and her stomach growled, letting her know it was still hungry. She resisted the urge to eat every bite of toast and fruit. If she had nothing else, she had her dignity.

Folding her hands together in her lap, she stared out the narrow window and longed for the sunny fields of home. A sense of desolation swept over her. She was no longer sure of her place in the scheme of things.

"I'm disappointed you don't like the breakfast I ordered for you," a deep, masculine voice said from the door. "Would you prefer something else?"

Roselynne looked up. Her eyes widened in horror, and she was, for the first time in her life, rendered speechless. The monster of her dreams stood in the door!

No, of course he wasn't a monster, she chided. No short red horns stood out from his black hair. No poison-dripping fangs protruded from his mouth. Instead she saw a man who had been beaten with ferocious skill.

Bruises and swellings covered part of his face, making it impossible to judge its true outline, which was further hidden behind a coal black beard. His mouth had been injured and was scabbed on the bottom lip. The flesh around one eye had been badly assaulted. She met his amused gaze and almost gasped.

His eyes were blue, the purest shade she'd ever encountered, like that of the summer sky over Ullswater Lake when all was peaceful and still. The lashes were long and thick and the same black as his hair and beard. This man, whom she'd thought a monster yesterday, had the most beautiful eyes she'd ever seen.

Beau watched the sight of his appearance register on her. "Not a pretty visage, I agree," he said, touching his jaw gingerly.

He stepped into the room. The door closed behind him, and Bowes turned the key in the lock. There followed the sounds of the minion's heavy-footed gait as he left them. Beau saw her struggle to overcome her fear as she realized they were alone.

"The result of a dispute with several of the guards as to the direction I should take upon leaving the Old Bailey. I'd a notion to see something of the countryside rather than the gaol," he continued as if they discussed the most commonplace event.

"I apologize," she murmured. "I didn't mean to stare." Her expression changed to one of compassion.

"No apology needed. 'Tis a sight to cause babies to cry and grown men to shudder." He grinned when she smiled slightly at his quip. He wondered if it would hurt as much to kiss as it did to smile.

His gaze went to her lips. Her mouth was quite attractive. It was small, reminding him of a rosebud not yet opened to the heat of the sun. Or the heat of his mouth.

A stirring inside recalled the dreams he had entertained during the night. He would like to undress her and discover all the sweet mysteries she possessed. During the night, he'd had visions enough about her womanly charms to fill a harem.

Enough of that, he admonished, feeling the fabric of his doeskin breeches tighten across his groin. He'd frighten her again. Assuming a casual air, he smiled guilelessly at his guest.

"Allow me to introduce myself, Miss Moreley. Beauregard Winston St. Clair, formerly of Virginia, lately of his majesty's finest accommodation." He waved a careless hand at their prison. "My friends call me Beau."

"You…you are from the colonies?" she asked. Her hands clutched the shawl tightly around her shoulders, giving him no clue as to her shape.

Her face was lovelier up close than from a distance. Her eyes were wide-set and gray in hue. Her nose was short and up-tilted. There was a slight cleft in her chin. Hers was the type of face that at thirty would still retain the freshness of sixteen and would remain so until old age, unless life intervened and turned her bitter.

In her eyes, he observed a sharp intellect. From her actions yesterday, he knew her to be a person of courage. An interesting personality, he thought.

"We Americans won the war," he chided on a humorous note. "The colonies are now states."

"I beg your pardon," she said.

He nodded toward the food. "Won't you accept my gift?"

She shook her head, causing soft brown tendrils to float attractively about her face. In spite of the mud on the hem of her gray dress, she had managed to keep herself fairly clean during her captivity.

"I have had breakfast," she said politely.

Beau felt his admiration for her grow. While he had been willing to accept a street urchin for a wife to thwart his enemies—whoever they were—he was more than delighted with her poise and aspect with every passing second.

"You'll hurt my feelings if you don't eat," he said softly.

She hesitated, glanced at the food, then at him. "Why is it important to you?"

He shrugged. "I think you will listen better and decide more accurately if your physical comforts are first seen to."

Giving in to his logic, albeit cautiously, she lifted a piece of toast and bit into it with even white teeth. Beau relaxed. She trusted him enough to eat his food. That was a good sign.

He ambled to the table and sat in the opposite chair, his every move controlled and careful so as not to alarm her.

Her hands were slender, with tapering fingers that looked capable of a hard day's work. As an impecunious vicar's daughter, she was probably used to doing for her father and herself as well as others; another positive attribute.

He judged her to be about twenty. Bowes said no one had asked about her, so it would seem she had no suitor. She was plainly a person of sense and compassion, and she might not be averse to aiding him if he put his plan to her rightly.

She wiped her mouth with the napkin and laid it beside her plate when she finished. "You should have a poultice for your bruises. If only I had my medicinals." She looked with pity on his countenance.

So, he had figured her correctly. "Thank you for your concern, but my bruises are of no consequence. They'll heal on their own. Would you pour me a cup of coffee?"

"Of course." She asked his preference for cream and sugar, and, ascertaining that he took neither, prepared the cup and gave it to him.

She was used to the genteel life. So much the better to be his countess. Yes, she would suit his purposes.

His gaze wandered again to the shawl she kept around her shoulders. Most likely she was on the skinny side, flat-bosomed and thin-flanked, judging by the slenderness of her wrist.

It didn't matter. As his wife and heir, she would suit his purposes very well, but only if he could charm her into trusting him and becoming his wife.

A savage hunger shot through him at the thought, so unexpected that he hadn't time to prepare and control it. It was a good thing he'd sat down. She'd probably faint if she saw the hard pulse of his desire against his breeches. He'd never wanted a woman the way he wanted this one.

Roselynne lifted her gaze to Beauregard St. Clair. Beau, to his friends, he had said. He seemed rational....

A peculiar look in his eyes startled her. It seemed to sear through her clothing to the very center of her being, causing a sharp ache on its passage. She grasped her shawl nervously and pulled it tightly around her shoulders. A grimace, almost of pain, passed over his face immediately thereafter.

"Is something wrong, Mr. St. Clair? Are you in pain?" she inquired anxiously.

His glance was startled. "I'd best be prepared for your discerning eye," he said with a slight laugh. "No, I'm not in pain. I just had an odd thought, is all."

She relaxed in her chair and picked up her cup. "And will you not share it?"

"Not now."

His smile changed, becoming wistful, she thought. That was a silly notion. He was far from wistful. She would say he was a man used to command, to having his own way or making the world conform to his ideas. The subjugation of prison life must be doubly hard on such a one. Her compassion for him increased.

He also stirred other emotions in her. When he looked at her, though his face was harsh to the eye, his gaze seemed heated with emotions she didn't comprehend. It roused strange impulses in her, which made her wary and on edge. A sense of self-preservation told her she should go.

Realizing she couldn't leave without the turnkey to guide her to the common cell where her father waited, she forced her gaze from his when he lifted his cup to his mouth.

His hand was broad across the palm, his fingers long and well cared for, she saw. The nails were clean and trimmed straight across the blunt tips. He handled the china cup as if familiar with delicate items and seemed wellborn in all respects.

If she had gone to him last night, she instinctively knew he would have treated her with the same courtesy he showed her this morning. The turnkey had been truthful when he'd assured her Mr. St. Clair was a gentleman.

But perhaps she was being fanciful. She pushed the thought from her mind and observed the firm column of his neck. His skin was brown and looked warm and healthy.

When he lowered the cup, she moved her gaze from his throat. The white linen of his cravat contrasted nicely with the deep blue of his morning coat. His shoulders were broad and tapered to a lean waist. She remembered the length and confidence of his stride when he crossed the room. He was a man who knew what he wanted.

"Why did you wish to see me, Mr. St. Clair?" she asked, reminded of the reason she was here.

He put the cup on its saucer. "Mr. Clayburgh mentioned a proposition to you, didn't he?"

"Yes." Her pose became wary.

He waved his hand as if putting aside her doubts. "Not the same one Mr. Bowes spoke of last night, I assure you."

A faint shade of red touched her cheeks. "Did he mistake your intent then?"

"No."

The brevity of his reply kindled her anger of the previous evening. "I thought not. I am not for sale, by Mr. Bowes or anyone." She rose. "I'm sure we have no further need for discussion."

"Please be seated, Miss Moreley."

His order was clothed as a request and spoken gently, but she had no doubt that it was a command.

"If you think to make me some deal whereby you will use me for your pleasure while promising to aid my father, you are off in your estimation of my character." She started for the door.

He was beside her in the space of a heartbeat, his hand closing on her wrist to detain her when she would have beaten on the portal.

A bolt of heat seemed to traverse her arm where he touched her. The burning sensation plunged all the way inside her. It frightened her to feel so turbulent toward a stranger, one whose nature she knew not.

"Don't be so hasty to judge. You've supplied your own reasons for my actions without hearing mine. It's true that I thought to amuse myself with you last night, but I've had another idea since then. Will you listen?''

They stared at each other, their faces only inches apart as he leaned toward her.

For a frantic heartbeat, she thought he meant to kiss her. She saw his lips move. His tongue quickly licked moisture across their cracked service, thus making them more pliable. She found herself caught between fear and a strange curiosity that urged her to wait for the outcome.

Had she, like her father, lost her wits? She knew nothing of this man. He appeared refined, but for all she knew, he might be thinking of strangulation rather than the tender act she envisioned. She held herself very still.

Slowly, with great deliberation, he released her and stepped back. ''Please,'' he said, ''will you listen, then judge what your answer will be?''

Swallowing the lump in her throat, she nodded. ''Yes,'' she whispered. ''I will hear what you propose.''

Chapter Three

"Propose is the correct word," he said with a chuckle. "How old are you, Miss Moreley?"

"I'll be twenty, come August," she replied. "Would you make your meaning clear, sir?"

"Beau. Call me Beau. May I call you Roselynne?"

She considered the request before nodding slowly.

"You are surprisingly wary for one so young," he commented.

"I have learned in the past few days that caution is the greater part of wisdom."

He gave her a glance filled with admiration. "My intentions are strictly honorable. I want you to marry me."

She opened her mouth, but no words issued forth. She shook her head slowly, disbelief of what she had heard plain in her face. "Do not jest with me, sir. I'm in no mood for funning."

Beneath her shawl, she locked her hands together to still their sudden trembling. He was playing a trick on her, or perhaps madness had seized his brain.

"I'm not jesting, Roselynne." He rose and paced about the room. "Let me tell you of my plight since I arrived on the shores of your fair isle."

Roselynne followed his movements about the room. He was not at all like Charles, she thought suddenly. His legs were well-shaped and thick with muscle that moved beneath his close-fitted breeches when he stalked the short length of the cell and turned abruptly toward her, his eyes narrowed in thought.

Charles was thinner. He practiced the languid air of the ton. Beau St. Clair, she knew instinctively, would have no patience with that attitude. His every motion was full of determination and purpose. She wondered if she would be able to resist if he was determined to have her to wife.

"Five years ago," he began, "I received a letter from a second cousin whom I had never met. The Earl of Rockdale. Do you know of him?"

She shook her head. "I may have heard the name, but I'm sure I never met him."

"He was something of a recluse, I think. His missive informed me his brother, apparently a young hellion, had recently died in an accident while riding along a bluff. The boy was thrown from his mount and broke his neck when he went over the edge."

"I'm terribly sorry," Roselynne murmured, automatically reverting to the role of the vicar's daughter, who heard many tragic stories.

"You may imagine my surprise when he told me that I was now his heir and that he wanted to know when I could come to England to begin to learn my duties."

He strode about the room once again, as if the small space wasn't great enough for the energy he possessed. An earl, she thought dazedly. He's heir to an earldom. She stared at his back when he paused before the window and gazed down into the street. It occurred to her that, from this view, he was quite comely in a very manly way. His tailored costume showed his masculine lines with great accuracy.

If only his face hadn't been so battered. Of course, common sense indicated that he wouldn't look near so formidable when some of his bruises faded and his swellings went down. She suspected his nose was broken and would sport a slight crook to remind him of his prison days.

"I replied that it was impossible at the time. We continued a correspondence over the next few years while I labored to get my plantation in working order after the war. Then I received a strange letter from my cousin. In it, he warned me to be very careful. He thought someone was trying to kill him, and I would be next, since I was in the direct line of descent.''

"How awful," she said, becoming intrigued with his story. She had always loved novels of danger. His tale sent a shiver of apprehension over her scalp.

"Yes." He strode to the table and stood beside her, so close that his leg brushed her skirt and she could feel his heat through the material. "Did Clayburgh tell you why I'm in prison?"

She shook her head.

"Murder."

She said nothing.

"They say I murdered my cousin for the title and especially for the considerable wealth he had amassed."

"Did you?" she asked bravely.

He pulled a chair close, sat in it and took her hand between both of his. "I swear by my hope of heaven that I had nothing to do with it."

"Then you didn't kill anyone?"

"No."

"I am relieved to hear it."

He cocked his head and stared at her curiously. "You believe it then? Without hearing the rest of my story?"

Roselynne licked her lips and considered her reply. She had always had good instincts about people. Perhaps that came of her father's close work with the folks in the parish. Lies always had a way of coming out, and she usually knew when the truth was being bandied about. Her father relied on her clear thinking.

"Perhaps you had better tell me the whole of it," she suggested, holding judgment. She eased her hand from his.

He rose and paced angrily. "My cousin arranged that I should come here, unknown to anyone but himself. We met at a crofter's vacant house and talked. He was distraught. More than one attempt had been made on his life, and he feared for mine."

"He sounds a good man."

"He was. We made plans to ferret out the culprit, and I left him at the cottage, expecting to meet him the next night at the same time. Instead, I was arrested by the local constable and his henchmen when I arrived there at the appointed hour. My cousin had been murdered the night before, his throat stabbed, then laid open with a knife. All evidence pointed to me, since his death was to my advantage."

"Because of the title and inheritance," she said.

"Yes."

"And you have no proof to clear your name?"

"None. I returned to a sailor's hostel on the coast—"

"Did no one see you at the inn who could vouch for your presence?"

"Yes, but the magistrate said I killed my cousin before I left the cottage."

"Then why would you return to walk into the constable's arms the next night?"

"For a woman, you are damned astute," Beau said, looking at her in admiration. "That is the argument Clayburgh used, but to no avail. No one would believe my story. I had no proof, other than my cousin's letter indicating his suspicions. The court said I preyed upon his fears and used the secret meeting to kill him."

"I can see their reasoning," Roselynne murmured.

He struck a fist upon his open palm. "By damn, but I would like to know the perpetrator of this misdeed before I hang."

"I will help you . . ." She realized the ridiculousness of that statement. "That is, as soon as my father and I are free."

He returned to the chair beside her. "You believe me?"

Roselynne ignored his bruises and gazed into his clear blue eyes. She saw strength, sutblety . . . yes, and arrogance and stubbornness, but no trace of subterfuge. "Yes, I do."

Reaching beneath her protective shawl, he grabbed her hand and brought it to his lips. He pressed an urgent kiss on it as if his passions were too much for verbal expression.

She felt a strange prickling all the way to her shoulder. It was not the first time her hand had been kissed in gratitude. A farmer in their parish had done the same when she had aided his wife through a difficult birth after the midwife had given up. Roselynne had been able to save the child, a boy. This kiss, however, was quite different from the other.

"Then you agree to the marriage?" he inquired huskily.

Roselynne stiffened and pulled her hand from him. Her skin burned from the contact. She had never felt so confused. This restive American disturbed her greatly.

"No, my lord. I did not say so. I only agreed that I trusted in the truth of your tale."

"My lord," he repeated. "In America, we don't care much for titles and such. A man must earn the respect of other men with the labor of his own hands and wit."

"That is the same here, but a title is inherited. Who stands to gain after you?"

His face hardened. "None that I know of. I'm the last male of the line. At first I was unwilling to forswear my American citizenship for a title, but then this bit of vile treachery was perpetrated. Now I'm determined to seek out the culprit and make him pay for his crimes. Unless I am forced to service the debt for him." His grin was reckless.

"Or her," Roselynne suggested. "What of female relatives? Is there one who would gain the wealth, or is it entailed with the title?"

"No, it is not. But there are no others at all. That is why you must marry me."

Her heart pounded at his insistence. "I don't follow your logic," she managed to say. His gaze was so compelling, she feared she would find herself agreeing before she could gain her wits and prevent it.

"As my wife you would inherit the property and income, else it reverts to the crown for the king to dispense as a favor to whomever he will. I wouldn't like to see that."

"Since you will be cold in the grave by then, your grudge isn't likely to bother King George." She lapsed into speculative thought. "Who is close to the king . . . and also knew the late earl?"

Beau shrugged impatiently. "Who knows? I care not. There'll be someone who will marry me for the gain. I am set upon it." His gaze settled on her. "You're a fool to refuse my offer. Money buys all the comforts of home, even in Newgate. It would buy your freedom, and, I've no doubt, that of your father."

It was her turn to pace the room in agitation. "What of my life? Would it not be forfeit, too, by the same cunning enemy?"

He caught her shoulders when she stopped in front of him. "Nay, Roselynne. I have a man I would trust as myself. He will guard you day and night until this mystery is solved if I am not on hand to protect you. You have my word."

"Where is he? He has not protected you so well."

"He only arrived this week. Please think seriously of my offer. I must have your answer soon or find another for my purpose," he cajoled, his deep voice dropping another note.

His fingers moved in tiny caresses on her, feeling her womanly warmth through the wool shawl and cotton dress. She had a delicacy of frame that pleased him. He wanted to touch her... all over. His mind became set on her, and he willed her to do his bidding.

When she raised troubled gray eyes to him, he couldn't resist the temptation of her mouth. His lips settled on hers.

The smoothness of her lips beneath his rough ones caused such a rush of desire, he had to fight his own emotions to stop himself from taking his husbandly rights before those rights had been granted. The nearness of her, the gentleness of her expression, reminded him of his dreams during the night in which he'd kissed her and held her in a passionate embrace.

He sensed her shock, then felt the beginnings of her struggle to be free. He tightened his clasp but couldn't hold her lips with his when she twisted her head away.

"Don't fight me, Roselynne. I need you," he whispered, using the most persuasive tone he could muster. "And you need me. Let's marry and thus fool the fate that awaits us."

"If I do, what will you expect of me?" she asked, her voice trembling. "Will I take your name only?"

The question seemed an insult to his tender dreams of wedded bliss and clearly indicated her feelings toward him. "I confess the thought of a child of my own intrigues me."

She again tried to free herself. "No, I won't. You can't ask it of me. No, let me go. Please."

"Go, then," he said. He went to the window and stood with his back to her, unable to quell his fury at her refusal.

* * *

Roselynne paused outside the common cell and tried to quiet her rioting emotions before entering. Mr. Bowes gave her an impatient glance. He had obviously written her off as daft when she'd demanded to be returned.

She tried valiantly to calm the trembles that shook her legs before she stepped inside. Her glance went automatically to the corner to check her father.

"Oh, dear, what happened?" she asked, going forward. Bowes slammed the iron door behind her.

Her father's coat was ripped along the shoulder seam and his fine white hair was disheveled. A bruise discolored his chin.

"'Twere a little scuffle, that's all," Henny said, sending a glare across the room toward Neddie. His burly friend, Hinkle, grinned and winked broadly at Roselynne.

Roselynne ignored the brute. "Who did this?"

Henny pointed a finger at Neddie. "He tried to get your da's coat, but I wouldn't let him have it. I did real good, except he wrestled the pot away." Henny chuckled. "It splashed some, but most of it went on the thief." She was highly pleased.

Roselynne inspected the damage, relieved it wasn't more than a few ripped threads. "Thank you, Henny," she said sincerely. "I must get him out of here." She glanced from her father to her new friend, uncertain what to do. Her tiny hoard of funds wouldn't extend to caring for three.

Henny detected her worries. "Now, don't ye go worryin' about me. I got nothin' they wants. Get your da to a safe place."

"Mr. Bowes," Roselynne called, making the decision. "Mr. Bowes, I would speak to you privately."

When he came to the door, she spoke in a whisper to him about a room for her father and herself.

"It'll cost you," he said.

"How much?"

"How much you got?"

She wasn't fool enough to tell him. "I'll give you a shilling."

He laughed as if she had told a hilarious joke.

"A crown then. That's all I'll go... until I see the room," she added, seeing the denial in his eyes.

He considered, then agreed. "Come along then and be quick about it. I got more to do than worry with the likes of you." He unlocked the door.

She rushed to the corner. "Come, Father, we're going to another cell."

"Too good fer us they be," the other woman sneered.

"Shut ye up," Henny advised. "Go on, ducks. Ye'll be better out of 'ere. Take yer da and go," she urged Roselynne, who had paused to look again at her.

Roselynne knew she dared not return to this cell. The resentment against her had coalesced into dislike from all except Henny at her escape from their common fate.

In the corridor, Bowes stopped after locking the door. "The coin," he demanded.

"Turn your back," she said, refusing to get the money while he looked.

With a snort, he pivoted heavily and leaned against the wall. "Guess you got something you think I'd want to see. I like the lasses with a bit of flesh on their bones."

Roselynne made sure no one watched, then removed the coin from a pouch tied around her neck and turned to the back so that it lay hidden under her dress and the thickness of her chignon. She quickly returned it to its hiding place.

"Here you are, Mr. Bowes."

He took the money as if doing her a great favor and lumbered off down the dim corridor. She followed quickly, pulling her father along without her usual gentleness. She was afraid if she let the turnkey out of her sight, he would desert them to a fate worse than the one she had left.

The room he showed them was in the same turret as Beau St. Clair, but one floor lower. It was a cramped space containing one narrow cot with a straw mattress on it and two chairs pushed up to a rough plank table that was pitted and scarred. The whole was dirty beyond imagining and smelled as bad as the common cell below.

"Take it or not," Bowes said, seeing an indignant protest forming on her lips.

"I'll need hot water and rags to clean it. And a fresh chamber pot. And mattress." She held the shawl over her nose and mouth while she spoke.

He grinned.

"How much?" she asked.

"Another two bits," he said.

"Turn around."

After she paid him and he left, she gingerly pushed all the trash and items she wanted to be removed next to the door. An old crone of a woman appeared in a few minutes. She set a pan of steaming water on the table, laid some rags next to it, and scampered out with an armload of debris. She returned once with a cleaner mattress and a blanket, then left with the rest of the trash.

Roselynne scrubbed the table first, then the chairs, bed frame and last, the wooden planks of the floor. The water was black when she finished, but the room smelled better. Glancing below to see that the courtyard was clear, she threw the water out.

Later, when bread and gruel were served for lunch, she purchased clean water and washed her father's face, hands and feet, then his clothing. With another coin, she bought firewood and started a fire in the hearth.

Soon the little cell was warm and as cozy as she could make it. When she had her father tucked on the cot for a nap, she bought more water and washed herself.

After another meal of bread and watery soup that night, she counted her money and, based on her day's experiences, estimated she had enough to last a week or more, provided she was very careful. Her father needed better food, and she must arrange for the barrister, it seemed.

The sky darkened into night. She stood by the window and watched the stars appear, one by one. A torrent of despair rose in her. She yearned to be free, to run across the fields of home, to stop by a crofter's cottage and eat a fried pie made from last year's dried apples and drink a glass of cool buttermilk.

An ache started and grew inside her. A sob rose to her throat. She placed her arms on the windowsill and buried her face in them. "Charles, where are you?" she asked, her voice thickened with tears and trembling with need. "Help us. *Please.*"

She sounded as whiny as Neddie, she scolded, trying for composure that seemed bent on slipping into self-pity. So far she had made it to this point without great tragedy. Surely she could hold out a while longer.

"A beautiful night, isn't it?"

Roselynne jerked her head up from its sorrowful position on her crossed arms. Her eyes darted around the small room behind her, but the voice hadn't come from that direction. She gazed outside the bars. Nothing there but the spires of London against the blue velvet of the sky.

"Do you think that bright star low on the horizon is Venus? I can't remember the star charts. It's been too long since I studied them."

She leaned against the bars and looked upward. A faint light shone into the darkness from the window above. "My lord?"

"Beau," he said, his deep, attractive chuckle wafting on the cooling breeze. "I'm happy to know you found accommodations more to your liking. Is your father with you?"

"Yes."

"How is he?"

She glanced at her sleeping parent. He had roused when she fed him supper and gone right back to sleep when she put him to bed after that. "I think he was terribly tired from the journey, but he sleeps well."

"That's good." Beau St. Clair sounded genuinely pleased. "And how about yourself?"

She lowered her head, hoping he hadn't heard her pitiful utterances when she'd called for Charles to save her. "I'm quite fine, thank you."

"Do you have a bed to sleep in?"

She smiled ruefully. He must think her as rich as a lord, as he obviously was. "I'll be all right."

"The night will be cold," he warned.

She shuddered as she remembered Hinkle's mention of keeping warm the previous night. She was glad to be away from him.

Unbidden, the memory of Beau St. Clair's kiss leaped into her thoughts, as it had many times since the event. His embrace had been warm, sheltering, restful.... She was appalled at the idea. Her mind was apparently none too steady this evening.

"My bed will be warm," he said, reading her mind.

She started and gasped.

"I've shocked you," he called softly down to her. "If we were married, we could sleep together in my bed. 'Tis comfortable with a feather mattress of finest down. I have a special license," he added, as if this were part and parcel of a sane conversation.

"You are mad," she admonished, "to think I would wed with one I don't even know. We have no affection between us."

"Perhaps it would grow. It seems to me that marriage would be an excellent way to get to know each other."

She thought of the gossip she'd heard in the parish regarding the surprises and shocks of the wedding bed. As the parish healer, she'd gleaned more information than most maids. The cottagers had been inclined to be frank. She laughed suddenly. "Yes, but one may learn more than one wishes."

Beau cocked his head to one side and listened to her laughter float up to him on the night air. At least his risqué teasing was driving the despair from her.

He wondered who Charles was. The duke? She'd not likely call him by name. The man might be a relative. Or a lover. She was far too lovely, in fact and spirit, not to have a serious suitor.

"Or one may learn of wonders undreamed," Beau said, his own voice going deeper and huskier.

She didn't answer, and he sensed she wouldn't talk further. His guess was confirmed when he heard the scrape of the shutter being closed. On an impulse, he called Bowes.

"I want you to take this comforter to the Moreley wench," he said, tossing a fur throw to the man. He threw a coin after it. "See that she gets a bed and—"

"There's not enough room for another bed, guvner."

Beau frowned. "A pallet, then. Surely there's room to stretch a mattress on the floor." The hard glint in his eyes caused Bowes's head to nod energetically.

"I'll see to it," he promised, tucking the coin away. He ambled out, leaving the door unlocked. He often "forgot" to lock it behind him.

Beau suspected the turnkey wanted him to try and escape so he could lay into him with his ham-sized fists again while two guards held him prisoner between them. However, he didn't intend to give Bowes the pleasure of breaking his nose a second time. He turned back to the window and gazed at the plentitude of stars now showing, his thoughts on the woman he'd asked to be his wife.

At his orders, Clayburgh had sought out the Duke of Wainsco to ask his help in speaking on the vicar's behalf to the king. If all went well—and with sufficient exchange of money—the charges would be dropped and Mr. Moreley and his courageous daughter wouldn't have to stand trial. Perhaps then she would reconsider his offer.

A cynical smile flitted over his lips. She was fast learning the true nature of the royal judicial system: money could buy privacy, comfort and, on occasion, freedom.

His imagination lent itself to producing many pictures of them as man and wife. He was certain she was a virgin, and he devised plans to seduce her so carefully that she would yield gladly and feel no pain, or very little. He wasn't sure on this score, never having had a virgin before.

A pang vibrated through him with great force as he thought of removing that damned concealing shawl from her shoulders. He wondered at the treasures hidden beneath that plain wrapping. It was driving him wild to find out.

He ran a hand through his hair. It came away wet. He made a face of dislike at the dark stain of dye on his fingers. He'd forgotten he'd touched up his hair when he bathed that evening. Thank God his beard and eyebrows were naturally dark so he didn't have to dye them, too.

It was a good thing his cousin had insisted he alter his looks before coming to England. It would simplify his plans not to have to keep coloring his hair, if he were ever free.

Freedom seemed a distant, if not impossible, goal just now. Thinking back on his life, he felt he'd been the slave of time, war and circumstances forever. He could scarce remember when he'd been young or happy, except for the few months with Mary.

Sadness erased the erotic musings of a moment ago. Mary, his sweet, gentle love, his fiancée. Mary, who had died and left him lonelier than he had ever been, more so than at the deaths of his dear parents and two sisters during the hard years of the war. Mary, who had been laughter and starlight. Oh, God...Mary.

He swallowed the stricture in his throat and put the sad thoughts away. That had been years ago; this was now. He wanted to live, he discovered. When had he started caring about life again?

Chapter Four

Roselynne stared at the old crone. "In town? You mean here in London? At his town house?" She couldn't believe it. The Duke of Wainsco had been in town for almost a week . . . and Charles was with him.

The crone nodded, smiled and held out her hand. Roselynne put a copper into it.

"Wait for my letter," she ordered and quickly penned a note on the paper the woman had bought for her . . . for a price. Every item in Newgate had a price, she had found. She folded the letter and handed it to the crone along with another coin. The woman grinned a nearly toothless smile and left the cell.

Roselynne sank into a chair, but only for a moment. Rising, she went to the window and opened the shutter, needing air and the sight of freedom in the open fields beyond the town.

"Good morning."

A startled frown settled between her brows. "Do you stay at the window all the time, my lord?"

"The view outside is more interesting than that inside," he replied. "Don't you think, given our circumstances, we could dispense with formalities and call each other by name?"

"No, my lord. It wouldn't be proper."

He sighed audibly. "I like the sound of my name on a woman's lips." Before she could respond to this, he spoke again. "Why were you angry a minute ago?"

Her fingers, which had been idly rubbing the bar, jerked in surprise. "Can you hear all that happens in the prison?"

He chuckled. "My hearing is exceptionally keen, but even so, it doesn't extend to all the corners of Newgate. I could hear your voice raised, but not the words."

Recalling what she had just learned from the old woman, Roselynne felt a painful cramp in her chest as if a vise squeezed her heart. She'd assumed her verbal message to Charles hadn't been delivered by the Ullswater innkeeper, and had engaged the old woman who worked about the prison to go to the Wainsco town house to ascertain the directions for a letter.

She still couldn't believe the duke was in town and had been for five days. Charles had come, too. It was inconceivable that he was in London and hadn't rushed to see about her and her father. "It was a minor thing," she said. After a brief hesitation, she added, "Thank you for your generosity. I ... The bedding was appreciated and useful."

She had planned to sleep in a chair with only her shawl for warmth during the night. The straw pallet and fur cover had been wonderful, and she hadn't been able to resist their comfort. She felt rested for the first time in days.

"It nearly choked you to say your thanks," he gibed. "Is it so hard for you to be grateful?"

"Only when I think of the reasons for your gifts, my lord," she said with some asperity.

"Which are?"

She leaned against the bars and wished she could see his face. He was probably laughing at her. "You wish to sway me to your bidding. I assure you, though, that I am not without a defender, who will soon be at hand."

"Who is this great knight?" he asked with a mixture of curiosity and amusement in his deep, pleasant voice.

"I will introduce you when he arrives." So saying, she returned to the chore she had started earlier.

Her clothing was spread before a small fire, and she turned it so that it would dry on the nether side. She drew the fur closer around her and rubbed her chin against it, enjoying the tactile caress of the rich sable.

A whiff of some spicy scent rose from its luxurious folds, and she knew it belonged to Beau St. Clair. It reminded her of the American—bold yet subtle, arrogant but gentle, with a lightness that reminded her of his humor and the way his chuckle drifted down to her when they talked at their windows.

Unbidden, a comparison of the two men arose in her mind—Charles, who apparently had done nothing about her imprisonment, and Beau St. Clair, Earl of Rockdale, who had offered her a means of escape. The painful tightness attacked her chest again, and she pressed a hand against her heart.

Perhaps she wasn't being fair. Charles surely didn't know of her problem as yet. He would be greatly distressed and shocked when he received her note. Even now, he was probably on the way to see her.

Taking herself in hand, she shook out her dress and held it nearer the fire. On the cot, her father slept peacefully. She hoped his mind was mending as his body rested.

When her clothing was dry, she dressed, then combed her thick mane of hair. This time she plaited it and formed an "eight" at the base of her neck to hide the bulge of the small purse. She nervously paced the floor while waiting for Charles to answer her note. He would come soon...surely he would....

Roselynne, restless and unable to sleep, pulled the fur throw tightly around her and went to the window. Opening the shutter, she gazed outside, so full of despair she wanted to cry and rant at fate. She fought the panic that rose inside her. She must be brave. Her father depended upon her.

Night lay upon the city. A fog crept silently around the buildings, hiding their foundations and giving them an eerie appearance. The wind was chill and deposited a film of moisture on her face. She stood there for several minutes, then heard the scrape of a shutter from above.

Her fellow prisoner had come to his window. She saw the flare of his light and inhaled the sweet scent of his tobacco when he lit his pipe. Neither of them spoke.

Her mind raced with a thousand unanswered questions. Fragments of thought, too faint to be fully realized before they were cast out by others, endlessly worried her tired brain.

The crone had assured her she had delivered the message to the butler, who had taken it directly to Charles. There had been no reply. *None.*

Her fears resurfaced. If Charles would not inform the duke of their situation, then she would have to find her own way out of this coil. If only she hadn't gotten herself cast into prison. She couldn't help her father from inside a cell.

A drift of tobacco smoke curled through the bars, mocking her worries. Beau St. Clair had offered her a way out. With his money to back her, she was sure she could free her father. This much she had learned in prison—money was the key to many doors.

Above her, she heard St. Clair move around his room. Often in the hours past, she had heard the restless pacing of his steps. A reluctant sympathy coursed through her. She wondered if he had found anyone else to be his countess.

For a moment, she thought of speaking to him. If nothing else, she could extend to him the comfort of conversing with another person who would understand his feelings, but further talk would serve no purpose. She reached for the wooden shutter.

"Goodnight, Roselynne," he said softly before she closed it.

She paused with her hand on the catch. One part of her, urged by desperation, wanted to tell him she'd reconsidered his proposal. Another part, afraid of the feelings he incited in her and of his expectations for marriage, shrank from the thought. Unable to choose, she closed the shutter. She'd wait one more day.

It was late afternoon before Bowes announced she had a visitor. She sprang to her feet, her knees weak with hope.

"Show him in," she said.

"Well, it might be against regulations 'n all—"

"No, it isn't. I won't give you another shilling, and I'll see that the king knows of your conduct—"

"All right. Don't get in a huff, girl." He grinned lewdly. "You want I should remove your father for an hour or so, give you some time alone with the gentleman?"

She hid her shock at his effrontery. "No, thank you. You may have Mr. Osgood come up."

Bowes nodded and lumbered out. She heard him muttering, "Hoity-toity," as he walked down the hall. She ran her hands over her skirt, regretting that she had no iron to smooth it. But at least it was clean. She glanced at her father, who sat quietly at the table. He, too, looked presentable.

"I wish you could speak," she whispered, placing her hand on his shoulder. "I need your wise counsel."

The door opened, and Charles walked in. He brought the scent of springtime with him, the freshness of daffodils and early roses, of pines and hemlocks. He looked crisp despite his languid air, and she was so glad to see him, she forgave his tardiness in appearing.

"Charles!" She threw herself into his arms and hid her face against the velvet of his brown morning coat, fighting the tears that clogged her throat. "I'm so glad you're here. Father and I are in the most dreadful muddle," she mumbled huskily.

After a few seconds, she realized his reluctance to indulge in an emotional scene. When she stepped back, he brushed at his coat, checking the pile of the velvet. She felt chastened for her conduct although he said not a word.

"Here, I'm a terrible hostess," she said, covering her awkwardness when she sensed his withdrawal. She brushed at her eyes. "Would you take some tea? I have some prepared."

He straightened his linen cravat. "Tea would be fine." His voice was so dearly familiar, she nearly wept again. He glanced around the tiny cell, and she almost apologized for its appearance.

Realizing she needed another chair, she gently moved her father to sit on the bed and invited Charles to the table. He asked about her health, and she inquired about his. She added two cubes of sugar to his teacup and poured a dash of milk left from the breakfast porridge, then she waited impatiently for him to taste the brew and make the usual polite comment.

"Very good," he said in approval after taking a sip.

"I am so pleased to see you," she exclaimed.

"The pleasure is mine," he returned. His gaze upon her was so remote she experienced a chill.

Suddenly she felt gauche with him, as if she had no reason to ask his aid. But that was silly. This was Charles, her very dear friend, who had spoken to her of his prospects quite earnestly no more than a month ago.

"What has happened?" he asked. He crossed his legs, and she noted the perfect shine on his shoes, the perfect fit of his breeches. He looked so... fashionable.

She explained her story to him in detail, leaving out only Beau St. Clair's outlandish proposal. "Has the duke spoken to the king yet? I'm sure his word will set things right."

Charles lifted his brows as if questioning her sanity. "I felt I should establish the facts before approaching him."

"Before approaching... Have you not spoken to him at all regarding us? Did you not get any message at the posting inn? You would have had to change horses there."

"There was a great deal of confusion when we arrived. The stableboys were excited about the gang of criminals that had gone through the day before. They told us nothing."

He glanced about the tiny room with an air of distaste and held his handkerchief to his nose to stifle a sneeze. Roselynne had the distinct impression that he was lying. She cast it aside.

"Father and I were in that group," she told him. "Oh, to think we missed you by only one day. All this could have been avoided. It is so frightening to be in prison."

"I'm sure it is," he said coolly. "But I fail to see what his lordship can do for you. I understand your father wrote a paper advocating that we all follow the American example and rebel against the king."

"That was not the way of it at all. He merely reflected that in a healthy society, the king rules by the will of the people. A tyrant rules by fear and subjugation."

Charles waved his handkerchief, stopping her flow of words. "An unfortunate observation for these times. Well, I will speak to the duke as soon as it is convenient—"

"Convenient," she snapped, her temper rising like the sudden release of steam from a boiler engine. "What has that to do with anything? My father and I need his help at once. You must speak to him immediately. Today, Charles, within the hour."

"One cannot rush into these things. The duke is preparing a speech for the House of Lords. I have been waiting for the most opportune time to present your cause." His voice was more than cool; it was frigid.

"Then you *did* receive my message," she said, knowing it was true. She could sense his unease.

They looked at each other for a long second, then he looked away. "I didn't think it of great consequence," he explained stiffly. "You haven't even come to trial yet."

She licked her lips and tried to speak calmly. "Charles, we've been prisoners for more than a fortnight. Do you realize what it is like, to be locked away and...and abandoned by mankind?" She didn't say by him, but she thought it. The faint flush in his face indicated he understood what was meant. "We...we are depending on you—"

"Naturally, you may be assured I will do what I can at the appropriate moment." He rose without looking at her. It was clear he would do nothing of the kind. He would not involve himself.

Roselynne stood by while he banged on the door. When it was opened, she saw the great, grinning moon face of Bowes and wanted to slap him. Charles bowed gravely.

"Good day, Miss Moreley," he said formally, as if he were a mere acquaintance rather than her champion, as if this had been simply a duty call, not a matter of her and her father's lives.

She realized she had allowed herself to think more of their friendship than he had, or else he had changed his mind now that she and her father were looked upon with disfavor by the king.

"Thank you for coming," she replied, just as coldly polite. She inclined her head regally in dismissal.

When the door closed and locked behind him, she stood there for a while, just staring at it. Something in her that had been tender, a bud that had sprung from the moist ground of her imagination, shriveled like a seedling caught in a late frost.

She hadn't been in love with Charles, but she had been fond of him, and she had assumed they would wed in a year or so, after a proper engagement period. Lately, due to her desperation, she'd allowed herself to see him as her knight and had envisioned a great love growing out of this time of danger. How foolish.

Love such as she'd dreamed of happened only to those intrepid heroines who dashed off on exciting adventures without regard to good sense. And they lived only in novels. She pressed a hand against the ache in her heart.

A sound behind her caused her to whirl about. Her father rose and moved to the chair he had used before Charles arrived. She dropped to the floor at his feet and rested her head on his knees the way she had done as a girl.

"Father, my accursed temper has done us in again," she confessed. "Charles will never present our case after I scolded him like a shrew. And I . . . I no longer wish him to. Did you hear? He was so . . . so selfish, and not in the least concerned for us."

Her father picked up a stray curl and stroked it over and over, but made no reply.

She swallowed hard against the depression that swept over her. "He doesn't want to speak to the duke for us. He's afraid for his position, or perhaps his prestige would suffer for knowing reprobates like us."

She sighed, a wobbly sound of mingled tears and woe. Her father kept smoothing the curl.

"I was going to ask for some money, in case it took a while to gain an audience with the king, but I couldn't when he acted so stiff and distant. My pride wouldn't allow it. It is difficult to believe I have any of that commodity left after what we've been through, isn't it?"

Looking up, she caught her father's eyes on her. He opened his mouth as if to speak. She held her breath.

"Ro," he said. "Ro."

"Yes, that's right. Roselynne. Roselynne," she repeated, and waited anxiously for him to say her name.

He looked greatly perplexed, then his expression became blank again.

"There now, don't fret. Your memory will return soon, and the words will come, too." She smiled as reassuringly as she could and stood. Her expression was resolute.

This was no time for her to sit around feeling sorry for herself. She had letters to write. With whom of the lords did she have the faintest connection? She concentrated deeply. None, she realized. Ullswater was so far from London.

Other than Wainsco and a country baron, she knew none of the aristocracy. Except for the Earl of Rockdale. "I will sleep on it. Mayhap something will come to me in the night."

But sleep eluded her and no idea was forthcoming with the dark. After an hour of restless turning, she rose and went to the window, opening the shutter as quietly as possible.

"Who was your visitor?" Beau immediately asked.

Roselynne cast an exasperated glance upward. "With your keen hearing, I'm sure you already know his name and the meat of our conversation."

He laughed. "For a fact, I do not. Mr. Bowes told me you had a man in your chamber. He was quite delighted to impart the news to me, thinking, I've no doubt, that it would be a sore prick to my ego. Mr. Bowes has a fine sense of humor and likes to tease, you may have noted. Especially me."

Beau quirked a sardonic brow as he admitted this last and fingered his broken nose. Bowes's own face had contorted into all manner of lascivious smirks as he announced that Mr. Osgood, a man of "high fashion" as "handsome as a lord" was calling upon Roselynne. Beau had gotten a glimpse of the man when he crossed the courtyard upon leaving, and he had thought Mr. Osgood looked a fop—overdressed and too refined.

The man must be Charles, the long-awaited loved one who was to save her and her father from their uncertain fate.

He kicked his toe idly against the stone wall, irritated by this turn of events. "Let me guess," he mused aloud. "Your handsome gentleman was the knight who is to champion your cause and free you. Is that correct?"

He waited anxiously for her reply. He hadn't been able to detect all the words of their discussion, but he was certain he had heard her voice raised in anger at one point. Perhaps things were not well between the lovers.

It suited his purposes for their friendship to be all to hell. He smiled grimly. Time was running out, and he had found no one else he would take as a wife, although Bowes had paraded half a dozen wretches before him. He had paid them for their time and sent them away. His mind was set on Roselynne.

"Stubborn wench," he muttered, then realized he was just as stubborn over this point. He would have her and no other.

"I beg your pardon, my lord?" She knew the title irked him, and she felt an unreasonable desire to taunt him. His money could buy him anything but his freedom, it appeared, or her.

"Nothing. Was my guess correct?"

Roselynne gazed across the street at the Old Bailey, where she and her father were still to be tried. She swallowed the hard lump of reality that filled her throat whenever she thought of her talk with Charles Osgood.

"I have seen few men, my lord, whom I would classify as knights of sterling quality. As for rescue, I have need of none. As soon as I present the facts, the lord high judge will attest to the error of the charges and set us free."

"So," Beau mused gently, "he had no suggestions that would aid you." When she didn't answer, he added, "My offer still stands. This very night you could be free, aye, and have the means to secure the best barrister for your father."

"What means have you of seeing to my freedom? It seems to me that, if we marry, I would be accepting another bondage with no assurance of throwing off the first."

"You'll be my wife, not my slave. As Countess of Rockdale, you can afford the fine for your release. In fact, we'll pay it before it's levied."

"Bribes," she scoffed.

"They work," he said, his voice hardening. "You've learned that much in the king's keep."

She thought of how fierce he must look at this moment. She was almost as frightened of this stranger who entreated her to marry him as she was of the men in the common cell she had left. He appeared to be a man of intense passions.

She couldn't bring herself to the point of accepting his hands on her. The sweet intimacy that should be shared in nuptial bliss, with soft words and tenderness to ease a maiden's qualms, would simply be a means of revenge on an unknown enemy. She would be no more than a pawn in either of their plans. It was a situation too strange to contemplate.

"I will not marry without love, my lord," she whispered.

He heard. "Tell that to your father when they hang him."

Her hand jerked on the bar as if jolted by lightning. "That was a cruel jest."

"It was but the truth, one that you had better make up your mind to accept if Charles Osgood doesn't save you, and I doubt that he will," he added. He spoke contemptuously, as if he'd seen Charles and his foppish mode of behavior.

"So, you do know everything," she cried. "Did it give you great pleasure to listen to my private conversation and hear him refuse to present my case to the duke, much less the king?"

"No. I didn't hear—"

"Were I a man and we were free, I'd challenge you," she spat into the night, her face pressed against the iron stays of her prison. "That was unconscionably rude."

Beau experienced a great relief. Her hero had not leaped to her defense. She was that much closer to accepting him, did she but know it.

"I apologize, Roselynne. Actually, Bowes told me the man's name. I couldn't hear your words, but you seemed angry at one point." He paused, but she gave no further clues to the development between her and Osgood. "Well, I think I will go to bed now. Dream of me, won't you? I dream of you, lying here beside me, snug in my arms all night."

A muffled sound, quickly suppressed, was all the answer he got. He grinned and added more food for thought.

"I would be a gentle lover, Roselynne, and not bruise a single petal of your delicate flesh. I give you my word."

"The word of a convicted murderer?" She heaped scorn on the phrase, but her heart set up a terrific beat as if it would jump out of her chest. She was afraid, afraid of her circumstances that were making her desperate and his promises that were all too persuasive in her present state.

"You know you don't believe that lie, just as I don't believe the ones against you and your father."

There was the hurt, she realized. Charles apparently hadn't been convinced they were innocent of crime, but she could see no reason for him to think them guilty of any charge.

Beau St. Clair believed her, and he didn't mind taking on her problems. But then, her fellow prisoner had nothing to lose. He was going to hang in a few days.

That would be an injustice. She believed him innocent of murder, but she couldn't marry him.

He was too frightening, a man of intense passion and dark moods, one who would demand much of a wife. And he would soon leave her a widow. That was the most frightening of all, to gain a husband and lose him almost at once, before they had time to know each other.

It was a strange contretemps that existed between them, she admitted. If life had been different, if their circumstances had been changed, even if he hadn't the handsomest face, once she had gotten to know him, she thought she would have liked him.

"Don't fret upon it," he called softly, sounding just like her talking to her father.

"I shan't," she said and closed the shutter.

But her dreams were strange that night and wouldn't let her rest. Hands touched her and stroked her ever so gently while soft lips—not harsh, bruised ones—kissed her mouth and throat, all the way down her neck....

She awoke with a start, her breathing fast and uneven, an odd heat flooding her body. The fur cover caressed her skin when she moved her head, and the spicy smell rose from its folds and filled her senses. It was the same scent she'd detected on him when he'd pressed close and demanded she listen to his proposal.

With the passage of five days in the private cell, she became frantic. "Father," she whispered, "we are almost out of money. Tell me what to do."

He looked at her with his sad eyes—she was sure they would have been sad had they held expression—and blinked.

"If I don't hear from Charles today, I am going to accept St. Clair's proposal tomorrow." She was silent while she thought. Aloud, she said, "Roselynne St. Clair, Countess of Rockdale. What do you think?"

She shook her head. "I cannot do it. I am too much a coward. Forgive me, Father." Her tears fell on his trouser knees.

The Westminster chimes reverberated on the noon air like a death knell. The walls of Newgate moaned with the sobs and shufflings of its human burden, the sounds muted by the fog that lingered over the city and hid the sun.

Roselynne carefully stoked the small fire in the grate with a pointed piece of wood. Finished, she straightened and put her hands to the small of her back where the pain of her monthly courses throbbed with a dull ache.

Her manner was distracted as she gazed about the tiny room as if seeking an answer to some insistent question in her mind. Seeing no writing on the wall or elsewhere, she paced the narrow cell from hearth to door and back.

She had given Charles one day and then another, but he still hadn't returned. The money in her purse was woefully low. She had counted it three times that morning but had detected no increase in its substance. With a rueful grimace, she acknowledged she had not miscounted or overlooked any coins.

"Mr. Bowes," she shouted. "I would speak to you." When the turnkey lumbered to the door, she requested that he contact St. Clair's barrister for her.

"Now you're showing some sense," he said approvingly. He was so delighted at her acquiescence he forgot to demand a coin for the favor and paid the messenger out of his own pocket.

Roselynne settled herself to patience, not expecting to hear further for at least a day. She was surprised when the door was unlocked and Mr. Clayburgh strolled in before vespers. In one hand, he held a basket of fruit; in the other, a wedge of cheese.

"Compliments of Rockdale," he said, placing the feast on the crude table.

"Please thank his lordship for me." She dropped a small curtsy as if St. Clair were present. Due to his frequent stream of comments or, surprisingly, soft singing from above her, she often felt he was. "Won't you take a seat?"

They took chairs on opposite sides of the table. The lawyer was first to speak. "Did you have a question concerning the earl's proposal? I have the papers drawn up—"

"No," she said quickly. "No, that's not it at all. I wish to speak to you on my father's behalf. Would you take his case?"

"On what grounds does his defense rest?" Mr. Clayburgh pressed the tips of his fingers together and studied the silent man who sat on the cot.

"You can see he is no threat to the crown in his condition. Is that not reason enough?"

"Would you like a fruit?" Mr. Clayburgh asked, ignoring her indignant query. He selected a peach. "These were grown in the Rockdale conservatory and brought to town only this morning. A new variety, I understand." Taking up a knife, he peeled the fruit in one continuous spiral.

Roselynne accepted a slice when he offered it. She remained silent, knowing that he was using the delaying tactic to think over his reply.

At last he spoke in a kind voice. "I think your father's best chance is to pay a penalty before his case comes to trial."

"A bribe," she said, correctly reading his meaning. "I have no money for it."

"How were you planning on paying my fee?" he asked, obviously amused. "Or were you appealing to the goodness of my heart? Have you not heard, Miss Moreley, that attorneys are notoriously lacking in that commodity?"

She smiled at his gentle teasing. "My father has an exceptional horse, a Newmarket possibility. I would pledge Athene to you."

"Athene, an excellent name. She is fast?"

"Fast and intelligent," Roselynne boasted. "We trained her ourselves."

His fingers steepled beneath his chin, as if he said a silent prayer. "You are a most surprising young lady."

"No, sir, only fortunate in having a parent of vast interests who included me in them." Her gray eyes lighted on Mr. Moreley with tenderness. "I must get him out of here. The cold and damp are bad for his health."

"And no aid in recovering his mind," Mr. Clayburgh added sympathetically.

"True, sir."

Roselynne waited while the attorney studied the situation. When he shook his head sorrowfully, she felt a great letdown of her spirits. "It is folly to think we can defend him. The paper itself speaks better than words of mine."

"You have read his essay?"

"Indeed I have. A most ingenious argument. The barristers of the Bailey have discussed it in detail. No, a bribe is the only way. For you, too. Naturally, if you should say I said so, I will deny it." He rose with a smile and held out his hand. "The price of a horse wouldn't cover the cost. You would do better to take my client's offer while it is still open. He has money enough for your purposes.''

Roselynne allowed her hand to be bowed over. When Mr. Clayburgh left, she studied the contents of her purse once more, then closed her eyes, fighting the fear that darkened her soul. Even if she sold everything they owned, she couldn't come up with the amount needed for a bribe.

Her father coughed, a dry hacking that worried her no end, and the sound spurred her to action. She must have money to keep him in food and what comfort this cell offered.

She went to the window and opened the shutter. ''My lord?''

''I'm here,'' he said quietly.

A puff of smoke swirled on the damp air. Behind her, her father coughed and sniffed. He was taking a chill. With reckless abandon, she left the window and added more wood to the fire until the blaze jumped in the grate. The room warmed, and she returned to the window.

''I would speak with you,'' she requested formally. She would use sweet logic on him, appeal to his better nature with the cruelty of her plight. He could not help but see her need.

''Yes?''

Beau knocked the dottle out of the pipe and watched it fall to the courtyard below, where it was extinguished with a hiss of moisture on the cobbles. His hands shook slightly, he noted, when he laid the bowl of the pipe on the stone and propped the stem in the corner. She'd sent for his attorney; that must mean she was ready to accept his offer.

''I have a horse of great merit I would sell to you.''

It took a full minute for her proposition to sink it. ''A horse?'' Beau repeated. He was first incredulous, then furious. ''Miss Moreley, I have no need of a *horse* of any merit, whether the fleetest or the most spavined in all England!''

''There is no need to shout, my lord.''

He modulated his next utterances, a feat of remarkable self-control, and said only part of what he felt. ''I'd like to do more than shout, I assure you. When I first met you, I thought you were a sensible female, not one given to extravagant notions, but I see I was wrong. You're like all the others and can't see beyond your own selfish wants—''

"Wanting to be out of prison is hardly an extravagant notion," she interrupted hotly, her temper erupting at his unfair comment. "Trying to protect my father is not selfish on my part, but a desire most basic to my soul and to my idea of loyalty and duty to one's own blood, a thing I wouldn't expect a person of your callous tendencies to appreciate nor your uncouth mind to comprehend!"

She gripped the bars with such force her hands ached, and she wondered why the metal didn't bend from her anger.

"I comprehend well enough that you would use me, or rather, my money, to secure your own ends, giving no thought to *my* needs nor to the bleak future that awaits me as surely as the night awaits the cold light of dawn. No, thank you, I have no wish for a horse, but for a wife—"

"I wouldn't marry you if you were the last available man on this green earth, sir!"

So saying, she slammed the shutter closed and threw another log on the fire. Shortly afterward, she removed her father's mended coat and his shoes and helped him retire to bed. Her anger still seethed that St. Clair wouldn't listen to her idea and accept Athene. "A much better mount than one such as he deserves," she said to the leaping flames, poking vigorously at the fire with a stick.

Of course, he would not get a chance to use the mare, she reasoned as her nerves calmed. She had been foolish to lose her temper. It had been one thing to offer Athene to the barrister, another to offer the mare to a man about to hang. Her impulsive notion had been an insult. She could see that now.

Rising swiftly from the chair, she returned to the window and opened the shutter again. "My lord?"

"What?" he snapped. He evidently wasn't over his temper.

"I apologize. I realize that you have no need of a horse you wouldn't have opportunity to ride. It was stupid of me to suggest the purchase."

Silence rained down from above like the drizzle that had settled firmly on the city with the coming of night. "It is no matter," he finally said.

She thought he sounded tired and discouraged, a condition she well knew. "Thank you." She hesitated. "Good night, my lord."

"Good night, Miss Moreley."

She paused in closing the shutter. "Roselynne," she corrected softly.

She ordered more wood, paid for it and added a log to the fire. It was time to retire, but she was restless again. Removing her dress and hanging it on a nail, she wrapped the comforter around her and paced the narrow path between her pallet and the fireplace. The sound of the key turning in the lock alerted her to Mr. Bowes's entry.

"Yes?" she asked, feeling a premonition that boded ill.

He removed from his mouth a splinter of wood that he'd been using as a toothpick. "Thought you might like to know that you and your da are on the court docket next month."

Next month. Her money wouldn't last more than three days. She could have Clayburgh sell Athene. The mare should bring enough to keep them in this cell until their trial.

"Thank you for the information," she said past the knot in her throat and glanced at the door, waiting for him to be gone before black despair overcame her. She mustn't cry in front of anyone.

"Maybe you'd better consider the nabob's offer," Bowes suggested. There was pity in his glance. "I think that's your only way out o' this mess."

Roselynne swallowed hard against the rise of tears. Things were bad indeed when even a Newgate turnkey felt sorry for her.

"Your advice is appreciated, Mr. Bowes. You have been most kind to my father and myself, and I..." The words stuck and wouldn't come out. She pressed a hand to her lips and clutched the fur closer about her chilled body.

Bowes shifted from one massive leg to the other. "If you want to talk to 'im..." he pointed toward the ceiling "...I'll leave your doors unlocked for a while, but I have to close them afore the night guard comes through."

"I...I must think."

"Don't be too long at it," he offered as additional advice. "Your time is running out." He left without locking her cell.

The drizzle outside turned into a torrent that beat furiously against the shutter. The cell walls closed in upon her, and she placed a hand upon the cold stone as if by sheer courage she could hold back the dark fate that awaited.

She'd never thought it would come to this. She'd counted so heavily upon Charles to come forth as her champion and save her and her father, but he hadn't. Only St. Clair's offer stood between them and possible—no, she must face the truth—*certain* death for her father. What the future held for her she couldn't contemplate. She'd heard such horrible tales of women convicts. . . .

A tremor coursed through her. She realized, wise or foolish, she must make a decision that would forever alter the course of her life.

Roselynne leaned against the wall of the landing. Her breath came quickly as she climbed, as if she ran rather than crept up the steps.

She smoothed the skirt of her dress and checked the chignon at her neck. Her appearance was as presentable as she could make it. Pulling her shawl close, she proceeded up the stairs.

Reaching the turret chamber, she knocked twice and waited. When no answer was forthcoming she knocked again, harder.

"Do come in," a sardonic voice invited.

As promised, the door was unlocked. She pulled the latch and stepped inside. The earl was sprawled in a chair, his long legs outstretched toward the leaping flames in the fireplace. He rose at a leisurely pace, his gaze never leaving her.

"Well," he said, obviously astounded at her entry. A smile matching his earlier tone spread over his face. "How delightful that you could call. Would you care for tea?" He was mockingly polite as he swept an elaborate bow in her direction.

"Yes," she said, hoping he didn't notice the quiver in her voice. She wished to appear calm and reasonable.

He made tea from a brazier on the hearth. "Please, be seated," he invited, glancing at her over his shoulder.

She took the chair across the low table from his, glad that her host couldn't see how her legs trembled. When the cup was ready, she accepted it from him and added sugar.

He resumed his chair and studied her over the rising steam from his cup. "How did you get up here?" he finally asked.

"Mr. Bowes gave me leave."

The earl frowned at her. "Mr. Bowes is fond of games. He sometimes leaves the cells unlocked in order to trap a person into escaping. Then he likes to take revenge for that boldness."

"I think he has pity for my father and me. He said I should talk to you."

"Mr. Bowes is indeed kind. Did he also mention the topic of our conversation?"

She ignored his cynicism. "He brought news. My father and I are to be tried next month. He says, as does Mr. Clayburgh, that money is the only way out."

"Bribes."

"Yes." She took a deep breath. "My lord, I...I will... That is, if you still desire..."

His gaze gentled. "What are you trying to say, Roselynne?" he asked in a softer voice. He reached out to smooth a strand of hair that hung over her forehead.

She flinched.

"I wasn't going to hurt you," he said stiffly.

"No, I know that. It...it was reflex on my part. I have grown distrustful of men recently."

"With good reason," he agreed. He inhaled deeply and exhaled with a sigh. "The night passes, and Mr. Bowes's intentions cannot always be trusted. How may I serve you?"

She twisted her hands together and tried to still the tremors before her courage gave out.

"Yes?" he demanded, becoming impatient at her hesitation.

"A-about your offer. If...if it still stands, then I accept." She got the words out in a rush.

He fingered his nose, testing its condition while he studied her face, his glance keen and intelligent.

"I could fix that for you," she said, on an impulse dictated by her years of caring for the tenants of the parish. "With clay to hold your nose in place and ice to keep down the swelling, I think it would grow straight with mayhap only a tiny bump."

"Would it bother you to marry me as I look now?" He waited without moving for her to speak.

Roselynne lifted her chin. "You are not handsome, my lord, but neither am I beautiful. I have seen examples of your kindness more than once, and I think you are a good man. I would be proud to be your wife."

For a long second, he fought some battle inside himself that she couldn't decipher.

"Of course, if the offer is not still open, I will understand." She held herself rigid while waiting for his answer. She realized he was her last hope. It was . . . daunting.

At last he spoke. "I have had my lawyer working on your release and your father's. The charges against you will be dropped. The king has agreed to a pardon for your father provided he sticks to his clergical duties when and if he recovers the use of his mind and leaves matters of state to the Parliament."

"What are you saying?" she whispered, not sure she was hearing correctly. She leaped to her feet, and he, too, stood.

"Tomorrow you and your father will be free to leave the prison when the papers are delivered to the gaoler."

"We will be free?" She could hardly credit it.

"Yes. You may go home or wherever you wish."

"My lord, how can I thank you?" she cried. She clasped his hand and brought it to her lips, then laid it against her cheek. "I will do all I can to aid you," she promised fervently. "I will work to clear your name—"

"Thank you. That will be a comfort when I am dead," he replied with sardonic amusement. He withdrew his hand and moved toward the door. "In the morning, Roselynne, I will ask you to marry me. Think carefully on your answer." His gaze slashed into her failing composure. "Come, I'll see you to your room."

So saying, he opened the door and indicated that she should precede him down the stairs.

Chapter Five

Roselynne greeted the dawn with a sleepless gaze. Without desperation driving her, she couldn't decide on the future.

She'd have rested easier, she reflected, if he'd accepted her decision of last night. It had been cruel of him to give her the choice of marrying a stranger in perilous circumstances or of walking away, free to return to her childhood home.

She couldn't ignore his needs and say no to his proposal after he'd freed them. Mr. Bowes would think her insane to quibble over it. St. Clair wanted a wife to whom to leave his fortune. By marrying him, she would become a countess. Most women would have leaped at the chance, in spite of the possible danger.

She pressed her hands over her burning eyes. Her foolish heart was still filled with dreams, but she must be practical. Her conscience demanded that she also be fair. To take without giving went against all she'd been taught.

He asked that she marry him and fulfill her duties as his wife. He wanted a child. That was natural. All men wanted an heir of their own flesh and blood. What he asked was very little in return for two lives. She sat up on her pallet, the fur clutched around her. She would marry him. 'Twas the only right course to take.

Roselynne waited impatiently for the summons. At last, Bowes came to the door. He bowed to her and showed her a gold piece in his hand before pocketing the money.

"You're wanted upstairs." He chortled. "Glad you've come to your senses at last. I'll take you to 'im."

She nodded, glanced at her father, then left the cell to accept her destiny. Breakfast was waiting when she arrived.

"Oranges brought from sunny Spain, I understand," Beau said, seating her as if they were a lord and lady at home rather than prisoners in a dreary cell at Newgate. "And bacon cured at the home estate."

"Is it a grand place?"

He shrugged. "Truth is, I've never seen it, but Clayburgh assures me it is." He sat opposite her. "Will you take tea or coffee this morning?"

"Tea," she said, wondering at this act they played. When she had difficult consequences to face, she'd as soon get them over with. "My lord—"

"Beau," he corrected firmly. "Eat first."

He carried on an inane conversation with her during the meal, his lightness of tone making her even more nervous. Finally, she finished the fruit, toast and eggs. "My lord," she began.

"Me first," he interrupted. He came to her side and dropped to one knee. "Miss Moreley... Roselynne, would you do me the honor of becoming my wife?"

For the briefest second, panic urged her to refuse, but she defeated the fear. A fatalistic calm descended upon her. What was meant to be, must be. "Yes," she said.

A blaze leaped into flame in his eyes, causing her resolve to waver just a bit. She had never known blue eyes could look so... so *hot*. He leaned forward until his face was on a level with hers, and she thought he would attempt to kiss her again. She forced herself to stillness.

"You don't have to agree," he said. "There are no strings attached to your father's freedom, nor yours."

"I—I understand."

"I don't think I do. Would you explain your reasons?" His keen gaze pinned her to the chair.

"They are complicated, but..." She swallowed, doubt arising in her mind. She struggled to overcome it. "I think you're an honorable man, and... and you've been more than kind to my father and me."

"You know that I want a wife in all the ways of marriage?"

She plucked at her skirt, unable to look him in the face. "Yes, my lord. I will do my duty."

"Duty," he repeated with a frown, obviously not pleased.

"I understand your desire for an heir of your own blood, and I shall try to give you one," she concluded, lifting her head.

His hands gripped her shoulders, and his gaze was fierce. "I need no heir other than a wife," he told her. "As for my desire..."

He let his eyes roam down her face to her throat, thence to her breasts, which throbbed hotly under the shawl. She felt faint.

"...My desire is for you," he whispered roughly, his lips inches from hers.

A long moment passed. "I see," she said.

"No, you don't," he contradicted, amusement in his voice. "But soon you will." He laughed, startling her. "I'll contact Clayburgh at once. We can be wed today, this very morning."

"My lord, just a moment. There are things to discuss and plans to be made. I—I must have a dress and see to a thousand other details before—"

"No," he said, jumping to his feet and taking a turn about the room, his actions full of leashed energy. He, too, preferred to act once his mind was set, she saw. "We have no time to lose. I cannot court you, Roselynne. Today is the twenty-fourth of May, only ten days ere I am to be hanged. You will have to give up maidenly expectations and accept our marriage as soon as may be."

Heat rose to her face. "You don't understand, my lord. I do not expect parties and such. I will even resign myself to this dress if need be, but there is another problem—"

"Well, what is it? Let's get it solved and proceed." He stood in front of her, his legs spread and his hands on his hips, a powerful, impatient male.

A tiny thrill raced through her at the turn of her thoughts as she gazed upon his manly frame. Except for his bruised face—which was healing rapidly—he would have been a very handsome man. He was compelling and strong in his personality; he was kind and generous. She felt drawn to him.

His caresses hadn't been exactly repulsive. He was somewhat overwhelming in his ardor, she admitted, but, now that she had accepted the idea of the marriage, she didn't find that so terrible an attitude for a husband. He had given his word that he would be a considerate lover.

Glancing up, she saw his eyes fastened on her shawl as if he could see beneath it to her breasts. She was glad he couldn't, for she would have been mortified to have him discover her nipples drawing into hard tingling peaks while she dwelt upon thoughts of his caresses.

She wondered how he would touch her when they married. Gently, he had promised. She remembered the kiss from his injured lips. It had been filled with restrained impulses. Inexperienced as she was, she knew there was more.

She found she was both attracted and dismayed by the thought of his touch. It remained to be seen which was greater—her fear or her curiosity. She pondered the strange sensations he'd aroused in her. His lips, when he'd kissed her...

Pulling her wayward mind back to order, she reminded herself of her problem. "I'm not, that is, I am . . ." She licked her lips and drew a deep breath.

"Make up your mind," he suggested with a sudden smile. "Either you are or you aren't." When she didn't speak, he added, "Roselynne, I am not the most patient of men."

"I am indisposed, my lord." She stared out the window.

"Indis . . . Oh." He sounded very disappointed. "It doesn't matter," he began, then stopped.

Her face went even hotter, and she thought she would die, simply die, of humiliation.

Beau looked at Roselynne and felt an indescribable tenderness at her embarrassment. For all her courage and quiet, mature ways, she was still a maid, with a maid's inhibitions and fears. He sank down on his haunches and took her clasped hands between both his.

"You are to be my wife. There is nothing we can't discuss, for we will know each other completely. There can be no shame between us. Do you understand?"

She hesitated, then nodded.

With one finger under her chin, he turned her face to his. His expression was solemn. "I vow to be as good a husband as I can, and I'll wait for you until you're ready to be my wife." He grinned wryly. "Don't make it longer than necessary. My days, as you know, are numbered."

On an impulse, she reached out and touched his rough, chapped lips. "Two days should be sufficient, my lord. Can you wait until then?" she asked anxiously.

He kissed her fingertips before she withdrew. "Yes. Will you not call me by my name? There aren't many living in this world, and only one in this country, who does so."

"Beau," she repeated. She smiled. "I am acquiring them, it seems. Beaus and Bowes."

He raised his brows in question.

"Mr. Bowes was quite gallant this morning. I think he is developing a *tendresse* for me. Or for the coins I earn him."

Beau chuckled. "I hope, even with this face, I am more to your liking, unless you prefer a...um...fuller-bodied man?"

His jesting reply soothed her nerves. "Nay, I'm not taken with him. Perhaps his manners are at fault."

"Then I will watch mine very carefully around you. I find I'd like you to be taken with me... as I am with you."

He was suddenly very near as he dropped down beside her once more. Knowing he wanted to kiss her, she held herself in check when her natural urge was to lean away from him.

"Is it so very hard to force yourself to endure my touch?" he asked, sounding almost wistful to her ears. He lifted his hand and caressed her cheek with his fingers.

"I beg your indulgence. I will get used to it, I'm sure," she murmured. "I admit I am curious..."

"About a man's kiss?" His breath fanned over her mouth.

"About yours." She spoke barely in a whisper, but he heard.

His hand slipped around to the back of her neck. He found her hidden supply of coins and smiled slightly before moistening his lips and settling them softly on hers.

Most of the rough tissue on his bottom lip had healed. There was only a pleasant raspiness as he moved his mouth across hers, slanting his head to one side before opening his lips. To her surprise, he stroked her lips with his tongue.

Tingles darted down her neck and lodged in some internal spot of great tumult. Her legs shook as they were inclined to do when she was frightened, and she felt the faint tremblings in her limbs creep up her spine as his arms tightened. Her nipples contracted even more. She wanted to rub herself against him.

"Open your mouth, Roselynne," he murmured, his lips still touching hers.

Suddenly she became aware of their position, of his thighs pressing against her knees, of his hand on her neck, the other lightly stroking her shoulder through her shawl and dress. Heat spiraled off into deep recesses in her body. Embarrassed by these primitive reactions, she pressed her lips together.

"Haven't you ever kissed a man? Charles couldn't have been very ardent if he never tasted the pleasure of your lips," Beau murmured, lightly grazing his lips along her cheek.

"Of course I've kissed a man," she replied stiffly. It had been her father, but she wasn't going to tell him that.

"Mouth to mouth?"

She tried to force herself to lie, but it wasn't in her. "Charles was a gentleman," she said instead.

Beau chuckled. Suddenly his tongue darted out and stroked the corner of her mouth. She gasped as shock waves veered off into the innermost parts of her body.

He at once followed the erotic attack with the searing contact of his mouth—open, wet, hot—on hers. She couldn't protest; she had no breath for it. Her lungs had ceased to operate. Her hands clutched his shoulders in an attempt to steady a world that had slipped completely out of her control.

It was even more disturbing to be staring into someone's eyes at this close range. His were evenly blue, as blue as a cornflower, with a slightly darker edging at the outer circle. When he closed them, she vaguely noted the dark sweep of his lashes against his cheeks before she lost all ability to think.

With bold caresses, his tongue explored her lips thoroughly, then sought the line of her teeth, pausing to run over the slight unevenness of the front two on the bottom.

When he leisurely swept inside her mouth, she felt excited, nervous, aghast and invaded, all at the same time. She sensed she should do something, but didn't know what. The novels she had read had made much of a kiss, describing bells ringing and the sounds of singing in the air like a host of heavenly angels.

She heard only the frantic pounding of her heart and the roar of her blood through her ears. When she thought she would faint from lack of air, she managed to turn her head.

"My lord," she said, a ragged whisper of sound.

He rested his forehead against her shoulder, his own breath loud in the still air of the cell. "I've shocked you again. I didn't mean to this time." A sigh of laughter escaped him. "Forgive me, Roselynne. I'm impatient, but my promise still holds. When the time comes, I will be gentle."

"Thank you," she said with simple dignity, regaining her own composure upon realizing he was as shaken by the kiss as she.

He moved from her slowly, reluctantly, she thought, and couldn't help the tiny conceit that bloomed in her. No other man had ever displayed a passion for her, and her vanity was piqued.

"Now I must send a message to Clayburgh to find out if the king indeed signed a pardon for your father as promised."

"How did you accomplish it?" It seemed a miracle.

He smiled into her eyes. "A donation to the king's depleted war chest in your father's name was sufficient to make his royal majesty see the true meaning of Mr. Moreley's essay. He also saw that a daughter would naturally defend her parent against a false arrest."

"So we are both free?"

"As soon as the decree arrives."

"I cannot thank you enough—"

"You are earning your freedom by becoming my wife. Perhaps with some danger to your life." He stared off into space for a long minute. "I wonder if I have the right to ask that of you."

"It matters not. I will do it," she declared.

She found she wasn't afraid. Somehow, they would find the criminal mind behind the murder of the old earl. . . . She realized she was thinking of her and Beau performing the feat together.

"We will succeed," she told him, her chin thrust out in defiance of whatever fate befell them.

He was solemn for a moment, then a smile broke over his face. "I think we will." He threw back his head and laughed heartily. "I truly think we will."

The pardon didn't arrive that day or the next. Beau paced his cell, furious with the king. "The old fool, he's being coy. The delay is merely a petulant reprisal on his part. Two can play that game. I'll halt the bank draft until you and your father are set free," he assured Roselynne.

She replaced her teacup on the table. A knock on the door distracted Beau.

"Ah, here's someone I want you to meet," he said when another man entered the cell.

The man was tall, taller than Beau by at least three inches, and pleasant to look upon, although he wasn't exactly handsome. He was stout of body and ruddy of complexion, with the quiet air of a thinker or clerical. His dress was simple: black breeches, coat and boots, a muslin shirt with a simple cravat. His hose provided the only color. They were striped with red and blue.

"Miss Moreley," he said, bowing in her direction.

"How do you do, Mr...?"

"Call me George," the man requested in a soft voice.

"He's to look after you when you get out of the king's boardinghouse," Beau explained. "Do as he tells you. You can trust him with your life."

She recognized the name. Beau had told her of the man who was more than a friend. George Myers had been the village ne'er-do-well, the son of a printer, before the rebellion. He and Beau had fought side by side in the war. When Beau was wounded in the chest, George had dragged him to safety and bandaged him, thus saving him from the British. Beau had made George his man of business after the peace and recommended him to others.

"I'm very glad to meet you. Beau has spoken to me of your courage and devotion as a friend."

George laughed, a surprisingly deep and hearty chuckle. "I only stay around to see what scrape he'll get himself into next.

The last time I had to help him out, it was a widow after him with matrimony in her eye—''

"Yes, well, that's of no importance," Beau interrupted, a flush creeping up his neck.

"Why, it was. She was dead set on having you—"

"She was ten years older than me and would take anything in britches," Beau snapped, glaring at his friend. "Enough of that. We have plans to make."

"If you say so," George said innocently.

He's about as innocent as a cat in front of a mouse hole, Roselynne thought. She glanced at Beau, who was pouring two glasses of brandy, and experienced a twinge of emotion new to her.

A widow, she scoffed. He would have to mend his ways if he was to be her husband. She discovered she had quite definite opinions on the subject. And none of them tolerated widows or any other liaisons.

"Here's to our success," Beau said, lifting his snifter and downing a large draught.

"I'll drink to that," George agreed. His gaze remained on Roselynne while he drank, as if he toasted her.

When he lowered the glass, he smiled at her. She smiled back, realizing with a pleasurable start that he approved of her and had liked her on sight. It was reassuring.

Beau scowled furiously at her. "Tomorrow we have the ceremony. The cleric will be here at three in the afternoon. That's the only time he has before evening services begin. Is that satisfactory?"

She nodded.

"George and Clayburgh will be our witnesses. Is there anyone you want to attend?"

"I know no one in London."

"So it's settled."

"Yes," she said. She pleated a fold into her dress. She would have to wear it. She couldn't ask for money.... Suddenly a thought struck her. Henny! She had promised to help the woman. "My lord," she said excitedly, "I would ask a favor."

"What is it?" Beau realized he was acting like a bull with one heifer. George seemed taken with her, and, while she was pretty in a wholesome way, she wasn't a great beauty.

"A woman is being held in the common cell. She was good to my father and me when we were in there. Could you have her case looked into and perhaps arrange to free her? I'm sure it would require only a small sum to pay her fine."

Beau was pleased that she asked him for the favor. "Remind me to have Clayburgh look into it. What is her name?"

"Henny. I do not know the surname, but I've no doubt Bowes can tell you."

He nodded and paced the room restlessly, his body moving with fluid grace and controlled energy. She watched him covertly, wondering exactly what would happen tomorrow night. Glancing aside, she saw George watching her and blushed painfully, as if he could read her thoughts.

A thump on the door prevented any further conversation. "Visitors out," one of the guards called.

Roselynne rose and held out her hand to George, who bowed over it. She then extended it to Beau, who turned it over and kissed her wrist. "Until tomorrow," he said huskily.

"Yes." She swept out of the cell and rushed down the steps to her own room. She had much to do to get ready.

Sunday morning dawned fair and sunny. The chimes pealed the hour throughout the city. Roselynne hardly noticed. Excitement beat through her blood with a rhythm all its own.

Her wedding day!

Once she had envisioned a much different spectacle, with a grand ceremony and her father reading the marriage lines. No, she mustn't think on that; it would make her sad.

She turned her dress before the small fire until it was dry, then she called the crone, who took it away to iron it. Standing in her shift and petticoats, Roselynne felt a momentary alarm at watching her only garment disappear. If the woman didn't return, she might have to wed in the fur comforter.

Fortunately, some forty minutes later, the crone had the turnkey open the door and brought the freshly pressed garment in. "A good job," Roselynne complimented, pleased.

She fingered the coins in her hand. "My father needs help with his bath. Will you see to it?"

The woman nodded and accepted a coin. Mr. Moreley was led away and returned, two hours later, clean-shaven and sweet-smelling, his clothing brushed and pressed.

"Why, you've even trimmed his hair," Roselynne exclaimed. "That was very nice of you."

The crone smiled proudly, but said nothing, as was her wont. She sometimes grunted a reply, but Roselynne had never heard her utter more than a word or two.

"Now I would have a bath. I need to wash my hair, too. Could you help?" She took the bag from around her neck and put the last of the coins in the woman's hands, then tossed the empty purse on the plank table.

When the woman went out, Roselynne set her father on the bed and stretched the blanket between the chairs to provide privacy for his bath. She unbraided her hair and ran her fingers through it until it hung in flowing ripples past her waist.

When the crone reappeared, two minions accompanied her. They carried a tub filled with water. The crone carried an extra pitcher. When the men left, she motioned for Roselynne to get in the tub. With a sly smile, she held out her hand.

"Soap," Roselynne said, delighted. She took it and sniffed. "Rose scented, too. However did you manage it?"

Not expecting an answer, she slipped out of her underclothing and stepped into the steaming water. Ah, the luxury of a bath all over. Ducking her head, she wet her hair and scrubbed it with the soap until it lathered richly. When she finished, the crone poured the fresh water over her head.

Roselynne stayed in the tub for almost an hour, until the woman tugged at her arm and pointed to the shadows on the wall. Time to get dressed. After drying off, Roselynne slipped into her fresh underclothes and her dress. She looked presentable, she thought. The gray went well with her eyes.

Now for her hair. She rubbed it until it was almost dry, then combed it vigorously until it lay in shining waves that ended in curling tendrils. Gathering it, she started to weave it into a knot at the back of her neck, but hands stopped hers.

The crone shook her head, indicating she should leave it tumbling loose about her shoulders.

"But it's so thick and wild," Roselynne said.

"Nay."

"Oh, all right, I'll leave it," Roselynne grumbled.

The woman scurried out. Roselynne stared out the window, lost in thoughts of the coming ceremony. No more than an hour left, she thought. She put on her hose and shoes.

An object in the toe of her shoe had her taking it off and giving it an annoyed shake. A bright copper rolled out.

Roselynne picked up the new penny and stared at it. "A penny," she said in a choked voice. "She put a penny in my shoe for luck."

Tears flooded her eyes and down her cheeks before she could gain control over her emotions. She had never pictured such a rushed wedding. She had no beautiful gown, no garden filled with flowers, no handsome groom waiting for her. And worst of all, no great shattering love that would sweep all else from its path, leaving her cleansed of the past and eager for the future.

Like a fishmonger, she had bargained—for her release from prison, which had not yet been gained; for a freedom that might prove even more perilous than Newgate.

Mr. Moreley rose from the bed where she had placed him earlier. He put a hand on her head and patted clumsily.

"Father, have I made the wrong choices for us?" she pleaded, but he didn't answer.

When Mr. Moreley moved away and explored the room, Roselynne dried her eyes and put thoughts of love and ecstasy behind her. She was a woman now; it was time to put childhood dreams away. There would be no handsome knight riding up to woo her and steal her away to some wonderful land beyond the sunset.

"Life doesn't follow a fairy tale," she explained to her father as if he'd questioned her motives. "We must live it as it is, not as we'd like it to be. There's no such thing as the passion described in poems. It is all fantasy and dreams."

Chapter Six

'"Tis Hobson's Choice. Take that or none."
England's Reformation, Ch. 4
Thomas Ward

Roselynne paced the narrow channel between her pallet and the cot. Chills swirled along her back. Now that her chores were done and her thoughts were free to roam, she could no longer deny her feelings. Fear, rough and urgent, stroked her nerves like an impatient lover. Her imagination supplied what her experience did not, and she wished fervently that she could hie away to some safe place and thus evade this mockery of a marriage.

She shivered and clasped her arms tightly around her. She was cold, but not because the fire had burned to embers. Pressing her hands over her eyes, she tried to draw a calming breath, but could not. No telling what would happen that night.

Would the man who was to be her husband understand her fears and act the part of the gentle tutor? She feared not. He had been in prison for months. He had been ill-used. Although he wasn't completely without sensibilities, he was an American. 'Twas a land of savages; the men who lived there, though they were once bold Englishmen, might have adopted savage ways.

A fragment of memory drew cold, bony fingers down her spine. He'd looked so sinister, watching their arrival from his turret window that first day, the shadows of the bars across his face.

Her nightmares returned to haunt her, and she rushed to the window, needing air and a sense of space. The sound of heavy steps on the timbers outside the door, then the turning of the key in the lock brought her around, her hands jerking up as if to fend off the devil himself.

The time had come.

She urged Mr. Moreley to his feet, glad she had an excuse to cling to him under the pretext of guiding him. Her knees felt like sausages not quite filled to sturdiness.

Bowes grinned hugely at her when he opened the door. He bowed as gracefully as his bulk would allow, and the scent of rose pomade wafted into her nostrils. To her astonishment, he wore a suit of red, gold and green velvet, and looked like a Christmas wreath.

"Mr. Bowes, how elegant you are today," she managed to say, her voice tremulous.

"Not ever' day we see a wedding 'ere, now is it?" he returned jovially, leading the way up the stairs to Beau's chamber.

Upon entering, her gaze collided with that of her groom and she instinctively recoiled. His perusal was so searing, she felt that she'd been singed by his intense regard. Flustered, she looked around the room.

The minister was already there, along with the lawyer and Beau's American friend. Roselynne realized she was the only female present and wished for a friend of her own.

Beau came to her, his expression unreadable after that first moment of uncontrolled hunger she'd witnessed. She realized anew that this was a stranger she would wed.

"So, you did come," he said.

She nodded, her throat so dry she couldn't have spoken had the room been aflame. An overpowering need to flee stiffened her knees. She glanced at Bowes, filling the doorway. There was no escape. She'd made her bed and now... Her heart beat so hard, it shook her entire body.

Looking at the deepening frown on her groom's face, she knew he had divined her feelings. If only he would say something, show some understanding of her plight. Yesterday she had convinced herself that he was a kind man. Today she needed evidence.

"We can proceed," he said to the clergyman, his tone brusque.

"Wait," she cried, desperate to delay the proceedings. From that moment on, she would know herself for a coward, but she couldn't help it. She must have another moment to compose herself. "T-there's someone I should like to have attend."

The men, all except her father who was peering out the window, stared at her as if she'd taken leave of her senses.

She appealed to Bowes. "Please, could Henny be allowed to come up... just for the ceremony?"

Bowes frowned while he considered. "It's 'ighly irregular, o' course."

Beau, with an impatient grunt, flipped a coin through the air. "Fetch the woman," he ordered, his eyes dark and brooding.

Bowes pocketed the silver piece and hurried out. Roselynne rubbed her arms as another shiver slithered over her skin. One kind word, she thought, but her groom said nothing, only stood there with that stony look on his face. It seemed as if he thought marriage to her was a distasteful task.

She was startled at this thought. He had everything to gain and nothing to lose, while she as yet had only his word concerning her freedom. For his information, she didn't want to be shackled any more than he did.

She snapped her back straight and lifted her chin. A ripple of anger warmed the chill attacking her body. She'd wager it wasn't often a person discovered a gently born maiden in the worst prison in the realm. He should count himself lucky that he didn't have to marry one of the poor wretches off the street.

At that moment Bowes returned, Henny in tow and looking like a fractious biddy about to flog him.

"Henny," Roselynne cried and threw her arms around her friend, her brief courage, born of anger, deserting her.

"There, there, ducks, it'll be all right." She held Roselynne to her pillowy bosom. "Is it true then? You're about to marry some nabob from Ameriky?"

"Yes. Yes, I am." Roselynne found her composure. "I'd like for you to be my witness. If you will."

"Why, I'd be d'lighted." Henny looked over the men. "Which one o' these fine gents is the lucky man?"

"I am," Beau spoke up. He and Henny sized each other up.

"Coo, dearie, and 'e's a prime one, 'e is," Henny declared, her eyes running over Beau's manly proportions.

Blood surged into Roselynne's face, then receded. She was going to be sick... No, she wasn't, she resolved, biting her lip.

"Let's begin," Beau said with all the joy of a diner finding a poison toad in his soup. He took her hand and pulled her forward to his side.

His hand on hers was like touching a hot iron, and she realized her own fingers were icy cold. He tightened his hold while he studied her face.

For a second, she thought of her girlhood dreams and the free spirited adventurer who was supposed to rescue her. She stole a glance at her groom's grim visage. Her rescuer was a wealthy nobleman, but the marriage might prove more of an adventure than she'd ever dreamed.

"We don't have to go through with it," he muttered for her ears alone. "The king signed the pardon for your father. Clayburgh has it in hand. Your fine has been paid, and you, too, are free to go. I won't hold you against your will."

She could hardly believe it. She was free. Her father was free. They could leave this fearful, disgusting prison and return to the gentle meadows and lakes of home. She didn't have to marry to save them.

"You must decide," he prompted her. He released her hand and stepped back, giving her room to think.

In his eyes she saw the bleak certainty of death awaiting him. Pity welled in her. He had so little time.

"Well, which shall it be, forward with the wedding or...?"

"Forward," she said, gathering her courage.

"Not if it bothers you this much." He faced the minister. "I think we'd best forget it."

Roselynne battled between relief and guilt. His disgust with her was plain, also the fact that he'd expected her to renege on their deal. That realization, more than anything, firmed her resolve. She would show him that she, too, was an honorable person. "I gave my word. Would you have me go back on it?"

"Nay, but I'd not force you, either."

"'Tis not force. I am . . . eager to proceed."

Cynical amusement flashed into his blue eyes, and she felt washed by summer warmth, as if the sun had just come out. His face had improved during the brief time she'd known him and he was almost handsome. More than that, he was a man of his word. He'd said he'd free them and he had. She'd keep her part of the bargain, God willing.

She waited while her groom studied her once more, then with a brief nod, he turned them toward the clergyman. The ceremony began. At the end of it, Beau produced a magnificent ring adorned with a marquis diamond and a band set with smaller diamonds. They slipped easily over her fingers, which were still icy.

He bent and touched her lips, causing her to jerk back in surprise. She hadn't expected the traditional kiss and hoped no one noticed her reaction. But of course, *he* had. He released her abruptly and turned away.

She looked at the rings. She was married. *Married!* She didn't recall the words although she knew she'd spoken at the times the minister stopped and nodded at her. She looked at Beau . . . the man who was now her husband.

Too late, too late, the pulse in her temple seemed to say. A headache began to throb across her brow.

"Congratulations, my lord," Clayburgh was saying.

George Myers clapped Beau on the shoulder while Bowes pounded him on the back. The minister smiled, glanced at his pocket watch and declared he had to leave to prepare for vespers.

Henny put an arm around Roselynne. "There now, ducks, it's done. Don't look so worried. Your young man knows what to do. Don't ye be a-fretting over what's to come this night."

Roselynne felt her knees getting weak again. Anxiously, she glanced around for her father.

"A toast," George Myers called out, going toward the other side of the cell.

She noticed the table then. A cake, small but perfectly decorated with forget-me-nots and roses entwined around golden rings, stood in the center. Fluted glasses and champagne bottles stood on a silver tray. A servant in black-and-gold livery stood quietly behind the table. Smiling, he poured the champagne.

Roselynne accepted a glass from George and went to her father. Tears gathered as she realized he hadn't heard one word of the ceremony. He should have performed it. "Here, Father, would you like a sip? You always enjoyed fine wines."

Her voice wobbled like the most woebegone of heroines in the romantic novels she had read. Behind her, the merriment built as the champagne was liberally poured. The servant brought two plates of cake and placed them on the windowsill.

Her glance collided with her husband's furious one, and she realized he'd cut the cake by himself. Apparently he'd expected her to act the part of the radiant bride. She turned away, unable to sustain his stare. Feeling like a specter at the party, she fed her father.

The affair took on a gay note as Henny flirted with the men and, her tongue freed by the third glass of champagne, told of her escapades. "Well, there 'e was, a-hanging out the window—'ow was I to know the bloke was married?—and there 'is wife was, ranting around the room, peering under the bed and in the cupboards—"

"An interesting friend you've acquired," George Myers murmured near Roselynne's ear. She replaced her father's empty plate on the sill. Her own was untouched.

She looked at Henny, who was twirling around, her skirts flying at that moment. "She has a kind heart."

"Aye. Like another I could name."

She met his kind glance and saw his meaning. "Nay. I have a vixenish temper," she confessed with a wan smile. "It has been the bane of my life."

"I hope to witness it one day," he teased.

Henny swirled about the room. "A kiss from the groom," she cried and threw her arms around Beau's neck.

"Aye, and from the bride," Bowes added. He pranced over, his lumbering girth threatening the strength of the timber floor, and clasped Roselynne by the shoulders. He gave her a smacking buss, which she accepted with calm grace.

The kiss between Henny and Beau was still in progress, she saw. George Myers and Mr. Clayburgh also claimed a kiss from her as a wedding token. The kiss across the room continued.

A silence crept over the little crowd. Storms of emotion swept through Roselynne. She wasn't angry, not at all. But this was going beyond the pale, she thought, when the couple showed no signs of coming up for air.

"I think it's time to depart," the barrister suggested.

Bowes tossed back his fourth glass of champagne and grabbed Henny by the neck. "Come on, woman. 'E's got his own plans for the night and they don't include the likes o' you."

Face flushed, throwing kisses and blessings to all, Henny bowed her way out of the room like an actress leaving the stage of a smashing success.

"I'll wait in the carriage," George told Beau and left.

Clayburgh stepped forward, papers in hand. "Here are the documents for you and your father. Shall I keep them in my safe?"

"Oh, yes, please," Roselynne replied. "May I read them before you leave?"

With a smile, he handed them over. She pulled off the ribbon and unfolded the pages. It was true. The king had pardoned her father. Her own release had been secured with a payment of one hundred pounds.

"Why, it's an outrageous sum." She glared at the lawyer. "My crime was not worth a tenth that amount."

"Shall I tell that to the king and repetition the case?" he inquired with a dry chuckle.

"Nay," Beau interjected. "The cost was small in exchange for freedom."

Roselynne looked at him, her gaze caught by his. A compelling light shone from the blue depths for a moment. She felt as if she'd drown in them. Or burst into flame, she amended, feeling the heat as his perusal became intense.

"I must go," Clayburgh said and broke the spell.

"Aye. Thank you for your work this day." Beau walked to the open door and saw the man out. He turned back and spoke to the servant. "Thank you for your help, too."

"A pleasure, my lord. Shall I take the old gentleman and go?"

Roselynne looked from Beau to the servant.

"Roselynne, this is Constantine, the earl's...the thir-teenth earl's...valet. He's willing to assume the same duties for your father, if you're agreeable."

"It would be wonderful to have someone help watch him. I worry that I might grow lax and he will become lost. It is lovely to have you, Constantine."

The man bowed to her. "I've always been called Connie by the family. It would please me if your lord and ladyship would continue the tradition."

"Of course." She felt so strange, as if she'd stumbled onto a stage and didn't know her part. The realization hit her that she was now a countess.

"The horses have stood long enough. You may leave. Tell the chef we'll have an early dinner. No later than seven," Beau said.

"Come, sir," Connie said to Mr. Moreley. "I have a room prepared for you at his lordship's town house." He guided Mr. Moreley out after Roselynne had kissed her father's cheek and bid him farewell.

She was alone with her husband.

Beau pulled out a chair. "You must be tired."

She nodded, relieved at his kind manner. In truth, she'd half expected him to grab her and haul her to bed.

"Sit and rest a spell. We'll talk later," he invited.

"It has been a rather unsettling day." She managed to smile as she took the seat. Her hands had become icy again, and she could think of nothing to say.

Beau went to the window and sat with his hip propped on the sill. She wished he would speak. She needed reassurance, but he had withdrawn into himself.

She noted that he wore the Rockdale colors, a black suit with gold threads woven through the waistcoat, with a simple white linen stock at his throat. A stream of late-afternoon sunshine fell upon his face, highlighting the startling blue of his eyes against his black lashes, which were long and curled at the ends. She caught her breath in wonder. Why, he was hand-some.

He turned to face her, casting his eyes into shadow, the lower part of his face darkened by his beard. The illusion faded. He was a man who'd been beaten, whose face was still somewhat bruised from his attempt at freedom.

"My lord—"

"Beau," he roared, coming off his perch and standing over her like an enraged lion. "I'm your husband. You'll call me by name, or by the heavens, I won't speak to you until you do."

"B-Beau," she repeated, hating the quiver in her voice.

She breathed easier when he moved away to add wood to the fire and stoke the embers into flames as the chill of twilight shaded the room.

"What were you going to say?" he asked.

"Only that your bruises look much better."

He touched his nose, then snorted as if unconcerned.

Her gaze settled on the locked door. "And that prison is a cruel place run by cruel men," she concluded.

"Aye." He paced the cell.

He stopped abruptly when she laughed. Nervous and unsure of his mood, she quickly explained, "You once said Mr. Bowes played a game, hoping you would be desperate enough to fall for it. Is this not a desperate thing we do, this strange marriage conducted in haste from a prison cell?"

Roselynne's nerves tightened unbearably when he continued to stare at her as if seeing her for the first time. The grimness seemed to leave him, and his expression softened, though he didn't smile at her. Other thoughts apparently occupied his mind. She sensed his restlessness and the primitive energy that drove him to resume pacing. He paused by the table.

"Here, let us drink to our vows." He poured them each a glass and stared deeply into her eyes while handing her the drink. After touching his glass to hers, he sipped from it, then rubbed his forehead as if he had the headache.

"Are you all right, my lor . . . Beau?"

He focused on her again. His eyes were like clear pools. She was drowning. No, she was burning . . . burning *and* drowning. The feeling was so confusing, it frightened her. She glanced about the room, but the reassuring presence of her father was not there. She gulped the champagne.

"To a happy marriage," Beau said, and she smiled suddenly.

He refilled the glasses as soon as they were empty. Roselynne realized she was quite giddy by the time supper arrived.

"Here, a bit more," Beau said. He tilted the bottle toward Roselynne's glass.

"No, I couldn't. Really."

He ignored her protest and tipped the rest of the wine into her glass. She lifted it to her lips and drank while he smiled at her in approval. Her head was in a pleasant whirl. It had been a delightful evening. Her earlier fears had been silly.

The candles sputtered on the table, burnt almost to the silver flange of the candelabra. He replaced them with fresh ones. "I think it's time we prepared for bed, wife," he murmured, giving her a wickedly teasing glance.

He'd flirted with her outrageously during the sumptuous meal of trout in mushroom and cream sauce, flavored with basil.

She peered through the shadows beyond the candles at the big feather bed. It seemed to sway and jostle as if upon a stormy sea. "I fear I will become ill if I move."

"Nay," he protested. "You cannot. Come, I'll play lady's maid for you." His gaze fired her blood.

She rose at his urging and walked unsteadily toward the bed. The room swayed dangerously, and she clung to his arm. He was as steady as bedrock. She leaned against him.

When they paused beside the bed, he untied the shawl from around her shoulders, his fingers nimble and quick at the task, and tossed the covering across the bed railing. Then his hands were at the buttons of her dress.

She stood still while he opened the first two, then another, and another. The cool air hit her warm flesh above her shift, and the shock of what was happening caught up with her. She covered his hands. "You mustn't," she scolded, scandalized.

His eyes, so gorgeously blue, were very near her own. They seemed to shine with an intense light. "It's all right," he whispered. "Don't go missish on me, Roselynne."

She spun around, almost falling as she turned her back on him. "I am not misshs ... sshs." She couldn't seem to command her tongue. Fright seized her as his hands touched her shoulders, pressing her to turn to him. She held her dress closed.

"I'm your husband," he coaxed softly. "There's no need for prudish modesty between us."

She tried to reason this out, but failed.

"I have dreamed of you nightly," he continued, his gaze hot and heavy upon her throat. She could almost feel him touching her.

He dipped his head and his lips brushed her collarbone, leaving a trail of heat there while chills raced along her arms.

His hands lifted hers, and he went to work on the buttons once more. *Husband.* The word twirled through her brain. Husbands could touch their wives. He was touching her, sliding her dress over her shoulders and down to her hips. He found the ties to her petticoats and unfastened them, too.

They and the dress fell from her to the floor in a frothy billow of material. She stood quite still in her shift and stockings and shoes.

"Sit," he said.

His hand pressed her shoulder, and she sat on the bed, feeling the feathers sink under her weight. She felt very heavy.

He removed her shoes, then untied her garters and rolled her stockings down and off her feet. To her amazement, he lifted her foot and began to rub it.

"Your feet are cold," he admonished. He massaged one, then the other, until circulation returned. With a smile, he bent and placed a kiss upon her instep, then her ankle. Heat throbbed through her.

"Why did you do that?" she asked.

"I like kissing you." He held her gaze while he rose, then leaned over her. His lips touched hers, softly at first, then with greater ardor.

Before she knew how it happened, she was lying back on the bed and he was lying beside her. The kiss continued unbroken.

His tongue joined in with the conquest of her lips, caressing her in a thousand ways. When she tried to turn her head and draw a deep breath, he invaded the interior.

It was like the other time. She felt strange—excited and nervous, fearful yet filled with longing. When his tongue gently rubbed hers, she tried to draw back, but couldn't.

His hands guided hers around his neck. She tentatively touched his hair. Finding the riband that held it, she released it and ran her fingers into the dark locks. It curled enticingly around her hand, as if to bind her to him.

"Yes," he encouraged, leaving her mouth to nibble on her ear. "I've dreamed of you touching me like that."

From deep inside, a beat like that of a drum began throbbing through her. This touching between husband and wife wasn't so bad.

She stiffened when she felt the brush of his trimmed beard against her chest. He kissed down her neck and along the delicate white lace topping her shift.

His hand at the fastening brought her dizzy mind back to the present and what was happening. Before she could protest, he moved away from her, shrugging out of his coat and waistcoat. They were tossed to the floor, then he returned and eased farther over her.

Through the fine material of her shift and the smooth cotton of his shirt, she felt the heat of his body as he rubbed against her. A gasp was torn from her at the sensations this caused.

His hand stroked over her hips and up her side. Before she knew what he was about, the shift fell open, exposing her breasts to his view when he lifted himself off her.

"My God, what bounty," he breathed, and arching down, he kissed first one, then the other. "What treasure."

Roselynne had never been so shocked in her life. She tugged her shift across her. Heat flooded into her chest and face.

"Nay, love," he scolded, pulling the material from her cold hands, "would you deny a starving man manna from heaven?"

His hand closed over her, engulfing that which hadn't been seen by another person since she'd been a child. She protested as best she could, but her mind had deserted her.

She felt suffocated by the strange, wild impulses he stirred in her. She tossed about, trying to free herself from him and the impulses, but he seemed to have grown extra hands. Where she closed and straightened with two hands, he opened and removed with a dozen or more. Suddenly all their clothing departed as if by magic, and his bare male flesh pressed against her equally bare skin. His kisses fell upon her face and throat and breasts in random order while he explored her completely.

"No," she cried when his hands—dear heaven, he was touching her *everywhere*—slid intimately between them.

"I will be gentle," he promised, soothing her.

"Please," she whispered, frightened not only of him, but of herself. Her body had become an alien thing to her, out of control and with demands of its own that she didn't understand.

"Don't be afraid," he murmured. "Lie still, love, and let me show you how wonderful it can be."

She heard his quickened breath, then realized her own sounded just as loud. She was being consumed from inside by a fire and from outside by him. The probe of his hard male flesh against her thigh catapulted her into action. With a convulsive surge, she heaved him aside and scooted away, not caring for dignity or modesty in her haste to be free of the web he had spun around her, binding her into immobility.

Hunched against the headboard, she crossed her arms and drew her knees protectively to her chest. Only the sound of their shallow breathing filled the space between them.

Heart pounding, she waited.

He shook his head as if to clear it, then he observed her for a brief moment. Rising, he turned his back on her and pulled on his breeches, giving her only a glimpse of his powerful male flesh. She doubted the vision of her own eyes. Nay, a man couldn't possess such an instrument. Why, 'twould be impossible for him to get his breeches on!

But there had been a certain pronounced hardness pressing against her thigh as he lay half over her. When he turned, she leaped under the cover, holding the sheet tight to her neck.

"You needn't look so outraged," he told her. "I won't bother you further. You have my word on it."

She said nothing. He went to the table and poured a glass of wine, sloshing it to the rim, then drank it down without another glance in her direction, his disgust with her obvious.

Instinctively, she knew she had insulted him in some terrible way. She still felt hot, somewhat ridiculous, and thoroughly confused by emotions too riotous for her to sort out. Perhaps if she'd talked to Henny beforehand, she'd not have been so shocked at his caresses and . . . and . . . whatever those other strange feelings had been. Nonetheless, she knew she must apologize.

She cleared her throat.

He ignored her.

"My lord," she began.

No reply.

She tried again, but still he ignored her.

Temper unfurled in her. She restrained it. A quarrel was all she needed after the embarrassing events of the night.

"Beau," she started anew. "I'm sorry for behaving so abominably. Please forgive me—"

He whipped around and stared at her, his eyes as dark as coals from hell, frightening her once more. Then she realized it wasn't anger but pain she saw in him. He seemed so . . . so desolate, so filled with despair. The impression lasted only a second, then he strode to the bed and sat down on the end, well away from her.

"Forgive you?" he said. "I promised you I would take every caution with you, then I rush upon you like a starving man at a feast. 'Tis I who wish for forgiveness, Roselynne."

"No, I was at fault. I acted missish, just as you said. If you would return to bed, I will . . . that is, I won't . . ."

He smiled at her. "There you go again, not certain if you are or you aren't, you will or you won't."

She felt much better at his gentle teasing. "Come," she invited, not quite so afraid of him after all. Clothed, he didn't look so formidable as he had naked. She scanned his body quickly. There was no evidence of . . . what had the village girls called it? His twig. Twig. 'Twas more like the tree itself.

He took a turn around the room and looked grim once more, but he spoke with great kindness. "It's been a long day. Go to sleep. We'll speak of our problems tomorrow."

So saying, he took a chair before the hearth and returned to the wine bottle, finding what solace he might from it.

Roselynne watched him from half-closed lashes. She sensed sadness in him and felt bereft. The evening had not gone at all the way she had envisioned, either in her girlish dreams or in her worst nightmares.

Her glance strayed to the shuttered window. Of course, the night was far from over.

Chapter Seven

Roselynne was wonderfully warm and comfortable. She yawned and snuggled under the covers, then became aware that she wasn't alone. The heat that was so blissful came from the man lying next to her!

With a muffled yelp, she eased away from him until their thighs no longer touched. Although the room was cold with the early morning chill, Beau slept with his torso bare, one arm flung over his head. She stared at his chest with its whirl of dark hair and noted a sickle-shaped scar on the smooth golden skin.

She wondered how he'd look without the beard obscuring his lower face and decided she was either growing used to him or he was becoming more handsome with each passing day. Without thinking, she reached out to touch him.

He moved, then muttered something under his breath, causing her to draw back. His lips had been gentle on her flesh when he had kissed her the previous night. A tightening of her nipples reminded her of where he'd touched her, his tongue spreading fire across her skin....

All the tumultuous feelings that had seared her yesterday returned, but she found they weren't so terrifying this morning. In truth, she quivered with a sense of excitement never before known.

While she nibbled on her lip, her blood warming with her own heated thoughts, Beau stirred. In a moment, he opened his eyes and looked at her, his gaze taking in her hair, which she knew must be a tangled mass around her shoulders, then sweeping down her shoulders to the sheet pulled across her breasts and tucked under her arms.

"Good morning," he said, a hint of a smile softening his mouth. His voice was deep and husky.

"Good morning."

She wasn't sure what to do next. Her shift lay too far away on the floor for her to reach it without exposing herself. She waited anxiously, nay, impatiently, for him to move.

"I'll start a fire to drive off the chill," he said. He slid from the bed, and she saw he wore linen smalls. She felt oddly disappointed. From a chest, he retrieved doeskin breeches and a shirt, then went behind a screen set in a corner of the chamber.

She lay in bed and listened to the sounds of his ablutions, her tremors receding. She realized it seemed very wifely to listen to the intimate sounds as he washed.

When he finished, and the fire was going, he glanced at her. "Are you going to lie slugabed all day?" he asked. "Breakfast will be here soon, and we have plans to make."

She started up, realized her state of undress and cast him an uncertain look.

His smile became sardonic. "I'll turn my back."

"Thank you." She sounded as prim as a governess.

As soon as he stared back into the flames, she leaped up and yanked on her scattered clothing as fast as she could. The chimes pealed the hour just as she fastened the last ribbon.

A knock sounded on the door.

Beau, after one look in her direction, opened the portal, admitting a footman carrying a large tray. Another followed with a silver urn in each hand. They spoke jovially and darted quick peeks at Roselynne.

"This is your new countess," Beau introduced her. "This is Sanders, that one Jim. They'll see to your comfort when you go to the country next week."

The men grinned and muttered that they were glad to meet her. Under Beau's direction, they quickly set out the meal. "Wait downstairs," he told them before turning to her. "My lady," he said, holding a chair.

Roselynne took her place and waited until Beau sat opposite her before picking up her fork. She was aware of his frowning perusal while they ate. Self-consciously she pushed her hair behind her shoulders. Her recently purchased comb was in the lower chamber along with her hairpins.

"Your hair is lovely," he said, settling back in his chair with a fresh cup of coffee when he'd eaten. "I've had your things brought up from the other room. Have you no other clothing?"

"Not with me. The soldiers wouldn't allow me to fetch anything when they arrested us."

"Damn," he said, setting his cup down with a clatter. "I've been a thoughtless bridegroom. You should have had a new dress."

"I had not the funds."

His frown grew fierce. "You have all the money of an earldom at your disposal," he contradicted in a harsh voice.

Roselynne was uncertain why he was angry. They had not discussed the subject and she wasn't about to make assumptions. Some men kept their wives in penury. "Am I to have an allowance?"

"After I am dead, you'll have it all," he raged at her. "And my plantation, too, although it's not so rich as Rockdale."

"I would like to purchase a few items," she admitted, gracious in the face of his temper. "If you would tell me the amount of the allowance—"

"Tell Clayburgh what you need," he snapped at her. "I'll not keep you on an allowance as if you were still in leading strings. You're my wife, not my offspring."

Roselynne was in no mood for his brutishness, especially when she could see no reason for it. However, he was being generous with her without knowing if she was a spendthrift. She lifted her chin. "Very well, my lord. Thank you."

He grabbed her wrist. "Beau, dammit, my name is Beau."

"Beau," she repeated. Funny feelings ran along her arm from where he touched her.

He released her. "Sorry, my disposition isn't the best this morning. It's not your fault," he added before she could apologize for troubling him.

"More coffee?" she asked, smiling at him. He was but a man, after all, and she'd watched her mother coax her father out of his ill humors all during her childhood. She freshened his cup, added hot water to her tea leaves and relaxed. "What shall I do first to gain your release?"

He looked at her in amazement, then he laughed. "Become the king's mistress."

"I do not find that amusing." She stared at him solemnly.

"Aye, I see you're serious." He sobered. "There's no avenue that hasn't already been explored by the attorney. Rest easy, Roselynne, my purpose for you has nought to do with the king."

The silence stretched awkwardly between them. She recalled all too well his purpose for her—to keep his inheritance out of evil hands and bear him an heir. He should have finished the task this morning. She'd been willing....

Astounded, she realized it was true. Perhaps he'd been a bit impatient last night, but he'd also been gentle. And he'd stopped when he'd realized her fears. In truth, he was a gentleman, and she no longer wished to avoid his touch. Besides, she'd given her word. He'd kept his part of the bargain; she must do the same.

"I know," she said softly. "I...I am willing...."

Beau waved away her confession. "You must be anxious about your father. The carriage is waiting to take you to the town house. George has gone over the accounts and will explain our finances to you. In my family, Roselynne, there were no secrets. We equally shared the good and the bad times. I'd like the same between us."

After she freshened up and bound her hair into a chignon, he laid her shawl around her shoulders. "Buy yourself a new cloak," he ordered. "A pink velvet one would be nice. With a hat to match."

With that advice, he called for the guard and had her escorted out of the prison. From his high window, he watched when she emerged into the courtyard and was handed into the carriage by Jim, who then clambered onto the back beside Sanders. The coachman cracked the whip and the carriage departed with his bride.

I am willing, she'd said.

He wanted her more than willing. He wanted her hot and panting beneath him. He thought of another who'd been eager for his kisses, who'd looked forward to marriage with him.

Mary hadn't been frightened by his touch. But she'd been in love with him and he with her. Roselynne had not the advantage of long acquaintance or the sweet wonder of love.

His throat constricted with emotions too confused and fleeting to be completely sorted out: sorrow for what hadn't been and could never be, vengeance toward the person who'd murdered his cousin and forced him into this harsh bargain, impatience with the restraint he felt toward Roselynne and with her fears.

No, he couldn't hurry her, for all her brave acting. He recalled her icy hands during the wedding and her tremors when he'd caressed her. However, he wasn't convinced her shivers had all been from fright. He thought he'd aroused her a tiny bit.

He felt an urgent need to share something of himself with her before he faced the hangman one week hence. He didn't want to go to his grave without showing her that passion could also be bliss.

As for a child, the chances were slim that he could get her pregnant in so short a time. To leave her with a part of himself, a new life... But he could not force himself on her and give her a complete disgust of him and the marriage act.

Ah, what a abominable coil life could be. Heat surged into the lower part of his body as he considered the pleasures he'd given up in deference to his bride's jitters.

He closed his eyes and recounted the treasures he'd discovered in Roselynne. Her skin...soft as a petal. Her hair...thick and fine. Lips as sweet as honey. God, what bounty!

Turning, he stared at the bed, visualizing her lying there, waiting for him to come to her. Her breasts had been full and firm, not overly large, but a nice handful. She'd tasted like pure ambrosia and her scent had been of roses.

Hmm. His bride, though modest, had some of the vanities of other women. She'd probably spent her last copper on scented soap. Enormously pleased with this insight, he sat down and prepared a list of items he wanted George to procure for him. Smiling, he planned the seduction of his wife. His blood stirred mightily at this enticing thought.

* * *

Roselynne couldn't believe this was her home when the coach stopped at a fashionable town house on Sloane Square. It was too grand, too imposing, too *rich*.

The footman waited for her to descend. She stepped down and stared at the elegantly carved door with its brass lion's-head knocker and crystal postern lamps. Two marble steps led to a marble stoop covered by a gabled roof. Flowers filled window boxes and an urn contained a giant fern.

While she was still gaping, George Myers opened the door. "Welcome home," he called out in friendly greeting. "The countess," he said to some unseen person.

She walked up the steps and into the house, dazed by the wealth unfolding before her. Why, Beau was as rich as Wainsco!

A bevy of servants lined the hall, which was inlaid with green marble tiles on the floor and cream watered-silk wall coverings. George introduced her to the housekeeper, a spinster with a cheerful nature and sunny smile, plus several upstairs and downstairs maids and footmen. All in all, there were fourteen in the household, including the laundress and her two girls, the coachman, a groom and two stable lads.

Her father, looking very dapper in new gray flannels, stood at the end of the line.

"Oh, Father," she cried and threw her arms around him. She felt as if it had been days rather than hours since they'd parted.

"Here now," George scolded. "None of that. Come into the study and we'll have tea, if you like. We're at your command."

Looking at the smiling faces of the staff, she realized it was true. She had fourteen servants, plus a business manager and a barrister, when all she'd had in the past was a day girl, who'd come in twice a week and helped her clean.

"Yes, thank you. Tea would be fine. Come, Father, we shall have tea. Thank you all for your kind greeting," she said to the servants, and followed George into the study.

The room was lined with tier after tier of leather-bound books. "This is a marvelous library," she exclaimed, reading a few of the titles. "Father will be overjoyed when he comes to himself."

She placed the older man in a chair and plopped on the stool at his feet. Seeing George's amused glance, she colored. "I am used to sitting thus at home."

He laughed. "You must do as you please. This is your home now. How was Beau when you left him? Did he say I was to attend him today?"

"No. That is, he didn't say."

"Probably other things on his mind," George said.

A knock on the door preceded a footman with a heavy silver tea service. A delicate fruit tart was divided among three plates. "Compliments of the chef to your ladyship," the footman explained. "And if you want something special for dinner, just let him know."

Roselynne was touched. "Please convey my appreciation."

She served George, then helped her father eat his treat before tasting her own. At any moment, she expected the lady of the house to appear, expose her for an impostor and order her out. "Did I really marry an earl?" she asked, explaining her qualms to George. "Is he really as rich as this house indicates?"

"Trust Beau," he advised, amused by her doubts. "He's as honest as they come, and he always lands on his feet. By the way, I'm to take you to the country estate before the week is out."

"Before? But aren't we to stay, that is, shouldn't we . . . ?"

"Stay for the hanging? Nay. Beau has forbidden it. You are to leave Sunday and be out of town before the event." He held up a hand as she protested, reminding him of funeral arrangements to be made. "It is all planned," he told her gently.

She studied her husband's friend through narrowed eyes. "I think there's something afoot. Tell me what it is."

But he would admit to nothing, no matter how she badgered or threatened. Her father was taken off by Connie for a walk, and Clayburgh, after first stopping by the prison, arrived to make sure she had encountered no difficulties. In the end, she had to be content to listen to the affairs of business from the two men.

"How much?" she asked, sure she had misheard.

"A half-million pounds," George answered. "In stock and bank notes. Now the estate has forty thousand acres...."

She nearly swooned. Wainsco had been the wealthiest person she'd ever known until that time, but Beau was even richer than the duke. It was almost more than she could comprehend.

"You'd best beware of fortune hunters when you're a widow," the barrister told her. "They will flock to comfort you like vultures at a carnage."

"Pray do not put my husband in the grave before his body cools," she said with asperity. She must start working for his release immediately. The king was first on her list.

Clayburgh stood and bowed to her. "I apologize. Now I must go to my office. George, here's a list of tasks for you, none too onerous, I think." With that, he left.

George looked over the list and chuckled. "Come, my lady, we have been given orders to shop this afternoon. Then you are to dine with your husband tonight. Will you tell the housekeeper or shall I?"

Roselynne reached for the missive, but George wouldn't give it to her. He tucked it into his pocket.

"I'll tell her," Roselynne decided. She had best begin by taking charge. She must establish herself quickly if she was to help Beau. She rang the bell and waited for the footman.

"I'll see you in an hour," George said and left her.

Roselynne sighed shakily. Her life had irrevocably changed. Time would tell if it was for better or for worse.

"A fine lady you made," Bowes told her, leading the way to the turret room and casting her many a glance over her shoulder. "Your groom be waiting for you. 'E seems a mite restless today."

Roselynne followed, feeling elegant in her pink velvet pelisse and matching straw hat with the white plumes fluttering from the band. Her hair was dressed in the loose, flowing curls of a shepherdess, the fashion now turning toward simple country styles after the excesses of the eighties.

She was still smiling, thinking of women, and men, too, who during the previous decade had worn their hair as high above their heads as they could pile it, when she entered the cell.

"You are in humor tonight," a deep voice said. Beau left the window and came toward her. "I wasn't sure that was you when you stepped from the coach. I see George carried out my instructions."

"You may be angry when you discover the cost," she warned, pleased by the admiring light in his eyes. "Thank you for the gifts. I've never had so many perfumes, silks, laces, hats, jewelry or... other things, not even at Christmastide."

She couldn't mention the other things to him, but her drawers in the elegant bedroom at the house were stuffed with night rails of the sheerest silk gauze in all colors, also corsets and chemises, petticoats and shifts of cambric, lawn and other fine fabrics so pleasing to the touch. Silk and cotton stockings had been purchased by the score. Never had she seen such plentitude.

He chuckled. "The pink becomes you. Now let me see the gown." He opened the pink satin frog closure and lifted the short wrap from her shoulders. "My God," he gasped.

Roselynne suppressed the need to place her hands over her bosom as she watched him lay the cape aside without taking his gaze from her. He took in her hair, her face, then her outfit.

The dress was rose silk, a simple gown laced over a stomacher of deeper rose with a wide sash to emphasize her narrow waist. Tight sleeves fell to her elbows and ended in wide ruffles of deep rose silk luxuriant with lace. She'd never had so fine a dress.

One thing had troubled her about it. She'd been appalled by the neckline, which the modiste, Madame Bertin, had assured her was quite proper. She shouldn't have listened to the woman, an émigrée who'd fled the troubles in her homeland. Everyone knew how bold the French were.

Her breasts would have been almost entirely visible except for the silk-and-lace fichu that draped around her shoulders and tucked beneath the front edge. The tight corset mounded her bosom into twin provocative peaks, visible above the fichu.

"I'll have the seamstress add some material to the top," she said, seeing how shocked Beau was.

"Nay," he murmured. "You are...incredibly lovely."

"Then you do like it? You don't think it a trifle...low?"

He touched a curl, then let his hand glide to the lace and follow its plunging dip to the valley between her breasts. His smile was somewhat strained. "You'll have all the men panting after you."

"My lord," she protested, heat rushing to her face.

"Beau," he corrected in a husky tone. "Our meal is ready. Please, be seated, my lady. Tonight I will feast doubly well."

His lingering gaze told her his meaning.

She tried not to feel vain, but he made it very difficult. During the meal, his gaze never strayed far from her, and she preened under his admiration. It was a heady sensation. She wondered what would happen once the meal was over.

Warm tremors whispered along her nerves as the meal drew to a close. When he rose and helped her up, she became flustered by his intent regard and swayed toward him. He took her arm.

"Here, take this chair. 'Tis more comfortable. We must make plans." He poured them each a small brandy, then stood at the hearth and sipped his. She noted he had not plied her with wine tonight, nor taken much for himself.

"Plans?" she prodded when he didn't speak. Her gaze went to the bed.

"I want you to be seen about town and introduced into society as the Countess of Rockdale. That way, there will be no doubt about who you are and your position to inherit. George will stay at your side and watch after your safety."

"All right." She wondered how she would gain entrance into the *ton*. She was gentle-born, but had no connections.

"Clayburgh will help," Beau said as if reading her mind. He smiled grimly. "And we have an ally. Wainsco has agreed to champion you."

"No!"

"I know you'll see your old lover, but you'll have to stand the temptation," Beau said coolly. "Wainsco is the only powerful contact we have."

Her pride wouldn't allow her to explain her revulsion at seeing Charles. Temptation, indeed. He had cast her and her father aside as if they were no more than curiosities at a fair. The thought still made her blood roil.

"Perhaps through him, you may meet the king," Beau added.

"I had planned to petition him."

"I thought you might. You're determined to save me, it would appear."

"I will do all I can." She wondered at his attitude. He seemed to be mocking her. Looking into his eyes, she saw his thoughts were on another matter. Heat poured into her from some unknown source as his glance roamed over her.

Silence descended between them. She felt devoured by his hunger. Tonight, then. She would be glad to get it over and cease this useless wondering. It couldn't be so bad, or matrons wouldn't laugh in their droll, knowing ways at maidens' shy questions.

"Take the lace thing off," he requested suddenly in thickened tones.

Her hands shook as she lifted them to the fichu. She pulled the ends free and let the silk fall into her lap. A shiver danced over her as the night air caressed her skin.

"You are beautiful beyond all imagining," he muttered. He seemed to be speaking to himself rather than her. "I had no idea. There wasn't a clue, not one, of such . . . riches."

"Thank you." A flush spread over her chest, wherever he gazed, and she was no longer cold.

"Come here."

She rose and went to him, compelled by a need she didn't understand. A sense of urgency drove her. Their bargain, that was what coaxed her to do his bidding. Yes, she would keep their bargain. 'Twas the only fair thing to do.

Her breasts trembled precariously above the lace with each shallow breath she took. She felt she might burst out of the bodice at any moment.

When he spread his knees and drew her inside the warmth of his thighs, she saw she was not the only one who strained against the confines of clothing. His manly staff pushed mightily against his breeches, and she could not avert her fascination at this evidence of his desire for her.

His lips went unerringly to the valley between her breasts, and his hands settled on her hips, his fingers started a kneading motion that made her knees weak in a moment.

"Ohh," she moaned when he licked and nipped the flesh above the silk. His caresses were like fire, gentle fire, flowing over her, making her hot, so hot.

He found the laces over the stomacher and pulled the bow until it was loose. The bodice dropped, and it took but a tug of the material to free her breasts. Then he gently suckled one breast until she had to clutch his shoulders to stay upright.

Dear heaven, no one had ever mentioned this stealing of the mind by the senses. She could think of nothing but where he was touching, except to wonder what he would do next...and when.

He brought her closer, enclosing her in his powerful arms so that she was pressed solidly against him. She was aware of his body, hard and masculine in its form, and held on tighter. When he drew back, she made a little sound of protest.

But he wasn't leaving her. Instead, his hands slid under her breasts, enclosed them and lifted them entirely free of her clothing. He kissed one taut nipple, then the other, causing sensation to rush into her innermost parts. She wanted...she *needed*...something more from him. Desperation seized her, and her hands clutched at him, silently pleading for more.

"Are you feeling brave tonight?" he asked, standing and pulling her to him.

She laid her head against his chest and heard the hard, even pounding of his heart. "Yes." She dared a glance at him. "What is this strange thing you do to me? I feel I'm under a sorcerer's spell when you kiss me and touch me like that."

He smiled, and his teeth gleamed with startling brilliance against the black beard. "It's the way between a man and a maid. And it gets better, believe me. It gets much better."

She found it frightening to be so under the control of another person. She'd never experienced anything like it. Her body reacted to his caresses without her volition, and she couldn't think when her blood rushed through her brain with a roar.

Before she had time to voice these fears, a knock had them both spinning toward the door. Before the key turned in the lock, Beau grabbed her cape and twirled it around her shoulders, hiding her state of dishabille from whoever entered.

It was George Myers.

"Beau, I have news!" he exclaimed, striding across the room after the turnkey admitted him. "I was at White's and guess what I've found . . . *who* I've found!"

"I've no idea," Beau said. He concealed his own condition by standing behind the table and offering George a glass of wine.

George took a gulp and waved the glass expansively. "William Spinner," he announced. He finished off the wine.

While the men talked, Roselynne took the opportunity to repair her clothing under the cape. After fastening the bodice once more, she looked around for the fichu. It was on the floor. She sat in the chair and, bending as if to inspect her feet for some reason, she scooped it up and out of sight.

"Who, pray tell, is William Spinner?" Beau asked. He brought her a glass and looked her over. A smile lifted the corners of his mouth, and his gaze was so intimate she blushed. "He'd better be damned important for you to interrupt an evening with my wife."

George darted a look at the newlyweds. "Oh, I'm sorry," he said. "Did I . . . I didn't . . ."

Beau chuckled. "He's becoming infected with your manner of speaking," he said to Roselynne, then again asked George about William Spinner."

"Spinner is a connection of the late earl's, a cousin by marriage, he claims."

Beau looked surprised at the news. "What has excited you about this man?"

"Why, don't you see? He's the murderer!"

"I'm afraid I don't see that at all. Sit down, George, and explain your reasoning. How did you meet the man?"

"I was introduced to him as your man of business, or rather, as Rockdale's man of business. Spinner looked amazed. He said he'd heard the earl had died and an heir was being sought abroad, perhaps in America."

"Why would that make you suspicious?" Roselynne asked.

"Well," George explained, "one, he shows up just before Beau is to hang. Two, he acts as if he doesn't know the heir was found, when it was all the news during the trial."

"Yes, even I recall having read of it," she agreed, "and London doings are not all that important in Ullswater."

"Perhaps he's been out of the country," Beau interjected.

"And three, there's the connection through his wife," George finished, a smile of satisfaction on his face.

"Who's he married to?" Beau asked. "No other kin was mentioned by the earl. He said I was the last of the line."

"That I don't know. I could hardly question the man on his marriage." George tapped his chin thoughtfully. "But he did ask about you and was amazed to discover you had married. If he had pretensions to the earldom, that would have dashed them."

"I must get Clayburgh to investigate, in case there is a claim." Beau glanced at Roselynne, then back to his friend. "Have you a carriage?"

"No, I came on foot straight from the club."

"Call a sedan. And hire a guard. I want you to take Roselynne home, then hie over to the barrister's and tell him what you told me." Beau paced the floor, apparently lost in thought while George rushed to do his bidding.

Before she could blink thrice, Roselynne found herself dispatched to the town house. George hastily bid her good-night as soon as she was inside, told the butler to keep the doors barred and hurried off into the night.

She went to her room, where a young maid named Ansella waited on her sleepily, helping her by unfastening the dress and then brushing the long curls that lay upon her shoulders and down her back after she was in her night rail.

"That will be all," Roselynne said, dismissing the girl after getting into the huge four-poster bed with its massive brocade hangings. Alone, she pulled the linen sheet over her and contemplated the evening.

It had been disconcerting, to say the least.

First there had been the leisurely dinner, then his command to remove the lace scarf from about her neck, then to come to him. She had done as he wished like one mesmerized.

All for nought. With the arrival of George, she had gone out of Beau's mind like yesterday's porridge. Without asking her preference, he'd sent her to the house like so much extra baggage. An insult, that's what it was.

She touched her lips, then let her fingertips glide down to her throat where he'd kissed her so hungrily, as if he couldn't get enough of her... until George barged in.

The more she thought of his callous dismissal, the angrier she became. She was not a courtesan to be ordered about at his whim.

He'd sent her home as if she weren't involved or concerned in the drama of his life, while he consulted with his barrister and man of business on a course of action.

If he showed so little regard for her, she would show the same for him. She gripped the sheet with both hands while tension curled her insides into knots.

Naturally she would continue to work for his release, but never again would she jump to do his bidding or go weak-kneed at his rousing kisses and caresses.

After making this decision, she turned to her side and tried to sleep. Tomorrow would be a busy day.

Chapter Eight

Roselynne paused on the stairs and surveyed her dress. The thin cambric was striped in a soft shade of gray green. Matching lace cascaded from the fichu, which came to her chin. She wore a riding jacket, called a caraco, mannish in cut and very tight-fitting, which was the current mode.

In the mirror on the landing, she quickly checked her hair— pouffed ringlets at the sides and a confection of lace and ribbon perched on top. Ansella had thought she looked "all the crack." She wished she felt as sure.

Head high, she entered the drawing room.

Clayburgh stood at once. Tall and formidable, the attorney wore a black coat, which looked very distinguished with his silver hair and dark eyes. "Roselynne. Countess," he corrected, his keen gaze taking in her appearance. Like her father, he seemed to see beyond the surface to her innermost thoughts. "Forgive this early hour, but I was most anxious to see you."

"Good morning, Mr. Clayburgh." She curtsied while he bowed over her hand, as if she were indeed a fine lady. From hoyden to doyenne in one bold move. She fought an insane desire to giggle.

"How is your father?"

"Fine, in his body. His mind is the same as you saw at Newgate." Her lips trembled. "Will you take tea?" she asked when the footman entered. "We also have coffee."

"Coffee."

Roselynne found comfort in the formality of ritual. She remembered going through the same with Charles in the little cell at Newgate. She had cast her hopes so high then; she must be careful not to expect too much of people in the future.

"Now, to our plans," he said, after assuring her the coffee was to his taste. "We are going to Radziwill's ball tonight. Wainsco arranged the invitations. Do you have a dress?"

She recovered from her surprise. "Yes."

New items arrived from the shops almost hourly. Beau had seen to it that she had enough clothes for a full season in town. She was amazed each time she looked into a chest or wardrobe.

"The duke will introduce you to Prinny."

"The crown prince?" Her eyes widened.

"I think he will be made regent soon. George is having one of his spells again."

The king's madness was whispered about, but not openly spoken of. "I see."

"If you charm the prince, it may advance your cause—"

"Can he free my husband?" She noted how easily the term came to her lips. *Her husband.* She perused the opulent room. She had gained everything upon becoming his wife; now she must help him.

"If he is regent, he can act for the king."

"Yes, but for now?"

"He is not without influence."

"Then I will do it."

Clayburgh smiled and stood. "I've no doubt of it. I shall come for you at nine-thirty. That should time us to arrive in the midst of the crush. You are to see and be seen, as the saying goes. The bonds you forge tonight may last a lifetime. I will guide you as best I can."

"Thank you. I have no qualms concerning your skill." She walked to the door with him.

"One other thing—listen to the duke's advice. I think he is uncommonly cunning."

A niggle of resentment reared its head. None of the men considered her capable of rational thought. They treated her like a green girl up from the country. She held back a retort.

"I'll try to be circumspect. Should I mention my husband and his plight to the prince?"

"Yes. You may engage his sympathy, and that would be good. The king would not be so approachable regarding an American. I need not tell you why, I think."

She returned his smile. "Beau and I have discussed that very thing."

The underbutler opened the door. "Mr. Osgood to see you," he announced.

"Ah, yes. Did you get them?" the lawyer asked.

"Yes, I have them." Charles hurried into the room, holding two envelopes. He, too, was dressed in the black coat that was fashionable at the moment, but his stockings and waistcoat were gaudily striped in red and gold.

"Your invitations to the ball," Clayburgh explained. "I'll run along to my club. Mr. Osgood, do you need a ride?"

"I'll walk to the duke's house, sir. It isn't far."

"Very well." Clayburgh bowed over her hand again, wished her a good day and departed in an elegant carriage.

"Roselynne," Charles said, his manner anxious.

"Would you take tea, Mr. Osgood?" she inquired.

"Please. I wish to speak to you."

She looked at the clock on the mantle. "I am in rather of a rush," she decided. She didn't like the look in his eyes.

"Roselynne." He caught her hand. "I was so worried. This hasty marriage...I realize you were desperate—forgive me for not seeing it sooner—but if only you'd been patient—"

She snatched her hand away. "It wasn't hasty at all," she declared. "It was love at first sight, a thing difficult to understand for those who haven't experienced it, but so it goes." She spread her hands as if helpless in the throes of a great passion. Let him think on that.

"Love," he repeated, his mouth moving like that of a fish out of water. She'd never realized how stupid Charles looked when he pursed his lips in distaste.

"Yes." She smiled dreamily while resuming her seat behind the tea service. She prepared a cup for Charles just as he liked it. "Love. 'Tis a wondrous thing, is it not? So tender, yet fierce." She drew her brows together in a ferocious manner, then smiled again. "Here's your tea." She replenished her cup.

Charles looked as if he wanted to shake her. The door opened once more and the underbutler announced, "Mr. Myers, m'lady."

George came in, bringing the freshness of the spring day with him. "Hello. I didn't know you had a guest."

"Hello, George. This is Mr. Osgood, secretary to Wainsco. The duke is championing me at the Radziwill ball tonight." She picked up the invitations. "Why, there's one for you."

George flung himself onto the small sofa where Charles sat, crowding the other man into the corner. "Don't be so surprised. I know how to make a leg and act the gentleman. It ain't so hard to ape your betters, is it?" He nudged Charles with an elbow and gave him an elaborate wink.

Charles was clearly affronted. He stood and straightened his tails, then stated huffily, "I must go." He marched out with nary a fare-thee-well to either of them.

George and Roselynne stifled their laughter until he was out the front door and striding angrily down the street. When Connie and Mr. Moreley returned from a walk shortly thereafter, the pair finally quietened.

"Oh, Father, sit here," Roselynne cried, jumping up and guiding him to a chair. She fixed a cup of cream-flavored coffee for him. "We are so terrible to laugh at poor Charles, but I never realized he was so pompous."

"An ass, that's what he is," George said equably.

"I once had thought to marry him," she said.

George looked amazed. "Damned lucky Beau came along," he commented, picking up a cup and indicating the coffee urn.

"Yes," she agreed. "Yes, I am." She thought of the evening and frowned. "Am I to dine with Beau before the ball?"

"No. He's busy—"

"Doing what?" she interjected. She thought of Bowes bringing him some woman to enjoy for the night and was furious.

"The lawyer brought him some letters and stuff that belonged to the old earl. Beau's going through them to see if he can figure out the connection with the long-lost cousin who's suddenly showed up on the eve of his demise. He said he has nothing better to do while we are partying."

Roselynne felt ridiculous for her momentary temper. Not that she was jealous, not at all; but they had taken vows, and she expected Beau to live up to them. *Fool.* He was going to hang in less than a week. This was no time for silly emotions. She must help him. She'd charm the prince or die trying.

When George bid her farewell after assuring her he'd dance with her that night so she wouldn't be a wallflower, she turned to her father. "How did you bear it, Father?" she asked. "I cannot stand the thought of his death even though there is no love between us. How much worse it must be to lose your heart's delight."

She took his limp hand and held it to her cheek.

"I remember the love you and Mother shared. Will I ever know a great passion like that? Will I? Oh, Father, I wish you would speak to me. I need your advice. I'm all mixed up inside and don't know how I feel. These matters of life and death, they intensify the emotions and put them in such turmoil. What shall I do about my husband? I feel I am a cheat. He has kept his part of our bargain and I have not."

She glanced about the lovely room, with its heavy satin draperies and silk undercurtains, the rose brocade sofa and chairs, the tables of fine woods and craftsmanship, the tasteful paintings.

"I have gained all and given nothing." She sighed shakily. "You taught me to always keep my word. I will. I promise."

Clayburgh laid his notes aside. "Her name was Alice. She was the daughter of an illegitimate son acknowledged by the old earl's grandfather. Spinner married her seven years ago, some said to better himself. There's no doubt he gained a fair fortune from her. She died in childbirth two years after the marriage. He has no claim to the title or estate, nor any favors due from the king."

Beau flicked an old parchment back and forth against his fingers while he considered. "It's probably coincidence that he returned at this time."

"Well, not exactly." Clayburgh's thin lips curved into his crafty lawyer's smile. "He was running aristocrats through the blockade in France and I understand things got a little hot for him. The good citizens who stormed the Bastille decided to behead him instead."

Beau laughed. "The rascal obviously belongs in the family. It appears we all get into trouble wherever we go."

Clayburgh agreed. "By the by, your wife is going to a ball tonight. Wainsco and your man of affairs will be there to watch over her, as will I."

Beau pictured Roselynne in a low-cut ballgown and groaned aloud. "Every man jack will be dangling after the soon-to-be widow," he complained. "I would give my eyeteeth to go."

"Hmm, could that be arranged?" Clayburgh thought about it. "Nay. Even our greedy Mr. Bowes would hesitate to let you out for an evening of fun and frolic. He would hang in your place if you failed to return."

"I think he doesn't trust me overly much, especially since I've refused several *favors* from him lately."

"He wants to gain your coins and can't understand why you don't accept the doxies he brings to you?"

"Damn, you are astute," Beau said in admiration.

The barrister smiled modestly. "With a wife like Roselynne, what man would take the leavings of the street?" He rose. "But that is a thing beyond Mr. Bowes's sensibilities."

Beau settled in his chair after the attorney left. He thought of George and Clayburgh and the duke fawning over Roselynne, of men holding her while they danced, their eyes free to roam her delicate curves, to speculate on what lay underneath. Speculate? Hell, the way women wore their clothes nowadays, little was left to the imagination. Her breasts— sweet and luscious treats—would be on display for all men to admire—all but her rightful husband.

By damn, it was too much.

He was forced to molder away in this rotten cell, unable to take that which was his in the sight of man and God. She belonged to him, and the next time she came to this cell, he would see that she learned just what that meant.

He laughed without humor. Nay. He could not frighten her. She had to come of her own accord.

One thought comforted him. She'd seemed to like his caresses the previous night, and once or twice he thought she'd looked at him with admiration.

Bah, the man who could read a woman's mind had never been born. He was a fool, hoping for something that didn't exist.

He picked up the brandy flask, stared at it a long minute, then set it down. Nothing would drown the fire in his loins, nor the jealousy that plagued him like a sore tooth. Rising, he bowed and then held out his hands. Uncaring that he was an idiot, he danced around the room, pretending to hold his bride in his arms.

Roselynne smiled at George, who was acting the gallant by waving the tiny lace confection that passed as a fan before her face. She had danced every set since arriving at the ball. The duke had done his job well. Everyone knew her story and thought it terribly romantic.

Matrons and debutantes had all gathered in the retiring room to hear how she'd met the Earl of Rockdale and wed him. She'd described him in the most handsome of terms, telling of his blue eyes and dark beard and charming accent. She'd even told the story to the crown prince, embellishing it with as much drama as she could.

If worse came to worst, she mused, she could go on the boards and make a living as an accomplished actress.

"An enchanting story, m'dear," the prince had said, patting her cheek. "I understand your plight, indeed I do, for I, too, am of the romantic persuasion. P'rhaps all will work out."

"Oh, do you think so?" she'd asked, giving him a wide-eyed look of innocence. She had a thought. She would ask the prince to intercede with the king. Misgivings rose in her mind. The prince, though only twenty-eight, showed signs of dissipation already, and everyone knew he'd repudiated and deserted Mrs. Fitzherbert, his great love, four years ago, so Roselynne hadn't much faith in his romantic notions. "If only the king could be convinced to stay the execution . . ."

She delicately touched her eyes with the lace edge of her sleeve, then smiled bravely at the well-fed royal heir.

"Dare say the prime minister could look into the matter, eh, Fox?" he inquired of his companion.

"If you so ordered, sire," the man replied.

"Well, we'll see," the prince declared, as if the matter was settled. Then he'd toddled off, some said to his mistress's house for the night, some said to a rendezvous with Mrs. Fitzherbert.

Later, riding home in the carriage with George and Clayburgh, she told the lawyer, "I'll not count on the prince. He didn't seem overmuch interested in my story."

"Don't be discouraged. You made a fine impression on the *ton* tonight, including the royal. I heard him commend you for your courage to Radziwill when he left. Didn't he say something about speaking to the prime minister? A good word never hurt anyone's cause, even if it should come to nothing else. Society's opinion does make a difference."

She couldn't see that it would help Beau at all. There had to be something else she could do. There is, her conscience nagged. Accept him as husband and bear his child.

Tomorrow was Wednesday. Only five days ere he hanged. She must act. And she must tell him of tonight's events.

"You what?" Beau glared at his wife.

Roselynne replaced the cup on the saucer. He was clearly furious with her, and she couldn't figure out why. She had roused herself before noon in order to convey to him last night's events. He wasn't in the least grateful.

"The prince said he would speak on your behalf."

"Damnation!" He took a turn around the room.

"You are not pleased," she concluded, disliking the quaver in her voice. She didn't want him to think she was intimidated by his fury.

He spun around. "Damned right I'm not. That was not your purpose in going to the ball. You were to establish yourself, not bargain like a street vendor for my release."

She leaped to her feet. "That was not the way of it at all. Wainsco spread the story of our circumstances, as *you* seemed to want. I merely supported the tale." Not being a tattle, she didn't mention that Clayburgh had encouraged her in her plan.

"And added your own twist by speaking with the royal dunce. Don't you know that he and the king are at outs with each other?" He clapped a hand to his forehead. "Every orphan on the street knows that." He glared at her again.

She was quite tired of his hard glances. Lifting her skirts, she headed for the door. "I will leave you to your megrim," she announced. "I had thought to cheer you with the possibility of a stay of execution, but I see 'twas wrong to think so."

He ran a hand through his hair, and she remembered doing the same. Apparently he had sampled her charms and found them wanting. A distinct hurt settled behind her breastbone. He'd cast her aside, ignored her all of yesterday and hadn't a kind word for her work on his behalf. So much for this notion of marriage.

"Where are you going?" he roared when she lifted a hand to the portal to summon the guard.

"Home. To the town house," she added nervously when he advanced upon her.

"Nay. You came to share lunch, and we've not eaten."

"I am not hungry, my lord."

"I am," he said.

He stopped beside her and surveyed her figure, outlined in the tight jacket and soft skirts of her outfit. He gazed deeply into her eyes, confusing her with his sudden change. She realized the heat of anger had been replaced by the heat of desire and was properly outraged.

When he lifted a hand to her, she drew back. He paused, then proceeded to stroke her cheek. "I missed your company last night."

She pressed her lips together and fought an urge to lean into his gentle strokings.

"I've wounded you," he said. "I didn't mean to. I know you acted on my behalf and I'm grateful. Will you accept my thanks?"

She nodded stiffly.

"And stay for luncheon?"

She hesitated, then nodded again.

"Good." He looped an arm around her shoulders and escorted her to the table. There, he laid out the meal with his own hands and with much revelry, teased her into eating a hearty meal of beef tongue pie.

"I am not a babe," she protested when he fed her bites of apple and nut meats after the dinner.

He looked her over until her skin burned. "Nay, I know that."

A blush spread over her when he glanced at the bed in the corner and back to her. Was he thinking...oh, surely not. 'Twas full daylight.

He sighed. "Clayburgh is due within the hour."

"He brings news of William Spinner?"

Beau shook his head. "The man is nothing to us. Clayburgh brings my will. The papers are in order, and you are officially my heir."

"Oh."

"You appear sad. Most women would be overjoyed to come into so great a fortune," he reminded her.

"I am not most women," she said with some asperity.

"No, you aren't, and I, for one, am glad of it." He turned his chair sideways to the table. "Come sit on my knee and let me fondle you. My moments for such pleasures are growing short."

She came to him, unsure that she should let herself be mollified for his earlier loutishness, yet unable to resist the wild sweetness of his kisses. She was, she thought, a wanton.

His thighs were firm as rocks under her, but unlike rock, he was warm and much more comfortable to perch on. He put his arm around her waist and held her close.

"Give me your lips, Roselynne," he murmured. "You are by far sweeter than any dessert I've ever tasted."

She turned toward him and slipped her arms around his neck. Her fingers slid easily through his thick dark hair when she untied the leather strip that bound it neatly at his nape.

The bruise around his eye had faded until it was hardly noticeable, and most of his swellings had gone down. She stroked his beard, which was silky-textured. His nose had healed with only a slight crookedness. If life were different...

The minutes sped away. When they heard voices outside the door, he muttered an imprecation and reluctantly set her on her feet. "Someday we will have all the privacy we could desire," he promised, bringing his breathing under control. "Will you return tonight?"

"To dine?" she asked, frowning while she considered her schedule. "I have a tea this afternoon and a soiree at the

Beauchamps in the evening, with a late supper to follow at the—''

"I'll be busy, too."

"Busy?" Sparks ignited inside her. "Does the turnkey provide entertainment for you?"

He threw back his head and laughed. "Not what you imagine, my sweet wife. Would I take Bowes's offerings when I have your kisses to sustain me through the long afternoon and night?" He pressed a kiss upon her parted lips just as the door swung open and the lawyer entered. "Nay," he whispered, answering his question. "I'll send for you as soon as I'm done with legal wrangling and you have a moment free from your gaieties."

In the carriage, she leaned her head against the satin squabs and envisioned the warmth of her husband's regard. Her breath grew short as she relived his caresses.

She wished Beau could take her to a ball. With his height and those blue eyes surrounded by black lashes, he would be the most distinguished man there. The other women would look upon her with envy. She remembered her girlish daydream of being carried off by a handsome brigand. It was almost true. If she could free Beau, they could sail for America and live there amongst the savages. . . .

With a start, she realized people were shouting. The carriage, which had been moving at a snail's pace, had stopped. She peered out. A carter was trying to make his mule obey, but was making the animal buck in terror as he beat the poor beast.

"Jump," someone shouted. "The carriage . . . jump!"

A rumble like approaching thunder had her glancing up the side street. A dray, laden with roofing beams, hurtled toward the intersection. Straight toward the carriage!

"Jump, m'lady, jump," Sanders screamed, leaping from the back rail along with Jim. The driver jumped squarely onto the lead horse's rear and thence into the street and out of the way.

Roselynne stared at the wagon coming as certainly as death. People shouted and ran, tumbling over each other to get to safety. Horses and carts went in all directions. It was a mad scene.

"For God's sake, jump!"

Springing up, she cast herself out the side away from the wagon as hard as she could. Her ankle turned upon hitting the damp, dirty cobbles and she rolled, skirts flying, until she smacked into the red-and-white post of a barber. She lay there dazed, barely hearing the great crash of wood splintering into a thousand pieces as the carriage shattered under the impact, and the screams of the horses as they were pulled to their haunches before the traces also broke into pieces. A long time seemed to pass.

"Here, m'lady, are ye all right?"

She stared up at Jim and Sanders and the other two footmen. A crowd of staring bystanders pressed behind them, all looking at her. She felt incredibly foolish.

"Help me up," she requested.

They lifted her to her feet. Her legs were trembling so, she had to cling to the two men for support.

"The driver?"

"He's all right. You're bleeding from your temple. His lordship will be right angered," Sanders added.

She saw the driver checking the horses. They seemed able to stand. She touched her temple, where pain throbbed hotly. Her fingers came away bloody.

"Here's a handkerchief," someone offered.

She pressed it against the cut. "I want my husband," she said, then realized how ridiculous that was. "Take me home."

"Poor lady. Near to killed, she was," the apple vendor remarked to the greengrocer.

"Aye. I saw the whole thing. Terrible, terrible," the grocer affirmed. "Why wasn't that wagon chocked? The driver ought to be locked up for that bit o' carelessness."

A constable rushed up and demanded to know what had happened. It was another hour before Roselynne was able to climb into a hired coach and retreat to the town house. The barber had cleaned and bandaged her head during the delay.

At the house, Ansella helped her remove her filthy dress and bathe, then Roselynne went to bed and slept for the rest of the afternoon and evening, missing the planned entertainments. She dreamed of gentle hands holding her, and called out a name in her sleep. Waking in the night, she realized she was alone and wept for no reason.

Beau balled his fist and beat it upon the table, making the dishes jump. "She's not to go out on the streets for any reason. I want you to move to the house—propriety be damned—and guard her with your life. See that she obeys." A faint smile touched his mouth. "And watch yourself. She's stubborn and may try to talk you into her thinking."

"So you agree it wasn't an accident?" George asked.

"I'm not sure. I never thought she'd be in any danger in London, but we can't take any chances. Hire more guards for the trip to the country. I don't want her hurt or frightened. You're to stick by her like a burr."

"I'll not leave her for a minute," George promised.

Pain mixed with jealousy shot through Beau. It was his place to stay by his wife, to guard and protect her. He wanted to kick the stone walls of the prison until they fell. Useless. His life was useless. Aye, and so was his anger. He must think of Roselynne. Her safety was the only thing that mattered.

"You're a good friend," he said wearily, settling back at the table. "Hire a couple of runners to investigate the dray and its owner. Perhaps they can ferret out the truth of the matter."

"I will."

Beau stared out the window at the twilight. "She's not to come here again. Make her obey. Tell the servants these are my orders and their positions are forfeit if they do otherwise."

After George left, he sat in morbid contemplation. He'd most likely never see her again. All his dreams of sharing the wonders of the nuptial bed were for nought. He'd never know the fullness of pleasure with her, never assuage her fears and release the passion he knew she possessed.

She probably hated him now. Aye, she should. It was his fault her life was in danger. Well, soon he would be dead and out of her life. She would be a rich widow, able to choose her own husband from every available man in the realm.

There was a possibility that he would live. His eyes reflected the tortures of hell as he considered the future. If he survived, he could still arrange to give her her freedom. He could pretend to be dead, returning to Virginia without any in England being the wiser. But first, he had a mystery to solve and a wife to protect.

He gripped the table knife as if it were a sword. "Someone will pay for this," he vowed. "Someone will pay."

Chapter Nine

Roselynne paced her bedroom. No word came from her husband inviting her to his cell, nor was she allowed out, although visitors came frequently to the attractive town house. All of society had decided to attend the hanging with her. Upon learning that, at her husband's request, she wasn't going, they immediately decided to shun the event in support of the tragic couple.

Wainsco had told her the previous evening that the king had been petitioned to postpone Beau's hanging while more evidence was sought in the case; he'd refused. At least Prinny had kept his word, she'd remarked.

Saturday had dawned cold and gray, and she was restless. A light rain fell off and on during the day. Her spirits sank into gloom. She was to leave London the next morning.

And Beau would hang the next. 'Twas a cruel fate for so young and prime a man. To die without fully realizing life. To never know the joys of hearth and home.

No, no, it couldn't be! He mustn't die! Dear heavens, she couldn't allow that to happen. He was not guilty, and no amount of evidence would convince her otherwise. She clutched her hands together and tried to think what more she could do.

There was nothing. Sick despair poked her like a sharpened pike, and she paced the carpet, desperate for an answer.

There was one thing, her conscience nagged. They might never enjoy the delights of a home together, but he had mentioned a child. He was a braw man, as the Scots liked to say, and he wanted an heir of his own blood. She must do her duty as his wife.

She jerked the bellpull.

"Tell my husband I will dine with him tonight. He may expect dinner at seven," she ordered the footman when he appeared.

Then she ordered a bath brought to the bathing room and began preparations for the evening. Since he couldn't come to her, she would go to him. An hour later, she was in her robe and rubbing her hair dry with a heated towel.

Jim returned with Beau's command: she was not to go out for any reason, and anyone who allowed it would be whipped.

"But you will take me anyway," she countered.

He shuffled his feet as if standing on hot coals. "Nay, m'lady. I cannot. 'Twould mean my job at the very least."

"Very well. That's all." She dismissed him without a kind word to soothe the worry on his brow.

"M'lady," he said, pleading for understanding.

But she turned her back and would have nothing to do with so cowardly a person. Even though they knew she was heir and would be their employer come Monday, they wouldn't disobey the master. He commanded great loyalty, she grudgingly admitted.

Well, she had things to do. If her husband thought to command her from his prison cell, he had better think again.

"We'll see," she muttered, brushing her hair without a care of tangles and pulls on her scalp. "Ansella," she called to the girl who was in the pressing room, ironing the gown she'd planned on wearing. A change of plans was in order.

"Yes, mum?" The maid rushed into the dressing room, pressing cloth still in hand.

"I've changed my mind about the dress. I would like yours instead."

"Mum?" Ansella questioned, her eyes going huge.

Roselynne laughed. "I've not gone daft. My husband thinks to confine me in this house to protect me from some imaginary assailant. I have a desire to visit him. It is of the utmost importance. Will you help me?"

Ansella chewed her fingernail while she considered the consequences, then, much overcome by romantic fantasy—she obviously thought the earl and his countess were as wondrous as the hero and heroine of any story she'd ever heard—she broke into smiles. "Oh, aye, mum. But there be a new dress just made for the parlor maid, never worn. It should fit you perfectly, for you're both slender as the swans of Hyde Park."

Roselynne smiled in relief. "And a dark cloak?"

Ansella was caught up in the drama. "Aye. Cook's be just the thing, a good stout wool, it is."

"Wonderful. But how will I get out of the house and to the prison? 'Tis far to walk."

Ansella waved a hand. "I was going to my sister's for an hour before dinner. You can come with me till we're out o' sight of the house. Can you afford a chair?"

"Yes. An excellent plan. I'll tell the housekeeper to add a coin to your pay packet."

"I thank you, mum. That would be nice, to be sure. Wait here." Giggling, she ran off to get the new dress from the pressing room and in a moment returned with it and the cloak "borrowed" from cook. Later, when Ansella finished her chores and was dismissed by the housekeeper, Roselynne was ready.

She went down the backstairs after Ansella signaled it was clear. Together they went out into the rain, hoods drawn over their hair and heads downcast in the drizzle. Roselynne carried a small valise.

"There's usually a chair to be hired near here," Ansella remarked, skipping along with childish glee.

"Good." Roselynne was feeling a bit shaky now that she was embarked on her adventure. Little shivers kept running along her back, but she was far from cold. She saw a hackney and waved it over, pleased at finding the faster vehicle. The coachman didn't descend, but waited impatiently for her to get inside.

"Luck be with you," Ansella called, waving up at her.

"Tell Jim to bring large portions for the earl tonight, for he will have a guest."

"Aye, I'll not be forgetting."

The chimes were ringing vespers when the carriage stopped on the wet cobbles of Newgate. She looked at the cold stone building. In the tower, she could see the outline of a long figure at the highest window and remembered that first day when she'd looked there and recoiled in fear.

All the meetings with Beau rushed before her eyes.

He had proven himself a good man, and she would carry into the world his child, God willing.

She paid the hack and hurried to the little back door she'd seen the crone use. She beat upon the portal. It was opened by the turnkey. She swallowed against the raw emotion crowding her throat.

"Good evening, Mr. Bowes," she said, displaying a flash of gold in her hand. "I've come to visit my husband."

"Aye, the man is lonesome, and has the temper of a mangy bear. You'll cheer him up a mite. Come along then." He held out his hand, and she placed the coin on his broad palm. He led the way up the back steps.

The room that she and her father had shared was dark.

"It's empty. Have you a hankering to see it again?" Bowes asked, chortling when she paused.

She hurried on. "No, thank you, Mr. Bowes. 'Tis a place I've no yearning for, I assure you."

As they neared the turret, she grew more apprehensive. Beau would probably give her a lecture for venturing out.

Bowes unlocked the door. "You have a visitor, guvner, one more to your liking mayhap than any I've brought you."

Roselynne gave the man a sharp glance. He'd better not be tempting her husband with wretches from the streets or she'd have a thing or two to say to him.

Not that Beau would accept anyone but her, she thought smugly, recalling his word on this subject. She stepped past Bowes into the neat chamber. Beau stood at the open window, unmindful of the mist that drifted through the bars.

"I don't want any of your doxies tonight," he snarled.

Had he taken them on another night? she wondered, her blood heating at the thought. She tossed back the hood.

"But a wife, sir?" she inquired sweetly. "Would you accept a wife?"

Her surprise was complete. He was dumbfounded. However, he recovered before Bowes had hardly gotten the key turned in the lock and lumbered back into the bowels of the prison. —

"What the hell are you doing here?" he demanded.

"I've come to visit—"

"Bowes! Bowes, dammit, come back here," he yelled, then strode over and pounded on the door. "Bowes! Come get her out of here!" He rounded on her. "How did you get here? I'll have Jim's ears for this bit of mischief."

"He doesn't know." She set the valise aside and hung the damp cloak on a peg. "I had to sneak out, since I've been held prisoner for three days." She tossed him an accusing glare and settled in a chair by the table. Remembering her purpose, she smiled . . . seductively, she hoped. "I wanted to see you."

"You've seen me. Now you can just get out of that chair and head back to the house."

"How?"

"How did you get here?"

"In a hackney."

She'd never heard anyone actually gnash his teeth. He stalked over and hit both fists on the table, causing a loud clatter. She flinched, but he took no notice.

"Have you no sense? Don't you realize there's a killer on the loose and you may be his next victim?" He paced the length of the floor and back. "Damn my soul for getting you into this coil. What the hell was I thinking at the time?"

Speaking calmly, she pointed out, "You freed me from a worse fate, if you will recall, and my father, too. I think you and George overreact. 'Twas an accident, nothing more."

Beau calmed marginally, but he was still far from predictable. She waited for further argument.

"Mayhap," he replied, slowing his pace about the room. He paused, then remembered his manners. "Would you like a glass of wine? Or I can prepare tea if you prefer."

"Tea would be lovely. I've always thought a hot drink went well on cold days. It's an uncommonly cool spring, is it not?"

"I don't know." He brushed aside her polite conversation and set about preparing tea on a tiny brazier. When it was ready, he realized he had no cream. "There's sugar," he said. "That's all I have."

"That will be fine," she said graciously. "Won't you be seated and join me? Beau," she added softly.

He cast her a glance, his eyes narrowing as if he wondered what she was planning. In truth, she didn't know how to go about seducing a man. She had only his example to follow, but it seemed inappropriate to hold him on her lap and fondle him. She stifled a nervous giggle at the image.

"Pray tell what you find so amusing. I could use a laugh," he growled at her. He flung his long, hard body into the chair and stirred sugar into the tea, tasted, then grimaced. "Tea is for old ladies," he muttered.

"It is a cure for many maladies." She tried to speak in soothing tones, to change his mood to one more amenable.

He laughed, a harsh sound of no merriment. "Not for a stretched neck." He took a large swallow and stared at her. "You look nice."

Her hand jerked, sloshing tea as she set the cup on its saucer. "Thank you. You seem in fine shape for one confined so long."

Slowly she let her gaze play over him. He wore top boots and buff breeches with a gathered shirt, and a leather jerkin to ward off the rainy chill.

He opened his mouth, but didn't speak. Instead he drew a deep breath and let it out. She watched in fascination as his chest lifted, then settled. Aye, he was in fine shape.

A gold seal dangled from his pocket, indicating he carried a watch. Her gaze flicked to the clock on the nearby table. She watched as it ticked off another minute of his life. Soon there would be none....

Tears filmed her eyes. She wished the supper would arrive so she could execute the rest of her plan. Glancing at the bed, she wished she was brave enough to start the events of the evening.

"It has been a busy three days...Beau. We have become the cause célèbre of the season, and I have met many lords and ladies, all of whom mourn our destiny. They think it terribly romantic, the way we met and wed—"

"They're all fools," he said.

"Yes, but well-meaning, I think."

He grunted, which she took to be assent. He stared stubbornly out the window, refusing to glance her way even once. The blue gown wasn't as low as her own, but it was in vogue

enough for the tops of her breasts to show. Her spirits drooped
again. He wasn't interested.

The hour passed and then another. A knock on the door
heralded supper. Jim gave her an aggrieved look when he entered bearing a large tray. Sanders glanced quickly at her and
his lord, then kept his gaze on the task of setting out braised
lamb and minted jelly, new potatoes with parsley and several
other dishes, enough to feed six or eight good-sized men.

"Shall I serve, m'lor'?" Jim asked, growing more nervous
with the lengthening silence.

Roselynne began to feel uneasy at the unnatural quiet. For
all the attention Beau paid to them, they could have been on
the moon. He had returned to his perch at the window.

Finally he glanced at the three of them, clustered at the table. She saw him observe the food and the two china settings.
He frowned, causing the two footmen to stir nervously. She
lifted her chin just as her husband spoke to the men.

"You may go. And take your mistress with you."

"No."

He pierced her with his intent gaze. "Yes."

"No."

Jim shuffled from one foot to the other. Sanders coughed.

Beau stood. "You're to leave," he said to Roselynne, his
tone hostile.

"Nay. I am spending the night. I have brought my toiletries
and . . . things," she ended lamely.

He flicked a glance at the valise, then another at her. She
gazed at him as steadily as she could. Had she been standing,
she was sure her knees would have sounded a drumroll.

"Wait outside," Beau ordered the footmen.

They left in haste, and he crossed the room to stand over her.
"You . . . will . . . obey," he ground out, one word at a time.

"Not in this." She gave him a sweet smile. "I am here. What
harm can befall me now? Perhaps someone is watching the
prison and, if I leave, will seek to hurt me." She speared a chop
and placed it on her plate. "This lamb looks delicious. Will
you not join me, Beau?"

Each time she said his name, she made it a croon, Beau
thought. His blood was running high, and if he didn't get her

out of the room, no telling what would happen. Ha! He knew exactly what would happen.

"Madam, if you do not leave, you will be ravished on the spot," he said, giving her fair warning. Let the stupid little minx know exactly what she was bringing on her own head.

A flush spread upward from the modest neckline of the gown and nestled in her cheeks. "I am depending upon it."

He opened his mouth, snapped it closed. "Then yes, I will join you." He went to the window first and waved the footmen home. The carriage left posthaste. "Your ride is gone."

"Some jelly?" she asked.

Her hands were steady when she handed the crystal pot to him, but his were not. A fine tremor had invaded his entire body, and he felt ready to explode with hopes and needs too long suppressed. If she had but an inkling of how he felt, she'd flee like a fox running from the ravenous pack.

"There'll be no going back this night," he said quietly, "no matter who comes to the door, no matter what their purpose. Tonight you will be mine, or I'll die trying to make it so."

"I understand."

"Do you? I wonder."

He carelessly put food on his plate, but ate little of it and tasted less. The room was cold, but he was burning with the fever of desire. She didn't realize how near the edge he was.

He must be gentle, he reminded his raging libido.

Desperation urged him to throw her upon the bed, toss her skirts up and have done with the rearing pain between his legs. That would be the easiest thing to do.

Roselynne ate the perfectly cooked meal without tasting a bite. Every time she looked up, she saw Beau and his intense regard—his gaze never left her for a second—and beyond him, the large bedstead with the fur throw neatly folded across the end.

She recognized the comforter. 'Twas the one he'd lent her. Tonight they'd sleep under it together, but before they slept, he would make her his wife. She knew part of the ritual, but not the whole of it. There'd be kissing and touching...intimate touching.

"Did I ever thank you for the use of the comforter?" she asked, needing a diversion from her turbulent thoughts.

"Aye."

His eyes feasted upon her like a jackal upon downed prey. She felt powerless. She looked anywhere but at him and the rapacious hunger of his gaze. "You devour me on the spot," she protested in a choked murmur when she could bear his scrutiny no more.

"I want you enough to do so," he admitted. "But I will try to be gentle. You mustn't always tax me unfairly, though."

Her head jerked up. "Unfairly? Me, my lord?"

"Yes, madam, you. You're beautiful, as you must know."

"How would I know?" she demanded, piqued at his accusing tone and intrigued that he found her, well, probably not beautiful, but at least presentable.

"There aren't any looking glasses at the house? I must remedy that before I depart this good earth." He poured more wine into their glasses and studied her in a brooding manner. "Clayburgh has told me how you have charmed all of London with your looks and smiles and wit."

"Londoners are easily diverted," she said, both disappointed and relieved at the turn of subject.

"You are charming, Roselynne," he said, his voice dropping very low and very deep. "Charming and lovely and all the things a lady is supposed to be. You're also a very desirable woman, leading a man's thoughts to conjugal bliss."

She dropped her fork, unable to pretend to eat.

"Are you finished?" he asked.

She nodded.

He put his utensils down. "Come to me."

It was an invitation, a command, a plea, and she couldn't ignore it. With trembling legs, she stood, but instead of moving to his arms, she picked up the valise. "I...I would change first and freshen up."

He looked her over from head to toe and back. "Don't take too long. I find I'm not the patient man I once thought I was."

"I have known it for days," she returned, barely managing a saucy smile before fleeing behind the screen.

"I'll build a fire," he called to her.

She heard him at the hearth and peered over the screen at him. He was kneeling, his haunches outlined by the tight fit of his breeches. Aye, an uncommonly fine specimen, she noted with pride and building excitement. And his speech was educated, as fine as any Englishman's.

She closed her eyes. Tonight she would pretend he was her highwayman, come to claim her and take her away to some enchanted land. If only they'd had time to fall in love....

Quickly, before her small store of courage evaporated, she changed into a gossamer-fine gown of softest pink, chosen because he seemed to like that color on her. With satin slippers on her feet for warmth and a silk negligee for a degree of modesty—not too much, for she meant to entice—she walked to the hearth and stopped beside him, determined to take the final step into womanhood.

She held her breath when he turned his head and followed the line of her slipper, then of her leg, visible beneath the sheer materials, on up to the crisscross of ribbons over and under her breasts and finally to her eyes. He rose, brushed his hands on his breeches and reached for her. "You're too far away," he said huskily.

She stepped forward until her breasts mounded against his chest. He could surely hear her heart pounding. "Is this close enough, my lord husband?"

"Almost, wife, almost."

He bent and lifted her into his arms. Her slippers went flying. And so did she. Without letting go of her, Beau flung them both on the bed, landing so that he was on the bottom and she squarely on top of him.

"Oomph!" she gasped.

"Did I hurt you?"

"No," she murmured, aware of his body beneath hers, hard and solid but warm, so warm. His manly shaft pulsed against her abdomen and her thoughts shattered. She gulped back fears and tried for a light tone. "But you should give warning when you plan a flying leap. It's disconcerting...." She lost her train of thought when he tightened his arms around her.

He smiled and his gaze became lambent, almost sleepy. She was mesmerized by his eyes, blue like water but hot like fire. He would consume her in the heat of his desire.

Turning so that they lay side by side, he leaned over her. "I gave you all the warning you're going to get concerning this night," he said just as his lips covered hers.

She steeled herself, expecting fierceness. She received only the gentlest of touches.

He stroked a long path from her neck to her thighs. His fingers had ever so fine a tremor, and an answering tension leapt through her nerves.

"Very pretty," he said, fingering the silk. He pulled the ribbon between her breasts, and the bow slipped undone. Then he did the same with the one at her waist. The negligee fell apart.

Her body was barely concealed by the sheer silk of the gown, but skillful use of embroidered flowers and vines hid and enticed at the same time.

His manhood surged against her thigh as he gazed at her with lusty intent. With one finger, he nudged the gown downward between her breasts and pressed a kiss in the shallow valley, causing her breath to catch.

"Now, how do we get you out of this confection?" he mused, a smile playing at the corners of his mouth.

Easing away from her, he unbuttoned the tiny pearls at her wrists and, with a caress, pushed the negligee off her shoulders. Lifting her as if she were a doll, he removed the wrap. He started on her gown.

Her hands stayed him. He looked at her, his gaze so fiery, heat raced over her skin and her breathing was labored.

"You're right," he said as if she had spoken. "It's unfair that you should be the only one undressed. Why don't you help me?"

He guided her hands to his vest. She pushed the soft leather jerkin off his shoulders at his urging.

"The shirt," he encouraged, seemingly in no hurry.

She lifted her hands to his shirt and pulled the cord at his neck. The bow released and the material parted. She unfastened the bone buttons at his wrists, then paused. He pulled the shirt from his breeches and raised both arms.

Biting her lip in concentration, she pulled the shirt over his head. Gathering both jerkin and shirt, she tossed them onto the nearest chair. His chest lay bare to her gaze.

"You may explore," he offered with a lazy smile. "Wait." he tugged his top boots off and dropped them, along with his hose, to the floor, then lay back on the fur throw. "Be my guest," he murmured with a wicked gleam in his eyes, as playful as a boy.

Her eyes informed her this was no boy, however, but rather a man full-grown that she dealt with. He took her hand and placed it upon his chest.

She glided along his rib cage with her fingers, paused and followed the line of a rib. She traced the crescent scar under his breast. The tactile caress of wiry hairs tickled her palm as she drifted upward to touch his nipples. To her astonishment, they formed into tiny balls, contracting the way hers did in the cold, or when he touched her there.

He chuckled and reaching out, brushed her hardened nipple through the satin rose that partially hid it from view. "Aye, we react the same, love."

A flush scorched her cheeks, and she wondered if she should be doing this. She drew back, uncertain.

"It's all right," he said, obviously recognizing her shyness. It annoyed her that he should be so knowledgeable while she was so ignorant of this act between husband and wife.

"You've not been married, have you?" she asked.

He pulled his gaze from the view down the front of her gown. A flicker of emotion passed through his eyes. "No."

"You seem to know a lot about—" She stopped, realizing she'd given away the path of her thoughts.

He touched her under the chin. "I haven't a wife and ten mewling children crying for their papa back in Virginia. You are the only female with whom I've taken vows. Ever."

"Yes, but . . . You are experienced."

He smiled. "Not so very much, but neither am I a boy fresh from the nursery." His eyes sparkled with sudden humor. "Enough of this, or you'll be accusing me of infidelities before I even knew you."

She glanced at him, surprised. His admission of limited experience pleased her, but she was in no mood for teasing.

He chucked her under the chin, then laughed at her indignant frown. "I know the way the female mind works. I was raised with sisters, and they gave their suitor the door if he so much as looked at another female while they were present." His tone softened, and so did his gaze, even as it grew more heated. "I see no one but my very pretty wife, and have not for days."

With that, he pulled her down to him and claimed her mouth in a kiss that sent thoughts of others out of her mind. He rubbed her back, swooping down over her buttocks to caress and knead the flesh into melting clay.

Slowly the world changed and she was lying on the bottom while he bent over her, his mouth ever busy upon hers.

He teased her lips apart with his tongue, then leisurely sought the interior of her mouth, encouraging her to stroke and play as he did.

"Touch me," he whispered, his lips still on hers.

She followed his lead as best she could, touching him the way he touched her, wanting suddenly to please him.

When he began a slow, plunging motion into her mouth with his tongue, she responded with an internal contraction that had her clinging to him. He rubbed against her, and she was once again aware of the hard strength of his body.

Tension built within her, beating against the wall of reserve that had curbed her impulsive nature for a lifetime. She heard her own breath, panting with the effort of control, yet there was something in her that rebelled against her efforts.

She longed to break free and soar. Blood rushed through her, hot and restless, seeking tranquility and finding only wild urgings that confused and agitated.

Beau pressed her against the mattress and leaned further over her, his leg crossing hers, holding her captive. She twisted under him, excited and uneasy.

"It's all right," he soothed, his voice deep and husky.

Even the sound of it caused a frisson to hurl along her scalp. His hands ran along her sides, gentling her as he would a nervous filly. She tried to summon courage, but her emotions were far too turbulent to heed the command. They obeyed only him . . . and the frightening passions he induced.

He continued kissing and stroking her for a long time. Her nerves began to quieten. She sensed his warmth along her side and over her thighs where his leg rested. She was lulled by the ceaseless stroking of his hands, the small movements of his body against hers.

"Better?" he asked.

She nodded and smiled at him. This wasn't so bad, after all. In fact, she quite liked the kissing and touching. Now that he wasn't so demanding, she found it pleasant.

"Let's take this off, shall we?"

He eased the flimsy night rail up. She lifted her hips without a word, then let him flip it over her head and onto the floor. Turning from her, he did the same with his breeches.

She waited, breathless, realizing that at last she would know the full measure of wifehood.

Then she experienced the searing presence of bare flesh on bare flesh, and for a moment, felt panicked by this intimacy.

"Easy, love," he whispered, kissing and nibbling along her cheek and ear. "It's not so scary. 'Tis a natural thing for a man to love his wife in this manner. Has no one told you?"

"Not the particulars," she admitted, her voice so strained she hardly recognized it for her own.

"Will you let me show you?"

She hesitated, then nodded. That was what she had come for.

"I'll touch you," he said. "Like this."

His hand slipped along her bare side, onto her hip, then across and between them. She gasped and squeezed her legs tightly together as eerie feelings skittered away deep inside her.

"And kiss you."

He settled his mouth on hers again and began the insistent stroking that fueled both fear and a great churning in her.

"Please," she said, turning her head, "do what you must and . . . and get it over." She would explode if he didn't stop soon.

"I won't be rushed. 'Tis a pleasure we'll not soon enjoy again, and I'll not miss a morsel of your sweetness."

So saying, he kissed along her neck and downward until he reached her breasts. He took one into his mouth and rolled his tongue around it, again and again. Soon she was filled with the urge to squirm and twist beneath him. She was frantic with a need that made her feel almost violent.

With his knee, he nudged her legs apart. She realized she'd relaxed her vigilance there while he suckled her breasts. His hand took immediate advantage and slipped between her legs.

Then he was touching her in a most intimate fashion.

She must have gasped, for he lifted his head and gazed into her eyes. "It's the way between a man and a woman and will give you great pleasure, if you will but take it."

She wasn't sure what she felt was mere pleasure. It was too strong, too gripping. It took her right out of herself, making her pant and gasp and move without her volition.

Suddenly he was no longer beside her. He had, instead, insinuated his thighs between hers and was nestled securely over her. She stared up at him, sure the moment had come. She glanced down between them. No, it wasn't possible. There was no space within her for that.

"I'll make it as easy for you as I can," he promised, seeing the direction of her gaze. He thrust against her gently. "He's a friendly fellow and means you no harm. Indeed, he would pleasure you no end should you permit it."

She didn't see how, but she remembered the giggles of the village brides and their intimations of enjoyment. Before her courage faltered, she nodded.

Beau studied his lady wife, sensing her fears but unable to soothe them. Perhaps it would be best to finish it now—he was near to exploding!—and let her see that it wasn't so terrible, as she probably imagined. She was excited, her body moist and hot, and she unconsciously thrust against him when he stroked her. But she was gentle-born and fought her natural feelings.

If only he had time to woo her properly, then she would come to him with all the fullness of her passionate nature freed. His blood soared at the blissful thought.

"Close your eyes," he said.

Her lashes flew open, then snapped closed.

A sudden overwhelming tenderness made him pause. Could he be gentle with her? He couldn't be otherwise. She trusted him, whether she realized it or not.

Moving his hand between them, he guided himself into position in the narrow channel and began to thrust very gently, pushing deeper with each stroke, pausing and letting her grow accustomed to him between the movements.

Her lips trembled open as her breathing quickened. Her face was still flushed. At least she hadn't gone pale with fright when he'd entered her.

He closed his eyes as sensation overpowered his mind. She was ready, did she but know it. Sweet heaven, how could anything feel so good! He held back as his body demanded prompt and immediate release. He must go slowly, slowly.

The entire tip was sheathed now. He pressed for more, easing past the barrier of her broken maidenhead, seeing the evidence of his penetration and again experiencing the soul-deep tenderness toward her.

Within another minute, he'd reached the far shore and was completely ensconced within her. "'Tis done," he whispered hoarsely, fighting for control.

Roselynne opened her eyes. Beau's face loomed over her, dim now in the flickering light of the fire, the candles having burned out long ago. Moisture covered his brow. His arms trembled at each side of her as if he was under great stress.

"Was it so terrible?" he asked.

She sensed his regret at having hurt her. Surprisingly, it hadn't been at all what she'd anticipated. She'd expected a blow, like that of a blunt sword, but instead there'd been a sting and a slight burning at first. That had been replaced by the feeling of being gently opened and then filled.

The way he filled her now.

"No. You were wonderfully kind."

He smiled at her words. "Kindness is far from my heart at this moment, love. I'm apt to ravish you at any second."

"I thought that was what you had just done," she said in surprise, worry darting into her eyes. It boggled her mind that she could accommodate his manly proportions wholly within her body.

He chuckled, albeit with a strained grimace. "It's not over yet, far from it."

"Oh."

"Give me your lips," he ordered. "And put some feeling into it this time around.'

"Oh," she repeated, indignant.

He kissed her as before, with many hot turnings and twists of his mouth upon hers until she was consumed in his heat. Wildness swelled in her when he began to thrust within her again.

She was once again attacked by the need for more from him. If only she knew what she longed for. It was maddening. She found herself pushing upward, responding to his ardent kisses with demands of her own.

He stroked her breasts, her sides and waist. She explored his back, the hard muscles of his hips and buttocks. The yearning grew and enveloped her.

"Beau," she cried, a plea for help or something—she didn't know for what, and she didn't care.

Again he slipped his hand between them. She bucked beneath him when he touched some secret spot that set off bonfires inside her. Twisting, grasping, she held on to his shoulders, wild for his kiss, his touch.

"Hurry," she panted, mindless of what she was saying.

"Love, I'm going to explode soon. Relax and let it go," he urged, moving faster in her. "Let it happen, love."

"I . . . I can't. Oh, help me." She was frantic with need, but there seemed to be a wall inside her and she couldn't hurdle over it. Again and again she came to a point . . . and stopped. She thrust wildly at him, needing him desperately.

"Sweet heaven," he gasped. "Roselynne, be still. I won't be able to . . ."

Then he moved with quick, frantic thrusts of his own, his body surging into hers like a storm tide. At last he stilled. Inside, she felt a pulsing and instinctively knew he had reached the goal she'd sought and couldn't find.

She let her arms fall to the sheets while he lay heavily upon her, his heart pounding against her chest. When he raised his head, he looked at her solemnly.

"Thank you," he said.

She didn't know what to say. He spoke as if she'd given him a gift beyond price. The fire within had subsided, and there was left only a faint sense of dissatisfaction. A quiet pride stole into her. She'd given him pleasure. She knew it. And she'd kept her part of their bargain.

"Did you get me with child?" she asked anxiously.

Beau would have laughed, but she was so serious. A flicker of emotion shuddered through him, and he had the sudden wish that she felt some tendresse toward him.

Why should she care for him? he thought. He had oft treated her with impatience and a show of temper. But there was kindness in her and goodness gleamed from her eyes. At times she'd seemed to like and admire him. He must content himself with that. It was all he had time for.

He moved to her side and clasped her to him. "Only God knows the answer to that. And only time will tell."

Roselynne was sorry she'd raised the question. The thought of his child could only cause him grief. He'd never see the bairn.

"Beau?"

"Yes, love?"

"I think you would be a good father."

He didn't reply for so long she thought he'd fallen asleep.

"I'd like to think so." With that, he sighed wearily and went to sleep, his arms still holding her.

She lay there, feeling strangely secure, and hoped some good would come of their efforts that night.

Chapter Ten

The morning came too soon. Roselynne woke at dawn's first light to the feel of her husband's kisses. Again he stroked and kissed her until he knew her body better than she ever had. She found the yearning not so great this morning and realized she was still tired from the tension of the previous day.

"I think it is no use," she finally said. She hadn't reached the goal he'd set for her and felt like a schoolgirl who'd failed to please her master.

"Aye," he whispered. He kissed her eyes closed and took her swiftly, then he held her and she slept again.

She woke after sunrise. Beau was up, making a fire to ward off the chill of the day. He wore the shirt and breeches of the previous night. When he saw she was awake, he prepared them each a cup of tea, then sat on the edge of the bed.

"Good morning, wife," he said, handing her a cup.

She took it gratefully. "Good morning. Husband," she added at his steady look. He smiled, obviously pleased.

They drank silently while light from the fire brightened the room and that from the sun brightened the sky.

"We must prepare for the day," Beau said, a note of regret in his tone. "George will be here for you soon—"

"I won't leave," she declared.

"Yes. Before noon—"

"No. I cannot leave you at the hour of your greatest need. I'm your wife. It's my duty—"

"Duty be damned." He leveled a cold stare at her. "We've discussed this. I don't want you here."

"That's too bad," she said, stung by his manner after their night together. "There are arrangements to be made—"

"If you mean my funeral, it's all taken care of. Clayburgh has my orders, and he's to follow them exactly as instructed."

"I am not a servant to be ordered about," she reminded him, her voice as cool as his.

She was foolish to be hurt by his curtness. Their marriage was but a bargain. The intimacy of the night had meant nothing to him; any woman would have done.

"But you will listen to me in this instance," he said in a stern voice. He changed the subject abruptly. "I have a surprise for you. Something you've mentioned to Clayburgh or George every day this week. Can you guess what it is?"

His sudden smile beguiled her, and she put aside her hurt and anger. He was the condemned one, and he had a right to peace and his last wishes. She racked her mind for a clue to the surprise. His fate had been the only thing she'd thought on constantly.

"What is it?"

"You'll see." The morning chimes rang out. "Up with you."

They rose and dressed, she behind the screen, putting on the maid's dress, and he before the fire, donning a morning suit of black with a blue-striped waistcoat. In less than an hour, the footmen arrived with bacon, bread and jam. George came with them. He and the two footmen were oddly quiet, as if death already haunted the chamber.

"Why can't I stay for the day and leave in the morning?" she asked when Beau urged her to hurry her meal.

"I have things to do today," he told her, impatient with her questions. "Some final strings to pull." He laughed grimly.

She thought he and George exchanged glances but couldn't be sure. They were plotting something, but Beau evidently didn't trust her enough to reveal it, not even after last night. Laying her fork on the plate, she stood. "I'm finished."

Beau at once helped her into the cook's wool cloak and handed her the valise. He couldn't have made it plainer that he couldn't wait for her to go now that he'd had his use of her.

"Good day, my lord," she said. "Perhaps we'll meet again."

Surprise dashed over his face at her formal tone, then he took her wrist and moved them away from the others.

"Roselynne... There's no time," he muttered, more to himself than her. "You'll have to be content with this—last night was the sweetest I've ever known. I'll remember—" He stopped, his hands tightening on her shoulders. "You must leave now."

Again he hurried her toward the door, and in a moment she found herself being helped into the Rockdale carriage with its shield of two golden lions rampant, an olive branch between them. She settled her skirts about her and surveyed the gloomy interior. It was similar to the one that had been smashed.

She was plagued with restlessness and a sense of failure. But she'd done her best by Beau St. Clair. She'd taken his name, tried to conceive his child and spoken to the prince on his behalf.

She tried to think of something else she could have done, but nothing came to mind. If he'd confided his plans to her, perhaps she'd have thought of something. Having shared the greatest intimacy she'd ever known, it seemed odd to leave without a greater show of emotion.

Naturally she hadn't expected him to fall madly in love with her. That happened only in poems and novels.

A commotion outside interrupted.

"Cain't say I've been too pleased at yer 'ospitality, meself. Now take your bleeding 'ands off me."

Pulling aside the gauze curtain, Roselynne stared at the sight in the courtyard of the gaol. Henny was being propelled along by the gaunt gaoler, whose bony hand held a thick hank of the hennaed hair. At the carriage door, he released her. "See that you don't return, woman. You've been nothing but trouble from the day you came here." So saying, he went back inside the grim, sooty building and slammed the door behind him.

"Well, I hain't rightly wanting to come back," Henny retorted. She swung around and glared at Jim and Sanders, daring them to lay a hand on her.

Roselynne opened the carriage door. "Henny, get in," she said, laughing and perilously close to tears at the same time, "before they toss us both in a cell and throw away the key."

"Bless me bones, if'n it ain't 'er ladyship," Henny cried. She jumped into the carriage, setting it to swaying on its leather straps. "Coo, don't you look fine."

"Bobby, let's be off," Roselynne called to the coachman.

They clattered out of the courtyard.

"Where're we going?" Henny wanted to know.

"To Rockdale," Roselynne replied.

The carriage swayed along the rutted track. The Rockdale household, arranged in several carts, lumbered along behind it. Inside the carriage, Roselynne and Henny looked at the countryside while Ansella slept.

"I've not been to Sussex, have you?" Roselynne had asked earlier.

"Nay," Henny had answered.

That had been almost the whole of the conversation since they'd left London. They'd gotten on the road at noon and were due to stop at an inn soon for the night. The trip had been well planned down to the tiniest detail.

Roselynne leaned her head against the squabs and sighed. They had turned off the Brighton road an hour ago and were going through a great woods. She thought of highwaymen lurking in the shadows. A brigand was not apt to be the gallant of her dreams.

A smile, mostly sad, softened her mouth as she remembered Beau watching her arrival at Newgate from his turret window. He hadn't been a prince of the road, but he'd saved her from an uncertain fate. And while he hadn't been exactly handsome, she'd thought better of him as she grew to know him.

A jingle of bridle drew her attention. George rode up beside the carriage. "We've arrived," he said.

They pulled into a driveway lined with river gravel and stopped. Servants and grooms bustled about, and soon Roselynne and her father were seated in comfortable chairs in a parlor. George joined them to await supper.

"I cannot eat," Roselynne said, standing and pacing the room. "We must go back. I can't let him die without a person to mourn—"

"Nay, you will not," George countered, standing before her.

"I must."

He shook his head.

"Tell me what is planned," she demanded.

His eyes narrowed. "What do you mean?"

"I am not stupid," she said in a low, fierce tone. "I know you plan something. Like this trip, nothing Beauregard St. Clair does is left to chance. You will tell me, or I will ride out of here immediately."

George glanced at Mr. Moreley, then at Roselynne. "All right," he conceded, seeing the stubborn glint in her eyes, "there is a plan. If it works, Beau will escape—"

"I knew it! Tell me the whole of it."

"He'll ride for Dover and a frigate to take him to France."

"France," she exclaimed. "And then?"

"I, uh, suppose he'll go to Virginia from there."

"And send for me later, after he is safe," she concluded. "Yes, I see the reasoning. If he doesn't make it—" She clamped her lips tightly together. "You must return to London."

"I can't. I'm to watch you." The task was clearly not to his liking.

"Nonsense. I am safe enough with all the outriders you've hired. You must return and watch, then ride posthaste to tell me the outcome of this escapade. If it goes wrong, there may be something you can do to aid him," she added.

George paced around the room. "Beau will have my hide," he muttered. "But what does it matter? If he succeeds, he may need my help. If he doesn't, then all is lost anyway." He turned to Roselynne. "I'll go if you promise to stay here until my return and not leave the inn for any reason."

She placed a hand over her heart. "I promise."

Excitement danced in George's eyes while he called for the innkeeper. "Your best horse and be quick about it." He turned to Roselynne. "I should be back by nightfall tomorrow. If I'm not, go on to Rockdale. Jim and Sanders are to stay by your side. Go no place without them." He strode out, shouting orders to the servants and stableboys.

Roselynne refrained from commenting on his autocratic ways, which were only a reflection of those of her husband. George had been chafing at his duty toward her, and now he could return and be in the thick of things. She suppressed a tiny hurt that her husband hadn't included her in the planning.

Ansella knocked and entered. "Your supper, mum." She directed a maid in placing a repast on the table, then the two girls bobbed and left, talking and giggling like old friends.

Roselynne took her father's hand. "Come, Father. Sit over here and eat while the stew is hot." Satisfied that he would eat on his own, she lifted her spoon, put it in the bowl and left it there while her thoughts ran in all directions.

"If Beau should make good his escape, then we will go live in the American states, Father. A place called Virginia. Would you like that?" She ate a bite of stew. "I think I would. The state was named for Elizabeth, the virgin queen, and sounds romantic."

Roselynne remembered her own state of virginity, or lack thereof. Somehow she had thought she'd be a different person after becoming a wife, but she wasn't. She still longed for love and adventure. She still wanted to understand the elusive yearning that had scorched her when her husband had kissed her.

The breath quickened between her parted lips, and her gaze became misted with memories of her husband's touch.

"How very much different it must be, to lie in the arms of the person one loves," she whispered. She closed her eyes. "There's more to it than I yet know. I'm certain of it. He seemed to gain great satisfaction." She caught her lower lip between her teeth and stared into the fire, remembering the strange, compelling ways a husband touched his wife.

"This accursed waiting! I can't stand it another minute." So saying, Roselynne rushed for the door and yanked it open. She drew back in alarm before exclaiming with a severe frown, "What is this?"

Jim and Sanders stood in the hall, bristling with pistols and knives. Jim hopped from foot to foot while Sanders answered in placating tones, "We're on guard, m'lady. Nought will harm you while we're here."

She didn't know whether to laugh or curse. The serious faces of the two men convinced her of their sincerity. "I should like to go for a walk."

"Nay, you can't. The master—"

"Is probably still deciding on which suit to wear to his hanging," she finished and was immediately ashamed. Death was not a subject for jests. "Tell the good dame I'd like some tea."

"I'll fetch it for you," Henny volunteered.

Roselynne looked at her friend in sympathy. Henny, too, was eager to leave the desperate quiet of the room. "Thank you, Henny. Why don't you take your luncheon in the grand room? I'd like some time with my father."

Henny's round face beamed. "That would be nice, dearie, uh, m'lady."

"Dearie is fine when we're alone," Roselynne corrected as Henny departed. She suddenly understood why Beau wanted to be called by name. It had a comforting ring when a person felt alone and friendless.

Beau must have felt that way in prison. He'd had few friends to cheer him. She clenched her fists until her nails bit into her palms. "I can't imagine him dead, Father," she said, taking the footstool next to his chair. "He is...was...so full of life."

Her father lifted a strand of hair and smoothed it between his finger and thumb. At that moment, Ansella brought tea and a light repast. "Shall I serve your da first?"

"I'll do it." Roselynne dismissed the girl. "Come, Father, this soup looks good. Chicken stock with egg noodles, one of your favorites." She helped him to the table and took her seat.

She crumbled bread into the broth but ate little. "He gave me breakfast that first morning," she mused, tears filming her eyes. "It was a thoughtful thing to do. He was always kind. And gentle. Aye, a good man." She laid a hand on her abdomen and wondered if his child grew there.

The afternoon passed. Twilight was nigh before she heard the pounding of hooves on the road and rushed to the window. George had returned.

She was out the door before Jim and Sanders could stop her. They ran after her into the inn yard, setting the dogs to baying and the horses to stamping and snorting.

"Well?" she cried. "Tell me the news."

George glanced around. "Inside."

Swinging down, he took her arm, and they returned to the parlor where her father patiently stared into the empty hearth.

"Did the plan succeed? Tell me," she demanded.

"I don't know."

"You don't know? Were you not there?"

"Yes, but there was a great deal of confusion. The scheme didn't go at all as planned." George took her arms and held her steady. "I fear he's dead. I saw him shot with my own eyes and believe no man could withstand such a wound."

She gasped and pulled away, despair flooding her. She had wanted him to live. She had wanted to join him in America, to tour that savage land with him and learn of its ways. She had wanted...

Her wants mattered not. Wishing wouldn't change a fate now completed. For all his bold plans, he was gone.

She choked back a sob and whirled on George. "Did you get his body? We must have a proper funeral."

"Nay. He leapt from the bridge, his hands still tied, and the current dragged him to sea. I waited while the river was searched, then rode as hard as the horses could stand to tell you the news. They found only his coat, washed up on a spit in the Thames, and a shoe, farther down the strand."

"His body wasn't found?"

"Not yet."

"Then there's a chance he lives."

George looked at her sadly. "A chance," he agreed.

She clung to that thought through the night and all of the next day while they wended their way south through the forest. At last they came to cleared land that stood ankle high in wheat. Orchards marched in stately procession along the road, with stone fences, all in good repair, on either side. They turned into a long drive between graceful yew trees.

Roselynne pushed the curtain aside and leaned her head out like a curious schoolgirl. Her eyes widened. The house came into view, a brick mansion of modern design, standing foresquare on a wide lawn.

"Father," she said, her voice hardly above a whisper, "look at this. Why, there must be two hundred rooms."

"Welcome home, Countess," George said, reining in beside her. His smile dispelled the worry lines that had knit his brow all day.

"Is this Rockdale?"

"Aye. All the land since morning, including most of the woods, is yours, according to Connie."

The valet alighted from the carriage behind them. "Welcome home, my lady," he cried, evidently overcome at arriving. "It's a fine country seat, isn't it? Robbie Adams had the rebuilding of it when the old earl inherited."

Roselynne climbed out. She looked up at the windows, hundreds of them, and saw curtains twitch into place as if dropped by dozens of hands. The manor must employ scores of servants.

George took her arm and escorted her to the front steps. Connie followed with her father. Henny and Ansella, awed into silence, crept up the stone paving after them.

The door opened and a tall, elegant woman, dressed all in black, bowed her head to Roselynne. "Your ladyship," she said. "We are pleased to have you home."

"The housekeeper, Mrs. Hunson," Connie explained sotto voce. "She's been with the family for ages, was born and educated here at Rockdale, and played with the late earl as a child. She's been a widow for several years."

"Thank you, I'm pleased to be here," Roselynne said to the woman. She walked up the steps and glanced inside the hall. Black onyx pedestals resided at each side of gold velvet sofas. Each held the portrait bust of a gentleman.

"The first thirteen earls," Mrs. Hunson said. Her voice and bearing were almost haughty, as if she considered them interlopers and would have closed the door in their faces had not manners forbade it.

A shiver ran over Roselynne, and she wished for the quiet cheer of the London housekeeper.

The mansion was both formal and beautiful. It was rather like a museum, but with flowers to brighten the foyer, it would look welcoming. She suddenly thought of the little house in Ullswater. There she'd been safe and sure of herself. Here...well, here she was the countess, owner of forty thousand acres and a prime country seat. She had a responsibility to her husband and his tenants, she reminded herself.

"Will you meet the servants now?" Mrs. Hunson asked.

"No, my father is tired and needs to rest. We'll take tea in the library. I'll see the rest of the house and meet the household after that."

She hoped there was a library, else she'd made a total fool of herself. Behind her, she heard Henny tell Ansella she'd be glad of some proper rest; her rear end was killing her after two days of riding.

The housekeeper's lips twitched into a shallow smile of amusement or disdain. Roselynne had no time to speculate on Mrs. Hunson's personality. She had more pressing matters to consider. She followed the woman into a large room.

"Oh," she gasped, looking past the magnificent glass-fronted cases that lined the walls and out the tall windows offering views of the lawn and flower gardens. Beyond was the sea. "I hadn't realized we were this close to the water."

"Brighton is just down the coast," George said.

"The view is lovely, isn't it?" Mrs. Hunson pointed out the window. "It was just there, on that rocky ledge, that young Harry, his lordship's brother, fell to his death five years ago." She turned to Roselynne. "His horse was stung by a wasp and pitched him off onto the rocks below. He broke his neck, although it wasn't a terribly long way to fall, about twenty feet."

Goose bumps appeared on Roselynne's arms at the telling of the tragedy. "Yes, well, that is very... sad. Could we have tea and toast now? And would you show Henny and Ansella to their rooms? They are my personal maids. The rest of the staff should have arrived by now. I'm sure you have rooms assigned."

The housekeeper nodded and swept from the room, taking Henny and Ansella with her. Connie seated Mr. Moreley and hurried out to see about their trunks. Roselynne stood by a window and gazed toward the churning ocean.

"You look like a prisoner yearning to break free," George said, standing behind her.

"You are close in your guess. I was just wondering *what* I am. I don't feel like a countess." She turned to him. "Am I wife, or am I widow?"

George shook his head. "For truth, I don't know."

"Neither do I." She turned and stared out at the sea. "I will give him a month to arrive or get word to us before I go into mourning. Does that seem reasonable?"

"I suppose."

"I cannot believe he's dead."

"Nor can I."

"Then we shall assume he is not." She walked to the huge double desk. Picking up a quill, she found a nib and ink and marked the day on the calendar.

The next morning, she marked another day off... then another... and another.

"Will he live?"

"That's in God's hands, not mine," the physician answered, throwing the old bandages into the fire and putting his tape and scissors into his bag. "He'd lost most of his blood before you called me to him. Did you find out who he is?"

"No."

Bernard Clayburgh walked the doctor to the door and returned to the sickroom. He'd been surprised when his client had shown up at his door, clothing soaked with briny water and blood. More surprising was the stubborn life that clung to the fevered body.

Clayburgh shook his head. The bold escape plan had surprised him. Beau had evidently hired a gang of thieves to disrupt the hanging. When people had realized their pockets were being picked, they'd reacted in anger and called for the soldiers to arrest the culprits. A brawl had ensued. When order was restored, most of the cutpurses were gone, and so was the prisoner.

The chase scene had been comic. Only bad luck had one of the guards spotting Beau just as he crossed the footbridge over the river. A lucky shot had nicked an artery in his shoulder and sent him into the tide-swollen river. That had been the last anyone had seen of Beau. Until about two in the morning when the butler had heard a thud at the back door.

"You are either incredibly lucky or have the strongest will to live I've yet seen," he remarked.

Black lashes opened on startling blue eyes. "Did he set my nose?" Beau demanded.

"Your nose is as straight as mud and plaster can make it," Clayburgh assured him, "just as you ordered."

The lashes fell closed.

"Vanity," Clayburgh decided. "He prizes his looks too much to go to the grave with a crooked nose. Or is it your wife you wish to please?"

With a smile, the lawyer settled in a chair and prepared to study the case he would present the next day. Beau had used good judgment in coming to his house. No one would look for a criminal in the home of an eminent barrister of the court. Nor would he turn Beau in. The case had too many interesting twists still to be resolved.

"Roselynne," the patient murmured.

Ah, yes, the widow. Perhaps he'd better clear his calendar and journey to the country for a change of scene. He chuckled, then he laughed aloud. He did enjoy complications.

Chapter Eleven

"Virtue is the fount whence honour springs."
Tamburlaine the Great, I, iv, 4, 1769
Christopher Marlowe

Friday, August 2, 1790

Roselynne woke to a familiar cramp in her lower back. She emitted a cry of disappointment and buried her face in the pillow. There was no child. For all Beau's planning, there'd be no heir to carry on his name.

It had been two months since she'd lain with her husband in the prison chamber, and she'd been sure she had conceived. Perhaps it had been only her own willful desire to make it true.

The possibility of a child had been a tiny ray of hope, warm and joyous within her, that had helped keep gloom at bay. Now even that was gone. She shivered and drew her knees up to her chest, sadness washing over her like a cold tide as she fought the tears that seemed too ready to fall of late.

She tried to picture her husband's face. Only a vague blur appeared, smiling or scowling at her through the misty fog of memory. Wrapping her arms across her abdomen, she lay there in the huge, lonely bed, missing that which had never been.

Finally, rising, she rang for Henny.

The woman bustled in, looking fresh in a new black dress and a crisp white apron with ruffles on the shoulder straps. Her hair was deliciously auburn, thanks to the henna wash.

Roselynne liked to breakfast with Henny and discuss the day, a ritual she clung to, although Mrs. Hunson looked askance upon the practice of eating with a servant.

Henny set out the meal and turned to her mistress. "Your eggs be ready, m'lady."

Roselynne couldn't convince Henny to be less formal. She missed the saucy cheer and familiarity of "ducks" or "dearie." No one called her by name anymore, not even George.

"Then we shall dine," she declared, forcing a smile.

She took her chair. Henny hesitated, then took the one opposite. She patterned her eating manners after Roselynne, breaking the bread into bites, adding a dab of jelly to the bite and chewing with her mouth closed.

"There's something different about you," Roselynne mused. "A twinkle of the eye, perhaps. Tell me what has excited you."

"Well," Henny began, "it were this way. I was down to the village yesterday and dropped in at the inn, as I've a notion o' doing, for a bit of a nab. The missus and I 'ave become friends, ye know."

"Yes, you told me about Widow Farkley."

"Yes, well, she asked . . . she wanted to know if'n I was interested in a job."

"A job? Henny, you've not thinking of leaving?" Roselynne demanded, shocked by the possibility.

"O' course not. Not so long as ye need me." Henny sipped her tea and wiped her mouth carefully on a napkin. "The thing is, I'm not much use 'ere in the 'ouse."

Roselynne saw to the heart of the problem. Henny was bored. The country house offered little excitement for one so active and interested in people as the talkative widow. Roselynne put her own needs aside.

"Why, you should go," she encouraged. "If it's something you think you would like. If it isn't, then you know you will always have a place in my household."

Henny beamed. "It ain't like I was going away. I could visit, or ye could come see me on my half day."

"Of course. That would be great fun." Roselynne put as much gaiety in her tone as she could muster. She already felt desolate at the thought of life without the tart-tongued widow to cheer her.

"Aye. And ye can bring yer da for the outing. The Widow Farkley makes the best plum trifle I ever tasted."

"A very good idea. It's settled then. When do you start?"

"Well," Henny said, "why not tomorrow?"

"Indeed, why not?" Roselynne smiled sadly and blinked as tears filmed her eyes.

"What ails ye?" Henny asked, leaning forward in the ornately carved mahogany chair. "I won't go if'n it causes grief."

"No, no, don't mind me." Roselynne dismissed the notion. "It's just that I find . . . I find I am not with child."

"Oh, that's too bad," Henny said, her sympathy genuine and caring. "I lost two babes meself, one at birth and another a few days later. Twins, they were. 'Twas a fever that took 'em."

Roselynne reached across the table and took Henny's hand in hers, ashamed of her own self-pity when the other woman's sorrow had been much greater. "Henny, I'm so sorry."

"'Tis past, and life goes on," Henny said. For a few seconds, she stared into the distance as if looking at the past, then she became brisk. She prepared fresh tea and served them. "Drink this. Ye'll feel right as a top in no time." She saw that Roselynne did as told. "Ye know, this might be for the best."

"What do you mean?" Roselynne asked. With any other person she'd have felt embarrassed at the intimate discussion, but Henny was a true friend, the only one she had who wasn't part of her old home and a childhood forever gone.

"When ye meet a new love, there won't be any ties to the old, that is, yer 'usband, the earl."

Roselynne gazed out the window at the restless ocean. "I can scarce remember what he looked like. Except for his eyes. They were bluer than the summer sky."

"A 'andsome man, 'e was," Henny said, wiping at her eyes with her napkin.

"Was he?"

"A fine man, a bonny man," Henny asserted.

Roselynne sighed. "I remember how he frightened me on that first day. He looked like a demon straight from the fires of hell, watching us from that barred window. He sent Mr. Bowes to bring me to him for the night. Do you recall?"

"Aye. And look at 'ow it turned out. A marriage and all."

"Yes."

"It's young ye are. There'll be another."

Roselynne finished the meal, her heart heavy at the thought of Henny leaving. "Remind Mrs. Hunson to give you your pay packet before you leave in the morning. I'll tell her to prepare it."

"I thank you. Now I'd better be about the day, or the old biddy will get in a worse snit than usual."

Roselynne laughed, but agreed with Henny's assessment. "She doesn't get much joy from life, does she?"

"Nay." Henny dropped her voice. "Widow Farkley says the 'ousekeeper and the old earl were lovers. She says everybody knew it. Mrs. 'Unson thought 'e would give 'er a neat sum and a place for 'er own in 'is will."

"Surely you're funning me!"

"I swear on me 'usband's grave."

Roselynne recovered from her shock. "The bust of the earl was made just before he was killed. He wasn't terribly old, only in his forties or thereabouts."

Henny touched her auburn tresses. "To be sure, forty's not old, not at all."

"Of course it isn't," Roselynne quickly agreed. She stood. "Help me into my widow's weeds, Henny. I think I'll go for a walk. It's a fine morning, and I've a wish to explore."

"Morning air's prob'ly not good for a body," Henny warned, but she went to the wardrobe and removed a newly made dress of black muslin with a snug jacket to match.

"Mayhap not, but neither is sitting indoors. I've explored every nook and cranny of this place, and I need a change of scene. My half boots, please. I'll walk along the bluff."

"Be careful. That's where the young master died, a-falling off his horse."

"I'm not going to ride, only walk."

To ride Athene nearly took an act of Parliament. Roselynne chaffed at the close guardianship of Henny and George, Jim and Sanders, one or more of whom were always with her except when she was in her own bed at night. It was wearisome.

Two months. It had been that long since she'd left London and her husband. She now understood and forgave his sending her away so hastily. He'd been plotting his escape. With George and Connie's help—she'd had the full story from them—he'd almost succeeded. Almost.

A month ago she'd donned her widow's clothing, determined upon the customary year of mourning. George had been against the idea, saying that Beau had forbidden it. But it was only proper.

Today she felt the need to mourn. The pain in her lower back echoed the painful emptiness she felt inside. It was a reminder of her barrenness.

Slipping down the back stairs, she left the house by a side door and strode off toward the shore, keeping behind the boxwood hedge so her guards wouldn't catch her.

She walked farther than she ever had, her eyes on the surging waves, but her inner vision was some fifty miles distant, on London and all that had transpired there.

Heat, not entirely generated by her fast pace, suffused her body. She couldn't remember the days in prison without also remembering the nights. Beau at his window talking to her; inviting her to his chamber. His ridiculous proposal. Her acceptance. Her initiation into womanhood.

She hugged herself tightly as a remnant of that explosive passion rippled through her. He had been gentle with her, but she thought she would have preferred something more robust. He'd left her tense, frustrated. She felt that way now, remembering.

The passions between a man and a woman—she didn't understand them at all, and between exploring ways to expose the old earl's murderer and trying to suppress those odd passions, she thought of little else.

If only she could speak to her father, but his mind hadn't returned yet. Oh, she should have asked Henny.... No, that might not do. After all, Henny could be a wanton, too; she certainly liked men. It was doubtful she could give advice on curbing the wild tendencies that rioted in Roselynne's breast.

Ah, it was too confusing. She'd think no more of it. From now on, her energies would be focused on clearing her husband's name. "I vow," she said softly, her footsteps as rapid as her thoughts as she climbed higher and higher.

At last she tired and stopped. She looked around, realizing the wooded cliff was one she'd not seen before. She stood on the bluff, which was about thirty feet in height, and watched a ship far out at sea. Going to Portsmouth, she guessed, to unload some exotic cargo from the east or tobacco and rum from America.

Turning, she spied a dim trail into the woods. Curious, she followed it until it opened into a meadow overgrown with daisies and cockleburs and pussytoes.

Avoiding the burrs and the pussytoes, which grew in damp places, she walked toward a tumble of stones that had once been a castle. Exploring, she found the remains of a great hall, and beneath that, a dungeon of dark stone still intact. The door, attached to rusty hinges, reminded her of Newgate. She dashed back to the sunlight.

She spied a rounded tower, twice as high as her head. It contained a stair made of stone wedges, each wedge carefully placed partway over the one below to support its weight. The steps were rounded at the narrow end of the wedge, and this formed the stable center of the spiral leading up to the next level.

She climbed cautiously, but the steps bore her weight without a tremor. A stone walkway, part of a thick wall, ran behind the remains of a parapet. She gazed all around, able to see the roof of the Rockdale house above the trees to the west and the church spire of the village to the east.

Only the murmur of the wind and the breaking of the waves on the strand assailed her ears. She was completely alone.

She closed her eyes and lifted her face to the sun, then raised her arms and let the breeze blow through her caraco. For a moment, she almost felt broad, masculine shoulders under her hands, almost felt arms close around her, pulling her into a warm embrace. She'd slept with her husband only twice, but now she found her bed a lonely place.

And her dreams. Sometimes she woke, hot and breathless in the throes of his lovemaking, tormented by the wild yearning he'd induced but not subdued. Her nights would have been easier had he never introduced her to those turbulent episodes they'd shared.

She sighed. Her few days of marriage seemed a long time past, so long she could hardly recall them. All that was left was this haunting memory of loss, as if she'd loved him.

She wasn't sure what that was anymore, for she'd never equated the gentle emotion with the wild longing Beau had aroused in her. Perhaps she only wanted to believe she'd fallen a little bit in love with him in order to explain the strange loneliness that sometimes came over her.

Remembering her vow, she considered the important task before her—to find the person who'd framed her husband with the vile murder of his cousin.

The problem was the lack of suspects. Neighbors had called, taken tea and expressed their sympathy, but she'd found no foul criminals in the lot. With another sigh, she decided she'd best return before George found her missing and sent out a search party. He'd peel her ears if he caught her out without a guard.

Along the road that wound to the north of her, she saw the post rider. She wasn't expecting mail, but she hurried down the steps and returned to the house as if eager for a letter.

"Bad news?" George asked. His face was flushed from his morning gallop, and he looked vitally healthy and in good spirits as he strode into the library.

Roselynne looked up from the note she held. "Mr. Clayburgh says he is coming to visit and bringing a guest. He doesn't want to miss my birthday ball."

George snapped his fingers. "I'd forgotten about that."

"I'm not having a ball. It wouldn't be proper." She plucked at the black material of her dress, pleating it into folds while she frowned in disapproval of Clayburgh's sensibilities. "The barrister knows that."

"You must. Beau ordered it. It was in his instructions—"

"I don't give a fig for his instructions," she said hotly. "It wouldn't be right, and I'll not do it."

George raised his eyebrows at her sharp tone, but shrugged and dropped the subject. "Mrs. Hunson said you were out of the house without Jim and Sanders this morning." He gave her a fierce frown.

The housekeeper seemed to have a thousand eyes. Rose-lynne lifted her chin. "I went for a walk."

"Hell's fires," George exploded. "Haven't you any sense? You're not to go about without—"

"I'm sick of being watched over like the crown jewels," she shouted right back. "I have a right to freedom. This is Rockdale, not Newgate."

He stomped over to the window, sat on the sill and peered down the road. "Do you think I like it?" he demanded. "I wish Beau was here to take over."

"So do I!" She returned his glare. George looked away first. "Will he come?" she asked after an edgy silence. She pressed a hand to her heart. "Is he on his way?"

George shifted as if the windowsill were suddenly very hot.

"What do you know that I don't?" she demanded, her voice low and intense.

"Nothing."

She shook her head, not believing him, yet not knowing what to think. "If he isn't dead, why hasn't he sent word to me?"

George tugged at his cravat as if the linen were too tight. "He must surely have drowned," he said.

She rose and paced the carpet. "If he lives and the two of you have left me in misery for all this long time, I'll never forgive either of you."

"He doesn't live."

"Swear it."

She realized it hurt that her husband hadn't trusted her with his plans. A marriage had to be based on mutual trust, if nothing else. She sensed there was some new mischief afoot.

George swallowed and glanced out the window as if seeking escape. "I can't," he protested. "I didn't witness his death with my own eyes, but it stands to reason. How could a man who was wounded, whose hands were tied, withstand the river?"

After a taut moment, she gave up staring holes into him, seeing that he wouldn't budge in his story. She pushed her let-

ters into a stack. "You've been going through the ledgers. How
fares the estate?"

He was obviously relieved at the change in subject. While he
explained that everything seemed in good order, she vowed to
watch and see what was happening.

After the meeting with George, she had lunch in the garden
with her father. "There is some mystery a-brewing, Father. I
can feel it in my bones. My husband issues as many orders
from the grave as he did when alive."

Mr. Moreley gazed keenly at the roses as if studying them for
a report to the horticultural society. "Rose," he said. He
looked at her.

"Yes, roses," she encouraged, her heart in her throat. "I'm
Roselynne. Do you remember?"

He frowned and seemed to think about it, then the expression faded. He stared again at the flowers, but with no comprehension in his gaze. She sighed and settled back in her chair.
It was the third time he'd spoken that week, but he said no
more than one word each time and immediately lapsed back
into blankness.

"Henny is leaving in the morning, Father. I'll miss her."

She fell silent, steeped in the haunting sadness, and they sat
in the sun until Connie came for Mr. Moreley.

"A nice nap we'll have," he said to the vicar, urging him to
his feet. He smiled at Roselynne. "You'll be enjoying yourself, soon, Countess, what with the company coming. Be nice
to have a stir, won't it?"

"You know about the barrister?" she asked. George must
have mentioned it to the staff.

"Barrister? I thought the man was of the leisure class."

"What man?"

"Mrs. Hunson said a gentleman had left his card this
morning. He'll be calling this afternoon. A relative, I understand."

Roselynne was thoroughly perplexed. She had no relatives
to speak of, only a cousin on her mother's side, but the woman
was married to a squire in the far north. They'd not be coming here. She went to find the housekeeper.

"Connie tells me we're to have a guest this afternoon," she
said, keeping a steady gaze on the haughty housekeeper.

"His card is on the tray on the hall table where they're always left," the woman informed her. "You weren't available when he arrived."

Roselynne kept a rein on her temper. No good would be served by reprimanding the housekeeper for snitching to George that she'd been out of the house without escort. "Thank you. That will be all. Oh, we may have a guest for dinner if this person really is a long-lost cousin."

Mrs. Hunson smiled. "He truly is. Mr. Spinner was married to Miss Alice this very month seven years ago. I dressed her in her bride's clothes myself." With that, she walked out.

Roselynne felt her knees go wobbly. Spinner! William Spinner! He'd come to kill her and put in his obscure claim to the Rockdale wealth.

The panicky thought had been absurd, Roselynne chided herself at dinner. William Spinner was a charming, elegant man in his early forties. He wasn't tall like Beau and George, but he was well built, with a threading of gray at his temples.

And he was a gentleman of breeding. She cast a sharp glance at George, seated on her left. He had sat in moody silence during the whole meal, and she was quite put out with him. Her father was at the end of the table, with Connie in attendance to help him.

"This place recalls many happy memories," William Spinner told her, peeling an orange in one continuous strip. "The earl and I rode together often. He was a bruising rider and would take any hurdle on a great red beast he called Greek Fire. It was a pleasure to watch them in action."

"What did the earl look like?"

"You've not seen his bust in the hall?"

"Yes, but his coloring, was it dark or fair? Did he smile often, or was he solemn?"

"He was all of those." At her puzzled glance, Spinner laughed. "His hair was blond, a darkish shade, and his eyes were blue, but he possessed black eyebrows and eyelashes. Aye, and his beard was black as a tar pit. A striking combination. The ladies were much taken with it. He was a man devoted to reading and thinking, but he entertained grandly on occasion."

"Did he never marry?"

"Nay. His betrothed died of smallpox before they wed."

"So did Beau's," George put in.

Roselynne turned a startled gaze upon the younger man. "Beau was betrothed?"

"Aye. Mary, her name was, the fairest lass in all Virginia, with pale hair and eyes as soft as moonlight."

Roselynne's heart contracted into a great lump in her chest. Beau had once loved a woman.

He'd lied to her. He said he'd never loved another. No, no, he said . . . she racked her memory . . . he said he'd never taken *vows* with another. But isn't love a vow? Isn't it the pledge of a heart for a heart, each to be held in safekeeping by the other?

She felt odd, as if betrayed by his former betrothal, which was ridiculous, and yet...it was another thing he'd not shared.

"And your wife, sir?" George inquired of Spinner, halting the turbulent thoughts that swirled in Roselynne's mind. "Did she not pass on, also, two years after the marriage?"

Spinner's hand jerked upon his wineglass. He caught the drop with his napkin before it splashed on his red-striped smallclothes. "Yes," he said, strain evident in his voice. "After the stillborn birth of our son."

"We need not discuss sad things," Roselynne said soothingly, giving George a stern glance. "You gentlemen may take port and cigars here or on the terrace, if you like, then I hope you'll join me in the library."

The men rose, including her father, who looked around the table with a vague air. His gaze lighted on Spinner, and he held out his hand. Startled, Spinner shook it. The vicar nodded and left the room, Connie at his elbow.

"Thank you," Roselynne said to Spinner. "He has been ill for some time now and does strange things."

"I'm sorry to hear it. I'm something of a philosopher myself and would have enjoyed a chat with him. I quite agree with his paper on prison reform." He smiled sympathetically at Roselynne. "It is an honor to have such a distinguished man in our family."

"Oh, I wish he were of his right mind," Roselynne cried. "He would so love to talk to you."

"Perhaps the day will come."

An idea came to her. "Where are you staying?"

"At the village inn."

"Why don't you visit with us? If you've the time," she added.

George gave her a fierce glare and shook his head. She ignored his negative reaction.

Spinner glanced from one to the other as if wondering about their relationship. "I'd be delighted. I've always loved this place."

George gave Roselynne a dark glance.

"Perhaps if you talked to my father he might start to remember," she said eagerly. "If it wouldn't be an inconvenience, of course. You're under no obligation to do anything but enjoy yourself."

"I'd like that very much. I want to help. After all, we are cousins, and what are relatives for, if not to help in times of trouble?" He gave George a cool glance before giving Roselynne his arm. "Permit me to escort you to the library. I say, you don't play an instrument, do you? I have a fair voice and would prefer a song rather than a smoke."

"Yes, I do play—"

"Then let us entertain one another. Do you play or sing, Mr. Myers?" Spinner asked. Hardly waiting for George's negative answer, he escorted Roselynne to the music room.

Roselynne realized he knew the estate quite well. He'd been married in the house, and he and Alice had lived here with the earl and his younger brother, Harry, for two years before tragedy struck.

Feeling much in sympathy with the man, Roselynne took a seat at the pianoforte. They played and sang for two pleasant hours. Indeed, he'd not lied. He had a fine voice.

Roselynne leaned on the parapet, her outward manner quiet, but inside she seethed with unsettled emotions. In a week she'd be twenty, an age that should signify wisdom and tranquility. She hadn't a soupçon of either.

Restlessly, she plucked at the black lace at her elbow. Since William Spinner's arrival a sennight ago, she'd not be able to steal a moment to herself. George had posted guards outside her door at night, and Jim and Sanders had dogged her heels every moment of the day. She was a prisoner, in Newgate or out.

Propping her chin on her elbows, she studied the chimney pots of Rockdale and mused on the inhabitants. George, as surrogate for Beau, acted like a distrustful father whose daughter had tried to elope to Gretna Green. He evoked her temper often.

William, on the other hand, had been an exemplary guest. She couldn't fault his manners. He was witty, amusing and cheerful. He'd taken on the task of speaking with her father for a while each afternoon. So far there had been no results.

Of the people at the house, including the servants, which numbered forty if one counted the stable lads and milkmaids, there was none she would classify as a murderer. Of the tenants and crofters, she could detect nothing but honest laborers.

She looked toward the church spire, where the village nestled out of sight behind the oaks and beech woods. Henny was happily serving table at the inn. She and Widow Farkley were fast friends and had included Roselynne in their circle. They'd invited her to tea on Thursday, and Henny had come to visit on her half day. Now that she wasn't in Roselynne's employ, she had reverted to using the pet names.

Outwardly, life was peaceful.

If only Roselynne's spirit would settle. Tranquility of the soul—how sweet that sounded. It seemed only yesterday that she'd possessed it. Her life had changed more than she'd ever dreamed the day the soldiers came for her father. She'd been a girl, kicking up her heels in the meadows of home like a fawn, with never a care for the world. She'd been secure in her ignorance of life.

As a woman, a *married* woman, she'd learned much. Her vision clouded as fragments of memories twirled like tops through her head. She saw blue eyes, a dark beard, a sensitive mouth, but she could no longer put them together to form a face.

"Beauregard St. Clair, where are you?" she cried, startling the lone gull that flew past the castle. "I'm lonely! Do you hear? And angry! Are you alive? Have you returned to Amer-

ica and forgotten you have a wife who waits for you? And why
didn't you tell me of your betrothal? Answer, damn you!''

She pressed a hand over her mouth. Never had she used such
a curse in her entire life. She was becoming demented.

A flash of light caught her eye. She glanced toward the post
road and gasped. There, riding a magnificent horse of pure
black, was the answer to a maiden's prayers.

He was a chevalier, the most wondrous of noble knight
about whom ballads had been written and sung. His hair
gleamed like freshly minted gold in the sun and blew about his
face in short curls. His shoulders were broad and clothed in
blue, the rich material edged in gold thread. He sat the spirited horse with the ease of a born horseman, and his every
movement bespoke control.

Spellbound, she watched his progress—he rode with another man, nearly as tall but not so wide of chest—along the
road until the pair turned onto the gravel drive of Rockdale
She realized they weren't going to Brighton, but to her home

"Sweet heaven," she exclaimed and raced for the circula
stairs. It must be Clayburgh and his guest. They weren't due
until tomorrow.

She would beat them to the house, sneak up the back stair
and freshen her toilet in her room before greeting them and
offering them a fruit punch or glass of chilled wine, she decided, her thoughts dashing hither and yon in her excitemen
at seeing new faces at the manor.

Picking up her skirts, she fairly flew down the shore path
As she dashed past the black oak at the corner of the stable, a
branch caught in the black lace of her fichu and yanked it free
Hardly pausing, she grabbed the triangle of silk and raced
around the stable, almost crashing into the two gentlemen
callers.

She stopped, her breath coming in great panting gulps as she
stared into the bluest eyes she'd ever seen. She felt a strange
sense of déjà vu, then dizziness washed over her.

"She's fainting," a vaguely familiar voice said.

"I've got her," replied another.

Strong arms lifted her from the ground as if she weighed no
more than a bantam hen. She wrapped her arms around his
neck and held on as blackness descended.

"My God, what treasure," someone whispered just above her head, then she heard no sound at all....

"My lady, are you all right? Countess?"

Roselynne opened her eyes. She lay upon her own bed. Her jacket was open, the stomacher and corset loosened so that she could breathe more easily. Mrs. Hunson leaned over her.

"I feel... faint," she said.

"You are in shock. Can you remember what induced the fit?"

Blue eyes, as blue as a summer day, she thought. That made no sense. No one, not even expectant ladies, fainted due to a pair of eyes. She shook her head.

"Do we have guests?" she asked.

"Yes, Mr. Clayburgh from the city. His companion is Mr. Hargrove, from the Colonies, I understand."

Roselynne started up. The housekeeper pressed her into the mattress and held a cloth to her head. "You must lie still. I have sent for ice. That will cool the fever in your brain."

"I don't have a fever. Help me dress, please. I must see to our guests. Hurry."

Her hands shook as she flung off garments and riffled through her wardrobes for others.

"My lady, you are ill," Mrs. Hunson protested. Her concern seemed genuine.

"Nay. I'm..." How could she explain that she thought she'd seen a ghost? "...I'm all right now. 'Twas but a trifle. I ran down the path and lost my breath, that's all."

Ansella returned with the ice and was put to work taming the disheveled locks instead of placing cold cloths on her mistress's brow. Mrs. Hunson left in a huff.

"Hurry," Roselynne urged her maid. "We have guests."

In another fifteen minutes, she was ready. She pinched her cheeks and rubbed her hands together, but nothing would bring the blood to the surface. She felt encased in winter ice as she clung to the top post of the banister.

Gathering her skirt in one hand, she took the first step toward finding out who waited for her down those stairs.

Chapter Twelve

Beau flicked the black lace fichu against the palm of his left hand, closed his fingers on it, pulled it free and repeated the act. Too restless to sit any longer, he rose and strode to the window. However, his mind wasn't on the view of the forest mantled in the green of late summer.

Roselynne. The image of her careening around the corner of the building had the power to shake him yet. He still couldn't believe what his eyes had seen. She'd been . . . bewitching!

Her hair had swirled in a wild mane of shepherdess's curls all the way to her waist. She'd been flushed and panting, from her run, he assumed. Unless someone had been making love to her.

He clamped his teeth together. He'd thrash any man who'd dared touch her.

He pulled the silky scarf through his fingers. She'd been carrying it instead of tucking it around her neck as modesty demanded. God's blood, her breasts had been exposed to all eyes, and that luscious treat he intended only for himself!

If she was playing the wanton, he would soon find out and put a stop to it. She was his. He'd see that she knew it.

Damnation. He couldn't tell her. He was traveling under the guise of True Hargrove from Virginia, come to visit Cousin Beau upon concluding a tobacco deal in London. Well, he would have to keep an eye on his wife as well as ferret out the murderer. He tucked the delicate silk-and-lace confection into his pocket.

The door opened and the butler announced, "The Countess of Rockdale."

Roselynne stepped into the sunny parlor. Her gaze skimmed past Clayburgh to the gentleman at the window. The sun backlighted his golden hair, forming a halo around his head, but his eyes held a wicked gleam as he looked her over from head to foot.

Devil or angel? she found herself wondering. She stared into his eyes, seeking a clue.

"Countess, let me introduce you to a relative," Clayburgh said, rising and bowing over her hand. "This is True Hargrove, the late earl's first cousin. You may imagine his grief when he arrived in London and heard the news...."

It took a moment for Roselynne to realize that the latest "late earl" had been Beau, and that the gentleman from Virginia was *his* cousin. That explained the eyes.

The cousin's eyes were as blue as a cornflower, with black eyelashes and eyebrows setting them off like sapphires in onyx. Unlike Beau's dark hair, this man's was blond.

She stared at his nose, his lips. Nay, he wasn't her husband. His nose was straight, his mouth generous in width. Beau's lips had been thinner, harder, his face half-hidden by a pitch-black beard. This man was clean-shaven.

The trembling in her legs stilled. "Welcome to Rockdale, Mr. Hargrove," she said when Clayburgh stopped talking. She'd vaguely heard something about tobacco during the introduction.

"First cousins need not stand on formality. Won't you call me True?" He took her hand in his and gazed into her eyes.

Tingles rushed along her arm and lodged deep inside her. He wasn't her husband, but he was much like him in height and breadth.

His perusal disconcerted her. It wasn't in the least polite, but naturally he was curious about his cousin's wife. No doubt the barrister had given him full details of the hasty marriage.

She removed her hand from his, disappointed, almost angry, that he wasn't the one she'd hoped for. "Of course."

"Are you feeling better?" the cousin asked, his eyes again swarming over her, lingering, she thought, at a point on her abdomen. Blood crept into her cheeks of its own accord.

"Yes, it was nothing. I ran along the path. It was most foolish. I was trying to beat..." She was rambling. "Please, be seated. I'll ring for refreshments."

"I took the liberty of ordering coffee," Clayburgh said.

Roselynne noted his tone. "You seem in good spirits. Was your trip pleasant?"

"Very." He flicked his coattails out of the way and sat in a chair woven in black and gold, the Rockdale colors, after she was seated. "True proved an able rider. We made the journey in record time. I do hate to tarry," he added with a sardonic smile.

Mr. Hargrove chose a place next to Roselynne on the sofa. The service arrived, and she poured coffee for the men, tea for herself, after passing the plate of shortbread biscuits.

"How do you take your coffee, Mr. Hargrove?" she asked.

"Black, Roselynne."

The emphasis on her name was a reminder that they were on kinship terms. She handed him the cup, aware of the warmth of his hand as she did so, and quickly moved away.

The cousin had a formidable presence. His face was comely and his voice a caress. He spoke in a charming drawl that invited the unwary to a dalliance. She'd best guard her virtue around him.

Confounded by this good advice, she lapsed into a discussion of trivia. "How did you find London, Mr. Har...True?"

"Diverting enough," he replied. "I like the country better. I'm more used to it."

"Mr. Clayburgh mentioned tobacco. Are you near the St. Clair plantation in Virginia?"

"Fairly close."

"So you were friends with Beau?"

He chuckled. "You could say that, although at times I was his worst enemy."

His smile was devastating, creating lines in each cheek that hinted at dimples but were more masculine. A very formidable presence. Ansella and the maids would swoon.

"But that is the way of youthful friendship, is it not? I remember falling out with my best friend in the parish at home many times. We always made up." She hesitated at his hard gaze.

"This is your home now," he reminded her in a low, dark growl.

"Yes, I know." She fidgeted with the lace around her neck. He made her uneasy, as awkward as a schoolgirl. But she was a woman, a widow with experience of life. She lifted her chin. "Tell me, how goes your father?" Clayburgh asked.

She told of the few encouraging signs they'd had and of William's kind help.

"Who?" Mr. Hargrove demanded.

"William Spinner. He, too, is a cousin, from the paternal side of the family."

"He's no kin."

Really, he was being quite rude. Not only did he contradict her, but he gazed overlong upon her with those disconcerting eyes that seemed to see every thought she had.

"By marriage, not by blood," she conceded, holding on to her temper. Autocratic traits obviously ran in Americans, judging by the three she'd met—Beau, George and now, the cousin.

"Where is Spinner staying?" True demanded.

"Why, here, of course—"

"Here!" he roared.

Roselynne drew back, alarmed by his manner.

Clayburgh had an attack of coughing. When it passed, he remarked, "Naturally a relative would stay at the house."

Roselynne glanced from one to the other as the men exchanged harsh looks. "And you must stay with us," she said. "Both of you." She hoped she didn't regret the invitation.

"One woman, recently widowed, with three men in the house?" True questioned. His gaze raked her black gown, paused at her abdomen and returned to her eyes. One black brow rose—in an insolent manner, she thought.

He looked at her as if she were easy prey for every man in sight. She would put him straight on that if he thought to take advantage of her! She managed a chilly smile.

"Four, actually. A friend from your country is also visiting. And my father is present, of course." Her temper frayed near the snapping point at his skeptical snort.

"A fine chaperon he makes, if he's as you say," he said, his tone one of censure.

She was a vicar's daughter, her morals so absolute she'd never considered that anyone, other than her own demanding conscience, might think her less than a lady of the highest order. She was furious that he, a stranger who knew nothing of her, would fault her judgment.

"Who, pray, sir, are you to tell me of proprieties?" she asked in icy tone, facing him like an opponent in the boxing arena, her hands clenched into fists, as were his.

"I'll tell you who I am—"

The barrister choked on his coffee and had another severe spell of coughing. The American pounded him on the back while Roselynne's anger changed to concern.

"A handkerchief," Clayburgh wheezed past his hand, which he'd clamped over his mouth like a vise. His shoulders were shaking, almost as he were laughing, but of course, he wasn't. The poor man was red in the face and emitting the oddest sounds.

True pulled his from his pocket before she could offer hers. He stared at the black lace as if wondering what it was and how it came to be there.

"That's mine," Roselynne shrieked, appalled that so personal an item should be in his pocket. She snatched it from his grasp and balled it between her hands. "Where did you get it?"

"It was left draped around my neck after I carried you to bed."

Her eyes widened in outrage at his words. "You prevaricate, sir! You did no such thing!"

He smiled and crossed his arms over his chest. "I assure you I did, madam."

"You had fainted," Clayburgh said, recovering from his spell.

The attorney supplied a cool voice of reason in the heated proceedings, making Roselynne pause and think. She remembered strong arms lifting her. "Oh."

"Yes, indeed, *oh*," the American mocked.

"Perhaps I'd best rescind my invitation," she said in a sweet voice, her eyes sparkling in triumph. "I wouldn't want to upset your refined sensibilities, Cousin True."

"Perhaps there is a solution," Clayburgh offered. When he had their attention, he continued, "I recall speaking to Lady Stanton, widow of a minor nobleman, at a recent ball. She lives in the neighborhood and has returned home. Perhaps she could be prevailed upon to visit and thus act as chaperon. If one is called for," he added hastily when Roselynne cast him an indignant glare.

"Give me her direction and I will write," she said, rising. She spoke to the cousin. "If you will excuse us."

"Of course," he murmured.

"One more thing," the barrister said. "We must get the invitations out if we're to hold your birthday ball. We have only a week to prepare."

"My dear sir, I am in mourning."

"I have orders to carry it through," he said.

"Nay, my husband cannot transcend the grave and enforce such a spectacle. I forbid it."

"She's right," Beau said. "It wouldn't be right."

"And what is *your* suggestion, Mr. Hargrove?" Clayburgh asked. "I have been instructed to invite the local people here in order to question them about the late earl's acquaintances."

Roselynne picked at the lace on the fichu. "I hadn't thought of that aspect of it. But we can't have a ball."

"A small country gathering, perhaps," Beau said, "with a few of the neighbors in for a picnic by the shore. After all, you must provide some entertainment for your guests."

She considered. "That would be acceptable." She went to a small rosewood writing table. "Tell me the widow's name again, and I will send Jim with a note. Do you know the local gentry?" she asked Clayburgh.

He hurried forward. "I have a list."

"I'll leave you two at it," Beau said. "If I could be shown to a room, I'd like to rest after the harried trip from town."

Roselynne glanced up in time to intercept the sardonic smiles the men exchanged. Such strange creatures men were, she thought. There seemed to be a deep friendship between the two, though they'd recently met.

And there was much of Beau in his cousin, she mused. The same physique and the same temperament. One thing she'd noted—blond hair appeared on both sides of the family, yet Beau's had been as dark as sin. There must be a gypsy strain in the blood.

"Ready?" Clayburgh asked, breaking the thought.

She started to pick up the quill, noticed the fichu and added it to the other around her neck. "Ready," she said. She retrieved the heavy cream notepaper from the drawer and began to write.

Beau followed Mrs. Hunson up the stairs. Her feet didn't make a sound on the steps, and her strange smile made him feel as if he followed a specter to some eerie fate.

"This is the earl's chamber," she intoned, stopping by an open door where a maid dusted the furniture and a footman laid logs for a fire. "The countess sleeps in here now. Alone."

She'd better damn well sleep alone, he fumed, his eyes on the huge curtained and canopied bed. He remembered how she'd looked when he carried her into the house and laid her there. She'd clung to him as if to life itself, her breasts mounded above her bodice and her cheeks rosy from exertion. He'd almost forgotten himself and kissed her.

Damn, but she was lovely. He'd missed her during his weeks of convalescence. She'd brightened his hours in prison, and while he was ill he'd wished for her caring ways, thus far reserved for her father. She'd have come if he'd sent for her.

He frowned, not liking the implication. He didn't want her acting from obligation or duty as she had the night she'd come to him in his lonely cell. He wanted her to come to him eagerly, without reserve, and find joy in their union....

An ache settled in the lower part of his body, and he forced his thoughts from temptation. He quickly scanned the rest of the bedroom with a bumpkin's rude interest. It was exactly as the earl had described it to him.

Beau knew the layout of the house by heart. And he knew the room he wanted. He hadn't yet contrived a plan to get it. His eyes narrowed. If anyone else had it, they'd be moved.

"I thought this chamber would do for you, sir," Mrs. Hunson said.

He almost gasped when she opened the door to the small suite next to Roselynne's bathing room. The very room he'd wanted. The woman was a witch.

"Or would you prefer a room farther from the sea? It bothers some people with its constant sound." Her smile gave him the chills, and her eyes, dark and opaque, gleamed with some inner mirth beneath finely arched brows.

"Uh, this will be fine."

"Very good."

She flicked back the undercurtains, which matched those in the master chamber, he saw. Yes, everything was as his cousin had told him. He relaxed slightly and took in the view of the sea.

"The twelfth earl died in this room, raving mad for want of his true love, some say," she told him. "The men in the family usually come to tragic ends. If you're interested in their history, here's a book." She withdrew it from a case and laid it on a table. Then she smiled at him again.

"Thank you. I think I prefer to rest now." His voice rang in the silent chamber like the plangent toll of a bell.

"I'll leave you then." She departed, closing the door without making one sound.

"Whew," he said, pursing his lips and letting the air out of his lungs in a rush. Just what he needed—an eccentric house-keeper to go with his infuriating wife.

He tossed off his boots and reclined on the bed. He was tired. He'd recovered from his loss of blood, but his stamina was below par. Perhaps he'd play the languid dandy for a few days, using the opportunity to sneak around and investigate the house.

A smile creased his cheeks. Thanks to a secret door, he now had access to Roselynne's room without using the hallway. Rising and going to the panel, he listened intently. No sound from the other side. Cautiously, he searched along the frame and found the release for the latch.

He pressed the button and the panel clicked open with a tiny squeak, disclosing the master bathing chamber through the slit. A picture of Roselynne in the bath sprang to his mind.

With a groan of rampant desire, he closed the portal and went to another beside the hearth. There, a twist of a lever opened a sliding door that led into the secret passageways of the manor. He looked both directions along the dark, dusty hall, then closed the door and returned to bed.

A satisfied smile settled on his face. He could also get into the master chamber from the passage. In fact, he knew a secret way into most rooms of this monstrous house. He could keep an eye on all its occupants. Including his beautiful wife.

He'd also rein in his temper. Clayburgh had saved the day with his choking fit that afternoon. Roselynne hadn't realized, when he'd gotten angry about her having three men in the house, that he hadn't included himself in the group. He had a right to be alone with her. He was her husband, by damn.

He quelled the renewed riot of desire this thought brought to him. He'd have to be careful. She'd almost guessed when she'd dashed around the stable and looked into his eyes. Hell, she'd known! Fortunately, she'd fainted before voicing the truth.

Later, she'd been unsure. There had been a bad moment when she'd entered the library, but his looks were altered enough to confuse her. He ran a finger along the ridge of his nose. When he'd gone over the bridge, he'd hit it again. Actually, that had been a stroke of luck. Having it set correctly had made a definite identification impossible for her.

She had looked different, too. Her figure had filled out a tad, making her breasts even more luscious. Her beauty made it hard to remember his plan for setting her free.

She could be pregnant. He'd dwelt on the possibility for weeks. It had taken all his control not to blurt the question as soon as she appeared in the library. Not even Clayburgh's coughing spell would have covered *that* blunder. Sweet heaven, but he longed to know.

Unable to stop himself, he relived the blissful night he'd spent with his wife. He could hardly wait to resume her education in those turbulent arts. There would be no need for haste.

His conscience nagged him. If she desired to be free, he shouldn't touch her. Besides, he had a villain to catch.

* * *

"We won! We won!" Lady Stanton cried.

She and Cousin True were playing at lawn bowls against cousin William and Rodney Witherspoon, the son of Squire Witherspoon. The squire, seated next to Roselynne, was telling her and Vicar Smith-Warren of last season's hunt when he had led the field to a near victory.

She was glad the fox had gotten away, but managed to say, "Oh, that's too bad," in a believable tone. If she had to smile much longer, she was sure her face would crack.

Lady Stanton clung to True's arm as the four players ambled back to the group seated under the oak tree. Servants bustled about, laying out a feast of cold meats and salads on tables draped in heavy linen.

Mr. Moreley and Mr. Clayburgh were already seated. George was off a little ways, examining a stone he'd found. Their little party numbered ten altogether, Roselynne counted. Of the local gentry, only a duke and his family, off to India on a tour, were absent.

"Oh, that was delightful," Lady Stanton declared, fanning herself with a languid air.

She'd been very active on the playing green, Roselynne noted. The woman had fairly leaped out of her bodice each time she'd bent forward to bowl. When she made a good showing, she'd jumped up and down, calling on Cousin True to observe her form.

Cousin True, looking angelic with his golden curls blowing around his face, pulled his blue coat on over his shirt and waistcoat. His breeches, also blue silk, fit his tall form perfectly, leaving no doubt about his masculine proportions. The man had no modesty.

Roselynne sniffed and glanced away, but the picture of his long legs and lean hips stayed in her mind. He was also a flirt. Since Lady Stanton had come to visit earlier in the week, he'd stayed glued to the vivacious widow's side, yet his gaze had often strayed, and Roselynne had found herself going breathless more than once at the searing glances he cast her... such as now.

His dark blue eyes had settled on the point where the fichu tucked into her bodice. Self-consciously she touched the rosebuds nestled in the valley between her breasts and moved away from the squire and vicar. A sardonic smile curled True's lips at her action. Honestly, she didn't understand him at all.

"A lovely nosegay," he said, coming over to her.

"Cousin William gave them to me."

"From your own greenhouse."

"It's the thought that counts," she said, lifting her chin. He was so . . . so irritating.

"Yet you refused my gift."

"It was much too dear," she explained.

The nosegay holder had been encrusted with emeralds among the gold filigree vines.

"Yet you accept the offerings of others, such as that young pup, with no complaint." He nodded to the foppish Rodney.

"Others gave only flowers or sweets or handkerchiefs. Your gift was valuable."

"It was but a trinket," he insisted, his gaze on the flowers again. He grinned, his teeth white against his tan, and she experienced a sweet ache inside. She looked at the sea.

"Black becomes you," he continued. "Some women can't wear it, but with the kiss of the sun on your nose and cheeks, you look very fetching."

Roselynne felt waspish. "And Lady Stanton? Does she not look fetching in her widow's weeds?"

The baroness wore silver edged in black, since she was near the end of her half-mourning year. The shade was very becoming to her high color and glossy black hair. Of course she did overdo the rouge pot a bit. And the black around her eyes was as vulgar as an actress. Roselynne halted her inspection. She was being a vixen and the good dame didn't deserve her ire.

He pivoted and perused Lady Stanton for a long minute, then turned back to Roselynne. He chuckled, but before he could speak, Rodney came to them. "I say, Hargrove, you're monopolizing the hostess. Lunch is ready," he said to Roselynne. "Won't you sit by me?"

"She'll sit by me," William countered, gallantly offering a chair.

"She's spoken for," Cousin True informed them.

"Indeed I am. I'll sit with my father and Mr. Clayburgh," she said gaily, taking a seat at the small table.

William at once took up a position behind her. "I'll serve you," he announced.

Beau watched the group settle itself at the three tables. He chose a place where he could see Roselynne each time he looked up. She was a tempting sight.

He felt a tightening in his groin. He wasn't the only one who'd noticed how lovely she was this morning. Rodney hadn't been able to keep his gaze off her, and at the moment, William, acting the gallant by serving her before taking a chair, was staring down at the creamy rise of her breasts through the thin black lace that covered them. Beau clenched his fork in anger and looked around for some excuse to distract the man.

At that moment, Roselynne's handkerchief was snatched by the breeze and sent tumbling across the lawn. "Oh, my gift," she said, jumping up.

"I'll get it." William dashed after the flimsy bit of cloth, a whimsy from Thea, which raced along the ground just in front of his feet.

Suddenly a knife arced through the air and landed point down in the ground, securing a corner of the handkerchief. William, startled, leaped aside, then retrieved it and the knife.

"I say," the squire cried, "a nice trick, sir, and well done."

Clayburgh nodded his head at the praise, accepted the knife from William, and resumed carving an amusing face on an apple. When he finished, he presented the apple to Roselynne. "I hope I didn't damage your handkerchief," he said.

She examined the lace after William gallantly returned the item. "Not at all. I am amazed at your skill," she complimented, turning the apple around to admire it. She glanced up at William. "Do be seated. You make me nervous hovering over me like that. It reminds me of times my mother used to scold."

He laughed good-humoredly, but remained standing. Beau decided he was going to punch the bastard in the nose if he didn't sit down. Some inkling of this must have gotten across to William, for he took a chair at the table with George and the vicar. Beau turned his attention to his own foursome.

"You weren't listening," Thea scolded, leaning very close so her perfume wafted under his nose.

Beau let his gaze become lambent. "I always hear what you're saying," he said with a cocky leer.

During the four days in Lady Stanton's company, he'd learned to play the impatient but resigned suitor to perfection. Thea had made it clear she expected his ardent attention, also that she set the pace. He forced himself to listen to her quips and to keep his eyes from Roselynne.

As soon as the meal ended, William returned to his place at Roselynne's elbow. Rodney took up position on the opposite side, casting the other men a challenging glance.

Beau and George walked off a ways to smoke. "God's blood, they smother her with their clumsy adoration," Beau muttered. He lighted the cheroot, then propped a foot on a boulder.

"Why don't you tell her who you are?" George encouraged. "She's going to be madder than a pegged hen when she finds out."

"Nay. She's too honest and open in her nature and might give too much away. I wish he'd croak."

This last statement followed the rising notes of a ballad as William sang of Lord Willoughby. Roselynne accompanied him upon a lyre. She was talented, Beau was discovering.

With little effort, she ran the household, conferring with the housekeeper, the cook and the butler every morning. Lunch was spent with George and Clayburgh, learning of the vast estate she'd inherited. She had her father attend each session on the off chance some remark might penetrate his fog and strike a memory.

A smile played about the corners of Beau's mouth. He'd chosen wisely when he'd asked her to be his countess. If only he could claim her. Damnation, he hated this sneaking around. When he found the culprit responsible for his cousin's death...

He whipped around and stared at Clayburgh.

"What is it?" George asked.

"Clayburgh. He's damned clever with a knife."

George raised his brows in question, then exclaimed as he followed Beau's drift. "And 'twas a knife that stabbed your cousin in the throat, then slit him from ear to ear."

"Aye." Beau blew out a streamer of smoke. "Have I brought the devil among us?"

"It's Spinner I don't trust. He, too, can use a blade. I've seen him peel a fruit with a skilled hand. Also, he needs money. Look how he sticks to our fair Roselynne like a deer tick to a bloodhound."

Beau laid a hand on his friend's shoulder. "As you love your life, guard hers. She trusts you more than she trusts me."

He dropped his hand and looked at his beautiful wife. A sudden hunger gripped him, a yearning for something he couldn't name.

"She's been around me for weeks and thinks of me as a brother," George explained.

A chortle escaped Beau. "Aye, and that's the only reason I haven't run you through this past week. I'm as jealous as an old husband with a young wife. Come, let us divert this group before I call those two out. I can't stand those calf looks the younger one gives her."

"Nor the bold ones from Spinner," George guessed correctly.

"I'd like to carve his heart from his chest," Beau growled. He tossed his smoke over the cliff into the sea, then strode back to the tables. "Enough of this dalliance," he called. "Let us perform deeds as men. 'Tis been a while since I've practiced with the bow. Who will challenge me?"

"I will," Rodney spoke up, an excited flush coloring his bony face and making his mustache look more than ever like straw pasted into place.

Roselynne sent a servant for a target while the men went to the weapons room to select their bows.

Soon after, the housekeeper appeared like an unwelcome apparition at her elbow. "Are you going to allow this, my lady?"

"The target practice? I see no harm in it, and our guests must have sport. Do you see a problem?"

"Nay, not if it pleases your ladyship. I wanted to be sure before I opened the room is all." She glided away up the lawn, the keys at her waist making a merry clinking as she walked.

Roselynne felt a shiver crawl up her spine. Perhaps she should retire the housekeeper. No. Mrs. Hunson was an enigma she meant to unravel if she could. The woman might have killed the earl in a fit of jealous rage when she'd discovered—by snooping through his desk?—he'd left her nothing but a regular servant's pension should the next earl not desire her services.

She let her gaze stray from one person to another as the younger men returned to the meadow with their weapons. George was the only one she trusted completely. She studied Cousin True. She hadn't a reason to distrust him, but she was wary of him.

A tremor entered her hands and a flush invaded her cheeks as she realized it was *herself* she didn't trust when he was around.

He made her feel strange, as if a cord tightened unbearably inside her when he was near. He popped into her thoughts at odd moments, even during her bath, startling and embarrassing her.

Watching him string his bow, she was reminded of his strength, yet he was a man who could be gentle.

When she'd refused his birthday gift as too dear, he'd plucked a wild violet from beneath the oak and tucked it into a curl at her temple. Her breath grew short as she recalled his touch when he put it there. She'd wished they'd been alone.

She bit her lip in despair. It was true. She was a wanton.

Chapter Thirteen

Roselynne paused in the common room of the inn. "You may have your ale here. I'll be with Henny." She indicated the door to the private chamber Mrs. Farkley called a parlor.

"I'll check the room out," Jim said. He took his duties as guard seriously.

Sanders took up a position by the door while Jim went in and looked the room over. Henny, setting out cups, batted her eyes at him. "Coo, I likes the men tall and long, to be sure."

Jim fled. Roselynne stepped inside and closed the door. "Henny, you are incorrigible."

"That I am, ducks, whatever it be. Come 'ave a seat. I 'eard ye 'ad a party at yer place this past Saturday." Her eyes were atwinkle, indicating she'd already heard all the gossip.

Roselynne sighed. "A picnic under an awning. The day was hot, but otherwise nice for it. It was my birthday." The party, four days past, had turned into a nightmare that haunted her.

After the archery contest—George had won, with Cousin True and William tying for second and poor Rodney barely hitting the target—had come javelin throwing, then the discus toss, then mumblety-peg with Clayburgh's knife. George, relaxed and enjoying himself, won most of them. As the afternoon wore on, the other three had become grimmer and more determined to win.

She didn't know how it came about, but a scuffle had ensued and suddenly three grown men, two of whom certainly ought to have known better, were in a brawl. George, Clayburgh and the squire, with the help of Jim, Sanders and several other servants, had had to put a stop to it. Thus had ended her birthday on that shocking and humiliating note. Naturally the tale had been too good for the servants not to recount.

"Aye, I remember. I 'ave a little something for ye." Henny pulled a packet from her apron packet, a paper twist with a blue bow around it enclosing a nosegay of dried flowers.

"A tussie-mussie. Why, Henny, how very thoughtful," Roselynne murmured. The sweets and trifles from her house-guests hadn't moved her as this gift did. This one had been planned, the flowers collected and dried during Henny's precious spare-time hours. "You shouldn't have bothered," she protested, caressing the tiny bouquet.

"Take the paper off. There's a holder," Henny said.

Roselynne did and almost dropped the gift when she discovered the nosegay holder. It was gold filigree with emerald leaves twined on a vine. "It—it's exquisite," she managed to say.

"A bloke what stopped at the inn sold it to me. 'E heard me and the widow talking about your birthday party whilst I was fixing the flowers. Said 'e'd bought it for a girl, but she wouldn't 'ave nothing to do with 'im." Henny looked up from pouring the tea. "A fair man with blue eyes that reminded me o' the late earl, yer 'usband. Ye wouldn't know of 'im, would ye?"

Roselynne nodded and examined the inset of gems in the tiny holder. "His name is True Hargrove, a cousin from America. It must be a hard land," she mused. "They breed hard men there."

"Aye. I've no doubt o' that. My man sent four letters while 'e was there, afore 'e died. I 'ad them read to me. 'Twas a land o' savages and the like."

"Yes." Roselynne held out the holder. "Don't you want to keep this for yourself? The flowers are enough for me."

Henny shook her head vigorously. "I bought it for you. H'it only cost me pin money, 'e was that anxious to be rid o' it. The leaves look like real jools, don't they?"

Roselynne saw she couldn't refuse without hurting Henny's feelings. She touched her friend's hand affectionately. "Thi is the best gift I've received, and I thank you for it. Has business been good since I last saw you?"

"Aye, and then some. Everyone dropped in to talk about the party—" She grinned at Roselynne but didn't mention the fiasco. "—And the folks what went to it. I understand Lady Stanton is staying with ye."

"Yes. She's a perfect guest and has helped me no end."

"It's said she 'ad 'er cap set for the late earl, but 'e wouldn't come up to scratch. 'Is mistress, I 'eard she was."

"He was a busy man to entertain all the mistresses he's reputed to have had," Roselynne said with a dry smile. "If one believes the gossip, which I for one do not."

"So all is going well?"

"True and William have taken a dislike to each other." She sighed. "Men are so wearying. They constantly try to best each other, whether at cards or archery. They compete at riding and swimming, which they do each morning in the sea."

"Why, 'tis a dangerous thing," Henny said, shocked at this reckless behavior. "What will they be doing next?"

"Swordplay, I fear. William mentioned he needed the practice, and True volunteered to be his partner. I cannot think why they dislike each other so."

Henny laughed uproariously at this. "Coo, dearie, I can tell ye that without setting eyes on the pair. They's two dogs and only one bone. Ye know who the bone is."

"Oh, Henny," Roselynne protested, heat rising to her face at the blunt statement.

"That be the way o' men. What does this William look like? Is 'e as 'andsome as the other?"

"No. He is older, but well kept in his appearance. And not so tall. Nor are his shoulders so broad."

"And 'is legs?"

"Not as muscular and long."

"And what else 'ave ye noticed about this American?" Henny asked slyly, a smile lurking in her blue eyes. "Is 'e well built all over?"

"Oh, yes," Roselynne began, then stopped as she met Henny's glance. The flush deepened in her cheeks. "You are teasing me."

"Aye. You're taken with the man, ducks. That's good—"

"I'm not," she cried, setting her teacup into its saucer hard enough to make the pottery ring. "He is the most disagreeable person. Why, we hardly pass a civil moment. It's . . . it's embarrassing for my other guests, I'm sure. I've almost given up speaking to him at all. He corrects me as if I'm a child!"

Her grievances, stored for over a week, poured out. Henny clucked soothingly and listened to every word. An hour passed before Roselynne ran out of complaints.

"I have bored you dreadfully," she apologized.

"Nay, I love to talk with ye," Henny protested. "Will ye come again next week?"

"I'd love to." She checked the clock on the mantle. "I have some chores yet to do. I'm visiting each of the tenants and learning their names and family members. All seems in good order."

"Uh, one thing," Henny said, leaning across the table and speaking in a whisper. "Ye might keep an eye on the housekeeper. I've 'eard she's a bit queerlike. Don't know in what way, but she might be crazy as a coot."

"I'll be careful. Thank you so much for a pleasant afternoon." She tucked the posy holder into her bodice. "I love the posy and will cherish it always."

She embraced her friend and said goodbye. Jim and Sanders were sitting at a table right outside the door. Leaning on the counter was a familiar masculine figure.

"Ready to go?" True asked, turning when she appeared.

"Where?" The posy holder burned between her breasts.

"Home, of course." His grin mocked her.

She ignored him. "My horse, please," she requested. Jim rushed to obey while Sanders checked the front yard to make sure no unknown assailants lurked about.

"All safe, m'lady," he called.

She started out.

Steps sounded right behind her, and True said for her ears alone, "I wouldn't be too certain of that."

From the parlor doorway, Henny laughed. "The devil be after ye, ducks." She grinned at True when he glanced her way.

Roselynne picked up her skirts and fled.

There was no getting away from the man. He stuck to her side like a burr, reining in his great black beast to the slower pace she set for her mare, Athene, which he'd looked over before she'd left the house that afternoon.

"Does she meet with your approval?" she'd asked sarcastically.

Beau's cousin had cupped his hands and hefted her into the saddle, then stepped back, pushed his hat up his forehead and grinned at her. "The ride will be gentle," he'd said.

Remembering the look in his eyes as he'd said those innocent words caused a tingle to race along her insides. His thoughts had been far from innocent, and a ride with him would be far from gentle. She was instantly appalled at her own thoughts.

Her mind had a will of its own. At night she dreamed haunting dreams, filled with longing. Always she saw blue eyes, but she could never tell if her dream lover's hair was black or blond. It was maddening.

She rubbed her brow, weary of her wayward thoughts. There were important tasks ahead of her. She must concentrate on those.

"Are you all right?"

His deep blue gaze held her eyes a second before she forced hers away. There'd been no mockery in his eyes or voice, only a gentle concern that disconcerted her as much as his presence did.

"Yes, thank you, Cousin True." She insisted on calling him by the title to remind her there was kinship and nothing more between them. "I have some stops to make on the way. Jim and Sanders will accompany me."

"I don't mind the ride," he said. "The weather is pleasant for it."

"I should think you'd be tired after your outing with Lady Stanton this morning," she said waspishly and immediately regretted the words, though her statement was true. He and Thea had ridden off and not returned until lunch, four hours later.

"It takes a lot to tire me," he countered in lazy tones.

She said no more. He was obviously determined not to quarrel with her...for a change.

The black stallion edged closer to Athene, prancing a bit. The rascal was flirting with the mare. Had Roselynne been in better humor, she would have laughed.

The pair did look well together, she admitted. The glossy black of the stallion contrasted beautifully with the silver coat of the mare. Both wielded the proud bearing of the thorough-bred.

When the stallion snorted and shook his head, one eye on the mare, Beau laughed and slapped the animal's neck. "None of that, old son. We have to stay alert." His tone implied understanding and great sympathy with the stallion's plight.

While they rode, she noted Beau's eyes never rested at one place long. He was vigilant, as if testing the air for danger the way a forest creature might. It came of living in the wilds, she thought, and wondered how it would be to go on a grand adventure to Virginia.

Putting aside her problems with her guest, she visited two tenant families in the neighborhood, learning much of the gossip around the parish from them. Her companion was surprisingly helpful in that regard. Later, they stopped by Vicar Smith-Warren's house to rest and water the horses on the way home.

The vicar was working in his garden, his shirtsleeves rolled up and his coat off. "Countess, I'm delighted to see you again," he called. "Come have a cup of cold spring water. Your horses will be needing a drink, too. A body could dehydrate, it's that warm today."

He pulled down his sleeves and replaced his coat before opening the gate and striding forward. His keen gaze studied her companion with interest, as he'd done the day of her picnic.

"You have the look of the St. Clairs," the vicar declared.

"He is kin from the distaff side," she said.

"Hmm, the eyes—"

"Beau's mother had blue eyes, as did mine," True explained. He glanced at the garden. "The harvest looks bountiful this year."

"Yes, a good year once the weather warmed. Come rest in the shade and we'll see about that drink. You men might talk cook out of a fried pie," he told the two servants.

Roselynne had no choice but to let True help her dismount, his hands hot and tingly at her waist. Jim and Sanders led the horses to the back of the vicarage while the pastor motioned the couple to follow him.

She and True took chairs under an apple tree while their host fetched cool drinks. After they'd quenched their thirst, Cousin True talked of America to the pastor. He assured the older gent that Indians didn't raid in Virginia anymore.

The cook hurried out before they left and presented the guests with a packet. "A bit of a sweet for your supper."

"Thank you." Roselynne gave her and the pastor a brilliant smile. Their simple kindness reminded her of her old home.

The gloaming cast a soft, buttery light over the fields and forest as her ensemble started toward Rockdale.

"I'd like to visit the graveyard before we return," she said, gazing at the headstones on the next rise.

Her escort frowned, but instead of refusing, he nodded. "You two may go to the house. The countess and I shall be there within the hour. If we're not, come looking."

"Aye, sir," the men chorused and rode ahead while she and Cousin True reined their horses toward the cemetery. It was the strangest thing—even her own servants obeyed him without question.

Roselynne was surprised that he'd approved the side trip. This dictatorial cousin seemed to feel it was his duty to take over the guardianship of her. He was even more protective than George, who'd driven her to madness with his caution.

She'd come to look upon George as kin, almost a brother, but this cousin—she stole a glance at him—didn't fit any comfortable niche in her life that she could find.

"Why did you agree?" she asked.

"I wanted to be alone with you."

The blunt answer, delivered without inflection or emotion, caused her to tighten the reins. The mare pranced sideways.

"Easy, girl," he crooned, patting the animal's neck. The black stallion rolled its eyes back at them. Cousin True patted his neck, too.

A tremor started deep inside her and gradually spread outward. "I'm a married woman." It was her only defense.

"A widow," he corrected.

"No—"

"Then why the mourning weeds? Beau wouldn't have wanted you to wear black. Soft colors become you better."

"You are too personal."

"Au contraire," he replied in a soft voice.

He dismounted and helped her down. She smoothed her skirt and tried to still the trembling that grew worse with every breath. It had been foolish to stop. She spied the cook's gift.

"The pastries," she said. "I do love them. Shall we have them now?" Quickly, she unhooked the string from the saddle and opened the oiled paper. Two golden brown, crusty fried pies nestled within. "Here, one for you and one for me."

She was acting like a ninny. She plopped down on a small marble bench, spreading her skirt so he couldn't join her, and nibbled on the treat.

He brushed her skirt aside and sat beside her, his legs on the opposite side of the bench. They ate in silence. When she finished, he handed his handkerchief to her to wipe her mouth and fingers, then he used it, his mouth touching where hers had been.

A strange ache attacked her insides. "I suppose we'd better go." She spoke in a whisper.

"Why are you afraid of me?" His dark blue gaze seemed to drill a hole right through her poise.

She fought for composure. A vicar's daughter faced all situations with compassion and dignity, she recalled from her mother's teachings. But he didn't play fair.

His leg pressed her thigh when he swiveled to face her. "Why does my presence upset you?"

"You are mistaken."

"No." He leaned nearer. "I think it is because of this."

His hands closed on her arms and he drew her closer . . . closer.

At the last moment, she sprang up. "I wanted to see the Rockdale gravestones." She hurried to the iron gates set within a marble archway. A stone fence surrounded the area.

The mechanism was rusty, and she couldn't move the latch. He opened the portals for her, and they entered.

"Look, the earls are placed in order. Here's the first and here's the last." She pointed out the obvious fact.

"Except for Cousin Beau," True said, stopping behind her.

She turned to face him. "Do you think him dead?"

He hesitated. "What do you think?"

"Answer," she cried. "I asked you first. Do you think I'm a wife or a widow?"

His smile was strained. "I know what I'd like you to be."

She spun away from him and clenched a hand on the cold stone of the fence. "I can't abide this uncertainty. If he lives, why doesn't he come for me? Doesn't he realize I need him?"

"Why?" True joined her and placed his hands on her shoulders. "Why do you need him?"

She shook her head, unwilling to confess herself a woman of uncontrollable impulses. She'd not put that knowledge in his grasp. It was enough that *she* knew how disreputable she was.

They stood without speaking, and slowly his touch turned into a caress. At first only his fingers moved, working the tight muscles of her neck and shoulders. She dropped her head forward in despair. His touch . . . oh, his touch.

After a long while, his hands glided to her arms and brushed up and down, finally settling at her waist. He massaged her there.

She felt his breath fan her neck—ahh, so warm—as he leaned forward and whispered, "A woman is soft here, boneless. Her ribs end above." He showed her. "And her hips begin lower." He swept down and cupped his hands over her hipbones for a second before returning to her waist. "A man likes to touch the soft places."

He kneaded her there for a long time, in the space between her ribs and hips, and her body reminded her of other soft places that wanted to be stroked.

She tried to gather her thoughts, to move away from his tender assault, but she couldn't command her limbs.

A sob rose to her throat and her breath labored between parted lips. Her lashes dipped closed without her volition. She clenched her skirt in nervous desperation as the strange wildness ran like sun showers over her.

His hands became still. She held her breath. Then, with excruciating slowness, they began to move, climbing her ribs,
their touch gentle, until they hovered below her breasts.

Lightning flashed through her, and she couldn't move.

"Roselynne," he whispered. "I can't stand it. I
thought...but it's no use...'tis more than mortal man can take.
I shouldn't...I must...God, I want you. Now!" He pulled
her against the hard tumescence of his desire and pressed his
lips hotly against her neck.

"Nay!" she cried, fighting them both.

She must be the most depraved of all creatures. This man
made her furious. He criticized her for the smallest thing. He
dangled on Thea's every word, played servant to her every
whim, yet his gaze, when he looked *her* way, burned with tantalizing flames, inviting her to throw herself into the inferno
of his desire. And, heaven help her, she wanted to.

With a mighty effort, she tore herself from him and ran for
the gate. He followed more slowly, his expression impossible
to read. "I think we'd better go," she managed to utter, her
eyes lowered in shame at her conduct.

"Aye," he said.

She had to accept his assistance in mounting, but once in the
saddle, she moved off swiftly, needing distance from him.

He soon caught up. She spurred the mare, and Athene, eager for a race, stretched into a run. The stallion trumpeted and
accepted the challenge.

Roselynne leaned forward in the saddle as emotion poured
forth from some untamed place inside her. She would be free
of him. She would leave him and the confusion he wrought in
her far behind.

The wind rushed past her ears and tears collected at the
corners of her eyes as they raced up the hill. The stallion came
alongside as they crested and plunged down the nether side into
the twilight world of shadows.

Side by side the black and silver horses ran, like two couri-
ers of the gods on an important and dangerous mission. A
hand reached for her bridle, and Roselynne turned Athene's
head, evading True's grasp. She raced off the road and across
the meadow.

Behind her, she heard him shout. She paid no heed. To flee
was to be free of the guilt and doubt and torment that had
haunted her from the moment she'd laid eyes on him. He be-
witched her, made her long for things she little comprehended. She had to go, for honor's sake.

When she heard the stallion's pounding hooves closing the
distance between them, she urged Athene faster... faster. He
shouted again, and she shook her head, denying the warning
in his voice that told her to stop, that she was being foolish.

The path narrowed, taking a sharp turn through the forest.
Tree branches lashed her sides and snagged on her clothing.
Still she fled. Suddenly the sharp scent of the sea hit her nos-
trils. The cliff. She'd forgotten the cliff.

Instinctively she yanked back on the reins, rising in the stir-
rups as she fought to keep the mare from plunging over the
abyss that opened in front of them.

Time slowed. Behind her, she heard her companion curse,
and she wondered if he could stop before running them over.
Athene reared and twisted to the side. Roselynne saw black
hooves strike the air beside her head as the stallion did the
same. She knew they were going to fall in a tangle of thrashing legs and hooves, that she and True would be crushed under the heaving weight of the horses. She kicked her feet free
and prepared to jump.

Suddenly an arm flung itself around her waist, and a hard
chest crashed into her shoulder, sending her spinning through
the air—forever, it seemed—until she landed on a bed of pine
needles and grass, her skirts up and her limbs tangled with
masculine ones. She and True lay there for several seconds.

"Are you all right?" he asked when they'd regained their
breath.

"Yes," she said. "The horses?"

She peered over his shoulder as he twisted his head to check.
Both animals were winded, but they stood on all four legs. The
black blew gustily and rubbed noses with Athene.

"They appear to have survived." He turned his piercing blue
gaze on her.

Roselynne pulled her riding skirt from beneath him and sat
up. No sharp jolts of pain stopped her movements. She stood.

"Why didn't you stop when I yelled?" he asked. His mouth was grim, as if he held fury in check.

From the corner of her eye, she saw his hands clench, relax, clench again. She couldn't explain she was fleeing from her own wanton desires as much as from his.

"Roselynne," he said, impatience creeping in.

"Athene was restless. She needed a good run." She shook back the tangle of hair about her face and defied him to question her further. "I had forgotten about the cliff."

He reached for her. She flinched, then bit her lip as a scowl darkened his brow.

"Do you think I'd hurt you?" he demanded, letting his arms drop to his sides and stepping back from her.

"Yes," she said, helpless to deny it. "Yes."

He said no more, but looked at her with such an expression of outraged male pride she couldn't bear it. She turned away.

He placed her on her mount once more, ordered her to wait and swung up onto the black. Leading the way, he took her home. She left him at the stable, instructing the boy on cooling the horses.

Roselynne found her father in the garden, sitting in a cane chair and watching the sky with interest. He didn't move or look down when she flung herself on the grass and laid her head on her arms across his knees.

"Oh, Father, I need your help. I am lost and drowning and frightened. I don't know myself anymore. What happened to the person I once was? Please, help me."

He lifted a lock of her hair and rubbed it between his fingers, then, very gently, he smoothed it into the tumbled curls and patted her head. They stayed that way until Ansella called her to dress for supper.

Beau watched the scene below his window with a scowl on his face. He should be horsewhipped. He knew it. He'd taken her by surprise and force—not the force of strength, but that of gentleness—and would have made love to her right there on the wall next to the entire line of his ancestors if she hadn't stopped him.

He was a scoundrel. Nay, he was worse. He'd taken advantage of her inexperience and confusion, and had frightened her with his need.

She didn't understand passion. She didn't know how it could overpower the most pious of good intentions. Look at all the saints that had fallen victim to it.

He heaved a deep breath of disgust with himself. He'd made her miserable and unhappy when all he'd wanted was to protect her from harm. A whipping wasn't strong enough. A flogging was the proper punishment.

Another thought, very human, intruded: *He'd do it again as soon as he got the chance.*

His wife had yet to be fulfilled, and he ached to show her how good it could be between a man and a woman. He wanted to teach her the glorious art of seduction.

It was so damned obvious that he made her nervous, that she was *attracted* to him, *wanted* him as much as he wanted her. He couldn't resist both their longing. It wasn't humanly possible. So there'd be a next time.

He ground out a low curse. Leaning out the window, he spoke to the old man who was now standing directly below him. "Your daughter, sir, is driving me to Bedlam. Aye," he said when her father gazed up at him with a blank stare. "I want her. She's mine to take by rights. She wants me, too. Not me as her husband, but me as his cousin."

Mr. Moreley nodded as if he understood.

"Sir," Beau said gravely, "I wonder if any other man has faced this dilemma. I want her to yield to me, yet I want her to be true to my memory."

Mr. Moreley coughed politely into his hand and ambled off a few feet to sniff a late rose.

Beau continued his monologue. "Only George and Clayburgh know my identity. If I were to return to America as Cousin True, leaving all to think Beau died, she would truly have her freedom."

Beau poured a stiff drink of brandy and swallowed it down. He gulped down another and returned to the open window.

"I don't know if I can do that. To leave her... 'Twould be the honorable thing to do. Yet, she does want me... Nay, she wants True." He frowned and pressed a hand to his brow.

"Why isn't she afraid of him as she was of me? I was the soul of patience with her in Newgate, as gentle as a shepherd with a newborn lamb each time we met . . . well, nearly each time."

Mr. Moreley gazed up at him.

"Sir," Beau said. "The truth is . . . I am jealous of my-self!"

Chapter Fourteen

Roselynne moved the embroidery hoop to the next flower of the doily and selected a pink thread for the rose. Her father rested near her. Lady Stanton sat at the pianoforte and listlessly played some popular airs. The men—True, William, George and Clayburgh—played whist at a game table of inlaid rosewood on walnut.

When her thread snapped for the third time, Roselynne gave a silent exclamation of irritation and returned the work to her sewing bag. After a glance assured her the others were busy with their affairs, she slipped out onto the terrace and closed the doors behind her.

The night breeze tugged at her shawl, and she wrapped it more closely around her. Less than a week remained of August. Soon the nights would turn cold as fall, then winter would settle upon them. She wondered what a change of season would bring. Perhaps an end to guessing and—

The doors opened and closed silently.

She squeezed into a corner of the wall, but he caught sight of her anyway. Cousin True walked over.

"Are you tired of our company?" he asked.

His voice was low and vibrant, setting up a resonance inside her that hadn't lessened with familiarity. It strummed deep in her now, stirring notes better left unsung.

"I wanted some air and a bit of quiet."

He chuckled. "You've had that all evening. I think Thea is put out with our absorption in the cards. We've neglected you ladies shamelessly."

"Not at all. I'm glad you find amusements for yourselves."

"You are inclined to solitude, I think," he mused. "Was your childhood lonely?"

"Why, no. My parents called upon the parishioners regularly and took me along."

"But was it a happy life?"

"Yes."

"So was mine. My sisters could vex me at times, but mostly I was happy."

"Until the war," she said.

"Aye." The quiet of his voice spoke of sorrows he couldn't express. "Being here with you and your guests reminds me of times in my youth when my mother sewed and my sisters played music while we sang. When I was a boy, my father dawdled me upon his knee and told me stories of sailing ships and faraway places. I miss them."

Her heart ached for the simple picture he painted. "It was the same for me," she told him.

"I wish nothing better than to have a family of my own one day, and a babe to hold on my knee."

Her heart clenched into a fist in her chest. To be done with the uncertainty of her present situation, to share a home, to bear a beloved husband's child—those were the things she wanted.

He took her arm, and they began to walk along the terrace. "My cousin liked children. Is there a chance that you will give him an heir?"

His hand tightened on her elbow, and the entire night seemed to become still, awaiting her answer. "There is no child," she said.

He made a sound, like that of a quick drawn breath, then he sighed. After a minute, he said, "You sound sad. Did you want it otherwise?" He stopped and studied her face in the moonlight.

"Yes. I, too, want a family."

He smiled. "Then that is something to look forward to, isn't it?" he asked. There was an unmistakable tenderness in his voice.

A child, she thought. His child. He would be a tender father. She suddenly wished...

No, she dare not admit it. Nay, she could not. But the thought wouldn't go away. She wanted his child. She wanted him for her husband. She wanted to share her life with him.

Dear heaven, she was in love with him!

Panic washed over her. She mustn't love him. It would be the height of folly to allow such a thing.

"You're trembling," he murmured, bringing her closer. "Are you all right?"

No. "Yes," she managed to whisper. "I think..."

Just as she was about to suggest they return, he stepped in front of her. Taking her hand in his and laying his other hand at her waist, he began to dance to the faint melody Thea was playing.

"I've wanted to dance with you for a long time," he murmured.

They turned around and around in the moonlight, stepping forward and back, forward and back. They were a couple on a music box, destined forever to go around and around, never speaking, never touching more than this. The thought was unbearable.

After another moment, he stopped and escorted her back inside the manor house. "Are you sure you're all right?" he asked, peering at her in the stronger light.

"I'm tired. I think I will go up now." She called good-night to her guests and made her way upstairs. Jim was in the hall, trimming a lamp.

"Good night, m'lady," he said.

"Good night." She went inside, closed the door and leaned wearily against it. Love wasn't at all what she'd thought it would be. She'd expected delight; she'd found uncertainty and an ache that wouldn't go away.

Roselynne watched the dawn from her window. Later, from the solar, she saw Cousin True and Lady Stanton gallop across the pasture on a pursuit of their own. She barely listened while William read to her from *The Tragedy of Julius Caesar*, although he had a fine voice. Antony's funeral oration caught her attention.

"But Brutus was an honorable man," William declaimed.

When he got to the part about the "unkindest cut of all," she was in full sympathy with the slain Caesar. Cousin True plied his attentions zealously to Thea, but when he was alone with *her*, he looked at her with such yearning, she was shaken.

But she hadn't much experience with men. He probably acted as all rakes did, ogling every female in sight. She'd not give him another thought, she decided, and immediately recalled his remarks about having a family and children. Oh, he was too unpredictable! One minute tender, another ardent...and then, off and running after Thea. Nay, she didn't understand him at all.

"I have an errand in the village," William said. "Would you accompany me? We could take your father for an outing."

"I have to see to my house," she said, giving him a kind smile when he looked disappointed.

"I shall invite Mr. Moreley and Connie to keep me company," he declared, earning her gratitude. "It's a fine day. Let's walk along the shore when we've finished our chores."

"That would be lovely."

When those three left, she went in search of George and Mr. Clayburgh. They were in the counting room, going over the estate rents and tenant farms.

"Ho, come in," George invited. "We're almost through with the accounting. You'll owe the king a tidy sum in death taxes, but never fear, you still have much wealth."

"Do we pay the taxes before we have proof of my husband's death?" she asked.

"Is there a reason to wait?" Clayburgh asked, his keen gaze piercing hers as if to ferret out any information she hid.

She rubbed her temples with her fingertips. "I don't know. I know he must be...gone...yet I cannot give up hope."

George came to her and dropped a comforting arm about her shoulder. "Don't be unhappy. All will come about."

"How?" she asked. "When?"

He shrugged and returned to the ledgers spread over the oak counting table.

"I will delay the payment of the taxes as long as possible," the barrister assured her. "We'll give St. Clair every chance of appearing."

"But if he appears, he'll be hanged," she reminded them.

Clayburgh smiled. "A contretemps that might be described as being caught between the hare and the hound."

She thought his humor ill-mannered. "I must go over the household accounts with Mrs. Hunson." She selected the ledgers and went to the library. The rest of the morning she spent with the butler, the housekeeper and finally the cook, until all details were planned and in order for the week.

Stretching her tired back, she returned the books to the counting room and went to her chamber. After washing her hands and smoothing her hair, she drifted out to the solar balcony. A very provocative, very feminine giggle assaulted her ears, followed by a very deep, very masculine chuckle.

Cousin True and Lady Stanton were in the garden.

On slippered feet, feeling like an interloper, she edged to the railing and peered down. Cousin True had a rose in his hand. Its flame red color contrasted favorably with the pale shade of Thea's bosom as he drew the petals along the scalloped bodice. The lady had discarded her fichu—or her companion had removed it.

Roselynne's first impulse was to flee, but nay, this was her balcony, her gardens. If the lascivious couple sported in public, then they had only themselves to blame if they were noticed. She'd not be driven indoors.

But when Thea lifted her face and wet her rouged lips, when Cousin True bent lower over her, tucked the flower between those mounding breasts and lingered only inches from the waiting lips, Roselynne retreated toward the solar, unable to look.

Passing under the trellis supporting a climbing rose she spied a large green caterpillar munching away on a leaf. She glared at the smug creature steadily destroying the plant, and without further thought, grabbed it between finger and thumb and, turning, flung it over the balcony.

"Aiiiieee!"

Roselynne froze.

"Here, be still. I'll get it. It's slipped down . . . stop squirming . . . Dammit, Thea, be still. I don't want to crush it inside your dress."

"Hurry," Thea screeched.

"I've got it. See, it's nothing but a harmless caterpillar, interrupted during his lunch. I'll put him on this shrub."

"Ugh, let's go inside."

Roselynne heard a rustle of skirts and quick steps on the flag stones. She released her breath. She crept back to the edge and looked over.

Cousin True grinned up at her. "A direct hit, Cousin."

Heat flooded her face. "I didn't..." she began, but couldn't push the lie past her lips. "It was an accident. I found it on the rose and..."

"And removed it. Very commendable," he said with a solemn nod. "It's a rare woman who isn't afraid of worms and such."

Telling her he'd see her at lunch, he disappeared from her view, a smug glint in his eyes. She clenched her fists. If he thought she'd done that only to interrupt their kiss, he could think again! At lunch, she was very kind to Lady Stanton and very cool to the men.

"One moment," Lady Stanton said. "I think I have a stone in my shoe."

Beau's smile hid his annoyance when the others of their party disappeared around the curve of the path. "Sit on this boulder, and I'll remove it." He unfastened her slipper and shook it out, then replaced it on her silk-clad foot.

"Thank you, sir. You are a true gallant." She smiled at him and let herself lean forward until their lips almost touched.

"Come, we'd best hurry before they come looking."

Thea pouted. "There's never a moment alone in this group. Why don't we go for a ride later, just the two of us?" She ran a nail down his cheek and tapped him on the chin. "I'd like to talk to you without interruption. Perhaps—"

"Ready?"

He cut her off before she could suggest he come to her room. He was fast running out of excuses not to be alone with her. The frustration mounted until he wanted to hit something. He was getting nowhere, either with the investigation or with Roselynne.

A frown marred his brow as he pulled Thea to her feet and set off down the path after the others, anxious to catch up and keep an eye on his wife.

Roselynne. Something was wrong there. She seemed pale and distracted of late. Rarely did she smile, and never at him. He'd been his most charming with her. When that had failed, he'd paid more attention to Thea. Jealousy didn't work, either.

Except in his case. He was damned jealous of the time she permitted George and William and Clayburgh to spend in her company, but it seemed she rarely had a minute for him.

He was beginning to think this whole thing a nightmare, that he had killed his cousin himself in some fit of greed and couldn't remember the deed. Not one single clue had surfaced to indicate someone else, and he was the only benefactor of his cousin's death.

He and Thea caught up with William and Roselynne in time to see William peering intently into her eye. With the corner of his handkerchief, he wiped out a cinder.

"There, is that better?" he asked.

Roselynne blinked several times. "Yes. Thank you, Cousin." She turned to the laggards. "There you are. We've decided to return to the house for an early lunch and go riding this afternoon. Will you join us?"

Beau noticed the annoyed scowl cross William's brow. So he'd wanted Roselynne to himself. Too bad. With a satisfied smile he started to agree, but Thea cut in.

"I need to go to the village. True has agreed to accompany me. We'll probably take tea at the inn."

"Why don't you join us?" Beau inserted, determined not to leave his wife with the person he looked upon as his rival. He ignored Thea's quick frown and gazed at Roselynne.

She hesitated just a fraction too long to sound casual. "I think not. I want to take tea with Father."

"We would get back in time," Beau said, his jaw stubborn.

"Then I suppose we can," she said, not meeting his eyes.

George and Clayburgh, who were inspecting the monthly records of the overseer of the rents, joined them for lunch and agreed to the outing. Later, while the others were changing, Beau went to the stable to check the horses.

The stable lad had six animals saddled and ready in the near paddock. Beau inspected Athene's girth and bridle. It was in good repair. With time on his hands, he idly ran his fingers over the black's girth ring, feeling the corded rope attached to it.

All at once, he realized the threads were fuzzy instead of smooth. He looked. Two cords were worn through. With a curse, he shouted for the stableboy and groom.

A few minutes later, a chastened groom stood in front of Beau, his head downcast. "Won't happen again, sir, my word," he said when Beau demanded to know why the tack hadn't been checked and repaired.

"It better not, or you'll be gone." Beau stalked off, his anger unabated.

If that had been the girth on Roselynne's saddle, she could have had a nasty fall; however, he was sure if there was mischief afoot, it was directed at himself. The girth knots could have been frayed by hand if a person was skilled with a knife.

A chill settled on his soul, and he had a sense of time drawing in, of events coming to a close. He'd be glad when it did.

Roselynne had no heart for the outing, but as hostess, she felt she had to do her duty. A vicar's family often had unpleasant tasks to perform, and she placed this in the same category.

George rode to her right and slightly ahead of the party, his gaze moving constantly over the land. William stayed close on her left, while Cousin True, Thea and Clayburgh laughed and talked behind them.

The black stallion was being fractious today, and she heard Thea exclaim when he took a nip at her gelding. Then the beast bounded up, pushing between Athene and William's horse, his teeth bared at the other stallion. William's steed decided the best defense was to fall back. With a proud shake of his head, the black took his place next to the silver mare.

"Now are you happy?" Cousin True demanded of his mount. The horse tossed his mane and sidled closer to the mare. True's leg brushed Roselynne's skirt. "Ease off, you great oaf," he scolded.

Roselynne ignored the laughter in True's eyes when he gave her an oblique glance. His gaze ran over her too freely, causing heat to suffuse her skin. She clenched her hand on the reins and stared at George, who had moved to the front.

After a mile in silence, Cousin True began to sing:

"There was a girl named Nelly
Fair as a hog's belly
Who lived in a town not far from my home.
Sixteen was our Nelly
When a sailor from Penselly
Stopped at the port; his eye, it did roam.
Hey-de-lie, Hey-de-lee
Who did he spy but our sweet Nelly?"

True turned in the saddle. "William," he said.
It was William's turn to make up a verse.

"The sailor was John Finn
With a heart black as sin
He'd love the lasses and leave them to cry.
Our Nelly had no schooling
But she wasn't fooling
When she said she with no sailor would ever lie.
Hey-de-lie, Hey-de-lee
Finn got nowhere with our fair Nelly."

William pointed to Clayburgh.

The song went from the barrister to Thea to George. Each added to the merry but unsuccessful chase of Nelly by Finn. George gave the nod to Roselynne.

"Nelly's refusal
Had Finn all a-skew-sal
It was her nays that did in our boy.
Upon my life
I'll take you to wife
You'll be my own, my pride and joy.
Hey-de-lie, Hey-de-lee
Finn at last won the fair Nelly."

The men hooted at this sentimental ending. Thea took up the cudgel for wary maidens. "You men would ever despoil us poor women and go on your merry ways were we not careful," she scolded, her darkened lashes used to effect on William and Clayburgh. "Nelly was right to hold out for marriage."

"Nelly must have been a vicar's daughter," Cousin True teased, his voice low as he leaned toward Roselynne.

She felt the warmth of his gaze and tried to harden her wildly beating heart against his attraction. "Perhaps."

"And as hard-hearted as another I could name toward us poor languishing males."

At her wronged glance, he murmured, "I meant Athene. See how she disregards the black's attentions?"

As if to disprove him, the mare nipped at the stallion in a show of irritation at his persistent nudges. The stallion drew back in surprise, then he nuzzled Athene's ear, not in the least put down. Cousin True laughed uproariously as Roselynne grimaced. Both she and Athene were taunted by outrageous males.

At that moment, a shot rang out from the woods and Clayburgh's hat went flying. Beau instinctively positioned himself between Roselynne and the direction of the shot. George, with a savage yell, rode toward the trees, his body flat against his mount.

"Guard her," Beau commanded Clayburgh before he followed George.

In the woods, they caught up with the culprit easily. The man was on foot, the pistol in his hand. "Eh, wot is this? Let me go, damme. Let me go."

George held the man by the hair. Beau leaped from his horse and took the pistol. He trained his own gun on the man.

"I ain't got no money," the man whined.

"What the hell do you mean, firing at us?" Beau demanded.

The man's eyes widened. "I didn't shoot at nobody. 'Twas a varmit, a fox wot had been in the henhouse. When he jumped on the log there, I fired afore he could leap down." He tried to peer around Beau. "Did I get him?"

"You missed," Beau said dryly. He stepped back a pace and lowered the gun from the man's forehead, but kept it at the ready. He glanced at George.

George shrugged. The story could be true.

"What's your name and where do you live?" Beau asked.

"Harry Connor, I am, a gamesman for the squire."

Beau questioned him further, but he stuck to his story. "All right, Harry Connor, I'll accept your story, but if I ever catch you with a gun pointed in my direction again, you'll not live to tell of it. You understand what I'm saying?"

"Aye, govner. It'll not happen again." The man was shaking.

"Let's go," Beau said. He handed the pistol to the gamesman, then he and George turned back.

William and Clayburgh had moved the two women to a copse of trees and stood guard in front of them. Beau waved to them that it was safe to resume the journey. The men put their weapons away and returned to the road.

"It was but a gamekeeper, firing at a fox, he said," George explained to the waiting group.

"The man ruined my favorite hat," Clayburgh complained ruefully. "You should have shook a shilling or two out of him to pay for the deed."

"I was never so frightened in my life," Thea exclaimed.

"Are you all right?" Beau asked, reining in beside Roselynne. She looked pale but composed.

"I'm fine," she said. "I wasn't frightened." Her eyes ran over him with a worried frown in them.

She'd been concerned for him, he realized. He felt a swelling sensation in his chest, as if his heart had doubled its size. If only they were alone. He wanted to touch her, to hold her, to kiss her until her lips bloomed like roses beneath his.

"Roselynne," he said on a ragged breath.

She glanced at him and quickly turned away. Her paleness receded as a blush spread into her cheeks. "Don't. Please." She spurred Athene into a trot.

Beau stayed at her side, his visage grim, his eyes watchful as they rode into the village and stopped at the inn. Henny came out to greet them.

"Coo, ye must-a smelled the custards, just out o' the oven, they are, and fresh peaches just peeled and sugared. Come into the parlor and I'll serve ye."

She led the way and soon had the table set with bowls of fresh custard and sliced peaches. A pot of tea was set before Roselynne and coffee before Thea for the women to pour.

"Excuse me," Beau said and went into the main room. "Henny," he called, loud enough for the others to hear. "Where's the necessary?"

"Out back. T'other side o' the stable. I need a jug o' cream from the spring house. Come, I'll show ye the way."

He followed her out the door. Once away from the open windows of the inn, he asked, "Any news?"

"Lady Stanton is in need o' money. The creditors be after 'er. They say she's looking for a rich 'usband, for she's already gone through the fortune o' the last."

Beau frowned. "I don't know about that. She's after me, but I've given no information on my finances."

"Mayhap she knows who ye are." Henny gave him a shrewd glance from under her lashes. Her blue eyes gleamed with sly amusement.

He grinned. "You've guessed."

"Nay. I thought so from the first moment I laid eyes on ye, when ye insisted I take the posy holder for the countess. Then when I saw ye look at 'er, I knew. Ye care for the lass."

"She's my wife, so naturally I care for her." A scowl passed over his face. "I'm worried that she'll be hurt. I forced her into marriage, knowing she couldn't refuse after I bought their freedom, and put her into danger." He told of the shooting.

"I know the man. Shifty-eyed and smelly, with reddish brown hair and rabbit teeth."

"That's the one. Do you know something of him?"

"Only that 'e tries to catch me eye." She spat into the dust.

Beau chuckled and patted her rounded behind. "All men do that. If I wasn't a married man, I'd try myself."

"Go on with ye." She gave him a push. "Oh, one other thing. A servant from the Stanton 'ouse says, well, the lawyer 'as been there with the lady. They, uh, was alone for a spell, and after 'e left, she paid their wages afore going back to your place."

"What?" Beau said, a yelp of surprise.

"That's what she said. I don't know the truth o' it."

His face darkened with rage. "There seems to be treachery in every quarter. I'll have to watch Thea more closely." He thought furiously for several minutes. "Spinner's been hanging around Roselynne like a fox after a hen. George never trusted the man, thinks he may have set me up for the killing of my cousin. Perhaps we were looking at the most obvious suspect."

"Would 'e get the estate?"

"Nay. All goes to Roselynne but the title."

"Well, no wonder 'e dangles after 'er. The sweet innocent. She'd never suspect deception." Henny studied Beau. "She's taken with ye, but it'll wound 'er to know ye've not trusted 'er."

"She's no actress. She might give away the ploy."

Henny shrugged. "No one likes being made the fool. Ye'll 'ave to win 'er forgiveness when all this is over. And 'er trust."

"I will," he said.

Henny smiled. "Ye're cocky, lad. The countess might not forgive so easy." At his fierce glance, she added, "But I've no doubt ye'll prevail." She pointed out the outhouse and went on her way to the spring.

When Beau returned to the parlor, he found his place occupied by William. Hiding his anger, he dropped into the chair next to Thea. Across the table, the barrister watched the group with hooded eyes. Beau realized Roselynne might not be the only innocent. Perhaps he'd placed his trust too easily by confiding in his wily lawyer.

Roselynne laughed at a quip from William, and Beau looked at her. His heart gave a leap in his chest. A feeling, both an ache and a joy, assailed him. He considered his desire for Roselynne and compared it to what he'd felt for Mary.

His passion for his fiancée had been different. It had been tempered by the gentleness of his love. Mary had stirred a caring, affectionate warmth inside him, making him want to be tender with her, careful of her feelings.

His wife also stirred tenderness in him, but of a different nature. It was fiery and primitive in its intensity. He wanted her with a fierceness that made him tremble when he held her and with a possessiveness that staggered him at the thought of giving her up.

A sense of danger overrode the other feelings, and he worried for her safety. Damn, but life was a tangled mess.

After Thea purchased a length of ribbon, they returned to the Rockdale manor. Roselynne was relieved when they arrived. She gave orders for a late tea and found Rodney Witherspoon ensconced in the drawing room, waiting their return.

"I say, I'm glad to see you," he exclaimed, bowing over Roselynne's hand and trying to kiss it.

She withdrew gracefully before he could press his lips to the back of her hand. "How nice to see you. Have you been served?"

"Yes." He indicated the glass of wine on the table and a decanter that had been nearly drained. "What I wanted to say was, the thing is, my father's decided to hold a musical next week. I wanted to tell you myself." He removed the invitation from his pocket and handed it to her with a flourish. "You're all invited."

"That's very kind. I think I must decline. I'm in mourning and it wouldn't be seemly. My guests can speak for themselves."

There was a chorus of protests. "If you won't go, then none of us will," William declared.

"There's no need to sit in sackcloth and ashes," Cousin True interrupted, his lazy drawl becoming crisp and stern when he reprimanded her.

Roselynne thought he looked remarkably like Beau with his lips thinned into a hard line and a frown tucked between his eyes. In fact, if he had had dark hair and a beard, they could have passed for twins.

She was attacked by a sudden dizziness and pressed her fingers to her temples to halt the painful rush of blood through her head. Sometimes she felt so odd, as if she were on the brink of some great truth that barely eluded her.

"Does your head hurt?" Cousin True asked.

"A little." She stepped back from his nearness.

"I think you should go to the musical," he continued. "Take your father. It might tweak his mind. You said he liked music."

"Oh, I hadn't thought of that." She dropped her hands and turned to Rodney with a smile. "We must all go or all decline, it seems, so you may count on our presence. If you've the time, I'll pen a note to your father."

"I say, that's good news. Company is sparse this year what with the duke gone to India or some wild place and the king having one of his spells. The royal prince is at Bath rather than Brighton this year. Have you heard the latest?"

Rodney related the gossip he'd recently heard and stayed for supper, although it was quite late due to the treat they'd had at the inn. They played guessing games until it was nigh on to midnight and much too late for her guest to go home. She invited him to stay for the night.

Finally she could retire to her chamber. Weariness produced a lethargy to her movements as Ansella helped her out of her dress and into her night rail, a modest cotton gown that buttoned to her neck. She no longer wore the sheer silk ones sent to her by her husband.

Climbing into bed after the maid left, she admitted Beau St. Clair had been a good man, generous with his money and gentle in his conduct. In fact, he'd been an exemplary person, kind and understanding of her fears in marrying a stranger. Her dear husband had been quite unlike his cousin from America.

True was impatient and demanding. His eyes devoured her each time he looked at her. He played Thea's coquettish games, then had the nerve to touch her and tempt her with his caresses. He even flirted with Henny.

Obviously, he'd been spoiled from the cradle. Well, handsome is as handsome does. She'd take a man not so fair to look upon, but one who would be true.

She wet her fingers and snuffed out the candle. After settling herself in the big bed, she determinedly closed her eyes, but sleep eluded her. She was still awake an hour later when she heard a door creak. The sound came from her bathing room.

Every muscle tensed as she sensed another presence enter her bedroom. The pounding of the sea matched that of her heart as she lay absolutely still. Broad shoulders passed between her and the window. In the moonlight, she recognized the gleam of golden hair.

Cousin True.

Her thoughts shattered and disappeared when he stopped by the bed and stared down at her. She kept her eyes closed to slits and hoped he wouldn't notice the twitching of her lashes.

He touched a curl lying on the pillow, then drew back as if burned. Finally, when she thought she would have to move, he turned and left. She threw off the covers and crept across the room on tiptoe, in time to see him go through an opening into his chamber. He touched the frame, the portal closed with a faint noise and her mirror once again greeted her.

A secret door, she realized. He could invade her chamber any time he wished. She felt angry and exposed, knowing he had watched her sleeping and listened to her troubled dreams.

The interloper! To take advantage of her hospitality...to spy on her in this dastardly fashion. She would evict him . . . right after she told him what she thought of his vile manners.

She stalked to the mirror and searched its frame at the same level she'd seen him reach to close it. At last, after much fumbling about, she detected a tiny knob in the center of a carved flower. She pushed down, not sure what to expect.

The door opened with hardly a sound, but it was enough to alert the man who stood before the window, cloaked in moonlight and nothing else. A candle burned on the table next to the bed.

As he faced her, Roselynne raised her fingers to her lips in shocked awe. He had a magnificent body, tall and straight and powerful. Dark hair grew in whorls over his chest and legs.

His manhood nestled in its own bed of curls. At her stunned perusal, it began to throb with life. Anger changed to confusion as a riot of emotions, too turbulent to be named, ran through her.

Flee.

She couldn't move. A cloud invaded her mind, and her thoughts disappeared in a haze of fiery desire. He was so beautiful. . . .

"Come in," he said. His gaze caught hers and she couldn't look away. She was trapped in the snare of love.

She shook her head, denying his husky command, but her limbs obeyed. She stepped forward, drawn by a force that dazzled the mind and left no room for retreat. One step...

His eyes seemed to blaze over her, as hot as pitch pine. Fear, anger, distrust melted, until only instinct remained, and she followed the ancient impulse bred deep into her bones—the pagan force of nature to join with the one mate right for her. She took another step, and another.

He waited until she stood no more than an arm's length in front of him. "I've thought of this often," he murmured and took the one stride needed to bring her into his arms.

His hand cupped her chin and lifted her face for his kiss.

Slowly his mouth descended. She watched, caught in a dream that seemed real, but couldn't possibly be.

His breath touched her face in a gentle whirlwind, stirring her pulses to a great tempest of need. She couldn't resist him. Lifting her hand, she laid it on his warm, nay, fiery hot, chest.

Let it last, she prayed as his lips touched hers. Please, let the dream last.

Chapter Fifteen

The kiss was slow, sweet. She was aware only of him and of the sensual arousal he stroked to life in her. His lips, often angry or disapproving of her, were now soft as new butter and gently enticing. His arms enclosed her in a haven of security, but she was aware of the danger in that heated embrace.

He was strong, and she felt fragile next to that strength, but not overpowered. She knew, someplace deep inside, that with a word she could control him, and thus control the passion that bloomed between them like rock roses along the sea-swept shore.

The scent of him filled her—a mixture of wine, tobacco, soap and talc, with a hint of some more subtle, robust fragrance blended into the whole. She inhaled deeply, drawing his essence into her.

He brought her closer. Through the thin material of her gown, she sampled the luxurious texture of his maleness. With caressing movements of her body and her hands, she explored the hardness of his muscles, the wiriness of his hair, and marveled at the blatant differences between them.

He moved his mouth over hers, and she savored the contact, now hard, now barely touching. He sucked at her lower lip, taking it into his mouth and running his tongue over it until tingles of delight swept down her throat. He nipped at her upper lip, teasing her by withholding his mouth when she arched up to him, wanting more from him.

His laughter played over her face, and she opened her eyes with an effort. She was taut and heavy with passion. She trembled as storms of longing passed over her nerves. They weren't so frightening as they'd been in her first exposure to this bliss. She felt strong and confident.

Love lent her the courage to venture down this road. She couldn't deny it, although she'd tried. She should remember her uncertain state—she might still be a married woman—but she didn't feel married. She perceived only the promise of ecstasy humming through her veins, drowning out common sense and all else.

"Will you stay?" True asked, his voice deep and husky.

His blue gaze pierced any defenses she might have mustered, and she could only nod. Yes, her heart repeated. *Yes.*

With a mighty sweep, he lifted her into his arms and carried her like a trophy to his bed. "A small thing but mine own," he whispered as he laid her upon the covers.

His smile, the gleam in his eyes, everything about him bespoke care and tenderness. Weren't those the outward signs of love? Again her heart answered, and she believed it.

"The night's cool. Shall I build a fire?" he asked.

She shook her head. The candlelight flickered as he covered her with a linen sheet. It gleamed on his golden body, tan from his bathing in the sea, except for a small scar on his shoulder and another on his chest, half-hidden by the dark whorls of wiry hair. Then he slipped into the bed with her.

"I have dreamed of this," he whispered.

His hands found the tiny buttons at her neck, and he opened the night rail to the last fastening. With fingers that lingered at several points, he pushed it off her shoulders, past her waist, her hips and finally her feet.

By the time he tossed it onto the floor, she was breathless with yearning. Her heart jolted when he lay beside her, his masculine thigh finding a place between her smooth ones.

"Ahh," he breathed as he bent over her, his weight balanced on one arm, his hand tucked under her hair to caress her neck. With his other hand, he stroked along her side, kneaded the indentation of her waist and glided up her ribs.

She couldn't suppress the sigh of anticipation when he closed his large hand over her breast. He kneaded gently, then began a playful lover's attack, circling, darting in for a quick squeeze, and circling again. He watched his handiwork and chuckled as the sensitive tip became more puckered.

"I think you like that," he teased. He looked into her eyes, and the smile on his lips faded.

Against her thigh, his staff throbbed with demands that could no longer be suppressed. She wanted him inside her, hard and warm, a part of her, sharing this rapture.

"Do you trust me?" he asked hoarsely.

"Yes."

"You're not frightened?"

"No." She could barely speak.

He moved over her, nestling between her thighs but not taking her completely. Instead, he ground gently against her, nudging her, coaxing her to readiness. She moved impatiently against him, wanting more. The yearning was wilder, making her almost angry in her need for fulfillment.

He groaned and buried his face against her neck.

He sought her most sensitive points with his lips and his hands until she writhed against him in a tempest she couldn't control. She was lost, mindless in the drive to ecstasy.

When she cried out in frustration, he arched over her, and with one sweeping plunge, he joined them, stroking deep within her, reaching all the hidden places.

"Ohh," she whimpered, locking her arms around him, holding him captive. When he moved, she clutched him more tightly.

"I'm not leaving," he assured her, pressing kisses all over her face when she moved her head and gasped for breath. "Relax, love. I'll take care of you."

"I can't," she whispered, desperate for that elusive contact that would release her from this torment. "I can't."

Then his hands and his body were touching her in a way that wrung a surprised "Oh!" from her. He smiled and kissed her rounded eyes closed.

"Take all you want from me," he encouraged. "Forget all else and take what you want."

She couldn't do otherwise. The wildness had her, and she was helpless in its grasp. The feeling surged, receded, re-formed, rose to excruciating heights, and finally broke into a glorious rush. She cried out, unable to control the tremors that raced through her as she at last found the release.

He absorbed her cries with his lips as his body crashed against hers in a pleasing fury. She vaguely realized that he, too, had reached the final goal just seconds after she did. His pleasure added to her own and she felt a return of the tension, then another series of tremors, fainter this time. They faded as he slowed, then rested his weight upon her and his forearms.

She stroked his sides, basking in the afterglow, feeling the passion fade into contentment the way laughter fades into a smile.

When he moved beside her, one hand cupped to her breast, she laid her hand on his arm, unwilling to give up the tactile pleasure of touching him. Impulsively, she turned her head and kissed his mouth and chin and jaw.

He opened his eyes, and they looked their fill of each other until she yawned and closed her eyes. He chuckled. "Sleep."

"I should return to my room."

His hand tightened on her. "Nay, I'll not give you up so soon as that. I have other plans for the night."

"Tell me," she invited, wanting him again.

"In a moment. You must let me rest. Men cannot rebound as fast as the fairer sex," he instructed her with wry amusement.

She was being too forward. He would think her a wanton.... She realized she had just proven the fact. She peered at him and saw no censure in his eyes. He was looking at her as if she'd given him the world. She felt the same.

Peace descended over her without dimming the tingle of excitement that anticipated her next lesson in lovemaking. She was eager to learn all of it.

Idly she stroked his chest, loving the tickling of the thick hair against her palm. Her sensitive fingers found the scar there. He'd probably gotten it in the war against the king. A pain raced through her. She couldn't bear that he'd been hurt.

She kissed the shoulder puncture, then traced the outline of the chest wound. It curved in a half moon over his lower ribs, almost two inches long. What had caused the sickle-shaped scar?

Her worry for him jolted to a halt. A sickle-shaped scar? Beau had a similar feature. And he, too, had been shot.

Roselynne raised up, her eyes wide with shock, the start of anger, and, deeper, a terrible pain. She lifted the candle holder from the table and held it over him. Blue eyes questioned her action, but she ignored them as she took inventory of her lover.

The bluest eyes and the blackest lashes, thick and curved— the envy of all women. Clean-shaven now, but had not his lips felt the same on hers during the kisses they'd shared in the prison cell? Clearly she remembered the way he'd played his magic upon her... just as he had tonight.

And his hair? She touched the silky, golden strands. There had been a slight coarseness before, but dye would do that.

The candle spluttered with a warning hiss and the scent of hot wax stung her nostrils. She brought it closer, her fingers shaking as the truth crashed over her like a wave upon the shore.

This man in whose bed she lay... this man who had just become her lover... this man was her *husband.*

The knowledge pressed against her heart like a sharp-tipped sword. He'd given her his name, had made her his heir, yet he'd not trusted her with the truth of his identity.

She replaced the candle on the table and pressed her fingers to her temples. The pain of Charles's rejection had been only a pinprick compared to the ache in her heart at this betrayal.

To ply her with ardent glances, to paint a vision in her mind of a tender family scene, to tell her they'd have no secrets between them, when all the time he'd been acting a part... And she, fool that she was, had believed him.

To think she'd grieved for him and their unconceived child; had fought her feelings for him, although they'd been natural and right. He'd caused her to question her morals, yet they'd been honorable by any standard.

He'd known nearly all her history, but had disclosed little of his. A caring husband would have taken his wife into his confidence and revealed his schemes. "You...you deceiver!" she cried.

"Shh," he cautioned, patting her thigh. "What ails you?"

"Don't touch me." Flinging the sheet aside, she tried to escape, but strong hands caught her arm and pulled her down.

"What the hell is wrong with you?"

"You dare ask," she said, heaping scorn onto the words.

He pinned her flailing arms to her side and slid one leg over her thrashing ones. "Stop fighting. I won't let you go until you tell me what has driven you to madness."

"I'll tell you," she replied. "Mr. True Hargrove. Mr. Beauregard Winston St. Clair. Mr. Whatever-Name-You're-Using-Today. Now let me go, you . . . you liar."

"Tsk, tsk, is that any way for a lady, the wife of an earl and a vicar's daughter, to talk?"

His chuckle was a blow to her love and her pride. She fought harder, desperation giving her strength.

"Be still and I'll explain," he offered.

"I want no more of your bargains." She freed a hand and cracked him in the jaw with a flying elbow as she struggled to be rid of him.

"Ouch," he said, catching her arm and holding both wrists in one hand while he examined his jaw. "I'll probably have a bruise there tomorrow."

Innate courtesy had her opening her mouth to apologize. "Release me," she demanded instead, hating the shimmer of emotion in her voice.

"Nay, love." He took her hands in his and gave her a look laced with indulgent amusement. "We'll not leave this bed until you listen to my reasons for the pretense."

"There's no justification for your actions. I'll never forgive you," she said, hating the quiver in her voice as tears pushed against her control. "Never."

The laughter left his eyes, to be replaced by tenderness. She looked away. She'd not fall for his tricks again.

"Henny said that was a risk I took," he murmured. "You are too soft-hearted, Roselynne, to hold a grudge forever."

"Henny? Henny knows of this? You told her, and you wouldn't tell me—"

He laid a finger over her mouth. "She guessed, and I didn't deny it. She's in a position to aid us in our endeavor to find the person who killed my cousin. She hears much at the inn."

Roselynne ceased her struggles, which were serving no purpose. She couldn't undo the past hour and must face the consequences of her weakness for this man. But not at this moment, when he still held her trapped half beneath his large warm body; not when she wanted most to bury her face against his chest and be comforted.

Gathering the tatters of her lost honor and her ragged pride, she forced herself to ask, "What have you discovered?"

"Nothing. Not one real clue." He sighed in frustration.

She wanted out of his bed. "This isn't the place to discuss it. If you will let me up..."

"You won't leave in a huff?"

It hurt anew that her anguish obviously meant little to him. She eased away when he released her. "Get me my gown. Please."

"I like you better without." With no modesty for himself, he retrieved her garment and handed it to her.

She turned her back on him to put it on.

"We must talk," he said, pulling on breeches and a shirt.

Roselynne hesitated. She needed to be alone, to tend her wounds in private, yet she must hear what he had to say. "Yes."

The night air was cold, and she wrapped her arms around herself. He handed her a quilted robe of royal blue, embroidered with a golden dragon hissing a fiery breath. While she tied the sash and folded back the sleeves, he knelt and built a fire.

The reasons for their marriage hammered through her mind. Not love but a desire to thwart a criminal had prompted Beau to offer for her. Those were the facts she must concentrate on. He had never deceived her with talk of love, not even while playing the role of his cousin.

But he'd not trusted her with the truth, either. Anger rekindled, and she held tight to it, clinging to the control it lent her. She glanced at the darkness outside the windows and felt the same. Where her heart had been was only blackness.

When the fire caught, he poured them each a glass of wine and sat on the footstool, a supplicant at the feet of his master. His gaze was gentle upon her face.

"I never meant to hurt you," he began, "but I was afraid you couldn't maintain a deception."

He smiled at her so tenderly she had to fight the melting of her anger. "Of pretending I didn't know you?" she asked.

"Yes. Your lovely face is so honest and open, your feelings so clear to see, I worried you might give us away, and all the planning would be for nought."

She'd thought she couldn't be more humiliated, but to have him know of her feelings and ignore them, then to use them for his own advantage as he'd done tonight . . . She blinked hard. Dear heavens, please don't let her cry in front of him.

"You aren't much experienced with the world, Roselynne. You expect good of everyone. I know the ways of men," he ended on a cynical note.

She gripped the wineglass and took a gulp to soothe her battered heart. "I'm sure that is true, my lord. You appear much more practiced at deception than I."

Impatience rippled over his handsome features. "Beau," he reminded her, a trace of exasperation in his tone.

She gazed at him without speaking.

He sighed. "This stubbornness will get us nowhere."

"I am not—"

"I referred to both of us. It's a trait we share." He sipped the wine in silence. "I must know everything you've found out. George says you're determined upon an investigation of your own and have met most of the tenants and crofters hereabouts. Tell me what facts you've discovered."

"Nothing of import, I fear. There is some gossip . . ." She hesitated and glanced at him from under her lashes.

He lifted one brow. "Do not spare my feelings. I've never thought my family was composed of saints."

"The late earl was rumored to have been involved with Lady Stanton. It's said she wanted marriage and he refused. She's in need of money."

Beau whistled in surprise. "Our Thea gets around," he said and grinned.

So he didn't care that his paramour had been involved with someone else. Roselynne bit her lip to quiet her rioting emotions as she remembered that *she* was his latest conquest.

"What else?" he asked.

"Ansella said Clayburgh was seen going to her house with her. They were alone quite a while. When he left, she paid the back wages owed to her servants."

"That I know from Henny," he said.

"Also, Mrs. Hunson expected a house and pension from your late cousin. She was also his mistress, 'tis said, although I don't credit the gossip."

Beau shook his head. "Mrs. Hunson? I can't see it."

"But then, lechery and seduction seem to run in your family," Roselynne reminded him.

He looked astounded, as if he were a shepherd and a lamb had suddenly turned and bitten him. Then he threw back his head and laughed heartily. She wanted to throw her wine in his face, but she stoically held her composure.

"I've lusted after no one but my beautiful wife," he said softly, raising his glass in a toast to her. His gaze took in her tumbled hair, his robe covering her, her toes peeking out from her gown, and desire leaped to life within those blue depths.

Heat poured into her face from a source deep inside. The anger melted a little more.

She wondered what Mary had been like. Mary, with pale hair and eyes as soft as moonlight, George had said. She'd probably been sweet and gracious, without Roselynne's accursed temper and the stubbornness Beau had accused her of.

Tears pressed with dreadful insistence against Roselynne's eyes. She wouldn't cry in front of him. She wouldn't. Love was a foolish emotion, anyway, encouraging bad judgment and hasty actions. She'd no longer be a prey to it.

"So," he mused. "We have two women who might have wanted revenge on Rockdale. George thinks Spinner has some plan."

"Does he say what?" she asked, forcing her mind to the problem at hand.

"Well, to marry a rich widow wouldn't be a bad idea." He gave her a meaningful glance.

"As if I would," she scoffed. She was through with men.

"And then there's the strange behavior of my barrister. He visits Thea for unknown purposes, may have paid her a large sum of money, again for unknown reasons, and says nothing. On the other hand, he saved my life when I turned up, half-drowned and nearly dead, on his stoop."

"Mr. Clayburgh is a complicated person. He likes problems—the harder to solve, the better." Roselynne contemplated her reactions to the man. "I trust him."

"By what reasoning?"

"My instinct tells me he's a good man. I felt the same about George when first we met."

Beau threw her a sardonic glance. "I don't consider instincts a fair judge of a man's character."

"My first ones about you were correct," she retorted, stung by his admonishing tone.

His eyes narrowed. "And what were those?" he asked with deceptive softness.

She knew she pushed his temper, but her wrought emotions made her past caring. "Wariness. A sense of danger. Deception. You thought me a gullible girl you'd use for your own ends—*as* you have done."

"We struck a bargain, you and I. Did you receive nothing from it?" he demanded, leaning over her knees so that his face was mere inches from hers.

"Yes, indeed. Let me recount my gains." She counted them off on her fingers. "You used me to thwart whoever plotted this sly revenge on you and your kin. You freed me and my father from one prison only to place us in another—where the danger is just as great, the way I see it."

"You have lived in a fine home for three months," he snapped. "You are clothed in silks and satins and have a household of servants to obey your every whim. All the men in the neighborhood pant after you like a pack of dogs after a—"

"Ohh," she cried, banging her fist on her knee. "This is too much. You're the one panting after the females, all of them. The gossip of your prowess is probably spread all over the parish."

"Spread by whom?" He stuck his nose right up to hers. "You, my lady wife, are the only one who knows a jot of my prowess. And I've had damned little opportunity to show it to you. You fawn upon William and George and that young cub of Witherspoon's with equal grace and give me only your sulks."

"That is not true. If I've been unfriendly, it was due to an attempt to dampen your lusty glances, which even the servants must have noted, they were so hot...."

She colored and her voice trailed to a stop as a grin began at the corners of his mouth and stretched over his face.

"So you noticed," he said softly. "I've had the devil's own time of it, trying to hide my feelings. You tempted me, and you knew it. There've been many nights that I had to fight myself not to come through that secret door to you."

"You must have lost the battle tonight," she reminded him, trying not to give in to the sin of pride because he'd been unable to resist. "The sound of the door was what alerted me. I followed to see how you got into my chamber."

"Curiosity killed the cat," he cautioned.

He was no longer angry. With the back of one finger, he stroked down her cheek, sending heat cascading along her nerves.

"Don't," she said, pushing his hand away.

"I want to make love to you again."

Her heart nearly leaped from her chest. "Nay."

"Yes." He cupped her chin, bringing her lips perilously close to his. "Why not? Wasn't it as wonderful for you as for me?"

She clamped her lips tight to keep from confessing that it had been more than wonderful. It had shaken her soul.

He nuzzled her neck and kissed her throat when she turned her head. "We'll have to be discreet. I don't want to alert Thea. Somehow I feel she's the key to our culprit."

At the mention of the other woman, Roselynne stiffened. She placed a hand at the center of his chest and pushed him away. Standing, she moved from the temptation of his kisses. "We are to continue as before?" she asked. "You're still Cousin True from Virginia, and I'm to act the grieving widow?"

"Aye, we must."

"I see." He would be free to ply Thea with his attentions during the day and to come to her bed at night.

He enfolded her in his arms. "Come back to bed, love, the night is short and my needs have been too long suppressed." His lashes dropped sexily over his mesmerizing gaze.

She fought her own battle with desire. She wouldn't be caught in his web of lust and deceit again. Pulling away, she demanded, "What if you get me with child? What of your plan then?"

A lambent smile played over his mouth as he let his eyes roam over her. "This case will be solved long before the babe comes." His eyes darkened with thoughts only too obvious.

"But if it isn't," she persisted, as stubborn as he had said. "What will people say when I am large with a babe too many months after the seed could have been planted by my husband?"

He frowned in irritation. Placing his hands on her shoulders, he spoke in reassuring measures. "I will call out anyone who dares slander you."

"Oh, yes, that would help mightily."

"What ails you now, my love?" He ran a playful hand over her breasts.

She slapped his hand away, hurt at the endearment, which he used all too easily and without meaning. "You are ever the rake," she accused. "You'd use me for your sport with not one thought to my reputation or honor, and my father in no position to defend my virtue...."

Beau stopped his lusty dawdling and drew himself up straight. "There is no need to defend your virtue with me. I'm your husband, not your seducer. If I remember correctly, you came to my bed readily enough and enjoyed yourself there as much as I."

"Ohh, you are crude!" She stomped off toward the open panel.

"I might be more so before the night is over," he warned. "You'll not leave this chamber until I give permission."

She turned at the door, every nerve quivering in outrage at his presumptuous order. If he came into her room, she'd scream the house down around his mulish ears. Jim and Sanders would shoot him at a nod from her. Which was nothing more than he deserved.

With great bravado she closed the panel and held it tightly against his entry. She knew she couldn't compete against his strength, but she thought he wouldn't use brute force.

After a couple of minutes, her reasoning confirmed, she went to her bedroom and got into bed. As she settled under the cover, a movement caught her eye. "Oh," she gasped.

Beau stood next to the stone chimney. His smile was one of arrogant male superiority. "There's more than one way to skin a cat, my dear." He stepped back, into blackness so absolute he seemed to disappear, except for his golden hair and a faint blur of a face. "Don't even think you can keep me out of your bed, Roselynne, if I choose to be there."

With that harsh advice, he vanished.

She lay tense and rigid for a long time. When she was certain he wouldn't return, she turned her face into the pillow, unable to stave off the terrible hurt of the evening's discoveries.

They'd had a bargain, made in desperate circumstances, but both had understood the terms. He'd wanted a wife. She'd accepted and done her duty. Tonight had been different. She'd gone to him with love, but he'd felt no such emotion.

She twisted restlessly, a blinding pressure in her head. She looked toward the shadowed panel where he'd stood. Next to it, the moonlight spilled over the windowsill onto the carpet.

Eyes as soft as moonlight.

Beau had known of her relationship with Charles—which hadn't been at all what she'd thought—but he'd shared nothing of his past feelings. He'd never mentioned Mary, with the pale hair and soft eyes. Mary, who had died.

Pity for his loss added to her own unhappiness. She lay in the lonely bed where thirteen Rockdale heirs had been birthed, and stared at the night, wretched now that her anger was spent. Beau was the fourteenth earl. It was possible she'd conceived the fifteenth that night.

She wondered at the future, but could see only darkness. Beau hadn't meant to hurt her. He could be harsh—like her, he had a temper—but he'd never meant to be cruel. Neither of them had been able to resist the passion that consumed them. If only desire could be turned to love.

Her father had told her that love grew deeper in marriage as a couple shared laughter and sorrow. She and Beau had shared many things—the uncertainty of their days in prison, the danger of the unknown assassin, the wild yearning that brought them together in spite of doubts and misgivings. She'd use those as a base to build on.

No marriage would work without trust, her father had said. If she won Beau's trust, would she also win his love?

Chapter Sixteen

"To lose thee were to lose myself."

Paradise Lost, IX, 959
John Milton

"Just a bit more, Father, and we shall be there," Roselynne encouraged, happy to have a free day with him.

Her guests were occupied with their own affairs. Lady Stanton had gone to her home to see to the household and give orders to her staff. Beau, George and William had ridden off to Brighton to witness a pugilist contest, and Mr. Clayburgh had left early in the morning on pursuits of his own.

She guided her father off the cliff path toward the ruins. "I know you shall enjoy seeing the castle. The construction is wonderful. Mrs. Hunson and Connie agree that it was built in the time of the second Henry."

They crossed the meadow and stood before the stones. Mr. Moreley studied the keep below the great hall. He even examined the hinges and lock on the gate.

Lately he'd taken to inspecting the house and gardens with grave intent. Roselynne found this a heartening sign, although he still didn't speak or recognize anyone. She was glad she'd brought him here even though the hike took the better part of an hour.

He pulled on the rusty iron bars. To her surprise the gate swung open easily but noisily on its hinges. She watched her father go inside and peer at the stone hearth built into the wall. It had probably served as a bed for the poor wretches locked in there by ancient earls of Rockdale. She wondered if the nobles had been a vengeful lot.

Thinking of her husband's ancestors brought Beau to mind, causing a quick stab of pain in her heart. She ignored it and sought the anger that kept despair at bay.

He'd not been back to her room since Saturday night. Thank goodness. She'd dreaded the possibility of nightly fights with him on his conjugal rights. As if he had any after letting her grieve for him!

He'd toyed with her, tempting her with his burning glances and ardent caresses until she was tormented by guilt and passion.

Her conscience reminded her he'd not been alone in that bed. Shame highlighted her cheeks in rosy pink. Yes, she'd gone to him. Perhaps, in her heart, she'd known he was her husband.... No, she wouldn't hide behind lame excuses. She'd fallen into his arms like the proverbial plum. Sighing, she turned to her father.

"Come, Father, let's look at the stairs. The stone masons were clever in their construction."

She led him to the steps and let him look at them before guiding him to the upper walkway. There, she pointed toward the horizon. "See the ship heading out to sea? Remember how I always wanted to go off on a grand adventure when I was a child?"

Mr. Moreley said nothing, but he gazed earnestly at the ship. Roselynne jumped lightly to the top of the parapet to sit a while. Her father did likewise.

The sky was deep blue on the horizon, as blue as Beau St. Clair's eyes. She bit her lower lip as a tremor invaded her.

"Oh, Father," she murmured, "I wish I could talk to you. My life seems such a charade." She paused. "Actually, what we did wasn't a sin, I mean, he was...*is*...my husband. But I didn't know that...so I guess it was a sin, only...it didn't *feel* wrong."

Her father coughed and cleared his throat vigorously. She waited to see if he would speak, but he fumbled through his pockets until he found the handkerchief Connie had tucked away, then patted his mouth with it.

"Damnation," she said. Roselynne pulled at the black lace of her sleeve until a thread loosened. Then, "I am becoming as wicked as he." Her eyes darkened. "Nay. No one is as vile as that deceiver. What I did, I did for love. I know that is no excuse, but it is the reason, truly."

She heaved an angry sigh and silently chided the tiny part of her heart that insisted on believing the look in his eyes had been love. She knew better.

"I shan't fall to temptation again, I promise you that." The memory of that night rushed over her like a spring tide, softening her anger in its wake. "No," she declared as if her father had spoken in Beau's defense. "I'll not soften toward him. It was a cruel trick he played, and I'll never forgive him."

Lost in her troubling thoughts, Roselynne forgot what she was about, and accidently ripped the lace right off her sleeve. While she stared at it stupidly, her father pressed the handkerchief over his nose and sneezed with a frightful sound.

"Oh, Father, forgive me. I had forgotten your sensitivity to dust and thought only of my own problems. I'll take you home." She urged him down from the wall.

The sound of voices along the wooded path caused her to pause before descending the steps.

"It isn't enough," an unseen female said in strident tones. "I must have more."

Roselynne recognized Thea's voice.

"No," a man replied. "We agreed on a sum. The bargain will stick."

Roselynne's eyes widened. The man was Clayburgh.

The couple came around the castle and stood inside the ruins of the great hall. The stairway turret funneled their voices to the second story. Roselynne put a finger across her lips to signal quiet and pulled her father to a squatting position between the stones of the parapet and the walkway.

"That was a year ago. I wonder what the new countess would say if she knew—"

"Do not speak of it."

Roselynne felt the icy fingers of fear creep up her spine. She'd never heard the barrister speak in such a tone.

Thea laughed mockingly. "You're still in love with her."

"Yes," he admitted, the sinister tone lessening.

"Then you're a fool," she scoffed. "Men are ever fools for a tender face."

"Perhaps it reflects goodness of heart, a thing you might not know." He spoke in his usual acerbic manner.

"When have I had a chance to find it?" she countered. "My father married me to a man thrice my age when I was but sixteen. My husband paid dearly for me. He was most disappointed when I didn't give him an heir. Neither had his first wife, but he beat me as if the fault was mine and not his."

"I haven't denied you had a hard life," he said softly.

Roselynne pitied Thea upon hearing this tale and thought the lawyer felt the same.

"It is no matter," Thea said, her tone changing as if she were weary of the conversation. "I must have money, Bernard. The creditors are hounding me unmercifully."

"How much?"

"A thousand pounds will be a help."

"All right. That will be all until next year," he warned.

"Yes."

Roselynne heard a step upon the stair and held hard to her father's hand.

"Let's leave," Thea said. "Ruins make me nervous. Perhaps they remind me of my life." She laughed wryly. "Too bad you never got over Alice St. Clair. I think we would have dealt well with each other. I would have been an asset, you know. As a hostess, I'm superb."

"I'm sure you are, but I would have required fidelity." The irony in his tone suggested the virtue beyond her ability.

"Perhaps for you I would have given it."

He laughed. "Do not perjure yourself, my dear."

"Am I under oath?" she inquired archly.

Their voices faded as they returned to the path.

Roselynne waited until she was sure they were gone, then she stood. A tug on her father's sleeve brought him upright. She led the way down the steps, anxious to return to the manor.

"Hurry, Father. I must tell Beau this news."

The bed seemed unusually hard and lumpy that night. She had dined at eight with Clayburgh, Thea and her father in attendance and had gone to her room shortly thereafter. It was now ten, and there was no sign of the three sportsmen returning.

They were probably drinking and wenching in a Brighton pub, she fumed, while she had important information to pass on.

The sound of hooves intruded on her thoughts. She sprang to the window in time to see the three ride around the side yard, heading for the stable. About time, she thought, relief at Beau's return overriding her petty jealousy. She rose and donned a robe.

She poked at the fire until she heard several calls of "good night" in the hallway, then went to the secret door. Pushing the knob, she opened the panel. Beau wasn't there.

Perhaps he was having a nightcap. He liked to sit in the library with a brandy and read after everyone else had gone up. After waiting another thirty minutes, she decided she'd have to look for him.

She returned to her room and left by her own door, slipping silently down the dark stairs to the lower floor. A light flickered from under the library door. She entered and closed the door behind her.

Only George was present.

"Where's Beau?" she asked, frowning in irritation. The man was never where one expected.

George put aside his brandy snifter, stood and looked at her cautiously. "Uh... who?" he asked.

"You can stop the pretense," she snapped. "I know who Cousin True is. Surely he told you."

George grinned. "He, uh, mentioned it in passing."

At the amusement in George's eyes, she wondered at the account Beau had given of Saturday night. "What did he say?"

George shrugged. "Only that you'd discovered the ruse."

"Nothing else?"

He looked at her with an innocent expression. "Is there more I should know?"

Color suffused her cheeks. "No. Where is he?"

"I assume he went to bed. He was anxious to return home, although William suggested we stay the night."

She was a little mollified to learn this. Perhaps he hadn't been wenching after all.

"Don't be too harsh on him," George said suddenly, his tone lowered to a near whisper.

Her gaze snapped to his. "He lied to me."

"He did it only for your good."

"So he says, but..." Unwilling to voice the confusion in her mind and heart, she turned from George's scrutiny.

"Aye, 'tis true," George defended his friend. "He has fretted over you from the day you were wed, especially since the accident with the cart in London. He'd never forgive himself if you were hurt in any way."

"That I don't believe." She remembered the pain of his deception. "He let me think he was someone else... and after I knew the truth, he showed no remorse, but regretted that I knew. What kind of person am I that even my own husband won't trust me with his identity? Have I given him cause to doubt my discretion?"

"Nay," George declared.

"Even now, he doesn't confide in me, but holds me at arm's length as if I were but a... a casual acquaintance." *As if he'd never lain with me and held me to his heart and joined his body with mine....* She put her hands over her face as tears threatened.

"Here, here, none of that. All will work out." George searched his pockets until he found a handkerchief. He handed it to her and put an arm around her shoulders, letting her rest her forehead against his chest while she fought for composure.

"Will it?" she asked wearily. "I've scarce slept for nights trying to figure out how."

Beau glared at his empty bed, then looked toward the panel that led to Roselynne's chamber with longing. Her bed would be nice. She'd be all warm and snug. If he entered, would she burn his ears with her accusations, or would she welcome him? If she were asleep and he woke her to passion before she realized what was happening... Nay, he couldn't do it.

She'd either believe he'd acted in her best interests or she could go to the devil! He was tired of it all—of worrying about his wife, of watching William and that green pup Rodney hanging over her, of catering to Thea, of snooping around like a mouse and finding nothing.

Dammit, he wanted his own bed with his own wife in it and a jolly tussle in the sheets and a family to watch grow to manhood or womanhood, as the case may be.

He sighed and stretched out, still dressed, on the bed. After a minute, he decided to make a quick tour of the house, just on the off chance he might discover something useful.

Rummaging through his trunk, he found a pair of soft moccasins and pulled them on. A black shirt rather than his white one, dark breeches instead of buff, and he'd be all but invisible in the dark. In a moment, he was wandering along the secret corridors, passing the turnoff to Roselynne's room with great self-control. He came to Thea's room and peered through the tiny hole that was the black center of a lamb's eye in a picture on her wall.

An imp of guilt prodded him as he recalled entering the bedchamber a few days before. He'd had no choice. Thea had insisted, and he couldn't have taken a chance on her raising her voice in anger if he'd refused. He'd managed to get away with the lame excuse of a pulled muscle in his back.

He put aside the nightmare that would have ensued if Roselynne had seen him leaving the other woman's room and concentrated on the present. Apparently Thea had found a more willing partner.

The murmur of voices from the bed was audible, but the words were indistinct. Beau pressed closer to the tiny hole and wished they'd talk a bit louder. A smile flitted over his mouth as he thought of knocking on the secret panel and asking Thea and her lover to speak up.

Was it Clayburgh with her? He'd wondered at the lawyer staying so long in the country. The month was nearly over, and they'd been at Rockdale for nigh on to three weeks.

"I tell you I can find out nothing," Thea said, throwing the covers off and clambering out of bed. She pulled on a robe and tied it at the waist with a savage jerk on the bow.

The man leisurely stretched, his face hidden in the shadows of the bed curtains. When he, too, tossed the sheet aside and stood, Beau couldn't suppress a start of surprise.

Spinner!

What the hell was the man's game? During the day, he plied Roselynne with adulation and attention, yet here he was, in the bed of a woman who'd shown very little interest in him, at least during the day.

As for the lady herself, Thea flirted with the other men without a jealous glance in Roselynne's direction; however, in Beau's observation of human nature, most people, male or female, were possessive of their lovers.

Meaningless affairs were commonplace in society, but Beau had a hunch there was more between these two than heat. Thea was careful of her favors, knowing those that were spread around grew less valuable.

"What are you plotting?" Thea demanded, watching Spinner pull on his clothing.

He merely smiled and quaffed a glass of wine.

She walked nearer, her manner threatening. "If you think to cut me out, think again. It was my idea that brought you here. I'm the one who thought of the plan."

"Plans change as circumstances alter," he informed her.

"I can send you back to your life of ferrying French aristocrats across the channel. If I should decide to expose—"

His hands on the lace at her throat stopped the torrent of words. "Such a pretty white neck," he said. "So slender, so delicate."

The softness of his tone enhanced its menace. A shiver visibly ran over Thea, then she smiled and shoved his hands away. "I have friends. The barrister, in particular, finds me quite lovely. And he knows what I know."

"And pays you well to keep quiet. One wonders what he would do should he learn you've babbled," Spinner mused aloud, mocking Thea's threat. "After all, the man was in love with Alice and hoped to wed her had I not intervened."

Thea kicked the train of her robe aside and went to a chair. "Ah, yes, and we known how charming you can be. Did you win the foolish girl with your sweet singing, or was it the languishing glances and soulful sighs? Roselynne might be more discerning than that poor child."

Spinner walked to Thea and took her hand. "Roselynne prefers me over the other cousin. You needn't worry. If I marry her, you and I shall continue as we are."

"You delude yourself if you think she will take you over the American. I have seen her eyes when she looks at him."

"We shall have to see how it all works out."

She gazed up at him, wariness in her expression. He stroked her cheek and leaned down to kiss her. At last she lifted her arms and returned the embrace, which lengthened and grew heated.

"Perhaps I put my clothes on too soon...." Spinner murmured.

Beau turned as they fell across the bed. He made his way back along the passage, which was as black and silent as he imagined a tomb would be, to his own room. He paused at a corner and unable to resist, turned it. At the panel to Roselynne's room, he stopped and peered through the peephole. She wasn't in bed, nor present that he could tell. Where was she?

His sleep these nights, what little of it he got, was tormented with dreams of her. The sweet way she smiled. The husky catch in her throat when she'd cried out during their lovemaking. The scent of her womanly perfume growing stronger as she became more excited. He frowned at the swelling in his own breeches.

Forget it. She was about as welcoming as a hissing cat.

He made his way to the lower floor and peered into the library. The sight that greeted him brought forth a surprised expletive. His wife was in the arms of his best friend!

By damn, he'd find out what was going on between them and put a stop to it. He punched at the lever to open the panel, but it refused to budge.

"Hell," he muttered. He peered through the hole again and saw George give his handkerchief to Roselynne. She wiped at her eyes.

His anger cooled, and his common sense kicked in. The scene wasn't a lovers' tryst like the one he'd just witnessed. George wouldn't encroach on another man's territory, and Roselynne wasn't the type to fall into any pair of open arms.

However, he decided with grim determination, if she wanted to cry, she should use *his* shoulder.

He pushed the lever gently, the latch released, and he stepped through the opening. The couple turned to him. George looked amazed, as if Beau had materialized out of the air.

"A secret door! How clever," he said, releasing Roselynne and going to the opening. He peered into the inky corridor. "Does the passage go all the way to the back of the house?"

"Yes," Beau said, his eyes on Roselynne.

She gave him one of her cool glances and took a seat in her favorite chair without a word to him.

"What's wrong?" he asked, going to her and perching on the arm of the chair. He lifted her face with a finger under her chin and studied her damp eyes.

"Nothing." She turned her head.

George, who was examining the panel, overrode her quiet utterance. "Everything," he said. "You two should talk."

"What's happened to make you unhappy?" Beau asked her.

"It doesn't matter." She glared at George.

"She's as pigheaded as you," he helpfully explained to Beau.

Beau exchanged a wry glance with his friend. "Then we're doomed to stay here all night. I won't leave until I know what the problem is."

"You know the problem. You're the cause of it," she informed him. Her anger was forced, but she used it to cover the wound of his deception. She'd thought they shared a great, passionate love. To find out otherwise made her see that she'd fallen back into her girlhood dreams. She'd never be so foolish again.

"Ah, yes," he murmured, giving her one of his perusals that burned her to the core. "Let's go upstairs and refresh our memory of the quarrel. I think I may have forgotten the fine details."

Roselynne drew herself up regally. "Have you not had enough of wenching after a day at Brighton?"

He shook his head. "There's no one I want but my wife," he averred in a low tone meant for her ears only.

"I think I'll leave," George said with a sardonic grin. "Can I get to my room from here?" He indicated the secret passage.

"Yes, I'll show you later," Beau said. "But first, I have information you should hear."

"I, too, have news," Roselynne spoke up, remembering the reason for seeking her husband out.

Beau took a seat on the sofa. "Go ahead."

"Father and I went up to the old castle this morning," she began. "While we were resting, Thea and Clayburgh appeared, but they didn't know we were there, too." She related the rest of the story to them.

Beau drummed his fingers on the sofa arm, his forehead knit into a frown. George poured them each a brandy as they tried to figure out what blackmail Thea held over Clayburgh.

"Perhaps he took a bribe," Roselynne suggested, remembering his ease in handling the same for her father and herself.

"He's too smart to get caught for that," Beau said.

She gave him a waspish look. "Tell us your solution."

"I have none, but I've another piece to add to the puzzle." He told them what he'd overheard in Thea's chamber.

George was astounded. "Show me this entire passage. Between the two of us, we can keep everyone under surveillance. I say, jolly fun."

They laughed at his imitation of young Rodney. Roselynne joined in, though her heart was far from merry.

Beau sobered. "I have a hunch all will be resolved soon. I think, whoever the person is, he's getting impatient and will make a mistake."

"Or her," Roselynne said. "It could be a woman." She thought of Mrs. Hunson and her strange ways. "It isn't Mr. Clayburgh."

"Why not?" Beau looked at her, his deep blue gaze sending another jolt of pain through her heart.

"A stabbing, that's too messy for him. So is a runaway cart. Besides, he was the one shot at that day we went to the village. Was that an accident, do you think?"

Beau and George exclaimed at the same time.

"What?" she asked.

"I was the one who was supposed to be with Thea," Beau explained. "She invited only me. I invited the rest of you."

Fright poured over Roselynne like a cold rain. Had someone really tried to kill him? Along with her fear, she experienced a fierce protective anger and unconsciously clenched her fist.

Beau took her hand in his and opened her fingers. "Don't worry. No one will hurt me."

"Have you magic eyes, that you can spot danger through the trunks of trees or behind stone fences?" she demanded.

"I'll be extra careful," he promised, "if my death would cause you grief."

He kissed her palm and stared into her eyes, his with a question in them. She wasn't ready to forgive him for his deception yet, but when she tried to look away, she couldn't.

Finally, George cleared his throat, and she managed to pull her gaze from the dazzling fire of her husband's ardor.

Red-faced, she rose and picked up a small portrait almost hidden by a vase on a shelf. It was of a young girl with blue eyes and tawny curls tied with a blue ribbon.

The hair stood up on the back of Roselynne's neck as a premonition hit her. "Alice," she said with certainty. "This is your cousin, Alice."

She carried the picture to Beau. He studied it, then turned it over. "Alice St. Clair, sixteenth birthday," he read. "She looked like my sisters when they were that age."

"Thea said Clayburgh was in love with Alice," Roselynne reminded them. She pressed her fingers to her temples.

"That's possible. He was my cousin's legal advisor for twenty years." Beau replaced the portrait and came to her. "Do you have the headache? Shall I ring for a powder?"

"No, I'm trying to think. Did we see a headstone for her at the cemetery?"

"I don't remember it, but I wasn't paying close attention." His rakish grin indicated his mood that day.

George stood. "It's late. Tomorrow we can try to make a whole cloth from the pieces we have."

"Aye," Beau agreed.

"Will you show me the passage now?" George requested.

Beau went to the panel and showed George and Roselynne the hidden lever. They snuffed the branch of candles and, holding each other by the hand, Roselynne in the middle, the trio crept along the silent corridor, occasionally finding a speck of light to brighten the absolute dark.

Beau and Roselynne left George at his quarters and proceeded to their wing. He showed her how to open the panel to her room.

She stepped onto the carpet, feeling its warmth under her satin slippers after the coolness of the passageway. She turned back to say good-night, but the words dried in her throat.

Beau didn't ask to enter, but the question was there in his eyes as he gazed at her from the dark.

"I . . . good night, my lord," she whispered and quickly closed the panel, her heart thumping. Would he accept her decision and go to his chamber? Or would he enter and demand his rights?

She couldn't decide which she preferred.

Beau stood in the dark and tried to reason with his fury at being left in the cold. She was his. Perhaps it was time he made that fact known to her.

He bent to the peephole and found her staring at the panel as if she expected him to burst through like an enraged bull and ravish her. Sweet heaven, he wanted to do just that. But he couldn't. He should just go to his room and forget it. He couldn't do that, either.

He was frustrated by her coolness when he longed for warmth and an invitation to return to her arms. Having her once was like being admitted to paradise and expelled after an hour. He hadn't had nearly enough of her sweetness.

The passion they'd shared Saturday night had been a revelation to him. Although she'd been as naturally responsive as he'd guessed she would be, he remembered more than the fulfilling of desire. He'd also found joy and contentment, more than he could ever have imagined.

He looked again. Roselynne had drifted out of his sight. She returned with a book, removed her robe and got into bed. After pulling a branch of candles closer, she opened the book and began to read. She obviously thought he had left.

His conscience demanded that he leave her alone, but the temptation was more than he could bear. He pressed the lever next to the chimney, and the panel slid silently open.

She glanced up when he stepped inside her chamber, and laid the tome aside. Her mouth tightened, as if attached to an internal drawstring. "Yes?" Her voice quivered slightly.

He sat on the end of the bed and let his gaze roam over her slender figure. Her modest gown didn't conceal the luxury of her breasts nor hide the effect of his perusal. He groaned with need as her nipples sprang to life and poked against the material.

"What do you want?" she demanded, a bit more the lady of the manor this time.

"You know the answer to that, my dear wife." He made his smile playful. "A moment of conjugal bliss would be welcome."

"That you have had." A hint of red entered her cheeks. She wasn't indifferent to him.

"I meant a kiss, a little something to tide me over until such moments become a nightly occurrence."

"That would be foolish." She clenched the edge of the sheet, pulling it more tightly about her.

He started to tease her more, but the flicker of acute distress in her eyes halted the words on his tongue.

"We're husband and wife," he reminded her, feeling wise and generous about their relationship. "Nothing we do together can be considered wrong as long as we both consent and enjoy it."

"If that is all you came for, you may leave. You are posing as another man, and I will not—"

"That's what's bothering you," he announced, satisfied he'd found the root of her problem. "You thought I was someone else, and you gave yourself to me. Don't worry, I don't hold it against you, although I was jealous of Cousin True for a time."

Instead of his magnanimity soothing her, it only seemed to stir her temper. "Oh," she cried, "will you ever remind me of that? You weren't so honorable. Taking another man's wife—"

"My wife," he said, riled at her accusing tone. All hopes of a pleasant interval faded.

"But you were pretending to be another."

So they were back to that. Henny had been right. Rose-lynne wasn't prepared to forgive his deception. "That was in your best interest," he informed her.

"And yours." She sounded sad. "You wanted to play the roving gallant."

He saw reasoning was useless. Once women got hold of a grievance, they were like a dog chasing a flea. "I didn't come to quarrel with you. There's something I forgot to tell you."

She waited, wariness in her expression.

"William plans to marry you and keep Thea for his mistress. Watch yourself around her. She may be the vindictive type."

Roselynne clutched the bed cover. "*Me?* William thinks to marry *me?* I think not! As for Thea . . ." She waved his suggestion aside. "She's too wrapped up in herself to worry about me."

"Don't rely on intuition too much," he warned, relieved at her vehement denial of William's hopes. She nibbled on her lower lip, driving him to madness with a need to do likewise.

"You're right, of course. There could be more to Thea than meets the eye. We must be careful."

"Yes." He continued to watch her. A frown puckered her brow, and she seemed deep in thought.

Mary would have approved of her, he realized and felt lighter of heart, as if he'd waited for her blessing on his marriage.

When Roselynne glanced up, his eyes met hers, and he longed to embrace her and once again share the wild sweet passion. It came to him that he'd never get enough of her even if they lived together for the rest of their days.

She looked away, and her fingers plucked at the sheet, a habit he'd noted when she grew agitated. "You must go before . . . before someone comes."

"One kiss," he bargained.

"And then you will go?"

"Yes. If you want me to."

He put his hands on her shoulders when she didn't reply and brought her forward until she rested against his chest. It was like holding an ember in his arms. He grew warmer by the second. With great restraint, he covered the sweet rosebud of her mouth and savored the taste.

With little effort, he penetrated the petals and discovered the warm, moist heat inside. He stroked her tongue and gloried in her response. With trembling hands, he rubbed up and down her back, then her sides. Such treasure.

"Umm," she mumbled. Protest or encouragement?

"Let me stay," he whispered when she turned her head.

"You can't."

"Why?" He nuzzled her neck above the delicate lace.

"If someone discovers you here, if they suspect who you are, you'll be arrested. The gaoler won't let you escape again." She added in a whisper, "I would not have you die."

"Why?" he asked, his throat so tight he could hardly speak.

She pushed him from her. "An innocent man would hang in place of the guilty one."

He was disappointed. "You would have justice," he said in a dry tone.

"Of course. Isn't that why we married, to thwart this person and restore your innocence?"

Beau reluctantly stood. "It would seem so."

He left her and returned to his own room, recalling the days in prison as he prepared for bed. He and Roselynne had been closer then than now, it seemed to him. Although she'd been afraid of him, she'd "done her duty" by him. Duty be damned! He wanted her to come to him again as she had the other night—of her own free will, because she couldn't deny the passion that ran like a mighty river between them.

Odd, now that they'd obtained the mutual bliss he'd longed to share with her, they seemed further apart.

He climbed into bed, resenting its emptiness. Although he longed to hold her and never let go, he had to give her a chance at finding happiness even if it meant she turned to someone else.

Chapter Seventeen

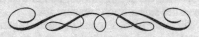

There. Roselynne stood back and surveyed her handiwork, then put her embroidery scissors and the glue pot away. With the dot of black paper over the tiny hole in the panel, no one could look into her chamber without her permission. The thought of Beau spying on her sent a rush of heat through her blood.

He'd probably watched her dress after her bath or while she shed her clothes for a nightgown. The thought was infuriating. Honesty forced her to admit it was also titillating.

Picking up a broad sun hat, she went down to the rose garden where she and Lady Stanton were going to pick and arrange bouquets for the house.

Thea was already there, shears in hand, working over a bush. "Hello," she said when Roselynne appeared.

Roselynne searched the woman's face for signs of dislike but could detect nothing. Thea maintained the same attitude from day to day—that of an amused cynic.

"Hello. The morning is perfect, isn't it?" Roselynne inhaled deeply. "The air seems fresher at this hour than at any other."

"Yes." Thea snipped roses and dropped them in her basket, then she pruned the plant. "You'll have new growth and a plethora of flowers next year. Your gardener doesn't cut them back enough."

"I'll tell him," Roselynne promised.

They worked for two hours, then took lunch in the pergola. Thea fanned herself with her hat while servants laid out salad greens dressed with wine vinegar and eggs and fresh ocean perch, caught at dawn by the men.

"August is almost over," Thea said, gazing into the distance. The ivy leaves cast shadows across her face, softening the faint lines at her eyes. "Time passes."

"Yes," Roselynne agreed.

Thea laughed, a strangely lonely sound with no humor. "You're young. Wait until you're my age—I won't tell you what that is—and you will know what *tempus fugit* means."

Time flies. Roselynne knew the Latin term well. A sense of urgency greeted her every morning. Each day that passed increased the chances of Beau being discovered and speedily hanged. Oh, yes, she knew.

She wet her lips. "How well did you know the thirteenth earl?" she asked. At Thea's sharp glance, Roselynne added, "I mean, as a neighbor. Did he pay calls frequently?"

Thea smiled. "You've heard the village gossip."

Roselynne colored. She was no good as an investigator. Her questions were gauche. "I was simply curious about the earl and thought you could tell me about him, if you would."

"After my husband died, I sometimes served as hostess for Robert. There was no love between us, but I thought we would marry. He preferred his life alone, though. He had an heir in America and was content." She paused, then asked, "Tell me, was Beauregard St. Clair as attractive as his cousin, True?"

Roselynne was disconcerted by the question. "In...in some ways. Beau's hair was dark, but his eyes were blue."

"Those St. Clair eyes. La, but they go straight to a girl's heart, do they not?" Thea gave Roselynne an arch glance.

"Y-yes," Roselynne admitted.

"Guard yours carefully, Countess," she advised. "There are those who would use it for their own gain, then leave it in pieces on the floor."

Roselynne's heart pounded against her ribs. "What do you mean?" she asked cautiously.

"A rich widow is indeed a prize catch." Thea would say no more. She snipped thorns from the roses so they could arrange them in vases for the house and gave advice on their care. "A teaspoon of vinegar or wine in the vase will make them last longer."

Roselynne brooded on the conversation but couldn't decide if Thea had spoken generally or if she offered a warning. She put it from her mind when the men returned from their excursion to a horse fair near Brighton. Beau...Cousin True, she must remember to call him...wanted to increase the Rockdale stock.

"I say, such a lot of spavined beasts I've never seen," Rodney declared. He eyed the poached fish on his plate hungrily. He'd returned from the fair with the others and accepted an invitation to a late lunch.

Thea and Roselynne sat with them, Roselynne watching as her father ate a good lunch. He'd gone on the outing and looked in fine color from the exercise. Surely his mind would return soon.

She sighed, saw Beau looking at her, and concentrated on the fruit ice the servant placed in front of her. She must tell him to stop, or his eyes would give them away.

"Don't forget, the musical is tomorrow," Rodney said at the close of the meal. He leaned over her hand and managed to kiss the back of it fervently before she could pull away. "I will see you then. All of you." He bounded off to the stable. In a minute, they heard his horse's hooves on the gravel.

"Impudent pup," Beau growled, but with a laugh.

"Many are smitten with your charm, dear cousin," William told her, also smiling. "Come, shall we walk along the shore?"

"I must read to my father before his nap."

"Before tea, then? I would like to speak to you on a personal matter." His glance informed the others he wanted privacy.

No excuse came to mind. She nodded vaguely and took her father's arm to guide him to his suite.

An hour before tea, William caught up with her on the stairs. "Are you ready to go?"

Roselynne could think of no graceful way out. "Let me find a hat," she said, resigned to the stroll.

They set off, and in a few minutes had reached the shore path. "Be careful. It's steep along here. Sometimes the edge gives way," William advised, taking her arm.

They climbed toward the ruins for a while, then, upon reaching the crest of a small rise, he brushed dust from a boulder with his handkerchief and invited her to sit.

She did so reluctantly. When he opened his mouth, she quickly said, "Look. A ship. I've always wanted to see exotic places."

William captured her fluttering hand between both of his. "Then you shall. It would make a splendid honeymoon trip."

He went so straight to the point she was lost for words even though Beau had warned her of William's plan. She remembered Thea's strange warning.

William sat next to her and stared into her shocked eyes. "You must know how I feel."

"Cousin William, please. I am recently widowed. It...it isn't seemly to speak of these things—"

"But I must," he declared. "My heart is so full, it cannot be denied, else it should burst with feeling." He smiled to show he jested, then became serious again. "Like young Witherspoon, I am smitten with your lovely face and charming manners. Before the line of your admirers grows to even greater length, I wish to secure my place. When the time is proper, I will ask for your hand, Roselynne."

"Please, say no more." She wished she were anywhere but at this place.

"Promise you will consider my—"

"Sir, I cannot!" She stood and took two steps before his hand on her arm stopped her.

"I have distressed you." He leaned close and studied her face. "Are you remembering your husband?"

"Yes." She nodded several times, relieved at the excuse.

"He is gone, dear Roselynne. You must allow another in your heart. Please say you will think kindly of me." He raised her hand and kissed it gently, giving her such a look of entreaty she could only agree.

"But of course I think kindly of you, Cousin." She dabbed at her eyes with her handkerchief. "I'd like to be alone for a bit."

"Let me take you back to the house."

"I will be all right. Please, leave me."

He reluctantly left. After a couple of minutes, she heard a rustling in the leaves close by. Beau stepped from the woods. She wasn't surprised. She'd known he or Jim would follow her.

"You heard?" she asked.

"Nay, but I can guess. He asked you to marry him."

"Not yet, but he will when my mourning is up."

"Over my dead body," Beau declared.

She closed her eyes against the painful picture. "Don't say that."

He sat beside her and put an arm around her. "You're trembling. Did he say something to frighten you?"

"No, it's just . . . I'm so tired of all this. Hold me."

He was startled at the request and studied her for a second before drawing her to his chest. His body began to react, and she stirred against him, sensing the turmoil she woke in him.

"I'm sorry. I can't hold you and not want you."

"I know," she replied wearily and laid her head against him.

He held her until she at last sat up and pulled her hat into place to shield her eyes from the sun.

"We shouldn't be here like this. What if someone saw?"

He grinned. "They'd envy me my good fortune."

"You jest, but I have a feeling something terrible is going to happen."

"Jim or Sanders follows wherever you go."

She pressed her fingers to her temples. "Not to me. To you." She gazed at him with worry clouding her eyes.

With an exuberant lunge, he caught her to him and gave her a kiss. "Don't worry. I can look after myself."

"Do you have eyes in the back of your head?" she asked crossly.

"Aye." He chuckled. "Come, we'll go for a ride. I want to check the cemetery for a headstone. Since you put the thought in my head, it won't go away."

"Yes, that is a good plan." She quickly considered. "If we can't find it, we'll ask the cook at the vicarage. She's been there for years, much longer than the vicar. Perhaps if I take tea with her . . . she may be more open if we're alone."

"I'll have the vicar give me a tour of his garden, or some such," Beau decided.

They hurried down the path and were soon off on Athene and the stallion. "What is your horse's name?" Roselynne asked. "I've never heard you say it."

"Midnight Fire. I call him the black. It's simpler."

"Your cousin had a beast called Greek Fire."

"The same bloodlines. He sent the black to me as a colt."

"The more I learn of him, the more I like him. He seemed a generous man."

A look of pain crossed Beau's face. "Aye, I liked him, too."

She was silent for the rest of their ride. After strolling through the graveyard and not finding a headstone for Alice, they went to the vicarage. Luck was with them. The cook was alone. Beau made an excuse about a problem with his horse's shoe and rode on into the village. Roselynne had a cup of tea and a biscuit with Mrs. Snelling.

"Cousin True and I were just up at the cemetery. There's been a long line of Rockdale earls, hasn't there?"

"Yea-up." Mrs. Snelling was from away, as the locals said, and spoke with a different accent. "I knowed the last two. Never met the young man from across the water, though. Too bad they hanged him before he came around."

"I saw a picture of Alice St. Clair. Mrs. Hunson said she was married at the house. Did you know her?"

"I did. A bonny girl she was, shy as a titmouse and as quiet. The whole family was given to thinking and reading."

Roselynne fidgeted with her teacup. "I, um, saw a tiny headstone for a baby. Would it have been hers?"

"It would. Died a-borning."

"And Alice died a few days later," Roselynne remarked as if remembering the fact. "But I didn't see her stone."

Silence bloomed in the sunny kitchen. Roselynne waited as she had learned to do on visits with her mother.

At last Mrs. Snelling glanced around as if to be certain they were alone, then she leaned forward. "They couldn't lay her in consecrated ground."

Roselynne gasped. "You mean she—"

"Shh," Mrs. Snelling cautioned. She whispered roughly, "it must-a been the shock of losing the babe. Unhinged her mind. Some say she jumped from the roof of the manor, but that's just talk," she added hastily, seeing the horror on Roselynne's face. "No one knows where the earl laid her, God rest her poor soul."

"How sad," Roselynne murmured, remembering her own desolation when she realized she hadn't conceived.

"Yea-up. Here, have another," the cook urged, pushing the biscuit platter closer. "They's plenty. I baked extra for the sisters up at the convent."

"What convent?" Roselynne inquired. "I've not heard of it."

"They keep to themselves, taken a vow of silence, they have. But they take in boarders if you've a mind for peace and quiet, so long as you don't talk to them." Mrs. Snelling leaned close to impart more news. "Some rich folks bring their relatives there to live, it's said. The sisters'll take them as long as they don't scream or nothing." She tapped her temple.

They chatted about the good sisters, then other matters for the rest of the visit. When Beau returned for Roselynne, Mrs. Snelling gave her a bundle of treats to take with them.

"Did you find out anything?" Beau asked after they left.

"Yes. Alice St. Clair isn't buried in the cemetery because, according to rumor, she couldn't be put in consecrated ground."

"Suicide? I don't believe it."

"Neither do I. She looked too gentle for violence toward anyone, including herself."

Beau rode in silence, obviously deep in thought, though his eyes moved constantly over the fields and woods, watching for the slightest movement. Roselynne remembered her other news.

"There's a convent off the Brighton Road, one not confiscated by Henry VIII, probably because the nuns take care of those who might be an embarrassment to the nobility."

"Illegitimate children?"

"No. Those whose minds have wandered. Mrs. Snelling says the sisters are grateful for help. Perhaps I will have Mrs. Hunson send over a haunch of beef?"

"As you wish. You have the running of the place. And do it perfectly," he added, giving her a warm smile. He spurred the black to greater speed. Athene increased her pace.

"Thank you, my lord."

His hand caught her reins and pulled the horses to a stop. "Don't get in the habit of calling me that unless you truly want to be a widow."

"You know I wish no such thing."

He chuckled. "Don't look so indignant, wife. I know your heart is pure, as is mine."

"Hah," she muttered.

He released her reins and swept a caress down her cheek. "Someday you'll believe all I tell you."

"Life doesn't go backwards. I'm no longer the green girl I was at our marriage," she retorted, her face tingling where he'd touched her.

"Aye. You're a woman. I remember that fact often." With that, he spurred the black, and they returned to the manor at a gallop, gliding effortlessly across the meadow, both riders and horses full of energy and high spirits.

Roselynne's portent of danger passed. They went to Squire Witherspoon's musical evening, which featured an opera singer who'd fled France and a quartet of musicians from Austria. Rodney stayed by Roselynne's side and introduced her to his aunt, whose visit was the cause of the entertainment.

On Sunday, Beau accompanied Roselynne and her father to the village church. Afterward, Connie and Mrs. Hunson escorted Mr. Moreley home while Beau and Roselynne had lunch with Henny and Widow Farkley at the inn.

In a moment alone, Henny told them Harry Connor, the gamesman who'd shot a hole in Clayburgh's hat, had spent more money than usual in the pub. She scowled in disgust. "I even let 'im kiss me out next to the well, but I couldn't find out where 'e came by the extra coins."

Beau pulled a red curl and gave her a buss on the cheek. "A woman after my own heart, you are."

"Go on with ye," she said, but she tossed her head with pleasure at his teasing. "Take the lass 'ome now. Clouds are coming up, and we're in for a storm."

She spoke truly. Before they'd covered more than three-quarters of the distance to the house, the wind brought the first drops of rain.

"Run," Beau shouted, spurring the stallion to a gallop.

Laughing like carefree urchins, they raced for home. The wind increased and pelted them with icy cold droplets. They were drenched by the time they reached the stable. Beau lifted her down and clasped her in his arms while they waited for the stableboy to appear.

"Let me go," she whispered, shivering.

"For a kiss."

"What if someone comes?" She searched his face anxiously.

"You'd better hurry before they do." His teeth flashed white against his tan in the dim stable. She lifted her mouth to his, and he took the kiss quickly. "Not nearly enough," he complained, releasing her and stepping back as a rustle of straw preceded the entry of the stableboy. "Ah, there you are. Wipe them dry and give them a bucket of oats for their supper."

"Yes, sir," the lad replied, taking the bridles.

Beau and Roselynne returned to the house. Mrs. Hunson greeted them at the door. "Terrible storm," she said, using her weight against the wind. "You must get out of those wet things. Shall I send hot tea to your room, my lady?"

"That would be lovely. Do you know where Ansella is?"

"She and one of the maids have gone to the berry patch. They'll probably stay with a crofter until it clears. I'll help you with your dress in a minute." She hurried off.

"I'd like to help you with your dress," Beau whispered, following Roselynne up the steps.

She ignored him and went into her room, shutting the door firmly in his face. A smile tugged the corners of her mouth. When Mrs. Hunson arrived, Roselynne was rubbing her hair with a towel. A footman built a fire and left.

"Now, let's get you out of those clothes," the housekeeper ordered, placing a robe to warm before the flames. She started on the row of buttons when Roselynne obediently turned her back and lifted her hair out of the way.

The rain burst against the windowpanes in furious blasts, driven by a wind straight off the sea. Drafts stirred through the chamber, and Roselynne was glad of the heated robe. She wrapped it tightly around her after stepping out of the wet dress and into a silk gown Mrs. Hunson found for her.

A young maid brought the tea, and Mrs. Hunson pulled a chair and a low table near the hearth. She dismissed the maid and poured the drink herself, along with a generous dollop of brandy. "There, that may help stop a chill from developing."

Roselynne took the chair and let the woman place the footstool under her feet. She accepted the cup of fortified tea and sipped it gratefully. "This is very good, Mrs. Hunson. Thank you."

The wind rattled the panes again.

"A broody day out," Mrs. Hunson said, fluffing out the damp dress and laying it over her arm. She gathered Roselynne's shoes, stockings and petticoats to be cleaned. "It was on just such a dark, foreboding day that Master Harry fell to his death."

Roselynne felt her scalp creep.

Mrs. Hunson looked at her, her deep-set eyes seeming to churn like a witch's cauldron. "He was angry that day, and no one could tell him not to ride." She swung her gaze to the window. "The earl was visiting the squire. He stayed the night, the weather was so bad, and came home the next morning to tragedy."

"How sad," Roselynne murmured, blowing across the hot tea and taking tiny sips to keep from burning her tongue.

"Yes. It devastated poor Robbie. He loved the lad."

"He must have been a good man."

"There was never another finer," Mrs. Hunson said in a fervent tone as if Roselynne had suggested otherwise. She poured more tea and brandy into Roselynne's cup. "He looked after his own. As all the earls of Rockdale do."

Her smile sent another chill along Roselynne's neck as the woman looked pointedly at her. She almost expected to see the earl appear from the grave to guard her.

"I must leave you now. Stay before the fire and rest. Shall I send supper to your room tonight?"

"Yes." She succumbed to the housekeeper's firm suggestion like a weak-minded child. "What about our guests?"

"Lady Stanton has gone to her home. The two Americans are in their rooms. Mr. Clayburgh left early this morning. I don't know his destination. Mr. Spinner went to Brighton to see a friend."

"My father?"

"In his room. Connie is reading to him."

"Good. All is in order." Roselynne smiled her thanks.

Mrs. Hunson replenished the tea and brandy, turned back the bed covers, and added another log to the fire before she left. The room seemed more cheerful when the door closed behind her, and Roselynne sighed in relief.

She drank the tea, sloshed the pot and discovered it held more and poured another cup. After a pause, she added the brandy. Soon she felt warm clear through and grew drowsy. Her thoughts drifted to her husband, and she sighed wistfully.

The panel slid open next to the chimney. "The devil take it," Beau muttered, closing the panel and inspecting it. He removed the dot. "I've waited forever to be sure she was gone. Why'd you cover the peephole?"

"Because I didn't want you or George spying on me," she replied. She should chastise him for invading her chamber, but it seemed too much bother. She yawned instead.

"Hmm." He glanced at her, then replaced the dot. He crossed to her, bent and took a whiff of the fortified tea. "You've been hitting the booze, my love. You're foxed."

"I am not." She yawned again.

"You need a nap."

"An exshu…exsh…a good idea." She stood—her legs felt wobbly—took another sip of tea and yawned her way to the bed. She shed her robe with provocative sensuality and climbed in, pulling the sheet up to her neck.

Beau stood by the fire, his own body heat increasing greatly at the sight of his wife in pink silk, her skin showing through in tantalizing glimpses. He picked up her cup and finished off the tea and brandy.

"No wonder she's foxed," he murmured, feeling the warmth spread through his system. He went to the bed.

Roselynne opened her eyes halfway. Her smile was relaxed, an open invitation to join her. He heaved a deep breath, but it did no good. God help him, but he couldn't resist her.

Blood pounded through him, reminding him he was a man. And here, in bed, smiling lazily up at him, was his wife.

He sat down and kicked off his shoes. In a moment, his clothing had joined her robe on the floor. When he slipped under the covers, she turned to him and snuggled against his chest as if they lay together nightly.

"Sweet heavens," he muttered. "I'll not last a second."

"Shh," she said.

Her breath fanned his chest, and he could feel the movements of her lips against his flesh. He was at flash point and tried to think of cold things, like standing out in the icy rain.

He managed to calm the raging need she'd incited within him. The thing to do, he reasoned, was to bring her to the same point. Then they could proceed from there.

He nudged her onto her back and eased the gown up. She obeyed his softly spoken orders without question. Then he tossed the gown aside and lay next to her, letting his hand slide over her curves and valleys until she began to move against him.

He smiled. She was as sensuous as a cat.

"Umm," she murmured when he cupped her breast.

He bent his head and took the tip into his mouth. He let his hand drift to her waist, then to the sweet mound that guarded the treasure he sought.

She moved her legs, giving him access, then to his surprised delight, she reached between them and softly stroked him.

He gasped as desire spiraled to maddening heights. Never had he been so aware of another, of the possibilities for pleasure that existed between them.

When she pressed closer, he slipped between her thighs and into the warm welcome of her body. She squirmed against him until they touched everywhere—lips, chest, abdomen, thighs.

She encircled his shoulders and ran her fingers into his hair, pulling his mouth to hers, demanding his kiss. He gave it to her. Holding himself back, he stroked her all over, giving her every nuance of pleasure that he knew.

Her body glowed in his arms. The smile had left her face, and she wore the look of concentration that only lovers knew.

"Beau," she said, a whimper of urgency.

"Easy, love," he whispered. He upped the tempo and heard her breath catch. She pressed her face against his shoulder, and he felt the imprint of her teeth—not hard, she was too much the lady to bite, but enough to know what she was feeling.

With a subdued cry, she clung to him, tremors running through her slender frame. Now he was free to soar. He plunged into her again and again, letting passion seize them both and fling them to the far, far shore. He poured himself into her and was lost to everything but her and their joining.

Beyond the passion lay peace. It settled over them like a blanket of the softest wool. He lay beside her and held her damp body against his, loath to let even air between them.

"Ah, love, for this, a man will take any risk, no matter how great. I think I'm addicted to your sweetness."

"Shh," she said. She kissed his chin, yawned and fell asleep.

He smiled, content to hold her while the rain lashed the windowpanes without mercy. It was a moment to cherish. He yawned. Soon he must return to his room. Soon . . .

Chapter Eighteen

"My lord! My lady! You must wake."

Roselynne woke from a beautiful dream. She saw Beau jerk awake as a hand prodded his shoulder. Putting his body between her and the intruder, he sat up, his fists ready to defend them.

Mrs. Hunson averted her eyes from the bed and spoke in a rapid whisper. "You must rise. There's been a tragedy, and the squire is here. He wants to see you, both of you, at once."

"What is it?" Roselynne leaned against her husband's shoulder and peered at the housekeeper. "What tragedy?"

"Lady Stanton. She's . . . suffered an accident."

"How bad?" Beau demanded. He started to move from the bed but stopped before revealing his lack of clothing.

"Most dire, I understand."

"We'll be down directly," he said, dismissing the woman. As soon as she left the room, he sprang up and began dressing.

Roselynne did the same. "Here, you'll have to do my buttons," she said, after slipping it into a black muslin.

"We're in for it now, my love," he murmured, kissing her neck before closing the buttons. "I fell asleep, and she found us."

"Do you think she will tell anyone?" Roselynne cast him a worried glance over her shoulder.

"I don't know. She's . . . ah . . . strange."

"It can't be helped. Hurry, we must find out what happened to Thea."

Beau returned to his room in order to exit from his own door and met Roselynne in the hall. Clayburgh was at the top of the steps. He waited for them.

"Do you know what this is about?" he asked. "The butler said everyone must report to the library."

"Thea has had an accident," Roselynne explained.

Was it her imagination or did his face pale?

They went to the library to find Mr. Moreley, George, Squire Witherspoon and Rodney already there. A footman finished building the fire and left, his eyes round with shock.

The squire bustled forward and bowed over Roselynne's hand. "So sorry to trouble you, my dear. 'Tis a sorry night to be bringing sad news."

"What has happened?"

"A terrible tragedy, I'm afraid."

"Something has happened to Thea, according to Mrs. Hunson. Can you tell us what . . . how . . . ?"

"Lady Stanton's mount returned to her stable sometime this afternoon. The groom found the beast, wet and shivering, when he went out to do the evening chores. He alerted the household, and they searched along the path from her house to Rockdale."

"And?" Beau asked, impatient with the details.

"That's the mystery of it," Rodney broke in. "She evidently decided to take the shore path. P'rhaps she wanted to observe the storm rolling in from the sea."

His father rapped him over the knuckles with the cane. "I'm the magistrate. I'll tell the story."

Rodney colored and went to stand by the hearth, well out of his parent's reach.

"The path had crumbled. It looked as if the horse slipped, and she fell off. Right over the edge she went. The horse must have regained its footing and run off." He paused. "Her neck was broken like a twig."

Roselynne pressed her hands to her mouth. Beau put an arm around her and pulled her tightly to him. George, with a warning glance at Beau, came over and put his arm across her shoulders. Beau relaxed his protective embrace.

"So it was an accident," he mused.

The squire looked from the three who stood together to Clayburgh, who leaned on the mantle near Rodney. "Nay. She landed on a bed of saltbush. Her neck was broken before she fell."

"Perhaps she hit it on a rock as she went over the side," George suggested.

"The rock that did the deed was found nearby, tossed into a bed of leaves." The squire's eyebrows, white but with a reddish hue, rose until they nearly met the old-fashioned bag wig he wore. He put his weight on his cane to relieve a gouty foot. "I'll have to ask where you were today. I'll start with you, Countess."

Beau stepped forward, his tone incredulous, his jaw belligerent. "You surely don't think she had ought to do with it."

"Don't know what to think as yet," the squire calmly stated. "Going to question all of you. Isn't one missing?"

Roselynne pulled at Beau's sleeve until he stepped back. "William has gone to Brighton. I assume he'll wait out the storm and return tomorrow," she replied.

"Hmm." The squire nodded. He turned to Clayburgh. "The servants say you were out most of the day, until an hour ago."

The barrister smiled dryly. "I rode with Thea to her home, as her servants no doubt have told you . . ."

The squire nodded.

". . . Then I continued on an errand of my own, a short ride in order to think. Later, I met a courier from my office at the pub on Brighton Road. The owner can vouch that we took tea in the private parlor. My man brought a copy of the late earl's will so that I might study it and advise Lady St. Clair on her duties. The paper is in my chamber. Shall I fetch it?"

"No one will go out of my sight until we finish this." The squire's round face assumed a dark expression.

"Sir, you can't truly believe Mr. Clayburgh did this terrible deed," Roselynne protested. Her knees trembled as she realized *someone* had done it. "It must have been an accident."

Mr. Moreley suddenly rose. Without looking at anyone, he came to Roselynne and offered his arm as if taking her for a Sunday stroll. She hesitated, then put her hand on his elbow. He escorted her to a chair, pulled his close and sat next to her.

The intent expression left his face, and he was blank once more.

Beau walked over and took up a stance to the side and slightly behind her. George did the same.

"And you?" The squire looked at George.

"I rode about the estate this morning. After lunch, I retired to my room and read. I rang for coffee and a fire when the storm blew in, so the servants know I was there."

"Yes, yes," the squire agreed, evidently having checked with the staff prior to sending for the countess and her guests. "Mr. Hargrove?"

Beau told of accompanying the countess and her father to church, lunch at the inn and the ride through the storm to the house. "I spent the remainder of the afternoon indoors and was napping until Mrs. Hunson woke me."

"That is true," Roselynne put in, then blushed as several pairs of eyes turned on her. "I mean, I did the same."

The squire cleared his throat. "By the by, I received a notice from London. The king's magistrate isn't convinced the earl died in the Thames. I'm to watch for a dark man with blue eyes and a goodly frame." He studied Beau, then George, then Roselynne. "The penalty for harboring a fugitive is severe."

"My husband was not guilty," Roselynne said hotly. "He liked and admired the earl, and would never have harmed him."

"He was convicted in a court of law," the squire reminded her with a stern frown.

"I say, p'rhaps Lady Stanton discovered St. Clair and he had to kill her to keep her from . . ." Rodney slowed to a halt as Beau and George each took a menacing step toward him. Roselynne glared, then turned her face in disdain.

Squire Witherspoon harrumphed. "I hope you can put us up for the night, Lady St. Clair. I have a constable and two guards with me as well. If it isn't too much trouble."

"No, of course not. I'll have Mrs. Hunson prepare rooms." She glanced at the clock. "It's past tea, but supper will be served early, if you can wait."

"Of course, of course," he agreed on a heartier note. He seemed ready to socialize now that his investigation was concluded for the present.

Roselynne rang for the footman. The next two hours were busy as she arranged rooms for the extra guests and ordered fires to be laid to drive out the chill and extra places to be set at the table. The squire told amusing stories of thievery and misconduct in the parish during the meal. Clayburgh joined in, often knowing details of the trials of the same individuals.

It was at once enlightening and macabre, Roselynne thought, smiling at the conclusion of a story about a wife who, in order to teach her husband a lesson on the evils of strong drink, had dressed like a demon and scared him into firing his pistol and shooting a neighbor's cow. Was the wife or the husband guilty?

"The husband," Roselynne said firmly.

"The wife," Beau countered. "She probably drove the man to hard liquor in the first place."

Clayburgh lifted his glass in a toast to Beau. "The jury agreed with Mr. Hargrove."

"Men," Roselynne sniffed. "Had there been women—" She stopped, remembering Thea. "We shouldn't jest."

"A long face won't change her fate," the squire told her philosophically.

Seeing that everyone was finished with the meal, Roselynne stood. "You may take your port and cigars here, gentlemen," she announced. "I'm going to retire, so I bid you good-night."

She went to her room, where Ansella waited, the bed already smoothed and turned back, her gown and robe warming before the fire. "Oh, mum, ain't it awful!" she exclaimed, helping her mistress with her dress.

Roselynne flinched at the horrified relish with which the girl spoke, then sighed. The tragedy would be all the talk for weeks, perhaps longer if it wasn't cleared up soon.

She looked at the rain hitting the window, and a chill spread over her. September the first. The month had started on a broody note, Mrs. Hunson would say.

"Yes," she replied to Ansella, "it is truly awful."

"And no one to mourn her, cook says," Ansella continued after Roselynne was in her robe, seated before the fire. The maid brushed the long curling strands until they lay in deep waves that flipped up at the tips.

"She had no family?" How little she knew of the woman who'd shared her home for almost a month.

"Nay, and her husband's folks had nought to do with her. I guess they didn't like her."

Tears clouded Roselynne's vision. "Thank you, Ansella. That will be all for the night. Have pleasant dreams."

"If I can, what with murderers loose hereabouts." On that cheerful note, the young maid put the brush away and left.

Roselynne was still sitting before the fire when the mirror panel opened and Beau entered from her bathing room. He came to her and took her hands between his.

"You look sad," he observed, sitting on the stool.

"Thea goes to her grave unwept, unloved and unsung," she said, paraphrasing a Greek tragedy she'd recently read to her father.

"Nay." He wiped a tear that slid down her face. "There's one whose heart weeps for her."

Roselynne pressed her face against his shirt, and he held her for a long while. "Let's go to bed," he suggested. "Tomorrow's another day, and likely to be a difficult one. Clayburgh will see to her affairs and . . . arrange things."

Gently, he shooed Roselynne into the large four poster, then he locked her door and his, leaving the panel open between. She looked a question at him.

"I'll stay with you tonight, but without the intrusion we experienced earlier. I spoke to the housekeeper. She informed me, with a sniff, that she was no tattlemonger."

"Oh!" Roselynne sat up, a look of utter horror on her face. "When she woke us, she said . . . she called you . . ."

"Damnation, you are right. She knows." He sat on the bed and removed his slippers and hose. "I think she has from the day I arrived. She put me in the room next to you."

"Do you think she knows of the panels?"

"Perhaps. She was raised here." He removed his clothing and got into bed.

"Sometimes people develop a fierce loyalty to the family they serve," Roselynne mused. "If Mrs. Hunson knew Thea was threatening to expose some scandal concerning the earl . . . ?"

Beau considered, then shook his head. "I can't see a connection. Besides, Mrs. Hunson was in the house when we arrived and later, when the squire came." He reached across Roselynne and snuffed out the candles, then clasped her in his arms. "It's late. We've thought on this enough. Now let's think on other things."

He kissed her slowly, deeply, his touch a reaffirmation of life and all that made it worth living. Roselynne clung to him, needing that assurance.

The days following the funeral were unusually quiet at the manor. The weather continued sullen and cold. Clayburgh handled the settling of Thea's estate, holding the old baron's sister and her pock-faced son at bay while he sorted the bills. Roselynne agreed to buy the land when the debts were settled. The sister-in-law had to be content with that. She and her son returned home.

William was interrogated by the squire. His story checked out. Although the friend he'd been visiting had left on a ship for America and couldn't be reached, the inn had a record of his stay.

Beau, George and Roselynne discussed the case several times. On Friday, they talked again but came up with no answers.

"Perhaps the earl, your cousin, was killed by a thief who chanced upon him at the cottage," she said to Beau. "Maybe Thea did slip and fall."

Beau shook his head, his fair curls gleaming like a cherub's locks around his face. "His signet ring and gold fob weren't taken, nor the silver buckles on his shoes."

"Thea wasn't thrown," George put in. "Beau and I examined the place. We think she dismounted and spoke with someone. There were tracks in the mud, a man's heel mark and small half boots. They'd have been washed out by the rain if they'd been made in the dust."

"And," Beau added, "she was with someone she knew well enough for her to turn her back to him, thus giving him the chance to hit her in the back of the neck and knock her off the cliff."

A chill tracked goose bumps along Roselynne's arms. "Mr. Clayburgh is the only one who hasn't accounted for his time. If we told the squire of Thea's blackmail, he'd be arrested."

Beau sat on the arm of her chair and rubbed her shoulders. "Aye. But the man didn't turn me in when I came to him half-dead."

"Yes, there's that," George said, in deep thought. He sighed and gave up. "I must go to my room and dress for dinner."

They were in the dressing area next to her bathing room with the panel open and both hall doors locked against intrusion. From this room, they couldn't be overheard even if someone pressed an ear to the door. Mr. Moreley sat before the hearth in her chamber. She was supposed to be reading to him.

George started out, then turned. "You know, Spinner lived here for two years, yet I've never met him in the hidden passages, something I've worried over from time to time. Do you think he doesn't know?"

"My cousin told me to tell only the next heir or someone I trusted as myself until the next heir was old enough." He smiled at George, then Roselynne.

George's ears turned pink. "Yes, well, I should hope I'm a trusted friend."

When he left, Beau leaned down to her. "I must dress, too. Shall I take your father to his room?"

"No, I'll ring for Connie. I'll see you later." She accepted his kiss and watched as he disappeared behind the mirror, his grin the last thing she saw.

"Father, it's time for supper. Are you hungry?" She didn't wait for a reply but pulled the bell cord for Connie and her maid. Then she stood by the window and watched the twilight deepen.

Her husband shared her bed every night now. It was the only time they had alone. If she was to gain his trust and thus his love, she'd realized they had to have a starting point. She would use passion as the bridge to his confidence and his heart.

His statement to George reminded her that he hadn't trusted her with his identity. She'd had to discover it for herself.

"I can't blame him for his caution," she said softly when her father came to stand beside her. "I bargained for my release from prison by marriage to a stranger. I gave myself to another without benefit of marriage, not even knowing if I was free of my first husband. He must think me without a shred of honor.''

Her father laid a comforting hand on her shoulder. She pressed her cheek against it for a minute.

"I long to speak of love, to assure him I'd die before I'd betray him to the authorities.''

Clutching her hands against her breast, she prayed for an end to this precarious existence. If there was a murderer about, she wanted him caught and put behind bars. She wanted to go forward with her life, to live openly with her husband, to love him without fear and bear his children.

"How does one win another's love, Father?'' she whispered. "He wants me, but is that enough? You told me marriage wouldn't work unless it was built on trust. Do you think me foolish to use passion as a key to gaining that?'' She fell silent as she thought on it. "Life is more difficult than I ever imagined, though you told me there would be times—''

The knock on the door was Connie, come to fetch Mr. Moreley. On his heels came Ansella, to help her with a fresh gown and to put up her hair in a Greek knot. It was time for tea.

Roselynne and her guests had barely sat down when Squire Witherspoon and the constable arrived.

"Won't you join us, gentlemen?'' she invited.

"Nay, we have business,'' the squire intoned. He leaned upon his cane and peered at the cozy company around the tea table. His gaze passed George, William, and Beau to land on Mr. Clayburgh. The constable moved behind the man, his hand on his pistol in his belt.

"Sir, what is this?'' Roselynne asked. She replaced the teapot on its trivet and stood. The men immediately rose. The constable whipped out the pistol and waved it around as if threatened with a riot.

"Ease off,'' the squire commanded the men.

"I think they've come for me,'' Clayburgh announced. His dry smile played about his mouth. He dropped his napkin across his plate and turned to the magistrate. "Isn't that it?''

"It is, sir," the squire replied. He nodded to the constable, who pulled out handcuffs.

"Wait!" Roselynne cried. "Why are you arresting him?"

The lawyer replied. "For the murder of Lady Stanton, I should imagine."

She remembered her first meeting with the man, when he'd come to her in prison on Beau's behalf. She also remembered that he'd saved Beau's life. "Nay, he didn't," she protested, looking at the squire beseechingly. "There is an error. I'm certain of it."

The squire patted her shoulder. "He was seen, m'lady, on the very path where she was slain after he'd left her at her home. And they'd quarreled at her house shortly before."

"We will get you the finest barrister," Beau promised. "Who do you prefer?"

"Myself." Clayburgh smiled, nodded a good day to the company and turned to the squire. "I'll go peacefully." He held out his wrists for the cuffs and accepted the arrest.

Beau and George went out with the men. Roselynne, in spite of knees that felt like jelly, rushed to the window. She watched as Clayburgh was helped to mount his steed and was taken away by the constable. The squire led the little parade and two guards drew up the rear.

"I cannot believe this!" She pressed her fingers to her temples. Hitting someone in the back of the neck and tossing them from a cliff was an impulsive act, and Mr. Clayburgh wasn't an impulsive man.

Beau and George returned in time to catch her words.

"It's hard to believe evil of those we know, even those we don't like," Beau said. "Come, sit, and we'll plan."

He led her to the sofa and encouraged her to pour the tea. She served each of the men, by now knowing their preference for tea or coffee and how they liked it prepared. She put two sugared almond biscuits on her father's plate. He and William were the only ones who hadn't commented on this turn of affairs.

"I'm so shocked, I can't think," she murmured.

"I myself am relieved," William stated. He leaned close and patted her hand. "You'll sleep better knowing there's no murderer upon the premises."

She couldn't resist a peek at Beau. A flash of humor tugged at his lips and was gone, reminding her that she slept very well at night, snug in her husband's arms. However, the thought didn't drive away her sense of foreboding.

"Then you think Mr. Clayburgh guilty?" she asked William.

"Aye." He stroked his chin as if considering some disclosure. "I have heard—although I dislike repeating hearsay—that there were other meetings between Lady Stanton and the man, many of which ended in quarrels. I don't know the cause of their dislike."

"Perhaps they were lovers, and she'd taken up with another," Beau suggested. His keen gaze lingered on William.

William returned the stare. Tension spun cobwebby threads in the cozy room.

"Perhaps," William said at last. "I've no idea of the lady's private life." He turned to Roselynne, signaling an end to the conversation with Beau. "If tomorrow proves fair, shall we ride to the village? A mummers' troupe is giving a show at the market hall. It may prove amusing."

"That sounds delightful. Father loved a good mime. I'm sure he'd enjoy it, too. Will you join us?" she asked George and Beau with a spritely humor she was far from feeling.

Both men declined, so she and William made plans. It seemed odd to plan outings as if they were on holiday when one of their members had just been arrested for murder.

After tea, she played while William sang. His choices tended to songs of unrequited love, which he rendered in tones of great longing while gazing at her.

Afterward, she retired to the library to read before the fire while he went off on a walk.

Beau and George found her still reading after they returned from a hasty errand. Beau looked disgruntled.

"The case against Clayburgh is tight. He has no alibi for the hours he rode about the country after another quarrel with Thea. She was definitely seen with a man while she was returning here, but the woodchopper was too far away to identify her companion, only that he rode a large horse, black and spirited."

"William's mount is roan and smallish," she said. She cast a worried glance at Beau.

His face hardened. "You know I didn't meet her. I was ... otherwise occupied."

"I didn't mean to imply you did, only that someone could have wanted it to appear that way." She toyed with a ruffle on her skirt. "Someone seems to be casting suspicion in all directions."

"Clayburgh's horse is dark," George reminded them. "Perhaps he is the guilty one. He might have killed your cousin," he said to Beau.

"How do you reason?" Beau selected two snifters and poured brandy. He handed one to George.

"Well," George drawled, thinking as he spoke, "with the earl and you out of the way, he'd be in position to advise the bereaved countess." He indicated Roselynne. "Be nice to have a half-million pounds at your disposal. People have been tempted by less."

"Assuming he could trick Roselynne," Beau said, pursuing the thought, "how would he fool you?"

"I'll be returning to Virginia at the end of the month. My passage has been booked since our arrival."

"With you gone, there'd be only Roselynne to curb his greed, if he is so inclined. She's gullible ..." At her indignant gasp, he added, "And the man's been an adviser to the St. Clairs for twenty years, so of course the earl trusted him."

Roselynne fought the rise of temper at Beau's assessment of her. He spoke in her presence the way some people did of children, as if they weren't there or couldn't hear.

"Think on this," she invited, devising a logic of her own. "With Beau hanged and no one to claim the title, it would have reverted to the crown to be given as the king wished. Recall that the barrister arranged the payment to the king's coffers to free my father and myself. We can assume he's done the same before, so the king owes him favors."

"By damn, there's motive for you." George looked at Beau, who said nothing.

Roselynne continued, "However, he couldn't know Beau would suddenly lose his mind and marry a fellow prisoner."

Beau frowned at this assessment of his intellect.

She let these facts sink in, then added, "I think him innocent of both crimes. He's cunning and intelligent, yes, but he's thoughtful, too. Why would he act on impulse when he's obviously dealt with Lady Stanton for months?"

"She was becoming unbearably demanding?" George suggested.

"Why?" Roselynne demanded. "What had changed in her life of late? It seems to me that a person changes only when pressed. She had a problem with William, too, you may recall."

"But his boot heel didn't match the one we found on the trail," George informed her glumly. "We followed him and checked the length. 'Tis different."

"Neither did Clayburgh's," Beau added. "So that came to nothing." He flung himself into a leather chair.

"Sanders may find out something. We have him following Spinner," George explained to Roselynne.

"You didn't tell me that," she began, then intercepted a frown from her husband to his friend. She realized he didn't mean for her to know the details of their investigation.

"I saw no need to worry you with our fruitless attempts to play the sleuth," Beau explained.

She hated the cool way he shut her out. "I see. In that case, I think I shall leave you two to your scheming and retire to my chamber." She put a marker in her book and laid it aside.

The two men stood while she made a dignified exit.

In the privacy of her room, she dropped her pose. Her heart ached with the evidence of his distrust. He had lain with her in this bed, had shared a passion so great she still marveled at it, and yet he wouldn't take her into his confidence. She was but a playmate, not a wife.

"You don't give her enough credit," George said in the silence after Roselynne's departure.

"The less she knows, the better for her."

"You hurt her with your secretive manner."

Beau leaped from the chair and paced the floor. "I don't want to involve her. In prison...when we married...I wasn't looking at things clearly. I didn't realize I was sending her into a nest of danger. I thought we'd quickly find the culprit and finish the case, but I was wrong."

George smiled slyly. "I don't think she minds. She seems happy enough to me. So do you."

Beau halted and spun around. A bleak expression passed over his face. "Life becomes more complicated when a man takes a wife. Roselynne's destiny is tied to mine, and it worries me. I've tried to make sure she's safe, but I'm afraid for her."

"Afraid?"

"What if she's left unguarded for a moment? What if this madman decides to get rid of her for some twisted reason?" he balled his fists. "I, for selfish reasons, brought her into this. I have to protect her as I see fit. Now, we must plan a trap, one with me as the bait."

"Spinner won't hurt Roselynne. He plans to marry her. But what will bring him into the open to attack you?"

Beau gazed thoughtfully into the distance. "If he thinks she has promised herself to Cousin True, wouldn't he feel compelled to get rid of the competition?"

Roselynne decided to change her rumpled gown for a fresh one before the evening meal. She started to ring for Ansella, then remembered she hadn't told Beau about the trip to the convent she intended to make.

A cow was to be butchered Monday morning, and she wanted to deliver a quarter section to the good sisters and pay her respects to the prioress.

Hearing William entertaining himself at the pianoforte and not wanting to be drawn into a musical with him, she went to the secret panel. Opening it, she crept along the black corridor, a hand on the wall at each side. She found the secret steps and went down to the first level. The passageway ended at the library.

She peered through the peephole to see who was present. Beau and George still talked. Good. She searched the frame for the lever to release the latch.

"And then what?" she heard George ask. She was startled at the angry tone he used.

"Then, when all is resolved, I'll return to Virginia."

"To stay?"

"Yes."

Roselynne froze.

"What of Roselynne? She might have something to say about being uprooted and moved three thousand miles away."

"She'll remain here."

"Are you crazy?" George laughed. "If I know anything of her, she'll be hell-bent on going with you."

"I'm sure she'll think it her duty," Beau remarked dryly. "But she'll stay here. I'm set upon it, so let's not argue."

"Answer me one thing. Why?"

"It's for the best. I'm thinking of her happiness." Beau stood and went to the table. "Would you like a brandy? I found an exceptional bottle in the wine cellar yesterday."

Roselynne straightened, her joints as stiff as someone three times older. With uncertain steps, she made her way to the stairs and up them to her bedroom. She closed the panel and leaned against it, every breath stirring a pain in her chest.

A chill shook her body, but her face felt hot and feverish. One thought echoed in the empty cavern of her mind. Her husband planned on leaving her.

Chapter Nineteen

Roselynne declined the fair on Saturday and church on Sunday although the weather had warmed and cleared. She'd felt too dreary to mingle with a cheery crowd and too restless to sit through a sermon, hidden behind her black veil of mourning.

Beau felt her head Monday morning and asked if she was ill when she refused an early morning gallop over the meadows, a pastime she usually enjoyed.

"You've been quiet the past few days," he noted. "Are you increasing?" He moved his hand to her abdomen.

She pushed him away. "No."

"What ails you?" he asked, sliding his hands over her breasts. "Is this a bad time of the month?"

Blood heated her face. She still wasn't used to discussing such things. "No." She shoved him away again.

He looked at the clock. "We have time for a frolic before breakfast," he suggested.

She was aware of his gaze on her, prying beneath the shield she'd placed over her heart. For her, their lovemaking had taken on a poignancy that was fierce and sad at the same time.

Knowing their time together was short, she stored each moment for the lonely nights ahead. She pressed each kiss, each caress into the pages of her memory, and every whispered endearment was written on her heart. If passion could forge a bond, they'd be forever bound.

"Yes," she whispered, pulling him down to her.

Words were forgotten in the urgency of their joining, but later, when he left her and she was alone, she brushed the tangles out of her hair and sat lost in contemplation, wondering why he thought it would make her happy to be separated from him.

She had news for him. She just might refuse to be left behind. If he wouldn't let her sail with him, then she'd book passage on another ship. He'd find a wife wasn't so easy to dispose of. If he was really thinking of her happiness, then he should ask her opinion on what *she* wanted.

"A quarter of beef and a yearling lamb," the cook confirmed, indicating the meat wrapped in oiled cloth for delivery to the convent. "I added a pot cheese."

"Good," Roselynne approved.

She had a gardener put a bushel of apples in the cart and told Jim and two laborers to be ready to leave at one. She returned to the house for a riding hat and gloves. Beau met her on the stairs and pulled her into his arms. He stole a kiss.

"Don't," she cautioned and moved from his arms.

"I have something for you."

She glanced down into the front hall to make sure no one observed them. "If we aren't careful, the hangman may have something for you—tied up in a pretty noose."

Beau laughed at her warning. He seemed filled with a reckless spirit of late, and she worried about him. Her father had once told her no idyll continued forever, that paradise wasn't without cost. She felt in her bones their time was growing short.

He removed a tiny, perfect rose from his pocket and tucked it in her hair. "Consider this a token of our vows," he proclaimed, then kissed her again.

The kiss lengthened until she was dizzy. She turned from it.

"I must go." She ducked her head and hurried out when he released her, her composure ravaged by his touch. Tonight, she decided, she'd tell him what she'd heard and have it out in the open. There'd be no secrets between them, he'd said. She agreed. A marriage wouldn't work if built on half truths.

Beau watched her leave, then, whistling a country tune, he dashed up the stairs and hid behind a suit of armor mounted on a marble pillar. Two minutes later, William walked out of the library, his face carved with fury.

Beau raced to his room and pulled on his riding jacket. He grabbed his hat and went out to the stable to order his mount saddled before William left.

"Say, William," he called, "wait for me. I thought I'd ride along the bluff and see what damage the storm did to the path. Do you want to come?"

William barely gave him a glance. "I've other errands this morning." He spurred his horse and started down the drive.

"Oh, too bad. Well, see you later. Lad, bring the black," Beau shouted at the loitering stableboy. He watched William ride off toward the Brighton Road. The scoundrel would soon cut into the woods and double back to the cliff, Beau was willing to bet.

A thought came to him as he placed his hat on his head and swung up onto the stallion. Young Harry had died from a fall on the cliff path five years ago after a wasp stung his horse. That was during the time Spinner had lived here with Alice.

A load of rock salt in a shotgun could do the same. Too bad George and Sanders were already hidden in the woods at the point where Beau planned to dismount and inspect the path, with the hope that William would appear. He needed to warn the men of this possibility. If William salted the black before then . . .

He made the ride without mishap. At the drop-off, the same where Thea had met her end, Beau climbed down, tied the horse to a tree well out of the way, and pretended to inspect the crumbling path in great detail.

After an hour, he gave up surveying the cliff from every angle except standing on his head. It was obvious their ploy hadn't worked. He gave a piercing whistle, which caused the stallion to throw up his head and rattle his bridle.

George and Sanders came out of the woods, guns at the ready. "What's happening?" George demanded, panting as he looked up and down the path. Sanders kept an eye on the woods.

"Not a damned thing," Beau said in disgust. He rubbed the back of his neck. "I thought sure the man would act. He would have had to be furious to bash Thea in the neck like that, and he looked murderous when he came out of the library—''

"What?" George asked when he broke off abruptly.

"Hellfire! Roselynne!" Beau ran for his mount, grabbed the reins and threw himself into the saddle.

"Wait," George called. "He'll not hurt her. That would be stupid on his part."

Beau sawed the reins as the stallion rose and pawed the air in excitement. He considered his half-baked plan to find and attack Spinner. George was right. He couldn't suddenly rush upon the man and accuse him of murder.

"You know," George mused, "we could be wrong. We haven't a clue that Spinner is the culprit."

"I don't trust him," Beau asserted.

"Because he wants Roselynne," George said dryly. "However, I don't trust him, either, and haven't from the first. He has a smooth and cunning manner."

Sanders returned with their horses. The two men mounted and joined Beau on the path. He led the way to the house, his countenance grim as he considered the ways a man might frighten a woman.

A half hour later they rode into the stable yard, dismounted, then burst into the house, to find Connie reading to Mr. Moreley in the library while Mrs. Hunson directed a maid in dusting and a footman in cleaning out the fireplace and laying new logs.

"Has Roselynne returned?" Beau panted.

"Why, no, only the men with the cart," Mrs. Hunson said. "The countess is taking some refreshment with the prioress before she returns, they reported."

At Beau's muttered imprecation, George reminded him, "Jim is with her."

Mrs. Hunson inspected a table for dust. "Actually, he isn't," she informed them. "His horse threw a shoe, so he went to the village to see the smith. Mr. Spinner volunteered to see the countess home."

"You seem distracted," William commented.

"Just enjoying the air and the view," she replied.

Roselynne realized she'd been lost in her own thoughts for many minutes. The sweet scent of the rose Beau had given her wafted around her on the breeze. She was still trying to figure out what he had meant about the flower being a token of their vows.

Perhaps it was some new strategy. "Cousin True" was becoming increasingly familiar with her in public, acting as if he had a right to touch her at will. Sometimes she thought he did it to taunt William, which seemed foolish to her.

She sighed and sat up straight. Her back ached.

Athene blew through her nostrils and shook a fly off her nose. Roselynne glanced up and saw William looking at her, his eyes flat and unreadable. She realized she'd gone off on another trail of thought.

"I'm sorry, Cousin William. I'm poor company today, I fear. I was thinking of...other things," she ended lamely.

"Quite all right." He paused as they came to a pub. "I shall rein in here and have a draught while you do your good deed, then I'll take you home."

"Fine. I shouldn't be long."

She and the two men with the cart ambled along the lane, which was bordered with yew trees like the drive to the manor. The name of the pub stuck in her mind. The Bedeviled Soul. She assumed it was a reference to the convent.

She put the notion aside as they drew up to a pair of stout wooden gates. One of the footmen rang a bell.

After five minutes a nun came to the gate and opened a tiny door. She looked out without speaking.

"The Countess of Rockdale," one of the men intoned. "We 'ave food for you," he added when this brought no response.

The woman shut the door. Another five minutes passed before the gates swung open, and they were motioned inside. Roselynne dismounted by a rail and tied the reins. The nun dropped a wooden bucket of water in front of Athene, who drank noisily, and motioned for Roselynne to follow her. Two other sisters appeared and began to unload the cart.

Roselynne walked quickly to keep up and soon found herself on a small sunny terrace. A table was prepared with two glasses, a pitcher of fruit juice and a platter of crackers and cheese.

The nun spoke, her voice hesitant as if she spoke from an unknown script. "We weren't expecting you . . . my lady. The prioress is ill with the grippe. Umm, your cousin, will be here." She turned to leave. "Soon," she said.

Puzzled, Roselynne sat down and waited. Footsteps, a whisper of sandaled feet on the paving stones, sounded almost at once. A sister scurried around a corner. Behind her came another.

The breath left Roselynne's body as the nun led a girl to the table and pushed her into the chair, then left with a soft rustle of cotton robes. Roselynne could only stare.

The girl had tawny hair, black lashes and familiar deep blue eyes. She hugged a doll to her breast and sang to it.

Roselynne breathed deeply, quietly, so as not to startle the other woman. Finally, she spoke, "Alice?"

Alice St. Clair Spinner looked at her, then went back to her lullaby. "Shh," she said when Roselynne cleared her throat.

Roselynne poured a glass of juice with a trembling hand. No wonder there was no headstone for Alice. The girl hadn't died shortly after childbirth. She'd . . . she'd . . .

Roselynne swallowed and looked at Alice in pity. The woman, who must be close to thirty but looked younger, had lost her senses. She'd been put away.

Smoothing the tiny row of gathers on her sleeve, Roselynne tried to figure it out. She leaped to her feet. She must tell Beau of this. His cousin Alice lived!

Alice glanced at the glass and nodded toward the pitcher. Roselynne poured another glass of juice and gave it to her. Alice drank half and replaced the glass. She smiled and put a finger over her lips when Roselynne started to speak.

There were a thousand questions she wanted to ask, but felt it wouldn't do any good. Alice lived in her own world.

To Roselynne's surprise, the vagueness disappeared from Alice's face, and she stood and bobbed a curtsy, her smile radiant, when another woman joined them.

"Good day, my child," the prioress said. "Go on with you and put your baby to bed for a nap." She watched while Alice, humming again, carried the doll toward a door in a long, low building.

Roselynne watched until Alice disappeared, then she looked at the other woman. She was very old, her face lined with many years and her back stooped with their weight.

"She's as gentle as a lamb," the prioress said. "Please, be seated, Countess. I see you weren't prepared for this. Had I not been sick . . ." She shrugged and took the vacant chair.

"I wouldn't have seen her, would I?" Roselynne asked.

"That was the earl's wishes. No one was to know."

"Why? I don't understand. Why?"

The prioress sighed. "The taint of madness. The twelfth earl was mad as a March hare. Robert, the thirteenth earl and a nephew, didn't want it known."

"**Alice**'s husband—"

"Thinks she's dead."

"How could this be?" Roselynne's thoughts chased themselves like a dog after its tail.

"He was away when the babe came. Early, it was, and she suffered so. They called me to help, for I was known for my healing in those days." The prioress shook her head. "We couldn't save the poor tiny thing. Nor the mother, as it turned out."

"So the . . . the *earl* put her here?"

"Not at first. A month passed and she kept crying and calling for her child. We hoped she'd recover if she was out of the house for a time. But she was no better here. Then, one day, she ceased her wailing. She'd found a doll, left by some young visitor who waited while her parents visited another. Alice has kept the doll, as you saw."

"Does no one know?" Roselynne asked.

The prioress hesitated, then nodded. "Mr. Clayburgh pays for her keep. He says there is a trust established for her lifetime, one that will continue even if something should happen to him."

Clayburgh! "He was once in love with her," Roselynne said softly, repeating Thea's words. Thea must have threatened to expose the truth about Alice, and Clayburgh paid her off.

"Yes. He loves her still, I think."

Tears welled in Roselynne's eyes. Her heart was tender toward anyone who loved so tragically. "I must go." She stood. "May I return and see her again?"

The prioress rose, her frail body trembling with the effort. She coughed alarmingly before she replied. "You are her next of kin and therefore have the say of her."

"Nay, there is someone—" She stopped, biting her lip. She couldn't explain about Beau yet. "Mr. Clayburgh has the stronger claim," she amended. "I must speak to him."

"He has been arrested, I understand."

Roselynne studied the woman. "For a convent with a vow of silence, you know much."

"A wise person keeps an ear to the whispers of the world."

They smiled, instantly liking and understanding each other.

"Next time, Countess, I'll show you our garden. We're nearly self-sufficient in everything but meat. Your contribution is most welcome. Thank you."

Roselynne bid the prioress good day and hurried to Athene, who was cropping grass growing under the railing. The cart was gone.

Leaping onto the mare, Roselynne urged her to a ground-eating gallop. She forgot about William until she arrived at the inn. He was waiting under a tree with the roan ready to ride, and he vaulted into the saddle when he saw her rapid approach.

"What ho," he said, catching up with her. "You ride as if demons chased you."

He seemed to watch her closely. A quiver of fear attacked her. She'd never noticed that William had black, beady eyes, like a rat's.

"I have the headache and wish to get home," she replied. That much was true. Mostly, she wanted to talk to Beau and tell him . . .

Suddenly pieces of information began to shift in her mind. Thea had been the earl's, then Clayburgh's mistress. She'd gotten money from Clayburgh. She'd also sent for William, according to the conversation Beau had overheard. William was Alice's husband, but he'd been told his wife was dead. These facts placed Thea in the thick of an intrigue of her own making.

Dear heaven, William had spoken of marriage to *her*. If he had married again, he'd have been a bigamist. He could have lived in sin for years without knowing it. The earl had been unfair in not telling him. Roselynne considered what she should do.

An odd distrust in the back of her mind made her hesitate to blurt out Alice's true situation to William. She'd discuss it with Beau first and get his views. After all, Alice was his cousin.

If William did know his wife lived . . .

Roselynne gasped as more pieces fell into place. If Beau had hanged, if he had died without marrying, then Alice would have been the only living heir. William could have brought her forward, and as her husband, he'd have controlled the estate, all except the title. He could probably get that if he wished, for a son if not for himself. A half-million pounds would buy a lot of things.

The problem with this scenario was herself. William would have to kill her . . . The runaway cart! They'd never found the driver for it, which was odd. And she most certainly would have been killed had she not leaped from the carriage.

She rubbed her temples as thoughts swirled. She knew she was near the truth.

"Are you unwell, Cousin?" William asked, reining in close beside her. "You're pale."

Roselynne glanced at him. His worry seemed sincere. Perhaps she was wrong to doubt him. After all, he'd asked her to marry him. Of course! If he didn't kill her, he could marry her and get control of the money. Assuming Alice and Beau were dead.

It would be a simple thing for a cunning mind to dispose of Alice when she was no longer needed. A chill swept over Roselynne, all the way to her soul. It would take an evil mind . . .

"Roselynne?"

"I'm fine, thank you," she managed. "It's just the headache. I need to get home." Warnings rang through her head, and she knew she was in danger. She smiled as if in pain and hoped her act was convincing.

He studied her. "I think not," he said, his beady gaze unwavering as he pulled a pistol from his belt. She saw he carried two weapons.

She gasped aloud. "What in the world!" she exclaimed. "Do you see trouble, Cousin?" She pretended to look for a highwayman.

He chuckled. "Do not dissemble, Roselynne. I think you saw someone you shouldn't have."

"So you do know of Alice," Roselynne accused. "The prioress said only the—" She stopped abruptly, realizing she'd revealed her knowledge.

She met his hard gaze without blinking, then her eyes narrowed. Athene was as swift as the wind and larger than his mount. But before she could put the idea into action, he grabbed the mare's long mane.

"I'd have no qualms about shooting her. Or you." All semblance of charm and kindness had evaporated.

Roselynne, looking into his face, believed him. He wore the smile of a devil.

Jim returned to the estate shortly after lunch. Beau met him at the stable.

"Did you see the countess on the road or in the village? She hasn't returned yet, and I'm worried," Beau asked him.

"Nay," Jim said in disgust. "I went by the nuns' place to see if she was ready to come home. She'd left, the nun said, and no one was with her. That Mr. Spinner, he said he'd watch out for her." The footman dismounted and shifted from limb to limb.

Relief swept through Beau. Spinner wasn't with her. "Where could she have gotten to?" he mused aloud.

Jim's face cleared. "She's probably at some crofter's cottage, drinking cider and bouncing a babe on her knee. 'Tis how she usually spends a free afternoon. The folks like to have her visit, she's so natural 'n all."

"Well, then, all is most likely well. Tend to your nag, then come to the house. In case I need you later."

But as the hours wore on, Beau's thoughts became morbid. Roselynne might have discovered something about William, and he'd found out she knew and had decided to kill her.

He stalked an angry circle around the library sofa, unsure what course to pursue. If he sent out a search party, Spinner would know something was up. But if he didn't and Spinner had Roselynne and she was frightened ... He was going mad with the uncertainty of it.

The clock chimed the hour. She should have returned by now.

He made a decision. "Jim, get Sanders. And find George."

A quiet inquiry to the vicarage and the cottages that lay near the manor wouldn't be thought out of the ordinary. He would caution the men to use discretion. When William and/or Roselynne returned, they'd be none the wiser if his fears had played him false.

"I won't." Roselynne crossed her arms and gazed at her captor without any show of emotion. William wanted her to write a note to True inviting him to a tryst at the castle ruins.

"Stubborn bitch. You're just like all the St. Clairs." William gave her a menacing glance. "Robert wouldn't loan me money when I needed it and look what happened to him."

"Did you kill him?" she demanded. "When you found out your wife lived, did you murder him and frame Beau, thinking to gain Rockdale and the inheritance?"

William gave her a feral grin, but ignored her questions. "I wonder how well dear Cousin True knows your hand. He's probably not seen it."

"Of course he has. Besides, why should you want him? He knows nothing of your duplicity."

Did William know True was really Beau? She thought not, and she'd never give the fact away, not even if William tortured her.

She plucked at her sleeve and realized the lace was torn and part of it was gone. Perhaps someone would find it and report to the manor, then Beau, George, Jim and Sanders would come looking for her. She feared for their lives. William was a man without feelings or scruples.

"This is your last chance," William said. "Write the note."

She shook her head, then grew still when her captor aimed his pistol at her. She breathed again when he lowered it.

"If aught goes wrong, I may need a hostage later," he decided with a contemptuous scowl at her.

He'd shed his veneer of charm like a snake's skin, and she saw the cruelty in his face. Poor Alice.

"I'll write the note myself," he said, after a period of thought. "I must have a culprit to account for your death, and he'll come if he thinks you want him."

He smiled at her through the bars of the castle dungeon. He'd put a chain and lock on the gate after forcing her inside.

"Just as you had Mr. Clayburgh to account for Thea's?" she asked with greater poise than she felt. Her knees went weak, and her hands would have trembled had she not gripped the bars.

He smiled. "That worked out well, didn't it? However, the evidence is circumstantial. If your lover is arrested for your death, he'll also be accused of Thea's. Everyone knew he dangled after her. I need Clayburgh free for my own purposes."

"Why would Cousin True kill me?"

William shrugged. "Who knows the mind of a madman? Perhaps he thought he would inherit as next of kin."

"You're the madman."

"Ah, I have it. You refused his suit because you and I have an understanding. He killed you in a fit of jealousy. I arrived and killed him, but alas, too late to save you."

With a satisfied air, he stuck the pistol in his belt. Going to a boulder, he sat and penned the note. Finished, he rose, grinning. "Soon I'll have all the Rockdale money. I won't have to grub for a living ever again."

Roselynne said nothing. No wonder Alice had lost her senses. William was a cruel, uncaring man.

She recalled Beau's gentleness. When she'd been frightened, he'd refrained from pressing his desire on her. Now that she understood the intensity passion aroused, she marveled at his patience with her.

William folded the paper and put it in his waistcoat pocket. Still smiling, he disappeared from view. In a moment, she heard him leave on his mount.

After a long silence, she whistled for Athene, but had no response. He must have taken the mare deep into the woods.

Taking a hairpin, she worked on the lock, but got nowhere at all. Heroines in novels could do wonderful things with hairpins and hat pins and such. Hers simply bent out of shape.

"Damnation!" she cried, rattling the bars of her cage, hardly noticing that she'd cursed and not feeling guilty about it at all.

The black skimmed along the trail at a rapid clip. Beau, his face grim, pulled to a stop and checked the directions in the note he'd received. Yes, here was the turnoff.

For all his strategy, he raged to himself, he'd not protected Roselynne at all. Someone—he suspected William—held her captive.

His eye caught a flutter from a bush. A piece of lace. He savagely tore it free and jammed it into his pocket, then followed the path through the woods. In a minute, he came to a clearing with an old castle on the other side.

After tying the stallion to a low tree limb, he walked in a semicircle, observing the pile of stones. No sign of William or his wife. And no cover to approach the ruins without being seen.

Hidden behind a tree, he assessed his chances of making it to the stone wall. He peered out. A bullet whizzed past his head.

Quickly, before his assailant could reload, he ran for the stones and flattened himself against them, his own gun ready.

"Come out or I'll kill her." William came to the front of the castle. He snapped the breech closed as he finished loading.

"He can't shoot me from where he is," Roselynne yelled.

Relief spun through him. She was alive. Beau crept closer to the opening and saw William disappear inside.

He peered around the edge of the arch. William had his pistol aimed at Roselynne, who was locked inside a cell. She stood at the bars of the door, glaring at their enemy.

Beau's heart gave a giant lurch. In that moment, everything he'd ever felt for her condensed into one simple truth. From the first moment he saw her, he'd wanted her, his brave, loyal, stubborn wife. Now he not only wanted her, he loved her, too.

"Last chance," William said and cocked the hammer.

Beau stepped out, his pistol skyward in his raised hand.

"Drop your weapon," William ordered, swinging around.

Beau did so.

"No," Roselynne cried. "Oh, you shouldn't have come."

"I got your note," Beau said.

"Not mine. William wrote it."

Beau sighed dramatically. "Damn. I nearly hamstrung the black getting up here to an assignation."

He hadn't gone a quarter mile before he'd decided the letter was a trick, whether she'd written it or not. His lady wife wouldn't have sent a crofter with a note inviting him to a tryst.

"Enough," William snapped. He waved the gun barrel at Beau. "Over here, against the wall, and no tricks."

Beau backed into a corner. "I can see why you'd want to kill me, but why her? Isn't that like killing the goose that laid the golden eggs?"

"I have another goose." William grinned.

"His wife, Alice, lives. I found her at the convent today," Roselynne spoke up. "Her mind had wandered, and the earl wanted everyone to think her dead."

"Even me," William vouched, "but when I discovered she lived, it was an opportunity not to be overlooked, a second one."

"Second?" Beau questioned.

"When Harry had his foolish accident, I was jubilant. I had thought Alice was next in line. Three months later, I was told she'd died, her allowance terminated, and all my plans for a life of leisure ended. I had only her marriage portion to sustain me."

Roselynne gripped the bars at this callous story. The gate creaked and trembled on its hinges.

"Do you think you can get away with multiple murder?" Beau asked. The curl of his lip indicated he thought William a fool.

"Yes. Now how shall I accomplish this?" William mused aloud, an evil gleam in his eyes. "I suppose I shall have to shoot you first, then her." He turned the gun toward Beau.

Fury hit Roselynne like a lightning bolt. She lunged against the prison bars with all her might. The gate gave way with a loud screech, and she stumbled forward as her weight broke the rust-held hinges.

The chain acted as pivot point, and Roselynne and the gate swung in a loose arc, hitting William with a jarring thud and knocking him to the side. His pistol went flying.

Beau dashed for his weapon, but William was as fast and nearer to his. He grabbed it and whirled to face Beau, who hit the ground and rolled as William leveled and fired.

"No!" Roselynne cried, flinging herself from the sagging gate like a madwoman. She didn't quite reach William, which gave him enough time to draw his other pistol. He whipped about and fired it as she leaped at him.

The bullet slammed into her. Her eyes opened wide in disbelief. She lifted her arm to look at the gush of blood from her side. Suddenly pain, unlike anything she'd ever experienced, hit her. It stopped her cold.

Time slowed to a crawl.

She saw Beau lift himself from the ground with a mighty heave of muscle and fling himself at William. She watched, through a strange dimness, as Beau locked his hands around William's throat.

William hit Beau with the butt of the gun, but Beau didn't let go. Both men fell to the ground and wrestled each other in a grotesque ritual of death. William's face turned blue; blood trickled from Beau's temple. Before she could tell the outcome of the struggle, the light disappeared entirely.

Chapter Twenty

Roselynne woke with a start of alarm. Fear engulfed her like a poison mist, and she looked around wildly. It took her several seconds to comprehend she was in her own bed in her own room.

She tried to rise, to shake off the remainder of the fear. The movement drew a groan from her. She had a terrible ache in her side. Confused, she touched her ribs and found them bandaged.

She heard another groan. The sound came from beside her. She turned her head and gasped as blue eyes opened and stared into hers. "Beau?" she murmured worriedly, remembering everything.

"Roselynne," he said at the same time, then moaned as he raised a hand to his head. He sported a bandage over his temple.

"Shh," she whispered and glanced around the room. "Where do you suppose William is?"

"He appears to be gone," Beau reassured her. "And we appear to be safe at home."

"But how did we come to be here?" She winced as she sat upright against the pillows. Her rib was surely cracked.

"That, I don't know," Beau said, grimacing when he raised himself up. He gave her an anxious and thorough perusal, which gradually changed to one of husbandly interest.

He stroked her cheek, a tender light in his eyes, and let his fingers trail along her throat until he reached the bow at her neck. "I find it doesn't grieve me overmuch."

"None of that," a voice spoke up from the hearth. Mr. Moreley rose from a highbacked chair in front of the fire. He closed a book and laid it aside. "Neither of you is energetic enough, I should think." He smiled as he came to the bed.

"Father!" A blush burnt its way into Roselynne's face. She stared in disbelief when he stopped by her side.

"'Tis I," he said, taking her hand and squeezing it to let her know he was alive and in the flesh.

She forgot her embarrassment at being found in bed with a man. "You . . . you can speak. You've regained your senses."

He nodded. "How are you feeling?"

She looked him over, still amazed at his altered appearance, and searched his eyes for any lingering illness on his part before answering. "All right. Except my side is sore. There seems to be a bandage. Are my ribs broken?"

"No. You have a flesh wound, not terribly serious but painful, I'm sure. And you, sir," he said to Beau, "you were beaten rather severely about the head and will have some bruises and lumps for a few days, and perhaps a headache."

"What happened to Spinner?" Beau demanded, his face darkening as he remembered the man shooting Roselynne. The urge to kill returned in full force.

"He's in custody of the squire. He'll live, but he probably won't speak above a whisper for weeks. You nearly strangled him."

"I wish I had."

"Thank goodness he's put away," Roselynne said. She reached up and touched her father's cheek. It was almost as if he'd returned from the grave. "When did your memory return?"

His smile turned a little sheepish. "It wasn't all at once, but in bits and pieces at first. Before it all came back, I realized you were in danger and decided to continue to act befuddled so that I might protect you." He smiled. "I found out much that way."

Roselynne frantically tried to remember all she'd said to him in his senseless state.

"More than you needed to know," Beau said with a rueful grin.

"But reassuring in some instances." The two men smiled at each other. Mr. Moreley continued, "I found people tended to speak freely in my presence. No one thought anything of a senseless old man wandering around the house and grounds."

"What did you learn?" Roselynne asked.

"Do you feel up to visitors?"

She and Beau exchanged glances. He nodded. "Yes," she said.

"I'll let others tell you the tale." So saying, her father went to the bell cord and gave it a pull. In a minute, Mrs. Hunson entered, followed by a footman and Ansella, each bearing a tray.

"Oh, mum, you're looking much better, you are," the girl exclaimed as she set her tray on a table. "You were so pale when they brung you and his lordship in, both of you near to death."

"Enough," Mrs. Hunson scolded, but she smiled kindly, her dark, deep-set eyes gleaming like a those of a witch over her favorite brew. "The staff asked me to relay our relief that you both are well." She bustled about, giving orders, then performing the task herself half the time.

"Ask the others if they'll join us," Mr. Moreley requested, returning to his chair, now turned toward the bed.

Mrs. Hunson served tea and a collation of meat, cheese and bread alongside a platter of sweets. She shooed the maid out when Ansella would have lingered, and spoon-fed Roselynne every bite. Then, checking that all was in order, she followed the footman from the room when he finished replenishing the fire.

"Mrs. Hunson seems . . . happy," Beau observed.

Mr. Moreley chuckled. "I've heard her story many a time while the maids dusted. It seems she married a farmer near here, and the earl gave her a sizable dowry. After a few months, he learned the man had beaten her, causing her to lose a child. He went over there, gave the farmer a whipping he'd not soon forget and brought her back to the manor. That was twenty-five years ago. 'Tis said she vowed to serve the Rockdales for all her life."

"What happened to her husband?"

"He tried to get the squire to force her back, but the squire ignored him. A few years later, he died of apoplexy while beating a mule. Mrs. Hunson inherited the land, and the earl arranged the farming of it."

"She told me the Earls of Rockdale looked after their own," Roselynne murmured, recalling the conversation. She smiled at Beau, who frowned but said nothing.

A knock on the door heralded the arrival of George and another man.

"Clayburgh!" Beau said. He pressed a hand to his head as the exclamation started an ache echoing around his skull.

"At your service, my lord," the barrister remarked dryly. His gaze flicked to Roselynne and he executed a bow.

"By heavens, explain how you came to be free, and make it quick," Beau demanded. "I'm totally confused."

"It was a ruse," George jumped in. "He and the squire suspected William all the time, but like us, had no proof."

Clayburgh poured tea for himself and George and took a seat. "We thought Spinner might become lax if he thought he was safe from discovery, so the squire arrested me instead."

"You must have hated that," Roselynne murmured in sympathy, thinking of her time in Newgate.

"Not at all. The squire gave me leave of his library, which is almost as good as yours. Naturally I couldn't leave the house and was under guard, but otherwise I had the freedom of the place. Sanders was in our confidence and, we learned, also in yours. He kept us posted on events here."

"Jim and Sanders have been my shadows for almost four months," she affirmed.

"But not when you needed them the most," George said. "We have your father to thank for leading us to you when William kidnapped you and lured St. Clair into his trap."

"Sir," Beau said, "how did you know where we were?"

"I was in the hall when the crofter delivered the note and listened while you left word with the butler to call off the search," Mr. Moreley explained. "When the men returned and the hour grew late with no sign of my daughter, George and I became worried. We didn't think you would detain her overlong, knowing others were concerned about her." He paused and fixed a twinkling gleam on his son-in-law.

Beau flushed. He'd hardly thought of the others at all in his haste to get to his wife.

Mr. Moreley continued, "When another hour passed, I decided I must give up my silence. I spoke and nearly scared George, Jim and Sanders out of *their* wits."

"But, Father, how did you know where William held me?"

"A lucky hunch," he confessed. "I remembered the castle and the cell there. Sanders went for the squire while the rest of us rode up as close as we dared, then walked through the woods."

George snorted. "As if we needed quiet. All of you were out cold, but we still had to pry Beau's fingers from poor Spinner's throat. You were holding on like a bulldog," he told his friend.

"I wish I'd killed the rascal."

Roselynne held a hand up. "Nay. I'd not have that hanging over you to be resolved in court." She turned to the lawyer. "William killed Beau's cousin. He said the earl wouldn't loan him money when he asked for it."

"He has confessed to it. Much of his success was my fault," Clayburgh said. "When Thea realized Robert would never marry her, she turned to me. One day she looked through my papers and discovered Alice was still alive. She wanted money in exchange for her silence." He sighed. "I told Robert it was a poor plan to lie about Alice, especially to William. After all, the man was her husband. But Rockdales have always been stubborn."

Roselynne gave Beau a loving glance, remembering how he'd held on to William and saved their lives. "Very stubborn," she agreed. "Thea said she'd sent for William. What was their plan?"

"I think she thought the American cousin wouldn't forswear his country, thus William could bring Alice forth and claim the estate should the earl suddenly die. Alice probably would have met with an accident in due time, then Thea could step in as his wife." A fierceness swept over Clayburgh's hawkish features, and Roselynne thought of Beau's face when William had shot her.

"But I did arrive," Beau said, "and William, out of some misbegotten revenge, killed my cousin and got me arrested for it."

"By marrying my daughter," Mr. Moreley said, "you ruined his scheme. One might say you threw a spanner in the Spinner works."

Roselynne smiled mistily. "Oh, Father, you have indeed returned with all your wits about you."

She settled against the pillows and sipped her tea as the men delved into William's reasoning. They decided William had come up with a new idea when he saw Roselynne—marry her, get control of the money, and have children free of the taint of madness. Thea had become furious when she realized he actually intended to cast her aside, and most likely threatened him with exposure.

"I think she tried to warn me of him," Roselynne mused.

"So he killed her in anger," Clayburgh ended, "and made other plans when he saw that you preferred the American."

"That was my doing," Beau admitted. "The plan was to use me, not Roselynne, as bait for William's anger, but it backfired."

She laid a comforting hand on his arm. "You came to my rescue like a knight of old." She smiled at the group. "I wonder if William shall like Mr. Bowes. The turnkey at Newgate is a most pleasant host, if one stays out of range of his fists." She glanced at Beau's nose, which still sported a tiny hump.

Instead of responding to her jesting, a darkness came over him, renewing her concern for his health. The story would be discussed for months to come, so there was no need to hear every theory this evening. She yawned deliberately.

"We should leave these youngsters," her father announced. "They're earned their rest."

She smiled at him in gratitude. When he came to her, she clung to him in a surfeit of love and kissed his cheek thrice before releasing him.

Mr. Moreley leaned past her to shake hands with his son-in-law. "I have much to thank you for, my lord."

"Call me Beau," he muttered, flushing. "'Tis I who should thank you, sir. Your daughter saved my life by distracting

William, then she took the bullet meant for me. You taught her uncommon bravery."

"Now he wants to be alone to show his wife how grateful he is for her help," George suggested, winking at Roselynne.

At Beau's scowl, he dashed from the room, laughter floating behind him. Clayburgh lingered after Mr. Moreley left. He cleared his throat, and Roselynne detected worry on his austere face.

"About Alice," he began and stopped.

"My cousin gave you the care of her," Beau said. "I see no reason for new arrangements if the present one suits you."

"I...thank you, my lord." Clayburgh turned and walked out, his lips pressed together against emotion he didn't want to show.

Pleased, Roselynne turned to her husband, who stared into space, his thoughts elsewhere. "So, all's well that ends well," she said, running her fingers along his wrist under the sleeve of the nightshirt someone had put on him. She vaguely remembered Mrs. Hunson tending her.

Beau got out of bed, pulled on slippers and belted the dragon robe around his lean waist. He added a log to the fire, then paced the floor, his face dark with turbulent thoughts. At last he spoke. "I haven't been a good husband to you."

Her heart, which had been soaring, drifted downward a few notches. She studied her husband. Why, he felt *guilty* for some reason. Oh, of course...because she'd taken the shot from Spinner instead of him. She smiled, feeling tender toward him.

"Perhaps you should let me decide that," she suggested. She let the sheet drop to her waist and gave him a flirtatious glance to encourage him to return to bed. She wanted to snuggle against him and bask in his warm embrace.

Her spirits winged upward. They were safe at last. No hangman lurked in the shadows to grab him away from her. No one threatened him with death. Beau didn't have to flee the country, and as for his concern for her happiness...a lifetime stretched before them, full of promises of wonderful things to come.

"From the first I thought only of my needs," he continued. "Our marriage would give the prison guards something else to think on, as well as thwart the killer, whom we now know was Spinner.''

"It had its advantages for me, too,'' she reminded him. She'd had enough of talking, but he seemed bent on confessing all. She leaned against the pillows and prepared to hear him out. Patience was a virtue she'd learned well as a vicar's daughter.

He paused, his eyes so bleak they appeared black. "I didn't sufficiently consider the danger to you." He dropped to one knee beside the bed. "I was arrogant. I thought I had arranged adequate protection, but you were nearly killed *twice* . . . and were in mortal danger all the time. Forgive me, Roselynne."

Ah, so that was the problem. She ran her fingers through his golden curls, remembering the day he'd arrived—her golden knight on his black charger. "I do,'' she said, smiling again.

He stood and resumed pacing. "I was also selfish. I desired you. Since I'd paid for your freedom, I thought that gave me the right to have you. I even wanted to leave you with a child.'' A grim smile flickered over his mouth. "Your gentleness and poise reflected my ability to choose well, I thought. You were perfect to be my countess.''

"All worked out in the end,'' she said, burning to speak of her love and have done with recriminations. She only wanted to hear one thing: his confession of undying love.

"No thanks to me.'' He stopped by the hearth and stared into the flames for a long minute.

The silence lengthened, and she plucked at the sheet, a growing uneasiness seeping into her.

He spoke again. "I'll return to Virginia as soon as I'm no longer needed here. I had intended to depart as Cousin True and let everyone think Beau had died, but too many now know who I am.''

She stared at him, unsure she'd heard correctly. "What are you saying?''

"I'm leaving as soon as I can find a ship.''

Her hopes for the future dimmed. Tears pressed urgently against her eyelids. For a second, she was afraid they'd spill over. She held in the cry her heart gave and spoke quietly. "I suppose I really can't blame you for wanting to be rid of me.''

He leveled a frown at her. "What are you talking about?"

"William realized right away, as soon as I left the priory, that I had information to disclose to you. He tricked me into admitting I had seen Alice. You were right not to tell me who you were when you came as Cousin True. I can't be trusted."

"Hogwash," he said. "You're the most trustworthy person I've ever met. In fact, it was your honesty that prevented me from telling you of the ruse George and I had concocted."

She considered his statements. He apparently admired her as a person, and he'd declared his passion for her, yet he seemed intent on leaving. It made no sense.

"It wasn't honest to take you for my lover when I thought you were someone else. I have no excuse," she admitted, "except it was all so overwhelming—"

"That was the best part," he interrupted with a hint of Clayburgh's sardonic humor. "Don't you see? You were attracted to *me*. No matter who you thought I was, you couldn't resist. Neither could I," he added on a soft note.

His gaze burned into hers, reminding her of their passionate moments together. He was remembering, too. Her sagging hopes revived a bit. "You at least knew who you were. I was left in ignorance. What of your promise that we should have no secrets, that we would share all things, the good and the bad, the way your family always had?"

She saw pain in his eyes and was sorry she'd mentioned his family. He had enough sad memories to deal with.

"You have my apologies for that. I was wrong to keep the truth from you." He resumed pacing. "I'll book passage as soon as possible," he said, abruptly taking up his plan to return to his plantation.

"For both of us?" She couldn't hide her eagerness to go on this great adventure with him. Surely he wouldn't leave her.

He gave her a long, unreadable look. "No. For me."

She said nothing. The ache in her heart was too great for words. She breathed deeply, forcing the despair to stay at bay. She searched for a shield, found anger, and reached for it blindly.

Men were callous, she told her bruised heart. They were unfeeling and thought of nothing but their own plans and schemes. He'd used her for his purposes, first to thwart the killer, then to slake his passion, and now...now he proposed to blithely sail off and leave her behind. As if they had no connection. As if their marriage counted for nothing!

"If there's a child," he said, staring out the window and looking like St. Stephen about to be stoned, "I'd consider it a kindness if you'd let me know."

She gasped in disbelief. The beast! He would even abandon their child. "I think not," she said, sitting up straight and glaring at him.

"What?" He looked at her stupidly, as if she hadn't spoken the king's English.

She crossed her arms and thrust her chin out. "If you go, you will take me."

"You don't understand. While I can't undo the marriage, I can give you your freedom. If..." He swallowed and took a deep breath. "If there're children...later...I'll understand and accept them as my own. Naturally I'll visit often enough to waylay any gossip."

It was the final insult.

"Ohh," she cried and flung the covers back.

Her fury was so great, she hardly noticed the pain in her side as she sprang from the feather mattress and stalked toward him.

"Do you think I have no honor at all?" she demanded.

She drew back and actually struck him on the chest, the first time in her life she'd ever struck another person. She pressed a hand to her lips, shocked by the violence of her act.

Beau caught her arm. He dropped his martyr pose and reverted to his normal dictatorial self. "Damnation, Rose-lynne, what ails you? I'm trying to tell you you're free of me."

"I don't want to be free. I want—" She was about to give away her love for him and _that_ she would never do, not now that he'd made it clear he didn't return it.

"Yes?" he demanded hoarsely. "You want..."

"I want to go to Virginia. Why must men always have the grand adventure while women stay home?"

"'Tis no adventure—"

"You're the one who wants to be free of our marriage and its responsibilities," she accused as her temper grew more heated. "That's too bad. You pushed for the bargain, now you must make the best of it. I've kept *my* part."

They glared at each other for a long minute.

"You've done your duty, right?"

"Yes," she replied.

"And now we must make the best of a bad bargain?"

It hurt that he viewed their marriage in that light. "If you wish to look upon it that way, yes."

"Fine," he snapped. He bent and, with a grimace, lifted her.

"What are you doing?" she cried, alarmed for his health and by the wicked light that flickered in his eyes. He'd surely lost his senses from William's beating.

"Carrying you to bed. That's where the best bargain is made and kept," he told her. "If you stay with me, then you must accept the consequences. I can't be near you and not want you."

He placed her in bed and started to strip off the robe and nightshirt.

"Wait," she said, confused. "Are you staying?"

He gave her an angry glare. "Truly, I don't think I can live without you," he admitted reluctantly.

She was astounded. "And you trust me?"

"Of course I trust you."

"But you shut me out because you thought I was too honest to lie?" she continued, trying to fathom his mind.

His patience ended. "I thought I could protect you that way." He lowered his voice and spoke again. "I love you more than life itself and wanted to keep you safe from harm, a task I failed at." He grimaced as he admitted his defeat.

He loved her! She could hardly take it in. 'Twas guilt that had made him talk this way. It made sense all of a sudden. He'd wanted to protect her. Failing that, he thought he must give her up. Her eyes began to shine.

"I think you did very well," she murmured. She held the cover up and patted the mattress beside her. "Come to bed and rest."

Beau studied his wife, perplexed by her invitation. She seemed to want him, and God knew he wanted her. Slowly he complied. His head ached from William's blows. His body ached from need of her. Did he dare believe the message he saw?

"You haven't told me how you feel," he reminded her. "Are you doing this out of duty?"

"No. I love you, too." She grinned at him.

He took her face between his hands and stared into her eyes. "Damnation," he snapped, "why didn't you tell me? I thought you must hate me for all I've put you through. I've felt guilty for forcing you into marriage."

She laughed, but he didn't give her a chance to answer. His lips claimed hers in a kiss of fire, of passion, of love at last free to express itself. She moved against him.

"Do you want...?" he began and hesitated. "Are you well enough for it?"

She nodded.

He chuckled. "Then, dear wife, tell me. And for heaven's sake, put some feeling into it so I'll know for sure."

She couldn't help but laugh. Her savage American had been as unsure as she had. She pulled his face close to hers. "I want you," she murmured. "I love you, more than I'd ever dreamed possible."

She waited for bells to ring and heavenly hosts to sing, but heard only the wild pounding of her own heart and his when he kissed her again. Then she touched him in ways he liked. She liked them, too, and all the ways he touched her.

He cupped his body to hers, guiding her legs to lie over his thighs, and showed her a new way to accomplish their joining. She closed her eyes as happiness rushed to unbearable heights.

He loved her. It was in his eyes, his smile, his tender endearments. He'd told her before, if she'd been wise enough to trust her heart. But then, he hadn't known, either.

She hugged this newfound happiness to her breasts and let the joy wash over her like a spring rain.

Beau reveled in her cries of delight and marveled at his luck in finding her at Newgate, of all places. One chance in a million. He'd taken it and won this prize—a woman beyond price.

After she slept, curled against his side, her hand lying on his chest, he gazed out at the night. For a second he thought he heard music or laughter, but the sound was as soft as the moonlight streaming in the window, then it was gone.

He tightened his arm around Roselynne, feeling her warmth all the way to his soul. She was passion and laughter and sunlight, all the things a man could ever dream of.

He was content.

* * * * *

HISTORICAL

CHRISTMAS

STORIES · 1991

Bring back heartwarming memories of Christmas past
with HISTORICAL CHRISTMAS STORIES 1991,
a collection of romantic stories
by three popular authors.
The perfect Christmas gift!

Don't miss these heartwarming stories,
available in November
wherever Harlequin books are sold:

CHRISTMAS YET TO COME
by Lynda Trent
A SEASON OF JOY
by Caryn Cameron
FORTUNE'S GIFT
by DeLoras Scott

**Best Wishes and Season's Greetings
from Harlequin!**

HARLEQUIN
Romance

A Christmas tradition...

Imagine spending Christmas in New
Orleans with a blind stranger and his aged
guide dog—when you're supposed to be
there on your honeymoon!
**#3163 Every Kind of Heaven
by Bethany Campbell**

Imagine spending Christmas with a man
you once "married"—in a mock ceremony
at the age of eight!
**#3166 The Forgetful Bride
by Debbie Macomber**

*Available in December 1991, wherever
Harlequin books are sold.*

HARLEQUIN

Romance

**This December, travel to
Northport, Massachusetts,
with Harlequin Romance
FIRST CLASS title #3164,
A TOUCH OF FORGIVENESS
by Emma Goldrick**

Folks in Northport called Kitty the meanest woman in town,
but she couldn't forget how they had duped her brother and
exploited her family's land. It was hard to be mean, though,
when Joel Carmody was around—his calm, good humor
made Kitty feel like a new woman. Nevertheless, a Carmody
was a Carmody, and the name meant money and power to
the townspeople.... Could Kitty really trust Joel, or was he
like all the rest?
